Verdict in the
Desert

Verdict in the
Desert

Patricia Santos Marcantonio

Arte Público Press
Houston, Texas

Verdict in the Desert is funded in part by a grant from the city of Houston through the Houston Arts Alliance. We are grateful for their support.

Recovering the past, creating the future

Arte Público Press
University of Houston
4902 Gulf Fwy, Bldg 19, Rm 100
Houston, Texas 77204-2004

Cover design by John-Michael Perkins

16 17 18 19 20 21   8 7 6 5 4 3 2 1

For Daddy

Acknowledgments

This book would not have been possible without the help of many people. Thanks to my friend and critique partner Bonnie Dodge, to Peg Weber at the City of Tucson Parks and Recreation Department for her expertise and to the wonderful people of Arte Público Press, especially Dr. Nicolás Kanellos, for helping me make the story better.

And thanks to my family for their endless love, support and belief in me: my husband, Jerry, and, daughters Marguerite and Gabrielle. They are my heart.

1
Summer 1959

MARÍA SÁNCHEZ CURRY left small bloody footprints down Lincoln Street. Under the full moon, they resembled a trail of flowers gnarled by the summer's heat. Clenching the image of the Holy Virgin on the scapular around her neck, she flinched as she walked over the dirt road. The slit across her forehead throbbed. Her neck felt pulpy and raw. But the bruises and bleeding were too little punishment. She should have been carrying a wooden cross of splinters and heartache. She should have struggled on penitent knees through a valley of death and bones.

Jesus. Sweet, sweet Jesus, she pleaded, but didn't expect any response.

The long-haired mutt in her arms yelped because she squeezed him hard. She kissed Oscar's head and cried out. The blood saturating her dress had painted his white fur a dark gray. Wetting her fingers in her mouth, she tried to clean his fur and tasted salt and guilt. She sobbed again, which left her thin knees feeble. Oscar licked her cheek as she wiped her eyes with the edge of her dress. Raising her face to the sky, she blinked. María anticipated judgment to drop on her like an angel's gilded sword from heaven.

Nothing happened.

Closing her eyes in prayer, instead she saw the image of Ben flickering behind her eyelids. She had never seen him so peaceful, especially considering her best kitchen knife had been plunged into the middle of his chest. Only a few moments before, María had watched her husband settle into death. Groans and red spittle dribbled out of his mouth. No cuss words or hosannas. Before his eyes became hollow blue glass, they betrayed a hint of surprise that she hadn't killed him sooner. She begged Jesus to bring Ben back to life and promised to be good from then on. No more disobeying. No more beer. She would be silent and absorb his slaps like water poured in the desert. But there was only the blood that bound them more than vows. So she had begun walking, not knowing where to go. Outside her front door, Lincoln Street was as dark at one end as it was at the other. She held Oscar tight while reciting her own novena of shame.

María didn't even notice a Borden city police car rounding the corner.

≈ ≈ ≈

Officer Rod Sawyer's sweaty back produced a sucking sound every time he shifted his weight in the patrol car. And his butt ached. He and his partner had driven around since dinner at Pete's Café downtown. Sawyer badly wanted a stick of gum because he had belched the hamburger special for the last hour.

Older and tough as tires, Officer Sam Jones drove their regular patrol route. He tossed his cigarette out the window. "You're going to have to get use to this, Sawyer. These long, boring nights."

"Anything's better than pumpin' gas at my old man's station. At least I don't have to scrub the dirt from under my nails or clean crap from the toilets."

"We got a different kind of crap on these streets."

Jones grinned at his own veteran police wisdom. And Sawyer needed to wise up. His younger partner itched for gun battles like the ones the New York cops fought in *Naked City*. He wanted to chase a speeding car full of criminals, track down killers and rescue slutty women in tight clothes. Sawyer saw himself as *Have gun, Will Travel*'s Paladin in a blue uniform but without a Richard Boone mustache.

Jones didn't blame his partner's daydreaming. It took the edge off the real police work, which mostly consisted of tagging drunken drivers, handing out speeding tickets and breaking up altercations between wetbacks and white trash.

Sawyer gripped his gun. "You'd think somebody needed a head busting tonight. Goddamn, it's slower 'n spit out here."

"You're watching too many cop programs on TV."

"I like westerns, too," Sawyer replied in his defense.

The radio flashed on. "Car 79, we got a report of a domestic at 1287 Lincoln Street. You're over in that neck of the woods, ain't you, Jonesy?" The male dispatcher sounded as bored as Sawyer.

"I know the place. We're on our way."

Sawyer sat up from his slump.

"Don't get excited. It's Ben and María Curry again. Those two fight like clockwork. I'm damn sick of them. A nosy neighbor woman calls when they go at it. Sometimes I feel like running her in, too."

Jones turned the corner onto Lincoln Street.

"There's a woman down a ways," Sawyer said.

"It's María. She's probably drunk and beat up."

When he got closer, he pounded on the brakes. María looked like a creature formed out of blood. "Oh, son of a bitch."

The officers burst out of the car.

Oscar growled as Jones grabbed the back of María's dress and pulled her toward the headlights. "I don't think all that blood came from her head."

Through her fear, María dared to smile, because punishment had arrived at last. The men's eyes were solid with it.

"What'd you do to Ben?" Jones asked and then let out a hard sigh.

"What's wrong?" Sawyer said.

"She can't understand more than two damn words of English." Jones summoned the rudimentary Spanish he had picked up from his years in Borden. He asked her again about her husband.

She lifted her finger and pointed to the house up the street.

Grabbing María's arm, Jones dragged her along to the patrol car. He stopped. "Wait. She's going to bleed all over my seats. I'll walk her back to the house. You drive and meet us there, Sawyer."

At the house, Jones passed María over to his partner. "Watch her and stay out here."

Despite his 270 pounds, Jones hustled when needed. Stepping onto the porch of the house, he wiped the perspiration stinging his eyes. He hated domestics. Couples beat, spit and cursed each other. But have a police officer step in and—bam—they transferred all their venom to him, as if he had caused their problems. Ben was inside, all right. Probably hurt, definitely tight and ready to mix it up as usual. Jones drew his weapon, which gave him confidence.

Footprints in blood led him through the door. The house smelled harsh from burning chicken. Rounding a corner of the hallway, Jones saw Ben sitting against a wall in the kitchen. The officer lowered his weapon. Ben's T-shirt was more red than white from the blood that created a shiny pool around the body. The officer counted at least six stab wounds. A black knife handle protruded from Ben's chest in what was probably the last blow.

"You ain't going to fight anybody no more, you dumb son of a bitch." Jones yelled out the door, "Bring her in!"

"What a mess," Sawyer said when he joined his partner. He tightened his grip on María, who shuddered and wept with equal parts frenzy and sadness. Shaking her as if she was a misbehaved child, the police officer found one of the few Spanish words he knew: "*Silencio*, dammit, *silencio*."

María put a hand over her mouth. With her other hand, she pulled her dog closer.

"Did you kill him?" Jones asked in halting Spanish.

She nodded. A ribbon of blood from her head wound had slid down her face.

Sawyer held María at arm's length. He guessed she was almost sixty years old, weighed one hundred pounds and measured a little over five feet tall. Tangles of long hair flew out of a salt-and-pepper braid on top of her head. Her eyes shrank to dots in an oval face from all the crying and swelling.

"How could this little thing topple that big man?" He kicked Ben's foot and answered his own question. "She managed somehow, because this boy got it good."

María started toward her husband. Sawyer tugged her back. "Lady, you did enough."

Inspecting the bottom of one of his shoes, Jones spit. He had stepped in the blood. "Damn domestics."

2

As the police officers were arresting María Curry, Michael Shaw was pulling a thorn from his palm. He looked up at his father's guests looking down on him where he had fallen on the grass. Michael laughed at their total lack of humor. Still, his drunken lapse barely generated a fuss in the garden party at his father's house ten miles from Borden's city limits. The party guests had seen his antics before.

On the way to the bar, Michael hadn't spotted the rosebush, and he stumbled. Although tanked, he instinctively put out his hands to break the fall. He now fully appreciated how those years playing football had prepared him for life.

When Jenny Shaw saw her husband go down, she gulped air. Her yellow silk dress rustled as she knelt to help Michael to his feet. One stroke of his hand composed his dark blond hair. Straightening, he buttoned his jacket over a once athletic body now in danger of going to seed.

He handed Jenny a crushed rose. "This is for you." He laughed at his joke.

Jenny took the rose, tossed it away and whispered into his ear, "It's only ten, baby. What'll everybody think?"

"That I started drinking at six," he whispered back.

Brushing off his tie and jacket, Jenny could do nothing but show her gracious smile and thank her lucky stars. Michael became even more charming when he drank, not violent or messy. Besides, she was not much of a woman if she couldn't handle a drunken husband. She had learned that lesson from her mother, who had plenty of experience with her father, The Lush. Jenny did frown when she saw Frank and Margaret Hideman staring at Michael. They were ranch people, country club people, rich as her father-in-law people. They actually knew President Eisenhower.

"Michael, maybe you should rest," Jenny said loudly enough for the Hidemans to hear. "You know you're still recovering from a cold."

"He's a little under the weather," she repeated to the couple in case they hadn't heard.

Michael rocked a bit. "Jenny, I'm feeling pretty damn good. Too good for this dirge of a gathering." His eyes cleared enough to recognize the older couple. "Frank, Margaret. What's the matter? Haven't you ever seen an intoxicated lawyer before? Hold it. Don't answer, or you'll tend to incriminate me."

The Hidemans melted away in disgust. Michael laughed, this time choking on his spit because he found himself so goddamn funny even if no one else did. Lacking an appreciative audience, he would slip away to his father's study and drink in peace until it was time to go home. But Byron Piggot cut off his getaway. Piggot the human safe deposit box.

"Oh hell." Michael swiveled away, hoping the stout banker got the message.

Instead, Piggot slapped Michael on the back, making him waver. "Mike, how you doing?"

"Me, I'm great. You know Jenny."

"Hello, Byron." She batted lots of eyelash.

"Saw that spill. You okay, Mike?"

"Michael just had a little accident. He's dandy." Jenny gripped her husband's arm with all the pale pink force she could muster.

"I hate those goddamn rosebushes," Michael said.

Piggot chortled, his pudgy cheeks lifting like a balloon. "What a character. Jenny, you know what people say, don't you?"

"No." She loved gossip.

"That Michael wins his lawsuits because the women on the jury fall in love with him and the men are afraid of his father." Starting light and friendly, Piggot's voice ended low and mean.

The inflection totally escaped Jenny, who held Michael's arm even tighter.

"You don't have to tell me I've got the most handsome man in town."

Michael sipped his drink at Jenny's delight in such an empty thing. Appearance amounted to one more burden he shouldered, just like his last name. Besides, she never really saw him—a man with greased feet staggering up a plate glass hill.

Piggot's fat face hardened. "You have to admit you have the world on the veritable string. Right, Mike? Not like the rest of us poor souls who have to work for a living."

Putting his arm around the banker, Michael leaned into Piggot, who was a foot shorter. "Byron, I plain forgot you bankers work so damn hard. Foreclosing on poor bastards, counting other people's money, giving away toasters."

Piggot's gray face darkened. "Excuse me. I see some people I want to visit." He left.

Michael called after him. "Come back! I want a new toaster."

"He didn't mean any harm, Michael," Jenny said.

"The fuck he didn't. I'm drunk, but I can still tell when he's firing cheap shots at *the* son of *the* Martin Shaw. You can't trust anybody here to tell you the truth, Jenny. Their lips are permanently puckered from kissing ass."

Her mouth formed a tiny circle. "You know I don't like it when you talk that way. All those swear words. You sound crude."

Michael groaned. He had come to despise that brainless Betty Boop pout she put on whenever she didn't get her way. Or how she mangled Broadway songs until he wished Rodgers and Hammerstein would break up their successful partnership. His wife wore naïveté like a suit of iron taffeta. But because of the amount of whiskey he had consumed and because she had no other defenses in this world, he allowed the pout to do its work. He pecked at her cheek. Her body smelled sugary and yielding. An overripe Doris Day.

"Sorry, Jen."

"Want to dance?"

"No, thank you. I'd rather drink."

The pout resurfaced.

Stepping back, Michael surveyed the crowd. Almost one hundred people milled about his father's luxuriant garden, hazily lighted by multicolored paper lanterns. Passing silhouettes in and out of the kitchen, Mexican workers kept tables loaded with hors d'oeuvres and distributed drinks to those too lazy to visit the bar. Shaped like the state of Arizona, his father's birthday cake remained formidable despite many pieces cut away. A six-piece combo played hit parade tunes as stick figures in pearls and ties danced. The occasional cha-cha brought out those adequately loosened by martinis and gin tonics.

Around the pool, other guests gathered in groups, shifting like chess pieces and exchanging inane chat. Pride at the

United States' additions of Alaska and Hawaii, along with speculation over what to do with all the hula dancers and Eskimo Pies. Worry about the flow of cigars, since Cuba had been taken over by that rebel fellow Castro. Wives giddily wondering how to get a copy of *Lady Chatterley's Lover* now that the post office had lifted the ban. And the usual question of why America didn't pound the communists into red powder. The guests invited Michael into the conversations with a "What do you think, Mike?" and didn't bother listening to what he had to say. Not that he had anything to say.

"They're all dead, Jenny. Can't you smell them rotting away?"

But she had drifted off to talk to a judge's wife. Her bouffant bobbed in enthusiasm as she listened to the older woman talk about recipes and other topics that bored the hell out of him. Michael took another taste of whiskey because his wife had joined the legion of wealthy corpses. He hadn't saved her at all and had probably even sped up the process.

His law books called that *magna culpa*. "Great fault."

Maybe Byron the banker did right to pile all the shit on the rich boy.

Jenny elbowed Michael in the ribs. "You should mingle. The best families in Mitchell County and the state are here. What an honor to your father."

That left him thirsty.

On his return trip to the bar, Jenny stepped in front of him and covertly rubbed against him. Her full breasts moved in a fleshy wave. "Lover, don't drink anymore. Save yourself for later."

Though he didn't mean to, he laughed. "Jen, I've gone past the lovemaking period right into the passing-out-when-I-get-home phase."

"Your loss."

Quickening his pace, Michael glanced down for any more rosebushes or other obstructions. When he looked up, the most daunting of all stood in front of him.

"It's my birthday, but you're doing all the celebrating, son. You didn't have to take a pratfall, you know. We hired the band for entertainment."

Martin Shaw was the kind of man people stepped aside for even if they didn't know who he was. With his dignified silver hair and stern countenance, he was the unforgiving Jehovah of the Old Testament in a three-piece suit.

"I wanted to perk up things around here, Father. This crowd reminds me of the Dead Sea on a Sunday night."

"When you were young, you talked about running away to join the circus. As a clown, wasn't it?"

"I just wanted to run away."

Jenny kissed her father-in-law, whose eyes never left Michael's face. "Wonderful party, Dad."

Josita Calderón, a short, chunky Mexican woman with white conquering her black hair, offered glasses of champagne from a silver tray. Her brown eyes were directed at the chins of the people she served. Jenny delicately took a glass.

Finishing his other drink, Michael grinned at his father and took the champagne. "Thanks, Josita."

"You're welcome, Mr. Michael," she replied with a heavy accent.

Michael saluted his father, who shooed Josita away with a sweep of his hand.

"Jenny, beautiful as usual. You light up this evening more than those lanterns," Martin said.

"You get more charming with age. Sometimes I do believe I married the wrong Shaw."

Michael winked at them. "It's not too late. I'm very progressive."

"What a thing to say," Jenny twittered and tapped Michael's arm.

His father did not smile.

"How does it feel to be sixty? The age of Geritol and prunes," Michael said.

"One should only consider the knowledge accumulated over the years."

"That's a really poor defense for growing old."

Martin cleared his throat twice, which signaled his displeasure. Michael smiled. Besides the law, he loved nothing better than pissing off his father. Childish, yes, but satisfying as ten-year-old Scotch.

Martin cleared his throat again. "Have another drink, son. There are plenty of rosebushes, and the night is young." Taking a quick step, he sidled up to a gaunt figure of woman in pearls and put his arm around her waist. "Why, Corky Longfellow, I haven't seen you since I sued your uncle. Come here and tell me about your liver operation."

Jenny wrung her hands. "You shouldn't have said those things to him. It's not father-and-son-like."

"That, my dear, requires affection."

Yet Michael could not but help admire how his father worked the crowd—a touch to the back, a warm handshake, a murmur in the ear. A goddamn master of disguise. Michael dug his hands in his jacket. "Jenny, I could use a nightcap."

"Please, Michael, no more."

"Don't worry. I'm through falling over the plants."

"It is getting late, and I'm so tired." She yawned. "I'm going straight to bed." She laughed at her invitation.

He wasn't listening. Something else had Michael's attention. He reached for her hand. "Did you ever see my old tree house?"

"Yes, I have, but this probably isn't a good time."

"Come on."

Michael pulled her to a gigantic oak at the edge of the garden. The thick tree trunk pushed against a ten-foot-tall wooden fence separating the yard from the desert beyond. His father's attempt to turn the garden into an eastern park with fall foliage had failed miserably. The Arizona heat had dispatched the other leafy trees, no matter how much water and care Martin's workers applied. The oak was the only survivor, which is probably why Michael liked it.

Michael looked up. "Wonder if my tree house is still standing?"

"That was more than twenty years ago. It's probably gone."

"Let's go see if it's there. It'll be fun." Michael began climbing.

"Get down here. You'll break your neck. Please." Jenny smiled nervously. Good. No guests around. Glancing up every so often, she started warbling "Some Enchanted Evening." As Michael climbed, a few leaves sprinkled down, and she picked them off her hair.

Michael didn't cry out when the bark scratched his hands. His slick leather shoes slipped more than once, and his heart stamped like a machine. His suit ripped somewhere, but he kept going. At last, he found his old tree house. The roof and walls had collapsed onto the warped platform. The boards squeaked when he stepped on them, so he put one foot on a bulky branch slightly beneath to balance himself. At thirty feet off the ground, however, the tree house was still a good spot for watching the world, especially under the radiant moonlight that showed him the way up.

Josita's husband, Diego, had built the tree house after Michael begged his father for one. Via rope, he would haul up vienna sausages and crackers that Josita had packed for him in a basket. Up there, he escaped the sounds of his mother and father arguing. Up there, he hid from his father, whose calls resulted in no good anyway, such as scoldings for bad behavior and good-byes as he went on his many business trips. Most times, Michael didn't even get a good-bye. His father just disappeared for days. But he climbed down when his mother called because it meant kisses and chocolate. Her voice was as feathery as the cream-colored comforter on her bed. His own blond angel with ruby red lips, plucked eyebrows and a martini glass in her hand. Her body smelled of bubble bath and mint. After his mother's funeral, he had climbed up to the tree-house every night for two weeks. At that height, he was convinced all he had to do was reach out to touch his mother in heaven. He used to hold out his arms to the sky until they ached.

Michael also planned to run away, to step out past the wall and into the desert. Instead of the French Foreign Legion, he would join the battalions of saguaros and transform himself into an invincible thorny solider. But he never left the safe place among the branches of his tree house with his vienna sausages and crackers.

The music from his father's birthday party in the garden below was faint, as if it came from another county. Michael glanced up between the branches to the moon and sky. Carefully balancing himself, he raised his arms out to heaven.

3

A FEW BLOCKS FROM WHERE MORTICIANS loaded the body of
Ben Curry into a hearse, kids charged in and out of the hall of
St. Catherine's Church on Quincy Avenue. Food and punch
stained their Sunday clothes. Shirttails flew behind as they ran
after one another. Their parents were inside having a good
time, which left them free to have fun on their own.

The hall's refrigerators held plenty of leftover food, but
guests had emptied one keg of beer. The groom's male cousins
tapped the other and sipped cold foam. People wiped at brows
with napkins, leaning in to hear gossip or jokes in English,
Spanish or a blend of both. While the band set up, relatives
cleared white butcher paper from the tables. The guests were
full after a meal equally American and Mexican. Ham and
turkey, mashed potatoes, green chili, salad, tortillas and the
chicken mole that had gone as fast as the three González sisters had dished it out from huge pots. Large women in flow-
ered aprons, the sisters were sought after for most Mexican
weddings, baptisms, funerals and other gatherings. They were
good cooks and charged reasonabe prices.

All widows, the González sisters swayed ample hips as they
rushed to clean up so they could be ready to dance. They had

15

a reputation not only for their mole, but also for knowing how to have a good time.

"Oh, no." Junie González's whole body shook as she scrubbed a stubborn stain on a pan.

"¿Qué?" sister Jo asked, not looking up from sweeping the kitchen floor.

Third sister Viola aimed a soapy finger at an older couple holding a large gift. "Get the food back out. Emilio and Celia Valdez are late, as usual. I bet they went to a funeral. They love a good funeral, 'specially when it's not theirs."

Emilio held his old fedora as he walked into the kitchen. "I'm sorry to cause more work for you," he told the sisters in Spanish. "We went to an uncle's funeral in Bisbee."

"What did I tell you," Viola whispered to her sisters.

"A marriage and a death. That's life," Emilio's wife said.

To ensure the older couple didn't bother them for seconds and delay their cleaning and dancing, the sisters filled two plates of food for each of them. Emilio sat and sopped up the red mole with a bit of tortilla. He announced his pleasure: "Muy sabroso."

Junie González bounced her hips as Sammy Flores and his band began to play. His fingers sped along the accordion keys, and his glossy cowboy boots kept time. Men gave robust shouts of approval as couples tipped hips back and forth and slid feet along the floor.

"Play rock 'n' roll," yelled the teenage guests after the band had gone through a few Mexican songs. Sammy obliged with his version of "Great Balls of Fire." His fingers skipped over the accordion as if the spirit of Jerry Lee possessed them. Sammy even had the identical wicked curls, although his were blue-black.

Sitting at the bridal table in front of the hall, Toni García rubbed her feet. Since six that evening she had wanted to ditch her stockings and the lavender-colored high heels. Hadn't she read something about someone dancing in bare feet at her sister's wedding? Was it in Shakespeare or Austen or the funny papers? She couldn't remember. Still, the sister of the bride had to maintain some dignity. She kept on the hose and massaged her aching arches and toes.

Behind her fabric crackled, lots of fabric.

With one hand, her younger sister, Carmen, fanned herself with a paper plate and with the other hand held up yards of white satin and lace. "This dress weighs a ton. I'm sweating like a pig."

"Have a seat, chicharrón." Toni added a hog's grunt.

"Thanks a lot."

"It *is* hotter than hell in this place."

"You don't have to tell me. You're not wearing all this satin stuff."

They listened to the racket, looked at each other and said simultaneously, "Great party!" They giggled like they were still kids.

"I've always dreamed of a wedding like this, Toni. Family, friends, *música*, the whole shebang. The only thing is . . . " Carmen began to cry.

Toni took her sister's hand. "She's here. She's watching." She wiped at Carmen's tears with a napkin. "Now, stop that, or your make-up will run and you'll look like the Lone Ranger."

Carmen sniffed. "So do I?"

Toni leaned in and squinted her eyes with exaggeration. "Nah, you're beautiful."

Their father, Francisco, rushed up to them. "Thank God, we had enough food. But I'm worried about how much beer we have left. I hope it lasts."

"If it doesn't, we'll tell everybody to go home, Pops," Toni said.

"That's not funny, *hijita*."

"Admit it. You're having a good time."

Lights reflected in Francisco's eyes as he smiled his answer. "Not bad at all."

He had removed his new black jacket and tie and rolled up his shirt sleeves. He pinned his rose boutonniere to his shirt pocket to remind everyone of his place as the proud father of the bride.

Carmen shook her head. "Check out John Herrera and Hugo Martínez near the door. They got that ready-to-fight look."

"Those two can argue over a fly on the wall." Francisco focused on the two young men. "In fact, I think that's what they're fighting over."

Carmen laughed and put her hand on his shoulder. "Not to worry. Víctor's cousins from Bisbee are the official bouncers. They're big as trucks. Nobody's gonna mess with them."

Francisco noticed Sammy waving. "Carmen, they're ready for the dollar dance."

"And remember to save me one later." Toni stood and straightened her father's collar.

"You can have your pick of dances." Francisco spun her around, amplifying his hip action. "Cesar Romero ain't got *nada* on me."

"You're more handsome than ole Cesar."

Sammy Flores called into his microphone. "Mr. and Mrs. Víctor Villaseñor, come on up here."

Carmen neared the center of the hall, her eyes widening with pride as Víctor emerged from a crowd of men. Slicked back, his dark hair picked up the lights. His partially opened dress shirt revealed a muscular chest. Although his face was flushed from beer and tequila shots, he maintained that calm she loved about him. Carmen hoped he hadn't had too much to drink. Yet the headiness in his eyes as he looked at her indicated she had nothing to worry about on their honeymoon. Besides, she had already had a taste of what waited for her.

Shorter and more compact, Víctor's brother Ramón helped with his jacket. "There you go, brother."

"If you want to dance with the bride and groom it'll cost you at least one dollar," Sammy told the guests in Spanish. In English, he added, "Don't be a cheapskate."

Male guests lined up in front of Carmen and female guests, near Víctor. Toni and Ramón held a box of dress pins. The hall lights were lowered, and Sammy began to play.

"I'm first," Manny Cabral said to Toni. "I baptized this little one, so I'm the first to dance with her at her wedding."

Toni held out a pin. "Well, Manny, you're going to have to pay one good ole American dollar."

He held up a ten. The González sisters whooped.

Carmen kissed his cheek. "Thank you, *padrino*."

He pinned the bill on Carmen's veil and took her around the floor. A few bars into the song, so as not to be outdone, Manny's brother displayed a twenty and took his turn dancing with the bride. In minutes, ribbons of bills trailed down Carmen's gown and veil and Víctor's tux. Sammy simply added another song to keep the dance going.

As the number of female guests began to thin out, Toni took a twenty-dollar bill she had hidden in her bra and tapped the shoulder of Manny's wife, who was dancing with the groom. "My turn."

Manny's wife reached up on her toes and kissed Víctor. "He's so good-looking. When are you getting married, Antonia? When will I dance at your wedding?"

"I don't know. I guess I'll have to start looking for a husband tonight." Toni pinned on the money and took up Víctor's hand, dancing him away. She had heard similar questions from almost every married woman at the reception.

"I bet everybody's asking you that," Víctor said.

Toni hung her head in dramatic despair. "Twenty-three and an old maid. I have nothing to live for."

He laughed. "You have lots to live for."

"Like what?" She smiled with suspicion.

"Like being twenty-six and an old maid."

Toni gave a laugh and squeezed his shoulder. "I suppose my father already warned you what'll happen if you don't make Carmen happy. You'll have to answer to us. That could get ugly, man."

"He told me. And you've already told me. But I love her a lot, Toni."

"I believe you. Besides, I put down a twenty-dollar payment on your promise."

When the dance finally ended, Toni and Ramón unpinned the money from the bride and groom.

"This'll add up to a nice down payment on a dinette set, Víctor." Carmen put the money in her white bridal purse.

"Or a new car."

"Keep dreaming, babe."

Afterward, Carmen and Víctor held hands as they visited guests. Toni watched and wondered how that lovely and generous young woman used to be her skinny little sister with missing teeth and knees like baseballs.

Finding an opportunity, Toni took a pack of cigarettes from her purse. She went outside to light up and kicked off her shoes again. She took care the ashes didn't fall on her billowy lavender bridesmaid's dress. Watching the people through the open doors, Toni smiled.

All so familiar.

Another celebration of their extended family, if not connected by blood, then by standing up at one another's weddings or baptisms. They were good friends who earned respect and the titles *padrinos* and *compadres*. During the years, they brought gifts for the holidays or no reason at all, empanadas filled with sweet pumpkin, bushels of chilies and lush tomatoes. Toni had dealt with unforgiving isolation in Phoenix for the past four years while earning a teaching degree. She missed the belonging of Borden. Now she had returned as a stranger desperate to fit in.

At the reception she chatted with the cousins and family friends, but a fragment of herself roamed elsewhere. She feared they'd notice the difference and consider her one of those Mexicans who had dreams reserved only for white people.

Many of her old high school friends celebrated inside. They had filled out to a comforting roundness, had kids running around and husbands who probably loved their cooking and warmth in bed. Toni imagined herself a chunky matron eating all the wedding cake she wanted with a little boy and man who'd ask nothing more of her than love and a good meal. How easy. But she had been attracted to the not so easy, which is why she'd probably end up a spinster schoolteacher wearing thick stockings and even thicker glasses.

She took a puff and grinned. Antonia Teresa García. Taking yourself way too seriously. Thinking too damn much. Again.

To Sammy's music, her body could not help but slant this way and that. Inside, her father danced past the open doors with her mother's sister, Lucille. She watched as he coughed into his handkerchief.

Footsteps ground the gravel. "What you doing out here? There's a party, if you hadn't noticed." Carmen carried a bottle of soda.

"I wanted a smoke, and it's so hot in there." Toni passed the cigarette to her sister.

"Damn, girl. It's hot out here, too."

They shared the soda as well as the cigarette.

"When I throw my bouquet, watch out for Susan López. She wants it real bad, and she'll squash you like a bug," Carmen said.

"I'm tough."

"I know you are. You used to beat up Jimmie Navarro in the fourth grade."

"And the fifth." Toni took another drag of cigarette and handed it off to Carmen.

Toni held her lips together tightly to keep from asking about their father's health. She didn't want to spoil the wedding, but promised herself that the minute Carmen got back from her honeymoon in Tijuana she would sit her sister down for a talk. Ever since she had returned home, she tried to raise the topic, but Carmen always changed the subject.

Her sister squirmed beside her. They often joked they could read each other's minds, and Toni guessed Carmen knew exactly what she wanted.

Francisco stepped out the door of the hall.

"Geez, it's Dad." Toni neatly tossed the cigarette into the dirt parking lot and waved to clear away the smoke.

"You girls always did sneak off and get into trouble." Francisco dabbed the sweat off his face with a handkerchief.

"Pops, you're thinking of the kids next door," Toni said.

Carmen gathered her dress. "Anyway, it's almost time to throw the bouquet."

Francisco motioned for them to get a move on. "*Ven, Antonia.*" He smiled mischievously as she put on her shoes. "*Hijita,* you could have finished your cigarette."

"What cigarette?"

To cheers and whistles, Víctor slid off Carmen's lacy garter in the center of the floor. He stretched the garter and snapped it into the air, sending it to the waiting hands of boys and men. The winner twirled the bit of lace around his fingers.

"You single girls get in the middle," Sammy announced into the microphone.

Toni muscled in front of the other women. Susan López's breath heated her neck. Susan weighed a good 200 pounds.

"Ready?" Carmen raised the prize. The bouquet of red roses and ribbons hooked into the air. Toni jumped, outdistancing Susan by a good foot, and caught the flowers.

Susan stomped her size nine heel. "It's not fair. You're the sister of the bride. You should let somebody else have a chance."

"Sorry," Toni shrugged. "I deserve something, since I didn't get a husband today." She flicked the bouquet in the air and caught it again.

Susan cursed.

At ten o'clock, a flurry of kisses, lots of tears and a drum roll sent Carmen and Víctor on their honeymoon. Too good to end, the party continued without them. Francisco danced with each González sister, who stepped lightly despite their girths. John Herrera and Hugo Martínez finally threw fists, and Víctor's cousins threw them out of the hall. Toni watched from the back door, relieved the unmarried sister of the bride was the most ignored person in the wedding party. That made slipping outside for another smoke so simple.

Walking to the back of the churchyard, Toni sat down on the side of a fountain located in the middle of a brick patio. She swore she tasted nectar from the nearby flowers. Placing her fingertips in the water, Toni wet the back of her neck. The splendid light of the full moon was like a vow she had not yet made.

In the fairy stories she had read, such a setting usually signaled the arrival of a prince to whisk the princess away to his rich kingdom. With no prince in sight, however, Toni was satisfied with the breeze she had waited for all night long.

4

ALL MORNING, MICHAEL FOUGHT THE URGE to lie down on the cool white-and-green marble floor of the Mitchell County Courthouse. The temptation always increased on Mondays after a weekend of drinking. Mondays were law and motion day. He and the other attorneys would sit in the front row of the main courtroom, waiting to ask a judge for a ruling, continuance, dismissal or some other legal favor. The lawyers sweated in their pressed shirts and gray flannel suits, with the creaky ceiling fans providing no relief in the summer. The temperature kept all the county clerks exhausted and in a bad mood.

The courthouse stood four stories high, at one time the tallest building in Borden, now dwarfed by the ten-story First National Bank, where Michael had a corner office on the sixth floor. An investor in the building, his father had a top-floor office that was three times the size of Michael's.

Despite the good view from the bank building, Michael preferred the courthouse, which echoed of experience instead of steel. He appreciated the elegant staircases of dark wood and the dome of stained glass depicting a cactus plant in the desert. He found it ironic that the glass shed a classy ambiance on the people below who waited to be sentenced for a crime or to complain about their taxes. Mostly, he loved the marble columns, because even when the weather reached 115 degrees outside, they were chilly to the touch.

His court business completed, Michael leaned against one of the marble columns while waiting for his client to get out of the ladies' room. Making sure no one watched, he gave in to his urge and placed his face against the column. The chill spread along his spine. Maybe, if he stood there long enough, he would transform into marble. So cool and indifferent for all eternity.

Unfortunately, the newly divorced Mrs. Jay R. Williams emerged from the ladies' room and cut his relief short. The paper work he had filed on her behalf charged adultery, but the circumstances were more colorful. She had unexpectedly shown up at her husband's office to have him choose fabric for his den curtains. There, Mrs. Williams had caught Mr. Williams dictating in the nude to his equally nude secretary. At the divorce hearing, the woman's broad, rouged cheeks grimaced at her soon-to-be ex-husband's lack of remorse. On the contrary, he appeared cheery, even after the judge ordered him to pay a hefty alimony.

"Thirty years of marriage all over so quickly. It's not decent." Mrs. Williams had a squeaky ingenue voice.

"So indecent." Michael checked his watch.

"You think you know a person, Mr. Shaw, but I didn't know him at all."

"He's a cad for treating you so cruelly. In the old days, he'd be horsewhipped."

"I have to say he was a good provider."

Michael patted her wide back. "You certainly won't have any financial worries. With the settlement, you can maintain your lifestyle."

"Such a load off my mind."

"The final divorce papers will be ready in a few weeks for you to sign. If you have any questions, please call me."

"I've appreciated your kindness in all of this terrible business, and I need some kindness now."

He shook her hand, and she tottered off on heels much too high for her swollen ankles. Michael felt sorry for the old girl. Her husband had disregarded her for a secretary with a tiny waist and welcoming mouth. All their children were grown and flown, so Mrs. Williams was destined to haunt endless bridge games at the country club, inflict herself on in-laws and spoil grandchildren. She would live down the humiliation by playing martyr to anyone patient enough to listen. Lots of Mrs. Williamses haunted the country club. Hell, he had represented half of them.

Locating the nearest drinking fountain, Michael popped three aspirins and slurped the water.

"Mr. Shaw."

Michael brushed water drops off his tie.

Behind him stood Judge Frederick Morton's secretary, a rod of an older woman whom Michael had never seen smile.

"The judge wants to see you in chambers. Right now," she ordered.

When Morton called, everyone had to snap to. "Mrs. Gillman, it would be my pleasure."

The closer the administrative judge neared retirement, the gruffer he became as every attorney in Mitchell County had discovered when Morton thundered at them from the bench. Michael affectionately called him "Mortilla the Hun." His empire encompassed only the county judiciary, but he ruled it with terror.

A collector of Indian artifacts, the judge exhibited glass displays of arrowheads in his sizeable office on the top floor of the courthouse. The place reminded Michael of an unhappy museum as the secretary directed him into the judge's chamber. Morton had a hefty build and a gray handlebar mustache. His mahogany desk held a lamp, a piece of paper and his folded hands.

"Summer appears to be a very busy time for criminal offenses, Mr. Shaw."

"When people sweat, they break the law."

"Witty, I'm sure, at least to those without a sense of humor." The judge had a voice just right for dealing out harsh sentences.

"Sorry, Your Honor."

"If I may proceed. The public defender's office is loaded down, Mr. Shaw. Your name is at the tip-top of the rotation list of private attorneys who agreed to handle overflow cases. You don't have any pending trials—I checked. So I'm assigning you to defend one María Curry, who is charged with first degree murder."

In his head, Michael went through all the swear words he knew, which were a lot. "But, Your Honor . . . "

The judge barely shook his head, meaning he wanted no excuses or argument.

Michael knew he was fucked. "Well, pro bono is part of the package."

"You'll receive the standard fee from the county. I know it's not what you're used to, but it's what you'll be paid at any rate, and it's all the county can afford."

The judge put his hands in his lap, an indication of dismissal. Mrs. Gillman handed Michael a file on his way out.

Michael slouched through the halls with the file in his hand, cursing whatever lawyer invented pro bono. "For the public good, my ass," he muttered and stopped for another drink from the fountain. A slap to the back nearly floored him, and he dropped his briefcase. "Jesus H. Christ."

Adam Stevens' broad face held a grin as he pulled at his ugly striped tie. In his work clothes Adam appeared like a stuffed sausage, because he never could find dress shirts that neatly fit his former-linebacker neck.

"How's the crime business?" Michael asked.

"Outstanding." Adam patted down the top of his reddish crew cut with the palm of his hand.

That habit drove Michael crazy. Bending down to pick up his briefcase, he moaned. His head felt ready to land on the floor, and he almost reached out to catch it.

Adam laughed. "You're a damn mess. Must have been a good party."

"I don't remember. And why are you grinning so much? Your teeth are blinding me."

"Mikey, I don't understand why you're considered such a hotshot lawyer when you're hung over all the time."

"Not all the time. Besides, my clients never know I'm hung over. I'm that good."

"What's doing today?" The freckles on Adam's face budged with his huge smile.

"Nothing much, a seal of approval on a divorce. Even you could have handled it." He and Adam played the insult game, which he regularly won over his friend. Michael speculated that Adam was waiting for the grand moment when he would score points on him and maybe win the game.

As they took the stairs down to the first floor, Adam continued to display his wide grin.

"What, Adam? You have the subtlety of a freight train at midnight."

"I heard Judge Morton ordered you in for an audience."

"The man's a veritable knife of sunshine in my life. He handed me, ah . . . " He stopped and checked out the name on the file. "The State versus María Curry, whoever she is and whoever she killed."

"While you partied with the elite of this town—to which I didn't get an invitation, I might add—said defendant carved up her husband in the less affluent area of this dreary place. The aforementioned incident involved one very large kitchen knife."

"Damn. I hate murder cases. They're so . . . long."

"I'm glad justice doesn't come into it. Let's go to Pete's. You can buy me lunch. Even if you didn't have it made in the shade with a rich daddy, you earn more money than me."

"I won't argue about that," Michael said.

As they opened the courthouse's wide doors, the summer heat pushed them back a step. Michael wanted to retreat to the sanctity of chilly marble.

Immediately, Adam drew his handkerchief up to his fore-head to catch sweat. "This heat could dry out a man's eye sockets in hours."

"Didn't we know a girl in high school who could do the same thing?" Michael said innocently.

Adam laughed. "Quit talking about the girl I married."

Minutes later, they entered Pete's Café, located a few doors down Main Street from the courthouse. The attorneys sighed lustfully when they entered the arctic air. Two months before, Pete had installed air conditioning, making his restaurant, the bank and Acme Theater some of the few businesses in Borden to display an enticing AIR COOLED sign in their windows.

Pete's investment paid off. Restaurant profits rose twenty percent after the sign went up. But if people didn't come in for the icy air, they came in for Pete's biscuits and gravy. Because of its proximity to the courthouse, lawyers and cops made it their unofficial meeting place, of course sitting in their own sections because they didn't fraternize. They were separated by education and how much pay they took home. They did share a love of Pete's food and the aura of law hanging in the air like the smell of bacon fat.

Slim and pockmarked, Pete Mason greeted his customers. "You boys in for the special?"

"You know it," Michael replied. "The best biscuits and gravy in the state."

"Damn right," Adam agreed.

Pete spread his arms. "How about that air conditioning?"

"Great," Michael said.

"Yup, that old movie theater ain't got nothing on me." Pete smiled as he set off for the kitchen.

Town lore had Pete picking up the biscuits and gravy recipe while serving a four-year burglary stretch at the Arizona State Prison in Yuma. He had shared a cell with a former New Orleans chef serving time for robbing a gas station. After his release, Pete borrowed money from relatives and established his café within view of the courthouse to remind himself of his past troubles and to stay out of them in the future. Since then, Pete had never earned so much as a speeding ticket. He joined the Chamber of Commerce, Elks and Masons. His community-service zenith occurred when old Sheriff Joss Bentley made him an honorary deputy for his support of the widow fund and letting deputies build a tab when low on cash. The photograph of Pete receiving his faux badge hung in a place of honor—right above the cash register.

Michael ordered the special, plus three large glasses of water from Mavis Mason. Pete's jovial wife had bleached blond curls rising six inches high on her head. Adam doubled the order.

"That'll be right out, handsome." Her eyes gleamed at Michael.

Adam feigned hurt. "What about me, Mavis? I'm devastated."

"Mr. Stevens, too damn bad." She toddled back to the kitchen.

When Mavis brought the water, Michael downed it in one long drink and started in on the other glass. He could feel the cold liquid flushing the alcohol out of his blood.

The specials soon arrived, and they attacked them. To Michael, Pete's stout gravy tasted of grease and fresh pepper-corns, something that went perfectly with an image of a homey kitchen occupied by a woman with round thighs and big tits fussing over a stove. Never being remotely close to such a circumstance, he was still pleased to think about it. The biscuits were sure to sop up any whiskey not diluted by the water. He began to perk up as he emptied his plate. "By din-nertime I'll be ready for a cocktail."

Adam put down his fork. "Shit, Mike, I've never seen any-body get over a hangover so fast. You've got the metabolism of a field mouse."

"While my college roommates puked their guts out after a night of guzzling, I'd be running the mile at midmorning, fresh as a daisy. Water and food were all I needed."

"One of these days it's going to catch up with you." Adam rubbed his ample stomach. "During high school and college, I ate like a horse and didn't gain an ounce because I'd work it off on the football field." He took a piece of biscuit, twirled it in gravy and shoved it in his mouth. "Now, everything I eat goes straight to my gut," he said with the fullest of mouths.

Huddled in the lower half of his law class at the state uni-versity, Adam had squeaked by the state bar. Despite their friendship since high school, Michael couldn't talk his father into giving Adam a job at the Shaw firm, even an unimpor-tant one. Michael believed Adam held a secret grudge against his family because that had forced him to get a job at more modest firm in town and, later, at the county attorney's office.

But Adam did have the smarts enough to manage a good living for the rest of his life. He had the abilities to work hard and follow orders without question, both unfettered by his mediocrity.

Michael placed his hands on the table. "Now, about this assignment. Doesn't the judge know I haven't tried a murder case in three years? All I've litigated is civil lawsuits. I even appeared before him last week. My client sued his own cousin for stealing cattle off the family ranch. This isn't exactly the stuff of a capital case."

Adam's eyes widened at Michael's vulnerability, a sure opening. "Sounds to me like you don't have the stomach for it anymore."

"I can still beat anyone you send against me." Michael sat back in the booth.

"Nothing so sad as a washed-up criminal lawyer."

"You tried one murder case and the guy confessed right after the voir dire. When I had your job, I took five to trial." Michael said this, not so much to rib Adam, but to remind himself of what he had accomplished. His friend usually brought out the worst of his fake bravado.

"I've heard those stories before, Mike. Never lost a case. Now you're Mr. Private Practice and making lots of dough in daddy's office way up in the bank building, among the vultures. Time to work for the little people."

Michael finished the third glass of water. "Hey, before I got that nice office, I worked for peanuts at the courthouse. That was damn well for the people, by the people and of the people." A smile broke his face. "I told my father I'd build character at the prosecutor's office. Too bad it didn't work."

"That's for damn sure."

"What can you tell me about this case?"

"Not much. Some Mexican gal whacked her white husband real good. A few jabs with the knife, then one right in
the chest. She even left the handle sticking out. Yech. But listen, Mikey, you won't even have to soil your manicured hands
on this one. It's open and shut."

"Good."

"I mean for us." Adam snickered again. "I got work to do."
He slid out of the booth, picked up his check and gave it to
Michael.

"Still playing ball on Sunday?"

"If you can get it up by then." Adam began to leave and
then wheeled back toward Michael as he unfolded his wallet.
"Oh, and about your new client."

"What?"

Adam took on an embellished Mexican accent. "She don
spika dee Inglis too gooda, sinior." He brushed his hand over
the crew cut.

Michael's headache reappeared like a shovel against his
temples.

5

SITTING IN A BLACK LEATHER CHAIR, Toni counted the long hairs Vance Johnson had combed over his glossy head. Her shoes were pushed together, and her hands rested on her lap. Her long hair had been pulled back into a bun. She had made the right choice with the dark suit that was bleak as a dry riverbed. When she left the house earlier that morning her father had told her she looked ten years older.

"Good," she had replied. "That's what I'm going for."

The principal of Washington Elementary School was reading Toni's application. His chest idled like an old motor. Ever since she entered his office, he had avoided her eyes. Even when he shook her hand, his eyes fixed on the playground outside the window or on the top of her head. As he read, his pug nose followed the lines on the paper, and he absently reshuffled the letters of recommendation from her college instructors. He pulled tissue out from his desk drawer and blew as if gray brain matter were a casualty. She jumped at the noise.

Finally, Vance Johnson spoke up. "Miss García."

"Yes." She gripped her hands more tightly on her lap.

The pronunciation of her name got caught in his throat like a piece of lettuce. Toni didn't want to correct him, at least not before she had a job. She didn't have to wait long.

"I'm sorry, we don't have any teaching positions for you, and I'm not sure when we'll have an opening."

With difficulty, she scooted up a little on the chair. "Should a position come up, I'm more than qualified. I graduated with honors and had a teaching job in Phoenix lined up, but I had to come home for family reasons."

"That's nice." Johnson's eyes went to the playground again.

From his indifferent manner, Toni could tell he didn't care a damn about why she had come back to town.

"Miss García, I do commend you for completing college. That is quite an accomplishment."

For a Mexican, she mentally filled in the rest.

He finally looked her in the eye. "We could always use help in the school cafeteria. It's good pay. And I see you worked in the cafeteria at your college."

"How about substitute teaching?"

"We'll call you."

Toni stood up and held out her hand. He barely brushed her fingertips. "I'll wait for a teaching job, Mr. Johnson."

He handed her the papers. "You're very welcome to try, but we may not have anything for a while."

"I'm not surprised."

"That's nice."

Toni shut his door and stood outside, not releasing the handle. Anger and frustration held her in place.

"Feeling okay, hon?" Johnson's secretary asked.

"What?" Toni said sharply.

"You're flushed. The heat bothering you?"

Toni's mood diminished with the woman's concern. "I'm fine. Thanks for asking."

"Well, be careful outside, hon. This summer sun is enough to fry your noggin'." The woman flaunted all her teeth when she smiled.

"I will."

About half a block from the school office, Toni took off her suit jacket. Her white blouse, once crisp from ironing, had become soggy tissue. She ambled to the bus stop. Last week, her car's transmission had gone. Her mechanic cousin Juan promised to fix it for free if she paid for a new part. She refused to let her father buy one. When he got mad, she reminded him of how he taught her to stand on her own. He still sneaked a little money into her purse, but she had to find a job to pay the rest.

When the bus arrived, Toni took a seat in the middle. An elderly Mexican couple boarded at the next stop and gravitated to the back, while two white teenage girls sat right up front. She had applied to every elementary school in Borden and gotten rejected by all the Vance Johnsons. Toni opened her folder and reread the letters of recommendation from professors, all describing Antonia García as a good student who'd make an excellent teacher. She closed the folder. Some future, working in a school cafeteria, serving hash and macaroni and cheese. She should have accepted the job for the money but didn't want Vance Johnson to have the satisfaction of seeing her take something less. Although aggravated at the rejection, she was more disappointed in herself. She should have reminded Vance Johnson there was not one Mexican-American teacher at a school filled with Mexican-American students. She should have told him how hard she would work and how she could make a difference in the classroom.

Should have, would have, could have.

Toni acknowledged her habit of thinking up speeches after the fact and when it was too late to do any good. The only time she had ever spoken up was to Mrs. Larson, the high school counselor. Toni wanted to apply for a scholarship to Arizona State and asked the counselor for help. Mrs. Larson called college difficult and expensive. Toni would be better off as a secretary or clerk or maybe a hair dresser. All during the conversation, Mrs. Larson spoke in an encouraging tone, which stung like a wet hand across the face.

At that point, Toni had had enough of the Mrs. Larsons in school and out. She stood up and grabbed her books. "I'm a straight A student and I'm going to be a teacher with or without you."

Mrs. Larson's mouth didn't close as Toni shut the door. She eventually found a teacher who gave her the help and recommendation she needed and got a scholarship. After all that, she still rode on a city bus, with no teaching job and no car. Less than ten years earlier, Arizona schools had segregated Mexican kids, like the Negroes in the South. What she really had hoped for was change and a little grace.

Lighting a cigarette, she pulled a piece of paper from her purse that reminded her to be at the county jail at ten the next day. She was scheduled to interpret for a woman accused of murder.

Toni had had no trouble getting the interpreter job, which wasn't even full-time or a county job at all, as it turned out. She was regarded as contracted help who would translate for criminal defendants who couldn't speak English. The county paid five dollars and fifty cents per day, unless the defendants had money. Then, they had to pay. To the county's chagrin, however, few of them could afford the cost. That's what a clerk had told her after Toni found the job advertisement in the newspaper.

Last week, Toni's only assignment was translating for a frightened young man who had illegally crossed from Mexico. He stole a car in hopes of heading to California to get a good job and send money to his parents in Hermosillo. When Toni entered the holding room in the jail, she stood taller than him in her heels. His delicate features were cast in dark skin, and his hair was black as a crown of evening. She could see him as an Aztec warrior greeting Cortez with awe and violence. She and her family called themselves "Mexicans" more than "Americans," but they were distant from that country by a generation or two. The young man made her feel as if she had met her own ancestor and witnessed how far apart they had traveled from each other.

The young Mexican held his eyes to the floor as she told him about the criminal charge. After the needed translations, he asked about her hometown in Mexico. She replied that she was born right there in Borden, Arizona, USA.

"¿Norteamericana?"

"Sí."

He shook his head soulfully as if he had been deceived by his own people.

On the hot bus, perspiration slid down Toni's back. "A shitty day," she said, but no one heard her above the rumble of the engine.

≋ ≋ ≋

Four blocks from her house, Toni stepped off the bus and onto a street full of children. They stomped barefoot through water sprouting from hoses and skipped in muddy puddles. Boys played baseball in the shaded street, calling time out for passing cars. A group of girls sat on porches and primped their blond dolls, made bald from continual combing. Other girls scooped up jacks, their eyes on the darting ball. Nearby, more boys hovered over marbles. They bragged over aggies as if they were jewels. On the sidewalk, larger boys tossed firecrackers left over from the Fourth of July. Their happiness forced Toni to smile, which she welcomed.

Pulling out her handkerchief, Toni wiped her forehead and neck. A little ways longer to her house, then a bath and nap, a luxury of the mostly unemployed. Her Ford rested in peace in the street, but her father's truck was gone.

Cooled by paloverde trees, the neat white house had dark blue trim, which were colors her mother had picked out. The two-bedroom house appeared smaller than when she was a child, as most things did. Out front stood a small statue of Our Lady of Guadalupe surrounded by a carpet of purple pansies. Everyone envied Francisco's green thumb, with his peonies the size of baseballs and fruit trees drooping with apples and pears. Each year, chilies, tomatillos, tomatoes and corn flourished in a large garden out back, and he would spread the ripened bounty among neighbors and relatives. As a kid, Toni had accompanied him on his rounds, carrying paper bags of vegetables and fruit for a young family living across the alley or the widow down the block, among others. She had waited patiently as her father visited at length with each and every one of them.

"Toni, Toni." Her Aunt Lucille ran from her house a few doors up the street.

"Hi, Auntie. You shouldn't run in this heat."

"I saw you go past my window. I called and called and you didn't even hear me." The thin woman wiped her face with a dishcloth.

Toni bent down and kissed her mother's older sister on the forehead. Delicate as the doilies she crocheted, her aunt spoke perfect Spanish, not the slang that peppered the language of North Park, the part of Borden prominently made up of Mexicans. Despite the heat, the older woman walked fast. Often, Toni felt dwarfed by her stamina. Her aunt had lost a sister, a husband and a son within twelve years of one another, but the loss only made her more determined to live.

"Come inside, Auntie."

"No, I gotta get back and finish my chicken enchiladas. I wanted to tell you I'll bring some over. I made too much. You know me. I cooked enough for an army."

"*Gracias*, Auntie."

Lucille's feet already started to move. "See you later."

Whistling in admiration at her aunt's ability to deal with the heat, Toni headed to the backyard.

Instead of buying a house as they had planned, Carmen and Víctor came up short of money for a down payment and asked to stay in her and Toni's old bedroom. Toni was prepared to sleep on the couch in the living room after moving back home. But her father presented her with the keys to the garage, which stood at the back of their long yard, near the alley. Francisco and Víctor had cleaned it out, painted it and added a kitchen sink, toilet and bathtub, turning the garage into a smaller version of home.

Toni had insisted Carmen and Víctor take the little house, but her sister, who could be as stubborn as their father, told Toni she was the oldest and deserved it. Toni believed the little house was a consolation prize because she didn't have a husband, and Carmen felt a little guilty about that.

Nevertheless, Toni gladly accepted.

Her little house. She loved the words. She had her own place for the books, records and other furnishings she had brought from the studio apartment in Phoenix. She could enjoy her jazz records, which her father didn't like, and read into the middle of the night, as she did as a kid.

About to open the gate to the backyard, Toni paused at the sight of Mrs. Sonia Hernández hanging wash next door. The woman reached on toes to hang sheets on the clothesline in the middle of her yard. Fortunately, she had her back to

Toni, who took off her shoes in hopes of slipping by the woman. It was only a hope.

Mrs. Hernández had the radar abilities of NORAD, as Toni and Carmen had learned when they tried to sneak home late during a school night. Mrs. Hernández had spied them through her window at the moment they thought they had succeeded. The next day, the neighbor happened to mention to their mother, Maricela, what time the girls snuck in. Their mother pretended to be stern as the neighbor passed on the information, but she didn't punish her or Carmen too harshly because she didn't like Mrs. Hernández. In fact, their mother made them laugh by accusing Mrs. Hernández of being a bruja, a witch who made everything go wrong in the neighborhood simply by talking about it. If a chicken died, if a car didn't start, if their dad farted a lot, they'd blame Mrs. Hernández's evil eye. The kind of woman who wanted to know everybody's business, their mother said, and what Mrs. Hernández didn't know, she made up.

That morning, the Hernández radar was fully functioning. "Antonia, where you been, girl?"

"Damn," Toni muttered.

The older woman spun around, and her dark eyes narrowed. With no possibility of escape, Toni stepped over to the wire fence separating their yards.

"So where you been?"

"Looking for work." Toni wanted to tell her to mind her own business, but answered politely. Best to avoid a Hernández curse, real or imagined, coming down on her family. "How's your husband? Dad said he got hurt at the mill."

Mr. Hernández was a round, friendly man who smiled a lot, which puzzled Toni because he actually had to live with Mrs. Hernández.

The older woman leaned on the wire fence, which whined under her weight. "That *viejo* is back to work already. Nothing serious, a cut on his arm." She tapped her chest. "But me, *ay ay ay*, it's a wonder this ole body is still going. I think I had another heart attack last night."

"Oh, no."

Mrs. Hernández made a quick sign of the cross. "I wanted to call the priest so he could bless me with the last rites, but my old man told me it was just tamale gas."

Toni shook her head sympathetically and tried hard not to laugh. Mrs. Hernández had complained of the same heart attack for the past ten years and regularly recounted miraculous recoveries from her ailment. If a neighbor had a disease, Mrs. Hernández had a better one.

"How's your *papá?*"

"He works way too hard at the mill and at home, but we can't slow him down." Toni edged back from the fence. "*Perdón.* I should go clean up and start dinner."

Mrs. Hernández chattered on. "Your *papá* is so proud you went to college. And it took four years? Ay, you could have been married and had babies in that time. You still speak Spanish, don't you?"

"All the time," Toni replied in Spanish.

"I guess now you'll be working downtown in some big fancy office and forget about us poor neighbors."

Mrs. Hernández mumbled something else, but Toni didn't understand. The woman had stuffed clothespins in her mouth.

Toni backed up to her door. "How can I ever forget about you?"

6

LEAVING THE COOL AIR OF PETE'S CAFÉ, Michael soon regretted not driving even the short distance back to his office. While his hangover had all but faded, a slippery layer of perspiration stayed behind. As he passed by the courthouse, he decided to sit down on a bench under one of the many mesquite trees surrounding the building. Cigarette butts were scattered underneath because the place was a popular spot for county workers to catch a smoke. Michael wasn't focused on the cases in his briefcase or those waiting on his desk. Not even the new one assigned by the judge. He thought about another murder case from years earlier. The State versus Marcus Fields.

At Harvard Law, Michael did well in classes—not at *Law Review* level, but enough to earn his juris doctorate with honors and still manage to have a good time. Upon his returning to Borden and passing the bar, his father expected him to work in the family firm. One day, however, Michael was flirting with one of the clerks at the courthouse when she told him about an interesting assault trial down the hall. He peeked in. Watching then—County Attorney Leo McCall in court inspired him to apply for a vacant deputy county attorney's job. Michael admired Leo's style of affability and sharpness before the bench. Michael also appreciated the passion of criminal law compared with the dry compost of civil, in which the Shaw firm not only specialized but excelled.

After Michael told his father he had landed the county job, Martin called him a fool. Michael argued the skills he learned there would ultimately result in higher fees when he later joined the firm. Martin agreed, albeit using the Grim Reaper expression he usually reserved for whenever Michael disobeyed his directives.

Within a few months, Leo had assigned Michael the case against Marcus Fields, who was a twenty-six-year-old ruffian and heir to one of Borden's largest trucking companies. Fields was accused of fatally shooting Lester Howard, a bricklayer who happened to be dating Marcus' old girlfriend, a hapless piece of ass named Shirley Walsh. Fields' defense attorney, a hired six-gun from Phoenix, had kidded Leo McCall about giving the case to a novice, namely, Michael.

Leo sputtered a laugh. "This kid right here is hungry. He'll eat your spleen and ask for seconds."

Burying surprise at Leo's confidence, Michael smiled at the defense attorney as if he had slept with his wife.

In preparation for the trial, Michael spent hours talking to witnesses and friends of the victim. He intricately mapped out the state's case on a blackboard in his tiny office. Almost every aspect of Fields' and the victim's lives earned typed pages in his file. He came to know them better than a relative. His girlfriend at the time, Jenny, pouted up a storm because he broke dates and missed dinners. He even abstained from heavy petting, drinking and playing Sunday football because he feared they'd diminish his edge.

In court, Michael did indeed taste spleen. He gouged a hole in the defense's case and worked it to a gaping wound with honed questions and objections.

The defense admitted that Fields and Lester had fought, but claimed the defendant's .22 pistol accidentally discharged when Lester tried to kick Fields out of Shirley's house. Michael's evidence revealed how Fields had stalked poor Lester for months before the killing. The defendant had also garnered a record of assault against anyone who happened to go out with his old flame.

Michael discovered his own style in court that was different from Leo's or his father's. He was strident when called for, sympathetic to the right witnesses and harsh to opponents. During summation, a female juror even cried as he talked about Lester teaching Sunday school and serving as a Little League coach. In thirty minutes, the jury voted Marcus Fields guilty of first-degree murder. Two deputies held back Fields as he lunged for his defense attorney. As they dragged him out, Fields cursed Michael and called him the fucking devil. Michael returned that with a wink.

Although he never admitted it to anyone, Michael compared that first trial to losing his virginity. The physical one had gone at age seventeen to Beth Vermont, a blond with an IQ lower than her bra size. The whole thing took place in his room at a party when his father was out of town. Beth begged for another try, but he declined, suspecting she really wanted to get knocked up in order to marry his father's money.

Sexual consummation with Beth Vermont and several others he could mention was not half as sweet as the moment the jury pronounced Marcus Fields guilty. He had found the law could be as skittish as a virgin he was trying to talk out of her panties, vengeful as a whore gypped out of ten bucks, seductive as a countess with state secrets. And he loved them all.

Michael perennially joked with Adam about his tenure at the county attorney's office, but he enjoyed the camaraderie built on the common mission of seeking justice instead of bill-

able hours. Over dinner one night, he informed his father he
wanted to run for county attorney after Leo retired. His
father's face was stolid, which unsettled Michael more than
anything. Without raising his voice, his father warned the
county job amounted to a career dead end. Michael could
expect to be prematurely aged by the aggravation of tight
budgets, heavy workloads and dealing with the criminal ele-
ment. At every opportunity, his father worked on him like an
artist chiseling at marble. He covered every angle of pending
failure until Michael began to wonder why he ever contemplated running for the county job in the first place. Michael
finally quit and went into the firm.

At the memory, his fingers hardened around the briefcase
handle. He got up from the bench and started down the sidewalk. Reaching the bank building, he glided through the doors
and up the elevator. The perspiration on his neck and back
dried quickly in the air conditioning. He waved to Mrs.
Whitehead, his grandmotherish secretary, to follow. Michael
put his feet on his large desk and closed his eyes. He pointed
to his head.

With a good-natured smile, she began rubbing his temples.
Her cat-eye glasses dangled from a chain around her neck.

"Will you marry me, Mrs. Whitehead?"

"You know I'm already married, and so are you, Mr. Shaw."

"Well, abandon him, because you're too much woman for
one man."

"Mr. Shaw, please." Her cheeks flushed pink.

Like Margaret Dumont in the Marx Brothers' pictures, his
secretary never got the joke. "Thanks, Mrs. Whitehead. That
did the trick."

She consulted her notepad. "The clerk's office called. Oh,
and I arranged a meeting with your new client, María Curry,
tomorrow at ten at the county jail. They found an interpreter

for you because the woman didn't speak English very well. The interpreter will meet you there. I checked your appointments, and that will fit your schedule."

"Anything else?"

"The Klingmans' attorney pushed back depositions until three tomorrow at their office, and the attorneys in the Raymond case want to talk about a settlement. You also have a new client. A Mrs. Douglas Sparrow."

"Let me guess, a divorce?"

"Good guess, sir."

"Mrs. Whitehead, won't you even think about leaving your husband?"

"Mr. Shaw, really." She left his office.

In his chair, Michael swung around to face the large windows behind his desk. He had never felt so good and capable as in that case against Marcus Fields. After he left the county attorney's office, he had searched for that same experience every time he went to court. But it was so elusive, like trying to snatch the sun's reflection in the gold and glass dome of the courthouse.

Swinging back to his desk, he went to work on the papers before him.

7

MICHAEL INHALED AS MUCH CLEAN AIR as he could manage.
He was about to enter the Mitchell County Jail, which was
located adjacent to the courthouse. When simmered by the
August heat, the smell of the place made him want to wail like
a toddler. Worse, it clung to his suits like smoke from a trash
fire. The stink mixed cigarettes, armpits, stale coffee and
whatever the jail cook had massacred for dinner.

Swallowing more clean air, Michael pushed through the
smeared glass doors. Several women, both white and Mexican,
sat on the scarred benches. Wearing teased hair and too much
lipstick, they waited for visits with husbands or boyfriends who
found it easier to do crime than earn a living.

The smell wasn't the only thing that made Michael want
to leave as soon as he entered. Deputy Herb Bell leaned
against the front desk counter. Six foot and slender as nerves,
Bell sprayed a fine mist with words ending in *s*. Worse, the
deputy talked more than an insurance salesman trying to fill a
quota. Bell used to man a desk in the sheriff's office in the
courthouse, until Michael and every practicing lawyer complained. Sheriff Bobby Maxwell reassigned Bell to the jail
because he figured no decent folk minded if the deputy spit at
prisoners.

"Why, Mr. Shaw. Haven't seen you in a coon's age." Bell's lips curled with pleasure.

Michael mustered a weak smile. Coon's age. That was the deputy's way of declaring himself one of the good ole boys, a good ole white boy, at any rate.

"How's it going, Herb?" Michael discreetly stepped back to avoid the mist.

Bell lit up like a bulb at anyone interested enough to ask. "Not bad. The jail does good business. This weekend, the wetbacks were partying like all get-out and spending their paychecks from the mill and the mines. We got so many in here, pretty soon cook'll have to put friholies on the menu."

To anyone within his squeal of a voice, the deputy put down Mexicans. They were the only people who had less power than Bell, Michael surmised.

"I need to see María Curry."

Checking the clipboard, the deputy sent a wiry finger down a list of names. "I'll take her down to interview room number 4. The interpreter's waiting in the hall. Wouldn't you know it. She's a Mex. One wet speaking for another. My, my, what a world." Bell chuckled.

That was the extent of Bell's wit. The heavy door buzzed and clicked, then rattled open like metal bones. Bell sent a grand salute. Michael took advantage of the escape and swept through the door. A young woman sat on a bench in front of the line of interview rooms. Her legs were crossed at the ankles. Her hands sat on her lap like a statue at rest. Her hair was in a black knot at the back, revealing sharp and high cheekbones and fluid neck. Never had a blouse and skirt been filled out so well.

Michael stared. She was pretty. But more than that. Her body emitted pure defiance with its straight back and her head up as if ready to pick a fight. And he believed she would.

Michael fixed his tie and walked over to where she sat. "Hello, I'm Michael Shaw. I'll be defending María Curry. You must be the translator." At least, he hoped so.

Toni stood up and stuck out her hand. Michael's mouth opened slightly at the straightforward manner. Usually, Mexicans kept eyes down. Her hand was warm as it was steady. Amber-colored eyes held his, as if they sized up his soul.

"Antonia García."

"I guess that makes us working together, Miss García."

She smiled a little. "That makes us working for María Curry."

Michael cleared his throat and opened the door to room number 4. "They'll bring her in a few minutes." Even through the stink of the jail, she smelled of honey and sage.

English and Spanish curse words were scratched into the dark blue walls of the small room, which held a chipped wooden table and three chairs. A clanking ceiling fan barely circulated air. Michael messed with his expensive briefcase. She changed her purse from one hand to the other. They kept heads lowered with a discomfort created from attraction. In the closed room, they both felt as if they were taking in each other's breath. He shoved a stick of gum in his mouth and offered one to her. They chewed in silence for a minute.

Michael couldn't stand it any longer. "I don't remember ever seeing you around the courthouse, Miss García."

"This is only my third job as interpreter. I recently moved back home from Phoenix."

Michael smiled broadly. "Why the hell did you come back to Borden? This is the town that time forgot."

"So why are you still here, Mr. Shaw?"

"I asked first."

"I wanted to be closer to my father."

"Ah, the sentimental type."

"Only when it comes to family. Don't you feel the same way?"

Without warning, Herb Bell brought María into the room. "Here she is."

The arrival made Michael happy because he didn't want to talk about family.

María shivered inside a huge blue jail dress. The skin under her eyes had been blackened. Her thin neck and arms showed vicious purple marks. Stitches lined up across her forehead. She looked like a mangled rag doll fished out of a garbage bin. The older woman brightened when she saw the interpreter.

Toni introduced everyone, since Michael's Spanish did not get past ordering beer and food at restaurants.

He motioned for both of the women to sit down. Taking a seat on the other side of the table, he pulled out a pad from his briefcase. "Mrs. Curry, I'd like to ask you questions about the night of your husband's death." He spoke loudly and slowly.

"Mr. Shaw, she's not deaf, and I understand English," Toni said.

His cheeks seared with embarrassment. He pushed at his tie. "Sorry. Now about that night . . . "

María ignored Michael. "Where's my little dog, Oscar? The police took him from me that night," she told Toni in Spanish.

"I don't know where he is," Toni said.

"Ay, my little boy. I tried so hard to protect him. Now he's gone." María started to cry at another loss in her life.

"I'll find him. I promise." Toni put her hand on María's shoulder.

María nodded. She believed the young woman. Her eyes held resolve, as if she had never been unsure of herself.

They continued to talk in Spanish. Feeling a foreigner in his own country, Michael waved his large hands in the air. "Wait, wait, what'd she say, Miss García?"

"She wants to know what happened to her dog."

"*Mi Oscar*, yes, yes." María had a dense accent.

"What dog? I don't know anything about a dog."

María again spoke to Toni.

"María says that Ben tried to kill Oscar that night. She was afraid Ben was going kill both of them."

"Oscar. Who the hell is Oscar?"

"The dog, Mr. Shaw," Toni said.

"Oh. Please tell her I don't know where her dog is."

After Toni translated, María sobbed again and wiped her face with her arm.

Michael gave the woman his handkerchief and cursed himself for not being out of the country when the judge assigned the case. The little woman in front of him didn't stand a chance in court, not even if he was fucking Oliver Wendell Holmes and Clarence Darrow rolled into one. She may have wielded the knife that night, but the word "victim" was probably stamped on her birth certificate.

He was going to go down in goddamn golden flames.

As María cried into his handkerchief, he got a closer look at the severity of the wound on her forehead. "Did your husband hurt you that night?"

The way he asked the question made Toni reevaluate her impression of Michael Shaw. At first his confidence practically filled the room like the scent of his expensive aftershave. He was handsome in a pampered way. His gem-colored blue eyes weren't as tough as his exterior.

Although the pricey suit fitted him well, he reminded her of a little boy forced to dress up on Sundays. His voice conveyed tenderness when he questioned María. Then again, maybe that compassion was a lawyer trick.

"You don't have to be afraid, María. I'm here to help," he said. "Did your husband beat you that night?"

María closed her eyes. Since her arrest, she felt as if she moved within a nightmare she alone had created. A place of dusk even in the daylight. The aching bruises and cuts on her body were just a reminder of her great sin and why she couldn't wake up from her bad dream. She opened her eyes.

"I made him mad," María said through Toni's translation. "I got home late from cleaning the motel. I was going to cook him a nice dinner, but he wanted my check to buy beer. I told him we had to pay the rent or we'd be kicked out. See, I really was the one to start the fight." María's voice was small as a tear.

"Okay. Now we start working," Michael said.

The questions and translations between the three of them advanced without effort. In her voice, Toni carried María's emotions and inflections, as well as her words.

"How long were you married to Ben?" Michael said.

"Fifteen years."

"Children?"

"God didn't give me any."

"The police say they often came to your house because of fights between you and your husband."

María's nod barely registered.

"Do you drink a lot, María?"

"Sometimes. I never used to, but I started to drink beer because Ben liked beer. It made life hurt less."

Michael tapped his pencil on the paper. He couldn't have said it better himself. "Other than the night he died, did your husband ever strike you, Mrs. Curry?"

She didn't answer. Michael looked at Toni.

"Please, tell him. He only wants to help," Toni told her in Spanish.

María held up her head. "*Sí.*"

"Several times?"

Disgrace clouded her face. "All the time."

Michael noticed the woman's hands were cut and bruised. "María, I know this is difficult, but you'll need to tell me about those times you were beaten. You'll also have to tell me everything that happened the night your husband died."

María's small face was wet with tears. "I know I'm in trouble. I didn't mean to kill Ben. I loved him, sir. But something broke in me that night when he went after Oscar. I know I'll never leave this place. God will punish me." Her sobs turned louder and her body quaked. Snot ran down to her lips.

Toni took out her own handkerchief to clean the woman's face.

Michael's jaw tightened. He couldn't make up enough lies to comfort his client. Then the interpreter spoke to María Curry in Spanish, and she turned almost serene. He continued his questioning.

"Thank you, señor." María took one of his hands in hers before Herb Bell took her away.

"What'd the hell did you say to her, Miss García?" Michael asked Toni.

She smiled. "I told her we'd find Oscar and take good care of him until she gets out of jail. I also told her not to worry because you're a very good lawyer who loves dogs."

8

LEANING AGAINST HIS BLACK JAGUAR XK120 roadster, Michael jumped away in a hurry after burning his backside. With two fingers, he loosened his tie under the noon sun. He noticed a scratch running the length of the hood.

"Goddammit."

He loved to speed at one hundred miles an hour along the back roads to his father's house, screech up on the gravel driveway and leave a gigantic dust ball near the front door. Now he and his British sports car were parked outside the dog pound, a city facility in name only. The decrepit brick building sat on dirt. Weeds sprouted from its eroding foundation. The tin roof buckled and radiated the heat. Inside, dogs howled and barked at their own impending death sentences. Why he allowed the interpreter to talk him into this he didn't know.

Yes, he knew why.

Toni came out of the door of the city dog pound carrying a small white mutt. The bun was gone, and her hair swung around a determined face. He opened the door for her and started the car. He planned to take her to lunch at the Mesa Inn, a charming out-of-the-way restaurant west of town.

"We arrived just in time, Mr. Shaw. The dog pound was ready to put Oscar to sleep."

He scratched behind Oscar's ear, and the dog's runty tail wagged furiously. "Hey, we saved this little guy. That's a good omen."

"Yes, it is." When he petted the dog, Toni noticed his wedding ring.

"What were you doing in Phoenix, Miss García?"

"Graduating from Arizona State. Surprised?"

"Of course not," he lied. "What's your degree?"

"Education."

"Teaching this fall?"

"No. I couldn't get a job at a school. That's why I became an interpreter."

"And a good one."

"It's not exactly hard to speak a language you learned growing up. Where'd you go to law school, Mr. Shaw?"

"Harvard." At that moment, he felt like a pretentious rich asshole in a sports car.

"As I thought. An Ivy League type of guy."

"What do they look like?"

She tilted her head. "Just like you."

Michael pulled into the restaurant's parking lot. "Over lunch we can talk about María. From what she told us, we might have a good case of self-defense." He almost believed it.

"I hope so." Toni rubbed the dog's stomach as she glanced at the front door of the Mesa Inn. She had heard of that place and its policies. "Mr. Shaw, they probably don't allow dogs in this place, and it's too hot to leave him in the car. I'll fix lunch at my house."

"That sounds great."

Pulling out, he glanced back. NO MEXICANS was printed on a small sign under the larger one that welcomed people to the restaurant. Shit. He felt like an idiot because he never noticed the sign before. Still, she didn't appear offended. Her wry smile hinted she had let him in on a bad joke.

"Head to the president streets, North Park," she said.

The streets in North Park had been named after American leaders and ran according to their terms in office. But they quit after Ulysses S. Grant. Michael had heard the city council agreed off the books to continue the street names in numbers. Council members didn't think it fitting the presidents should be honored with roads that had become so populated with the poorest people of Borden. A few Negro families, Indians off the reservations and Mexicans, the largest number of inhabitants. Most of them were born in the United States. Their ancestors had fought off Apaches and hard times with the rest of the state, but apparently none of that mattered to the city council. It still voted to save the rest of the presidents for the newer and more affluent part of town.

Driving in North Park, Michael gripped the wheel more tightly. He had crossed an invisible boundary. The Mexicans he passed shot him looks that could melt the paint on his car. He sped up.

"How often do you get over to this side of town, Mr. Shaw?" Toni enjoyed odd warmth over his obvious discomfort.

Michael grinned and lied again. "Pretty often. I know lots of people over here."

"Sure you do."

He ignored her skepticism.

"Here's my driveway." Her father's truck was gone, and Toni gritted her teeth. He worked swing, taking the extra shift despite her pleas for for him not to do so. "Come on, I have a place around back."

As Michael parked out front, Toni wished they had come up the back alley. Mrs. Hernández was watering her front lawn. The older woman didn't bother to hide her gawking at Michael as they walked to the backyard. Toni couldn't run. Best to face the enemy.

"*Buenas tardes*, Señora Hernández."

Mrs. Hernández's mouth rotated up. "*Buenas tardes*, Toni, señor."

"Tomorrow it'll be all over the neighborhood I'm sleeping with a rich gringo," Toni whispered to Michael.

"Really?" Michael turned his head and put on a lewd smile for Mrs. Hernández.

He followed Toni to her place, which turned out to be a garage. Inside, however, it was a home. Cheap imitation Persian rugs covered new linoleum. Indian blankets and multicolored pillows decorated a single bed that doubled as a couch. In one corner, books filled a shelf; in another, a door opened to a small bathroom. Album covers of jazz and blues artists were tacked up on one wall, right alongside pictures of Jesus praying on his knees and the Virgin Mary.

"Sit down, please. I'll fix sandwiches." Toni pointed to a worn stuffed chair in the corner.

Near the window over the bed she started a standing fan that pushed air into the room. She opened an old refrigerator in another corner that made up a tiny kitchen area. A white tablecloth and sunflowers in a vase topped a wooden table.

Michael liked watching Toni's relaxed movement about the room, propelled by a sense of home. As she passed by him, he no longer smelled honey and sage, but soap and lotion. She got out milk and poured some into a bowl for Oscar. Carefully choosing a record, she placed it on the player sitting on a chest of drawers. Within seconds, Billie Holiday sang "God Bless the Child" as Toni worked on the sandwiches and occasionally threw ham Oscar's way.

"There you go, boy."

She turned and saw that Michael stood near the door, still holding his briefcase and examining the room with a slight mix of curiosity and disbelief. She put down a piece of bread.

Vance Johnson stood there. Mrs. Larson the counselor stood there. Toni wiped her hands on a dish towel.

"Did you think I'd serve you tacos and beans for lunch? Maybe a little shot of tequila on the side."

"What?"

"Why are you staring?"

"I'm looking at the jazz albums, for Christ's sake."

"Were you expecting mariachi music, Mr. Shaw?"

"Did anyone ever tell you you've got a chip on your shoulder the size of the Grand Canyon?"

She came from around the table. They only were a few feet apart.

"You've never visited this side of town. You've never even had a Mexican friend." Her voice lowered with disdain.

"Hold on."

"Your big house is probably full of Mexicans. Cooking your dinner, cleaning your toilets. Doing jobs white people don't want. But then, we don't mind being poor and uneducated, do we? We're ignored except when you want someone to hoe your crops or do your dirty work. Isn't that what you're thinking?"

"You don't know what I think."

"You're not denying anything."

Michael set down his briefcase and took one step toward her. She didn't move.

"You're so observant." She had nailed everything, which made him mad. "My father's house is full of Mexicans—in the kitchens and the fields. Some of those people I've known all my life, and I still don't know the names of their children. Feel justified now?" He picked up his briefcase. "But you can't stand there and tell me you had lots of white friends and that you didn't learn to distrust us like we distrusted you. Gringos don't have the market cornered on prejudice, Miss García. Now excuse me. I'll find another interpreter for María Curry."

Toni hadn't expected the truth, and certainly not from this man. Vance Johnson and Mrs. Larson had vanished. She touched Michael's arm. "Mr. Shaw."

"What now? Want to insult me some more?"

"I'm sorry."

The change in her voice was enough to make him stay. "Well, I apologize for raising my voice. That's terrible behavior for a lunch guest."

"And I'm glad my father didn't see how I treated you, especially when you're helping someone who really needs it. The sandwiches will be ready soon, Mr. Shaw." Toni set plates and napkins on the table. Billie's singing soothed the little house.

"Michael, please. After we fought, we should at least be on a first-name basis," he said and took a seat.

"All right then. Call me Toni."

He swore her eyes became a deeper color of brown. "Toni. I like that."

"People tell me I have my mom's temper," she said.

"People tell me I have my father's money."

She laughed.

"I do like your house, Toni. It has character, and you can't buy that with any amount of money."

The compliment made her smile. "It's good to have your own place."

"So you can bring home rich gringos?"

"A Harvard one, to boot." She put a ham sandwich on his plate. "Not on the Mesa Inn's menu, but it'll do."

He didn't pick up the sandwich. "Toni, I didn't volunteer to defend María. A judge appointed me."

"You could have said no."

"I really tried."

Toni smiled and threw Oscar another piece of ham.

9

WHENEVER A METAL DOOR CLANKED in the jail, María Sánchez Curry thought of the beaches of Puerto Vallarta. The concrete enclosing her stank of piss and cleaners, which only brought to mind the smell of salt and moisture wafting over her like baptism water. When the women inmates cried at night, María remembered the waves hushing at the shoreline. She looked through the gray metal bars and saw the thickness of green rising on hills and palm trees saluting the wind. The two places were as far apart from each other as God was to the cell in which she sat. Hundreds of miles away lay the town where she was born. And the ocean, a color bluer than God's eyes. Waves undulating with the heart of the world. Sand the same color as soil washed clean of sin. Whitecaps winking at her. As a girl, she believed the Almighty watched as she stood on the beach and prayed to be rescued from loneliness.

Her father was a hulky fisherman, so their family always ate the catch that was too small or damaged for him to sell at the market. Her mother worked at a fruit cannery. That left María to take care of her younger brothers and sisters, who were thankless and mean. When her father wasn't on his boat, he drank and called María his "ugly little fish." *Pececita fea*. He sang it out as his eyes glazed from tequila and spite. María looked in the mirror and realized his description was more accurate than cruel. She did have an insignificant face, large eyes and lips like fishing line. Her body was straight as a boy's.

Meanwhile, María's mother offered no protection from the taunts. The woman worked, ate, slept and ignored her own children. Her mother remained passive as a windless day when her husband slapped her or pinched her breasts before shoving her into their room at night.

That was María's life, and she thought she might as well have changed the direction of the tide. Still, sometimes she wished her beloved ocean would sweep her father overboard and fill his lungs with salt water. After such a fantasy, however, she felt so terrible she'd run to the priest for confession.

Men paid no attention to María as a young woman and looked right through her, the older she became. After her sisters and brothers married, her parents expected half of the money she earned at the cannery. María spent her nights sewing in her room while her parents argued in theirs. Only at the beach did she feel alive.

One afternoon Ben Curry sat down on the sand next to her. He actually looked at her, smiled and asked her name. She returned the smile, hiding her mouth with her hand because her father said she had a fish smile. And Ben told her, "You shouldn't hide."

That winter, fancy hotels cropped up along the beach for rich tourists who were beginning to discover the beauty of her home. On her way to work, María passed the steel structures and knew she'd never make enough money to see the inside of one when they were completed. Ben supervised an American crew building the Mexicana, a behemoth of luxury. Some days, she would see him as she passed the construction site. He spoke Spanish perfectly. He said he had lived near Mexicans all his life in a town in Arizona and had an ear for the language.

With protruding ears, piggish eyes and only wisps of reddish hair left on his head, Ben was not handsome or even young, but then her years had gone, too. He did show powerful arms under his short-sleeve shirts and looked as if he could crush her, which excited María. He began to come by for her after her shift. They would remove their shoes and walk along the beach. She said little of her life, only of her love of the ocean. Ben talked about his work and how the rest of the men on the job were incompetent. He had an opinion about everything except family, which made María worry he was married. After a few weeks, he admitted to her that no one in the world would care if he lived or died. He hated his loneliness as much as she hated hers. María fell in love right then. She had long abandoned any hope of getting away from her mother and father, who told her she was destined to take care of them in their old age. But when Ben kissed her, his warmth moved inside her and weakened her legs. His arms held her so tight, she couldn't breathe. It was as if he was taking her breath and giving her his. She had never been kissed before.

María began wearing lipstick and bought new dresses. She paid no mind when her father called her a *puta*.

After two months, Ben announced he was headed back to the States. When he turned to leave, María grabbed his arm. "We don't have to be alone anymore," she had blurted out. "Take me with you."

"Take me with you," María repeated in her cell at the Mitchell County Jail.

She lay back on the lumpy, smelly bed. She had killed Ben, the man she loved. The man who had finally looked at her. The clank of a metal door came from another part of the jail, and she again thought of the beach in Mexico. She thought how far she had come to this place with no view of water the color of God's eyes.

10

Toni adjusted her suit jacket and entered the courtroom, which immediately reminded her of a funeral parlor. It had hardwood floors and dark wood on walls and railings. Tall windows behind the judge's bench had been shuttered closed and muted the sunlight. People talked in muted voices, as if they did not want to disturb the deceased. Rows of chairs as if for mourners. How could justice reside in such gloom?

The ceiling fans creaked like her father's knees, and everyone wiped at sweaty foreheads. Still, Toni shivered. She felt as cold as Ben Curry in the grave. She shivered for María, who sat at a table up front. María wore another drab jail shift.

"I don't like this place," María whispered to Toni when she joined her.

"This is the first time I've been in a courtroom, too. You and I will stick together and get through this."

María sat up. "I'll try to be brave." Knowing Oscar was safe helped.

Toni had listened patiently to all the instructions about what her dog liked to eat. "Shreds of chicken. Warmed-over Spanish rice. And he loves strips of dried tortilla. You'll see how he drags them onto his bed to chew them. But don't give him any fish, Toni. It will give Oscar gas, and then you'll be sorry."

Under the table, María's legs were restless. "All the white people look at me with blaming eyes," she said.

Toni glanced around. María was right. She recognized disdain. Toni held María's hand. "Don't worry. Everything will turn out all right. You'll see."

Toni also wanted to convince herself. She had the notion the walls of the courtroom might fold over on María and encase her like a coffin. The only person who could hold them back was Michael Shaw.

When he entered, he winked at them. On the first day of a trial, Michael always attempted to show optimism for his clients. "Good morning, ladies." But he couldn't stand the hope in their eyes, so he glanced over at prosecutor's table to size up the opposition. Unfortunately, Mitchell County Attorney Joe Brennan sat there.

Brennan's wire-framed glasses mirrored the overhead light as if the man had no eyes. After working together in the county office, Michael had learned Brennan could be brutal to people both on the witness stand and off. Coworkers had joked, "Best not turn your back on Brennan unless you have a death wish." Brennan loved to wear sharp three-pieces suits and to humiliate anyone who couldn't fight back or wasn't well connected. He was ambitious in life and dangerous in court.

"Joe." Michael mustered his most professional voice.

"Michael."

"Didn't expect to see you."

Before Brennan could answer, Ben Curry seemed to have risen from the dirt and come through the doors of the courtroom. María screamed.

"Who the hell is that?" Michael asked María, who crossed herself and shook with confusion.

"She said she doesn't know," Toni answered after translating. "He doesn't look happy, whoever it is."

"That's the deceased's older brother, Daniel." Brennan looked meaner when he smiled. "He came from Prescott to make sure justice is done for his kin. It will be."

Daniel Curry strode up to María, who cowered as if confronted by an avenging spirit. He had more hair than his dead brother and was thinner. Other than that, they could have been twins. The work clothes he wore were worn in places but were clean and pressed, although they smelled of beer and cigarettes.

"Damn you. You killed my only brother." He pulled María up by her collar. "He was all the family I had."

Toni shot up from the chair and put a protective arm around María, who turned limp with fright. "Leave her alone."

Michael stood up and grabbed Curry's arm, forcing him to release his grip on María's dress. "Now back the hell off."

Curry did so. "Greaser murderer," he barked at María.

"Shut up, or I'll see you're tossed out of here," Michael said.

"You and what army? And just what the hell is a white man doing standing up for that piece of brown trash? You turning against your own?"

"My own what? Morons like you?"

Deputy Herb Bell rushed from the back of the room and pulled at one of Curry's arms. "You'll have to settle down, mister. This ain't no way to act in court."

Brennan also stood. "Deputy, he'll be fine."

"Are you nuts? That man's a menace, Joe," Michael said.

"All rise," said Bailiff George Roy, who stepped into the room without noticing the scuffle. "The Superior Court of Mitchell County is now in order. The Honorable Milton M. Hower presiding."

But everyone in the room already was on their feet, either involved in the fracas or watching.

"What in the Sam Hill is going on in here?" Hower boomed.

They all looked at the judge and froze.

"Nothing, Your Honor," Brennan said.

"Good. Then everybody take a seat. And if I see anything like this again, I'll place the lot of you in contempt."

Bell released Daniel Curry, who sat in the front row of the gallery and fixed a hateful stare at María. The deputy returned to the back of the courtroom, and its regular decorum returned.

"Can we start?" The judge wiped his brow. "Mr. Brennan, your office filed a direct complaint instead of first going to a justice of the peace or grand jury. Is that correct?"

"Yes, Your Honor."

"Very well. Let's get on with the arraignment. It must be ninety-five degrees in here, and your shenanigans don't help."

Buttoning his jacket, Michael shook off the uneasiness about Ben Curry's brother. He was relieved that Hower had drawn the case. The judge lived by the rules-of-criminal-procedure book but was fair. With thick white hair and a square jaw, Hower resembled Zeus on the bench, hurling down rulings instead of thunderbolts, and Michael knew it was best to avoid being a target of one.

The bailiff read the criminal charge: "That María Sánchez Curry did willfully murder a human being, Benjamin Samuel Curry, in the first degree on or about August 18th, 1959."

"How does your client plead?" Judge Hower asked.

"Not guilty," Michael said.

"Any input on bond, Mr. Brennan?" the judge said.

Brennan adjusted his thick glasses with a slim finger. "This is a capital case. The state requests bond be set in the amount of fifty thousand dollars."

"Mr. Shaw?"

"The defense asks that María Curry be released on her own recognizance or at the very least her bond be lowered. She's a longtime resident with no prior criminal record. She's gainfully employed at the Santa Fe Motel as a housekeeper and regularly attends church."

"Mr. Brennan?" Hower dotted his brow with a white handkerchief.

"Your Honor, we fear this churchgoing woman will flee to Mexico, which is her native country."

"My client is now a citizen of the United States. Besides, Your Honor, she doesn't own a car. What's she going to do, Joe, stroll across the border?"

"Defense request denied," the judge said.

"Thank you, Your Honor." Michael sat down, lowered his head and muttered, "For nothing."

Hower took a sip of water. "Gentlemen." He dragged out the word for better impact. "Because of the extreme heat this time of year, as you know we do not hold lengthy trials. Unlike the Acme movie house or the bank, this ancient courthouse doesn't have any fancy air conditioning, at least that the county can afford.

"Fortunately for the wheels of justice, we're at the tail end of summer, so we'll set the trial for the end of September. That'll give you plenty of time to prepare, unless you intend to take a long vacation." He paused to let the joke sink in, even though he knew no one dared laugh out loud.

Hower abruptly stood and stalked out of the courtroom. Everyone rose quickly to catch up with him.

"Court adjourned," the bailiff announced. The few spectators left.

"I'll be back to see you hang." Daniel Curry glared at María. He left, mumbling.

"We'll miss you," Michael called after him. If the brother was an indication of Ben Curry's temperament, it was a wonder his client was still alive. He turned to María. "You didn't know your husband had a brother?"

"He never talked about him, Mr. Shaw," Toni translated for her.

Deputy Bell arrived to return María to jail. María held Toni's hand and wouldn't let go.

"Come on." Bell grabbed María's shoulder.

"Please, you'll hurt her," Toni said.

"Don't tell me how to do my job."

"My client is very scared. As a favor to me, go gentle, okay, Herb?" Michael asked.

"Okay, Mr. Shaw."

"Don't worry, María." Toni pressed her cold hand. "I'll visit, and I'll say a rosary for you every day."

"Thank you, Toni. I am sorry for being so afraid."

"We'll be strong for you."

Leading María away, the deputy loosened his grip. But Toni noticed he pushed María through the door.

"That son of a bitch," Toni growled.

Busy talking with the prosecutor, Michael had not seen the deputy's action.

"Mike, I'm glad to see you haven't lost your touch with the judge," Brennan was telling him.

"He's still mad because I won twenty bucks off him in poker last Friday."

"Want to bet on the outcome of this case?" Brennan slapped two books together to emphasize what he considered a witty remark.

Michael smiled. "Why Joe, I'd love to win another twenty bucks."

Brennan cleaned his glasses with a handkerchief. "You still like to make jokes, or try to. Well, this case won't be so funny. See you at trial." His eyes brushed over Toni as he left the courtroom.

Michael sat down at the defense table. "I hate that guy."

"He reminds me of this kid in school. The bullies picked on him like clockwork. But you didn't feel sorry because he had evil eyes," Toni said.

"That's Brennan. What he lacks in conviction, he makes up in pure malice."

Toni glanced around the room, now quiet and more oppressive with its sharp corners and dead flags. Taking off her jacket, she pulled a cigarette out of her purse, remembered where she was and put it in her pocket. "I didn't realize courts took the summer off."

"It's for the best. Otherwise it'd get so hot in here, the jury might convict the judge. Then again, during hunting season, all the scheduled trials seem to magically disappear or else get settled."

She smiled and picked up her purse to leave.

"Hold on, Toni. We're not taking it easy. I'd like to start interviewing María's friends and neighbors today. I'll need your help. I don't know if they'll talk to me."

Toni nodded. "Anything for María. But before we go, you need to get rid of that tie. You look like a cop."

"Hey, I like this tie."

11

STANLEY JAMES SERVED A PRACTICED SMILE along with beer and mixed drinks. He called all his customers "buddy," even the women, but no one minded because the alcohol was cheap and his jokes, funny. The bartender turned at the sound of the bell over the door. A well-dressed man and a pretty woman entered. He could spot a lawyer a block away, and they usually meant trouble in one form or another. Lawyers had clean shirts and no conscience.

"Hiya, buddies," Stanley called. "Welcome to Willy's."

Because of the dim light inside, Toni could not see for the first few steps into the bar and proceeded carefully. When her eyes adapted to the dark, she saw four Mexican men in work clothes with mugs of beer in front of them. They were probably mill workers winding down from a double shift. At the end of the bar, a white woman wearing a low-cut blouse delicately sipped her drink. Hamburgers fried somewhere, the odor of beef mixing with that of stale beer. The bar appeared to accept any customer, Mexican, white or black, as long as they had money.

Michael focused on Mr. Stanley James, whose name he had obtained from the reports of police officers who regularly broke up fights at the bar, including those involving Ben Curry. With burly arms and an affable face, the bald Negro bartender was the type of guy to whom people told their problems just to hear him say, "Damn, ain't that a bitch." Such a man knew everything that went on in the place, but getting him to cooperate as a witness might be a challenge. To smooth the way, Michael reckoned Stanley might be more talkative as a bartender. He ordered a beer.

"What'll you have, Toni?" Michael asked as he drew up one of the barstools.

"A soda, please." She sat down next to him.

After Stanley set the drinks in front of Michael and Toni, he returned to washing glasses. He tried to ignore the lawyer, although he didn't mind serving the woman. The bartender wiped his hand over his whiskers and wished he had shaved that morning. "We have ladies' night every Wednesday, where the gentler sex gets fifteen-cent drafts. I put in a new jukebox five years ago. What'd you like to hear?"

"She likes jazz," Michael answered.

Stanley's face lifted. "Got one you might like."

He stepped down from the bar. Stanley stood less than five feet tall. While the bartender slipped over to the jukebox, Michael and Toni both bent over the bar. The floor was raised a good two feet, with steps on one end. Ella Fitzgerald's "A-Tisket, A-Tasket" started up.

Toni smiled at Stanley. "She's one of my favorites. By the way, something smells good."

"Best chiliburgers in town, Miss Buddy."

"Nice place, isn't it?" Michael asked Toni.

"I feel at home."

Michael was delighted she had picked up his strategy of wooing the bartender. "Me, too. I can make this my second office." He drank down his beer and ordered another, plus a finger of whiskey.

Toni noticed that Michael was going through the alcohol with the ease of a man who enjoyed more than an occasional cocktail.

"I bought this place five years ago from Willy Knight." Stanley put stubby fingers on the clown-red suspenders he wore over a white shirt. "But I didn't think a bar named Stanley's had the right ring, so I kept it as Willy's. I did raise the floor behind the bar. I like to be eye level with people. You can tell a lot by doing that. Like you, buddy. Tell me what you're up to."

Michael introduced himself and Toni, then told Stanley why they were there and what information they wanted.

"Shit," replied the bartender. "Sorry, Miss Buddy."

"You don't have to apologize. I've heard worse," Toni said.

"What can you tell us, Stanley?" Michael said.

"That you mean trouble."

"Ever see Ben Curry strike his wife?"

Stanley rubbed his grizzled chin. "I get lots of customers in here. It's hard to remember everything that happens."

Michael smiled. "I do believe you're pulling my leg."

Wiping the bar in front of Michael, Stanley didn't glance up. "You ain't going to go away, are you, buddy?"

"Nope." Michael noisily sipped his beer. "If you don't talk now, I'll be back tomorrow and the next day."

"I'd like your business and your money, but having a lawyer in here might ruin the reputation of my bar."

Toni laughed.

"Stanley, tell me about Ben and María Curry." Michael's voice had the right combination of friendliness and threat. "I like you, and I don't want use any of my nasty lawyer wiles to get you to talk."

The tiny bartender shook his head in resignation. His ability to know when he was licked had saved him a lot of time and ass kickings in the past. "I can see you mean to stay here until I answer."

"You're very wise."

"And you're good."

"How nice of you to say so. Now, answer the question, if you please."

Stanley opened up a bottle of Coke and chugged half of it down before he replied. "Ben and María usually came in Friday nights. They lived a few blocks away and came on foot, so they told me."

"And they fought?"

"Dammit. Okay, yes. They fought like Jake LaMotta and Sugar Ray Robinson, but what married couple don't fight, especially when they've knocked back a few beers?" Stanley refilled their drinks. "Ben could be pretty ornery. He picked fights with everybody in the place until I threatened to kick him out permanently. Ben thought he was always right, and you couldn't tell him no different. You know the type."

"Intimately. Did Ben hit María while they were here?"

Stanley scratched his chin.

"Stanley, did you see Ben hit her?"

"When he got drunk, which he did all the time. He'd sock her or push her down until I told him to go home. Then they'd be all lovey-dovey the next time, until Ben got tanked."

"Did María ever hit Ben?"

"Not that I can remember. Never saw a woman take so much shit from a man. Excuse my language again, Miss Buddy."

"That's all right, Mr. James," Toni said.

"Did María ever get drunk?" Michael started in again.

"Lot of times. María is what I call a crying drunk. When Ben got mean, she'd cry into her beer. One time she had a few too many and yelled back. Ben slapped her hard across the face and knocked her to the floor. I threw him out and barred him for a full week."

"Thanks, Stanley. One more thing. We'd like you to tell a jury what you told us."

The bartender picked up a glass and quickly began wiping it. "Oh man. I knew you'd be up to no good. I hate to get involved. It hurts business. You know, a bartender's job is to listen, and that's all."

"I'd really hate to subpoena you, but I will."

"That ain't friendly."

Toni leaned toward the bartender and touched his arm. "María's facing a death sentence or life in prison. Please, Mr. James. You can really help her."

Stanley pulled back. "Okay, okay."

"Thank you," Toni said.

"This is exactly why I'm a friggin' bachelor."

Michael smiled. "You're a good man, Mr. Stanley James. Now I'm ready for another beer. And we'll try two of those famous chiliburgers. Fine with you, Toni?"

"Yes, thank you."

Stanley chortled and started cooking.

"Excuse me. I'm going to the ladies' room." Toni slipped off the tall barstool and fell against Michael, who took her arm to steady her. From the corner of her eye, Toni noticed the Mexican men stared and whispered. Her cheeks singed as she passed them. When she returned to the bar, Michael examined an elaborate model of a cathedral made from matchsticks.

"Toni, Ben Curry made this, if you can believe it." Michael handed her the model church, which had a foot-tall spire and double doors that opened.

Even in the dim light, the model church had so much detail that Toni expected to see Mass going on inside. "This is beautiful."

"Ben gave it to me last Christmas because he said I was a good guy and didn't water down the booze. He did pay his bar tab."

"I guess that's the only good thing we can say about him," Michael said.

"The poor dead bastard."

The bartender served Michael and Toni the burgers and grinned. "I'll tell ya, Mr. Shaw, you know how to get people to talk. You'd have made a pretty good bartender." Stanley refilled Michael's beer.

"That's the best compliment I've had all day."

Stanley James put another nickel in the jukebox.

≈ ≈ ≈

At her kitchen table, Bonita Ramírez shaped small pillows of dough between her hands. Meanwhile, Michael looked through Bonita's screen door and right into the kitchen window of María's house next door.

Uncertain at first, Bonita had welcomed Michael and Toni inside after Toni explained in Spanish that he was María's attorney. "Then you are welcome in my house," the woman pronounced in English.

As Bonita talked, she rolled the dough between her hands and then flattened it with a rolling pin, which made a soft thump thump thump on the table. She picked up the thin dough, slapped it between her hands, and placed it on a hot griddle. Bonita didn't wait to ask Michael or Toni but gave them each a hot, crisp, brown tortilla slathered with butter. Her cheeks were full even when she didn't smile. She was like her kitchen, warm and neat.

"*Gracias.*" Toni rolled up the tortilla and ate.

"*De nada*," Bonita said in a melodic voice. "Please, Mr. Shaw. Eat, eat."

"Thanks." When he lifted the tortilla flat, butter dripped down his arm. A grease stain spread on his cuff and notebook. "Damn."

"Mrs. Ramírez . . . " Michael wiped his hands on a napkin.

"Bonita, *por favor* . . . " Bonita said.

A smile came easily to Michael. The woman treated them with graciousness and generosity as she gave him another napkin to wipe his hands and sleeve. That made it easier to ask about María.

"We've lived next to each other ever since they moved to Borden. María's a good woman. She cleaned for me when I got sick in the hospital. We go to Mass together every Sunday and Holy Days of Obligation, not to mention Wednesday bingo at the church." Bonita made more tortillas, putting warm ones in a bowl under a clean, damp dish towel. "María became peaceful at church, as if she knew her husband couldn't touch her there."

"What'd you think of Ben Curry?"

"*El Diablo*. God rest his evil soul." Bonita crossed herself automatically whenever Satan's or Ben's name came up. She pointed toward María's house. "I seen him punch or slap her when he got drunk, and it seems he was always drunk. But you can't say nothing 'cause they're married. You can't interfere with a man and his wife. One time, María even came over with a black eye and broken arm. *Pobrecita*."

"When did that happen?" Michael wiped up more butter with a napkin.

Collapsing on the chair, Bonita fixed her own tortilla, which she folded in half. "At Thanksgiving time last year. María told me she fell at work, but I had heard her screaming, and I knew he did it, that *cabrón*. Another time, he chased

María down the street with a butcher knife. Everyone in the neighborhood saw that. How's the tortilla?"

"Good. Do you remember when Ben Curry went after María with the knife?"

"New Year's Day. I wanted to go help her, but my husband warned me to stay away from Ben because he was crazy. Loco. He said, 'Ben's gonna come after you with that knife *también*.' Ben Curry had the eyes of an animal out for blood."

"Did María ever tell you that Ben beat her?"

Bonita's whole body jiggled with a "no."

"I can't believe that."

"I think she was too ashamed, Mr. Shaw."

"Bonita, did you see what happened on the night that Ben Curry was killed?"

The big woman shook her head. "Me and my family went to see my cousin. We got home in time to see Ben Curry carried out."

Michael put down the tortilla and asked Bonita to testify on María's behalf at the trial. Chewing her food slowly, Bonita cleaned her hands on her apron. "My husband won't like it. But I'll go if you need me. María's my friend." The woman stood up, her large eyes ready with tears. "No matter what he did to her, María stayed with him all those years. She even wrote me a letter from jail and asked me to say a rosary for Ben."

"A rosary?"

"So that his soul won't stay in purgatory and will go to heaven," Toni said.

Bonita dried her face with another napkin, gave her approval at the explanation and started rolling more dough. "Eat. I have more."

By the time they left Bonita's house, the sky had melted into orange as it prepared for the night. Michael liked this time of day, when the world seemed in balance. For once.

"I've never felt so welcome in all my life. I think she wanted to adopt me." He took off his jacket.

"She was just being hospitable," Toni said.

"Well, after three tortillas and butter, I'm glad you talked her out of making us dinner."

"It's a cardinal sin at my house to send anyone home without their stomachs full. My father is the unofficial patron saint of hospitality. Anyone who visits us is served a meal as fast as he can cook, even if it only amounts to potatoes and hamburger meat in a tortilla. When my mother was alive, she poured coffee while my father served up the food."

"In my house, you'd get a cup of coffee and a Fig Newton, if you're lucky."

"Do all lawyers make so many jokes?"

"I'm just trying to impress you. Is it working?"

"I'll let you know." Her eyes darkened, however, as she glanced at María's house. "I keep thinking about what must have happened that night." She lit a cigarette and offered him one. He declined.

"I've gotta go in and check out the place. I'll drive you home."

"I'll go in with you."

"It'll probably be pretty bad in there, Toni."

"I can handle it. I hope so, anyway."

Crushing out her cigarette, Toni followed him in and at once wished she had stayed outside. "*Madre de Dios.*" She couldn't keep her attention away from the large, jagged blood-stain on the kitchen floor. A sin to behold, but also enticing. "I've never seen anything like this."

Her pretty face hardened at the chaos—the tossed around furniture, smashed glass, the smell of rotting food from the kitchen and the bloodstains scattered on the floor and wall. Michael felt like he had slain something priceless in Toni, which grieved him.

A framed photo of María and Ben, both smiling on a beach, was smashed on the floor.

"María's really in trouble, isn't she?" Toni asked.

"Want me to lie to you?"

Toni shook her head, picked up the photograph and placed it on the television set. On a shelf near the kitchen were several of Ben's intricate matchstick creations: a cabin, a ship, a skyscraper and a fine castle with turrets and tiny red flags flying. She imagined Ben patiently building at the kitchen table while María crocheted. The happy couple. Toni held up the castle. "How could a man who made something so beautiful hurt a woman?"

"Life's not that damn black or white. Even the worst killer loves his mom, and the victims aren't as innocent as they claim. That's the biggest lesson I learned when I prosecuted criminals." Taking the castle from her, Michael placed it back on the shelf.

"You're talking about María, too. As small and as scared as she was, she grabbed that knife." The blood on the floor completed the sentence.

"Ever seen the ocotillo, Toni?"

"What?"

"The ocotillo. A desert plant. It can grow taller than a man, with striking red blossoms, like the top of the plant is on fire. But its stems are covered with thorns."

"The good and evil, the beautiful and the thorny. You sound more philosopher than lawyer."

"Lawyers make more money. Let's get some air."

They sat on the wooden steps of María's house. Clouds slipped over the moon as the peach sky melted to purple and then black. From there, they could see Bonita's house with its windows open and hear lots of friendly voices from within.

Michael cocked his head. Across the street from María's house lived the woman on the top of the prosecution's witness list, in fact, the star witness. A hand parted the curtain, and a slice of face appeared.

"Who's watching?" Toni puffed on a cigarette.

"Lorna Dean Richards. She called the police that night. She called every time María and Ben had a fight."

"She's probably dialing the cops right now, reporting two very suspicious characters at a crime scene." But Michael didn't smile as she had hoped.

He motioned his head toward the house. "Sorry you had to see that, Toni."

"It made me think about my parents. Isn't that strange?"

"Did they fight?"

"The only time they ever argued was while they were cooking. My dad complained my mom put too much salt in the food. Their tempers grew hot and died down as quickly. Mostly, I can only remember love between them." Her cigarette glowed as she took a drag. "That love was so strong I can still feel it sometimes even though my mother is gone." She had told this man more than she intended. His face held no betrayal but something else she hadn't expected. "Why are you smiling?"

"I can't ever remember when my parents didn't fight. Nothing so messy. No fists or flying furniture or blood like we saw inside. But simple, plain, solid hatred, hard and tall as the Great Wall of China."

"*Lo siento.*"

"What does that mean?"

"'I'm sorry.' It sounds nicer in Spanish."

"I'm sorry, too."

"It's getting late."

Standing up, he held out his hand to help Toni up from the porch step. "Thanks for today, Toni. You did a good job."

She took his hand. "So did you."

Through the front window of her house, Lorna Dean Richards drank coffee and watched the man and woman drive off in a fancy car. She did call the police to report two suspicious people going through the Curry home but was told that the defense attorney had permission to be there.

She closed the curtain. She was more than ready to tell her story in court about what had happened the night Ben Curry was murdered. More than that, she enjoyed the peace.

12

MOST OF THE MEXICAN MEN who worked the open hearth furnace at Arizona Steel & Iron called it *la boca del infierno*. The mouth of hell. After all, demon sparks made the air taste silvery and bitter, and the molten metal flowed out of giant buckets like devil's blood. The machinery hissed their names in that black and charred place. If they tripped and fell into the melted steel from the furnace, they'd bypass purgatory altogether and land right in the fires of torment. To most of the men who worked there, hell couldn't be as bad as a double shift.

But Francisco García never tired of watching the fountains of molten metal. He admired this world with its veins of hot steel and a mechanical heart that throbbed. Glowing and fatal, the liquid iron reached a temperature of almost three thousand degrees as it was poured into the cars, sending off golden butterflies of sparks. The cars carried their loads to the rolling mill, where the metal was cast into strong steel bones. His own bones rasped and protested so much now that he took power from the ones he helped create.

He had come to prefer this hellish world and its belly of seething iron over that of the outdoors. Under the sunniest of skies, he had been forced to pee on the side of fields and live in filthy labor camps with holes in the walls. He had had to put up with farmers who paid shit for his efforts and looked at him as if he would rape their women.

As a boy, his first memory was of sugar beets. The large, leafy plant opened like a bouquet stuck in the ground. While his mama weeded, he played off to the side of the field with his most valuable possessions, three tiny rusted cars he had found. He made elaborate roads and towns, using sticks for stop signs. He spit in the dirt and built mud houses. Wearing a man's shirt and straw hat, his mama frequently glanced at him, putting her hand to her eyes to shield the sun. When she spotted him, she would wave. He swore she had a halo of gold around her head, like the saints in the little book they would look through at night under the light of the kerosene lamp. Making sure he was safe, she would return to work chopping weeds for hours with a short-handled hoe.

In a clearing between two fields in southern Idaho stood a gathering of shacks and a rundown shower house with two stalls to accommodate the hundred or so farmworkers. There were stinky outhouses and a tiny store owned by the farmer, who gladly took back the money he had paid the workers. The place had been called Ramona, after the farmer's only child.

After work, his mother cooked a dinner of beans and chicken in their shack, where Francisco could see through cracks in the walls. Outside, other camp residents sang and talked around fires in metal barrels. His mother was slender, and Francisco wondered how she ever had the strength to labor beside the men all day, weeding the beets. Her newly washed black hair hung past her waist, but her eyes seemed far away, as if on the journey ahead of them. A trip to the next field, the next crop. His father had left before he was born, and when he grew up, he never forgave the man for abandoning them. She had no photos of his father, only saying his name was Carlos and that he had come from Sonora, Mexico.

One night, his mama kissed him as she always did and made the sign of the cross on his forehead. He heard her whisper prayers, and then he fell asleep beside her on the squeaky old bed. Her body was feverish, as if she carried the sun inside her.

She did not wake.

"Mamá, get up!" Francisco screamed the next morning.

When she wouldn't stir, he ran into the labor camp and shouted for help. He cried as the other workers shook their heads and covered her with a threadbare blanket. Finally, they had to pry his hands away from her so she could be buried in a small cemetery outside of the nearest town. With no money available for a proper marker, someone fashioned a cross from two metal bars and scratched her name on them: ISIDRA GARCÍA.

Francisco was eight. He was sent by the state to live with his mother's brother in San Antonio, Texas. His uncle's family also followed the crops, and the next year Francisco joined them in the fields, bending over plants, eating on wooden pallets and trying to find a place to pee behind trees or bushes. He had given up on any schooling because the family traveled so much. His only regret was not learning to read, but his Aunt Mila and Uncle Edgar taught him to take pride in whatever he did, even in the lowest of jobs. On his nineteenth birthday, Francisco heard a man in a bar talk about a new steel mill in Arizona that paid decent wages—even to Mexican people. The mill did not care if you had an education, only a strong back, the man said. Francisco knew he had to take the chance for a good job, one where he could stay put, plant his own roots and build a better life.

Before he left, he received a blessing from his Aunt Mila and five dollars from his uncle, along with a book about Emiliano Zapata that had many photographs. He stole a ride on the railroad and hitchhiked until he landed in Borden. At first sight of the mill, he felt its might. In the office, a scrawny white man gave Francisco a friendly smile and helped him fill out his application because he didn't read. Francisco was grateful because the man gave him respect and even spoke Spanish, although it was the fancy kind with the lisps. Thanking God for his fortune, he was hired and started work the next day. With his first paycheck, he began saving for a house, all the while living in a tiny boardinghouse with ten other workers. His new job was among the fires and metal instead of the sun and earth, but it provided a way to mold his life as he wanted, like the steel he was molding into wire or bars.

After Francisco married Maricela, it took three years to save for a headstone for his mother. He and his young family traveled to Idaho, and he cried at her grave. For years following his mother's death, he dreamed of her standing in the fields, wearing the white dress they had buried her in. In his dreams, her straw hat shone like the full moon. Her hair moved in the breeze until she faded away and became the wind kissing his face.

In the flash of the steel fire, Francisco glanced at his watch and wondered how long he had stood in the middle of the cavernous building over the open hearth. His memories came to him more often now than in his younger days. *You will soon be part of memory, of the past,* he told himself as he glanced again at his watch.

Once inside the locker room, Francisco slowed. The inside of his chest blazed hot as the furnace. He stumbled into the bathroom and leaned against the wall, yielding to the burning. Recognizing and giving in to its command over him became the only way to force air back in his tortured lungs. He waited and breathed what air he could manage. Sweat soaked his shirt. At last, the pain let go, like a fighter who was tired of walloping an opponent. He straightened up and wiped the sweat from his eyes with his handkerchief.

If he had stayed tending to the crops in the fields, he might have been crippled from years of stoop labor. He could have been poisoned by a crop doused with bug killer, lost his arms in a harvest machine or been buried under sacks of seed or grain. All that, and he would still have had to pee on the side of canals, live in shacks with holes and wash in rusted water in farm labor camps. The ache in his lungs amounted to small cost for the good living and the dignity he had found in a place as dark and hot as hell.

≈ ≈ ≈

Toni held onto the chain-link fence while she waited for her father to come up the stairs from the tunnel connecting the mill to the outside world. The mill smokestacks jutted into the sky from the gigantic black buildings that resembled stranded arks. When she and Carmen were kids, they begged their mom to let them run the few blocks to the mill entrance to meet their father. During an extra shift, the mill supplied him a meal—usually a tired ham and cheese sandwich, chips, an apple and cookie. She and Carmen fought over the food, mostly the cookie, pawing through the gray box.

"Where's our lunch, Daddy?" Carmen would ask when he emerged from the tunnel.

Often, they found nothing but waxed paper.

"I got hungry and ate it all," he said at those times.

"That's okay," Toni would say.

She would put her hand in his, and they all would walk home. The mill reminded her of a palace where an evil duke lived with his dragon, similar to those in the storybooks she read in the school library. Hills of coal that fed the great fires were like bumps on a dragon's back. She often glanced back to make sure the dragon didn't follow them home. As a grown woman she was not fully convinced there was no monster and vaguely anticipated the pulse of scaly wings flying out from the mill.

She gripped the fence more tightly, watched for her father and waited to apologize. That morning they had argued. She had called him stubborn as a mule for not going to a doctor. Before he went to work, the persistent cough again took hold of his body until his eyes reddened with tears and he gasped for air.

"It's only a cold. Don't be a nag," he said once he could talk again. His voice became so intense, it left no room for argument.

She had learned not to quarrel when he sounded like that, and he sounded like that whenever she brought up the cough. She could get nothing more out of Carmen, no matter how much she begged or bullied.

When Toni had arrived home from Phoenix for good, she was glad she wore sunglasses so her father could not see the immediate worry in her eyes when she noticed how he had aged. On her previous visits home for holidays, she rationalized away his appearance to hard days at the steel mill. Now his thin, grayish hair had changed to white, and his dark skin had soured to sallowness. More and more, his pace slowed, as if he lugged the whole of the mill on a chain around his ankles. The first time she had heard that cough, she felt her own lungs ablaze. With each visit home, the spells grew more frequent and violent. Life had once again proved that it did not always cooperate with happy expectations. So she packed her car and left Phoenix to be with her father. She told him and Carmen she was moving back because she had missed them. Not a total lie, because she did. However, returning to Borden meant giving up a teaching job and self-reliance. Starting over. But her father was worth all she could give.

"Toni, you're daydreaming again."

"What? Oh, hi, Jesús."

Jesús Torres carried his black metal lunch pail under his arm. His unbuttoned shirt revealed a sculpted chest. Unlike her father, who disliked using the mill showers, Jesús wore clean clothes. Ready-to-go-out clothes. And Jesús did like to go out, which was one of the reasons they broke up while in high school.

"I heard you were back in town. Did you miss me?"

"No." She smiled. "How long have you worked at the mill?"

He put down his pail and ran a comb through his hair, still wet from the shower. "About four years. My dad got me in. He's a foreman now. Hell, it's all right money. I even bought a house."

"That's great, Jesús. You should be proud."

"So you're a teacher?"

"I got the degree. No job yet."

"Didn't hire you at the school, huh?" He grinned.

"Nope."

"Well, I'm glad you're back. You're still a knockout. Maybe I'll call you. You know, like old times."

"We broke up, remember?"

Jesús playfully slapped his head and laughed. "I forgot about that."

"I didn't. I busted you making out in your old truck with Emilia Montez when we were supposed to be going steady."

"Oh, yeah. That was dumb. If it means anything, I was thinking of you at the time."

"Baloney."

Jesús had been polite if tenacious about her sleeping with him. She held him off because she didn't want to end up like her best friend, Juanita, pregnant and uneducated. She wanted children someday, but not to conceive them in his Ford truck. Still, he could be hard to resist, and at times she'd had to fight back her temptation with a two-by-four.

Jesús kissed her on the cheek. "Maybe I'll call you anyway, okay, Toni?"

"Maybe I'll answer," she called to him as he walked away. Toni did not notice Francisco coming out of the tunnel, lunch pail in hand and exhausted.

"Toni, who's sick? What's wrong?" he said.

"I wanted to walk you home, that's all."

"Thank the Lord. ¿Cómo estás, hija?"

"Bien, Papá, and you?"

"Not bad, but I'm getting too old for all this." Francisco waved to Jesús as he drove off in his brand new Ford pickup. "Well?"

"Well, what?" Toni said.

"You know, getting married."

"I have to fall in love first."

"Oh, is that all?"

Toni took her father's lunch pail to carry, and they headed home. "Sorry about this morning, Pops."

"I don't hold grudges."

"That's what I love about you. Now, me, I'm like Mom. I hold onto grudges like they were gold."

"How's your court job, hija?"

"Doesn't pay well, but it's interesting."

"Will that lady get the gas chamber?"

"She's got an excellent lawyer." She felt her cheeks warm for some reason. "I mean, he's one of the top lawyers in Borden, and I think he really cares about her."

"Rich?"

"As a king."

"And he still works hard for that lady?"

"Yup."

"Then he sounds like a good man."

"Yes, he does. How was work?"

"Busy." Pride in his job made him forget the smoldering fire in his chest and soreness in his bones. "Our steel built this country."

"That means *you* helped build this country."

Francisco lowered his head a bit. "Sorry you didn't get that teaching job. Next year might be better."

"I didn't even get the chance, Pops." Toni spoke in Spanish. The language created an intimacy between them. "It's hard not to . . . " She stopped.

"What? Hate, get mad? You can't keep that up every day, Antonia. It hurts you more than them. Besides, getting mad isn't going to change somebody who can only see you're Mexican and nothing more than that."

Francisco's thumb pointed back at the mill. "We got the worst jobs at first, but we worked hard and earned their respect. I made enough money to buy a house and support a beautiful wife and two beautiful daughters. That's not too bad for someone who can't read or write a lick."

"Not bad at all."

"The best you can do in this life is work hard and love God and your family."

She took his hand. "And don't stand for too much shit from people."

"I'm glad your mother didn't hear you cuss."

"Why? Mom always said 'shit.'"

As soon as they entered the house, Toni rushed to check the pot. The cooking beans smelled of earth and salt and had boiled to a fine light brown tinged in pink. She checked the flame on the gas stove, but the heat from the pot made her instantly weary because the house was already sweltering. Although she had opened all the windows before she left for the mill, the temperature refused to budge, not even for the fan she had bought.

Francisco went to the bathroom. Soon Toni heard the shower running. Wiping sweat from her forehead, she stirred the beans. Her hand brushed the pot. "Dammit."

"What happened?" her father called from the other room.

"I wasn't paying attention and burned myself."

Toni placed her hand under the cold water and enjoyed the cool stream of relief.

As soon as Francisco had toweled off and dressed, he emerged from his bedroom and was gripped by a coughing spell.

Toni rushed to him to him with a glass. "Here, sip this."

The coughing subsided after a while, but his eyes became bloodshot, and his chest rose and fell in quick movements.

"You're going to see a doctor. I can be as stubborn as you. I'll carry you there if I have to."

"Stop," he managed to yell.

Her eyes blinked.

"Sit down, Antonia." His voice barely reached above shallow gasps.

Toni knelt down beside him.

"I did go see a doctor."

"And?"

"My lungs are filled with metal dust from the mill. It's tearing my lungs apart bit by bit until they won't be able to hold any air."

"Can the doctor cure you?" She choked on the words.

"No. You can ask him for yourself. He's a nice man."

Toni began to cry.

"My lungs probably look like little ingots." He gave a smile.

"Don't joke about it!"

"I'm sorry, *hijita*. Sit next to me." Francisco explained as if Toni were a child: "We all are heading to death, Antonia. You know that. There's nothing else to do about it but live a good life."

"We have to get you to a specialist."

"Unless they have a miracle in their pocket, what can they do? Just pray for me."

"You should have told me sooner." She hugged him hard until he gently pushed her away.

"If I had, then you would have wanted to come home. I wanted you to finish your schooling."

"That doesn't matter." She wiped at the tears.

Her father took her shaking hands in his. How rough they were from calluses, like the cracked desert. His fingernails were bruised and multicolored from years of hard work. Toni never realized how small they were.

"See, no matter how many times I wash them, I can't get the dirt from under my nails. I'm not complaining, because that's how I earned my living. But I did all that so your hands, and Carmen's hands, won't be like these." The coughing made his voice gruff and low. "I think the beans are burning."

Tears blurred her eyes as she lowered the gas flame and stirred the beans.

"Antonia." Her father stood beside her. "The beans are salty enough." He took his handkerchief from his back pocket and wiped her cheeks. "If we eat them, we'll all feel like crying."

She washed her face in the sink and went into the living room. Sitting down in his chair, Francisco held out the newspaper to her.

"Now, read me the paper, *por favor*. I want to see what that Eisenhower is up to."

After her father fell asleep in his room, Toni cleaned the house and checked him every twenty minutes. On his high chest of drawers was a shrine with jar candles decorated with Jesus unveiling his Immaculate Heart. Next to those was the foot-tall statue of the Santo Niño de Atocha, the Holy Infant, wearing finery and a plumed hat and carrying a basket and staff. The outstretched arms of a taller statue of the Virgin Mary held rosaries, medals and scapulars. Whenever she and Carmen passed the dresser, they would cross themselves, which they had learned to do from their mother. Toni lit one of the candles and prayed for a miracle.

Once before Toni had asked for divine help, when her mother lay in a room at St. John's Hospital. Her mother's once-beautiful black curls had been transformed into gray and brittle strands, as if life had already deserted them. Wracked with pain, her mother wailed until nurses gave her shots of morphine. In the few moments of her mother's lucidity, Toni recognized the feisty, loving woman who had played dolls with her and Carmen and sung Frank Sinatra songs as she cleaned the house. How easily she had laughed. How she had loved to dance. Mama's kiss on her cheek forever sweet and soft as she bid them good night.

During catechism, the nuns had taught Toni about the black mark marring every baby's soul as a reminder of man's ejection from paradise for disobeying God and how baptism washed away the original sin. When her mother died, Toni swore that black, ravenous mark had returned and expanded within her because of another sin. Namely, her anger at God for taking her mother away from them.

A little after four in the afternoon, Toni checked on her father, who still slept. She went outside to wait for Carmen to come home from her job as a hairdresser at the Moreno Beauty Shop on Grant Street. Toni paced and smoked.

"He told you, didn't he?" Carmen said as soon as she saw her sister.

"Why didn't *you* tell me?"

"He said he'd tell you in his own time."

"Oh God, Carmen." She threw down her cigarette.

Carmen put her arms around Toni. Sitting on the curb in front of their house, the sisters held each other, sobbing as quietly as possible so as not to wake their father.

Love and prayers were never enough to keep death away, Toni knew. It would come as surely as man had lost paradise.

13

MICHAEL HATED SURPRISES, especially when they made him late to dinner at his father's house. He didn't want a lecture on punctuality, because it gave him indigestion. Ignoring his complaints, Jenny continued to guide him down a street of well-set homes. The neighborhood reminded Michael of a cheerful Norman Rockwell artwork with pink-cheeked, happy people. He disliked those paintings because they hid the true state of the world.

"We won't be long." Jenny sat half off the car seat. "Wait, pull over here."

Michael glided to a stop in front a two-story white house with columns and a FOR SALE sign. Fat pink flamingos stood guard in a flower bed. Jenny jumped out of the car in her pretty cocktail dress, the pearls bouncing on her chest.

"It won't hurt you to have a quick look at it," she called. "Isn't it perfect? Janie Hitchcock told me about it at lunch, and I rushed over to see it. The pink flamingos match the pink kitchen, and one of the bathrooms is pink, too."

"Who lived here? The Easter Bunny?"

Jenny pulled him along as she peeked into the front window of the empty house. She dug into her purse. "I've got the key."

"How the hell did you get that?"

"I have my ways, Mr. Nosey."

Her flirtations tired him. "Jenny, we can do this another day."

She had unlatched the door. Michael smelled dust and saw mouse prints.

Jenny swept up the large stairs, then slowly down, arms open to welcome guests. "Don't I remind you of Loretta Young? There's three bedrooms, two baths and a rec room. And a big fireplace in the living room and master bedroom." She turned and sprinted the rest of the way up the stairs.

Michael followed. "For God's sake."

"In here."

Jenny stood in the middle of a spacious room with white carpeting and floor-to-ceiling windows. "This is the master bedroom. Isn't it gorgeous?"

"Right out of *Life* magazine. Can we go now?"

She took his hand. "I know I promised not to pester you about buying a house, but this is what I call perfection."

She led him to a smaller room across the hall. "This could be a nursery. In yellow, I think. Then we could paint it blue if it's a boy." Suddenly she headed back down the stairs. "Come on, Michael. I have to show you the kitchen."

Opening cabinets and rubbing her hand over the counter tops, Jenny coughed a little at the dust, though even that held a charm for her. "All modern appliances. You've got to see the yard." She opened the back door and almost skipped along the manicured lawn and garden.

"We're going to be late for dinner." Hearing his father whine over their tardiness didn't scare him at all. But he wanted to avoid talk about buying a house because his excuses began to reflect a lack of substance.

While Jenny inspected the patio and barbecue pit, Michael strolled to a square hole in the back of the yard. The hole must have measured about twenty feet square and about fifteen feet down. "What the hell is this?"

"Oh, that was going to be a fallout shelter." Scrunching her nose, she glanced into the hole. "The owner said he didn't really need one anymore because nothing will save us if the Russians dropped the bomb. But he had a great idea for what we could do with it."

"What?"

"Turn it into a swimming pool."

"Great."

"The owner also says he'll let us have a generator and all the dried food we'd ever want for a bargain price."

She hugged herself and spun in a full circle to appreciate the whole property. "Perfection."

As they drove to his father's house, Jenny pretended to read *Photoplay* but kept looking up at Michael. "Well?" she said from behind the magazine. "The house? Isn't it gorgeous?"

"Very nice, Jenny."

"You promised we'd talk about a house and children after we got settled."

"Did I?"

"It's almost three years now, Michael. How much more settled can we get? I could be the happiest woman on earth with a house and a baby."

Michael tensed behind the wheel.

"I know you want to wait. But your career is going great, and I'm not getting any younger. I'm twenty-three years old. It's time we had a family."

"You talk like we're on a damn time schedule. Life's not like that. You can't plan anything."

She squeezed his leg. "We *are* on a schedule. A lovely house. An adorable baby. It's something we can count on for the future."

Michael tried on Jenny's vision. Him in a ridiculous velvet smoking jacket in that monstrosity of a house with dusted furniture and dusted lives. He'd be marking time in a place with pink flamingos, which just made him all the thirstier for a drink. Jenny kept reading her magazine and smiling at the image of happiness he had a hard time keeping in his head. He might have loved her once, but now he couldn't remember why.

At a country club dance he had complimented her dress. When she admitted she had the dress copied from one Audrey Hepburn wore in *Roman Holiday*, he should have realized she didn't have an original bone in that voluptuous body. He thought she might help his loneliness, but unfortunately he mistook her vivaciousness for spirit and became all the more isolated. Then again, her willingness not to make demands had attracted him the most. Although lately, that was all she did.

"We can talk later, Jen."

"It won't be on the market forever."

"Then we weren't meant to have it."

They drove for miles without more words, a space as dry as the land they passed. Concentrating on her magazine, Jenny refused to talk in order to show her irritation with Michael. She would do whatever it took to make him see her dream for that house. She began to sing "Bali Ha'i."

Up ahead, Michael noticed two Mexican men repairing the fence surrounding his father's vast ranch. Their hats were down over their eyes, and their backs were curved. "That's back breaking work," he said.

"What are you talking about?" Jenny said.

"When I worked on the ranch a few summers during college, it damned near killed me."

Jenny didn't bother to look up from the magazine.

"Come to think of it, those people really run the farm and ranch, not us."

"Michael, you say the weirdest things." Licking a finger, she turned the page. "Besides, lover, they were made for hard work."

14

PABLO FLORES LIKED TO WATCH MICHELLE GÓMEZ wash dishes. How she shifted her weight from one leg, then back again, while scrubbing pans in the kitchen. If the radio was playing, it could be a dance. Wouldn't that beat all? Dancing and carrying on in old man Shaw's kitchen? The place could use a little dancing. It was like a big, fancy graveyard. Pablo scratched his head. He couldn't understand how Michelle could resist him after the six long months they had worked together. He had nice clothes and a Chevy with tuck-and-roll upholstery. Lots of other girls swept their heads in his direction when he entered a bar.

"When you going out with me, Michelle?" he asked again.

"When you stop working in this kitchen." She didn't turn away from washing the pots.

He leaned on his broom and pointed a thumb his way. "I got plans."

"What you gonna do? Become a butler?"

"I ain't breaking my back at the mill or on some stinking ranch. I don't want to be an old man by the time I'm thirty, like my father. Hell no, woman." He picked up a silver pot and smoothed his hair. "Come on, Michelle. We'll go driving and dancing. We'll howl at the moon like a pair of wolves."

He howled.

Michelle laughed. "No wonder us Mexicans can't get anywhere."

Pablo pointed to the dining room where the Shaw family was working on the first dinner course of mushroom soup. "That bright-future stuff only works for people who came over on the *Cauliflower* and those other ships."

"Ay, that's *Mayflower*, dummy."

"I don't care if it's the *Sunflower*."

Michelle put her hands on her hips, despite their dripping soapy water. "I'm going to finish high school and go to college. We have to depend on ourselves, on our own people."

Pablo laughed. "What people? A bunch of Mexicans?"

Jim Jordan, the Negro cook, prepared the chicken cordon bleu at the counter. He rubbed his white whiskers in aggravation at Pablo's constant play for the pretty girl.

Josita entered carrying a silver soup tureen and chided them in Spanish. "Shut up, you two. I could hear you in the hallway. All you do is talk and talk and play around. The young want too much, too fast."

Jim, the cook, bobbed his head in agreement.

Pablo and Michelle took up their work again. Pablo inhaled with satisfaction because he just knew he was wearing Michelle down.

Jim spooned the chicken onto the china dishes, which Josita placed on another tray. He added green beans and mashed potatoes.

"How's it going in there?" Jim said.

"Pretty quiet, so far."

"It's early yet. Old Mr. Shaw can't help but tell young Mr. Shaw how to run his life. They'll get into it real soon."

"That's the way Mr. Martin treated his first wife, God rest her soul. She didn't have a moment's peace," Josita said with a sigh at her aching bunions.

Jim's cigarette dripped out one side of his mouth. "Old Mr. Shaw should leave that boy alone and let him have his own life."

"Never has and never will."

Jim added a garnish. "Now off with you, and we'll see you at the next course."

Picking up the tray, Josita headed toward the large dining room where the Shaw family sat around a long table. To Josita, they were like an advertisement in one of the home magazines she saw in Miss Melody's bedroom, everything clean and unreal, like wax fruit.

"Josita, take away the soup dishes first before you start serving the entrée. Do I have to tell you every time?" Melody Shaw's fake sincerity caused Josita's bunions to ache all over again.

Michael shook his head. His latest stepmother jumped on every opportunity to display her breeding, or at least, what she wanted people to think was class. Truth was, Melody came from the middle-class side of town, but her large bosom had gotten her out of there. Melody had begged Michael to call her Mom, but he could barely manage to hold a conversation with her painted cherub face. He slurped the last of his soup as loudly as he could.

"I ran into Judge Hower at lunch the other day. He said it was gratifying to see you back in his courtroom," his father said.

"Did he mention he refused to reduce the bond for my client?"

"I'm sure he had good reason."

"He probably worried about that woman coming after him in the night."

Jenny sensed a rising argument. Her husband and father-in-law never yelled. But their civilized quarrels made her want to bite her nails down to the nubs. She hoped to divert them. "Michael is really working hard, Dad. I have to tell him to slow down all the time."

"Thanks Jenny," Michael said, "I'll lie on my own."

Josita removed his soup bowl with her familiar chapped hands. Michael smiled. Her returned smile hinted of the front gold tooth he loved as a little boy. He even once asked Josita if she could pull out the tooth so he could wear it for a while. She laughed so hard she cried. He had spent a lot of time in the kitchen with her, doing his homework, watching her cook and learning Spanish words, which he had mostly forgotten. She baked him chocolate chip cookies, and he taught her to play checkers. He told her what he had learned in school when his stepmothers didn't have the time or interest to listen. Every summer, he accompanied her when she took lunch to her husband Diego, an amiable fellow with a thick mustache who could fix anything on the ranch or at the house. After he grew up, she became a passing figure in his peripheral vision.

Michael realized he hadn't really looked at Josita for a while. White now streaked her black hair, and her body was fuller. Her calm face was mostly unlined by age, although she was almost sixty. He still loved her gold tooth.

"Michael?" his father said.

"What?"

"As I was saying, your client confessed. You might consider having her plead guilty and hope for leniency." Martin sipped water. He never drank alcohol.

Melody pepped up her hairdo with one hand. "I hope you two aren't talking the law. I'll be bored to tears."

"My darling, since when aren't you bored to tears?" Martin said.

His wife just giggled, the insults soaring over her curls.

Michael finished his wine. "Confession or not, we're going to trial, Father." He watched Josita fill his wineglass. "There are mitigating circumstances in this case."

"You have more important ones."

"I can handle those and everything else. Don't worry about me. Besides, providing the best defense is part of those darn lawyer rules."

"You're very argumentative tonight. Save it for the courtroom. Joe Brennan has the killer instincts of a mountain lion, even though he does look like an accountant."

By the end of dinner, Josita could hardly wait until she got to her small home on the ranch. She would put on the terry cloth slippers her son had given her last Christmas. Then she would say her rosary and fall asleep well beside her husband. For now, she went into the kitchen for the coffee.

Jim put out his cigarette when he saw her. "Thank God, this night is almost over." He filled the silver coffeepot and placed éclairs on paper doilies on a glass plate. "So who's winning in there?"

"Don't know, but young Mr. Shaw started hitting the brandy."

"That's a bad sign."

Holding the pot and the plate of éclairs, Josita entered one of the sitting rooms off the dining room. Michael sat in a big chair like a lost boy with a brandy glass in his hands. Old Mr. Shaw stared out the window. Miss Melody thumbed through a magazine. Mr. Shaw's young wife wiped the lipstick off her teeth. How sad, these white people with all their money having no fun and not talking to one another. Noise and laughter lived in her house, along with yelling and cursing, too, but each room was full as life itself.

Melody held her cup out for Josita to serve her more coffee. "Jim did a first-class job with the chicken. Very tasty. He's not a bad cook once we get him to wash his hands and stop using lard. And thank goodness for Josita here. I don't know how I'd run the house without her."

"And when was the last time you had a raise, Josita?" Michael asked. Josita stiffened, leaving him ashamed for putting her on the spot. All he wanted was to needle his father.

Martin cleared his throat with annoyance. "We pay you well, don't we?"

"Yes, Mr. Shaw." Josita stared at the carpet.

"Michael, I suggest you think about your future instead the future of our Mexicans. Right, Josita?"

"Yes, Mr. Shaw."

"Sorry," Michael told Josita when she offered him an éclair. She nodded. He was glad to see she had on her forgiving smile—the one he had always received whenever he broke dishes in the kitchen or did something stupid when he was a kid.

"You can go now, Josita." Martin added a spoon of sugar to his coffee. "Michael, I guess you heard Joseph Grant is retiring next month."

"I won't be sorry to see him go. He's one of the meanest sons of bitches to ever sit on the bench."

"You might consider putting your name up for his position. You have a definite advantage with civil and criminal experience, and the Shaw name can't hurt. View it as a step up."

"To where?"

"A political future. As a senator, even governor."

"I thought you hated politicians."

"Not when they're named Shaw."

Michael swirled his drink. "I have to admit, I've always dreamed of being elected dog catcher."

Martin put on a contemptuous stare, the kind from which others keeled over. Michael just took another drink.

"Your grandfather had nothing and built an empire in the desert. He knew the importance of ambition and hard work."

"Don't you mean he knew how to work everyone else for slave wages, filch state land grants and rig a few elections? I've read the history books, Father."

Jenny and Melody sat still, expecting the disagreement to escalate.

"You don't know the first thing about sacrificing for your family. But I'll teach you, if it's the last thing I do. Excuse me, I have several telephone calls to make." Martin took the stairs to his study on the second floor.

They all watched him go.

"And that, my dears, ends the sermon for tonight. Next week, the Reverend Shaw will talk about how to turn shit into gold." Michael drained his brandy glass.

On their way home, Jenny snored a little. Michael drove past the Mexican workers walking on the side of the road. The headlights of his roadster flashed on the men, who went straight ahead as if it was the only way to go.

15

As Toni and Michael crossed Lincoln Street, he took off his jacket and slung it over his arm.

"Seven in the evening, and it's a cool ninety-nine degrees," he told Toni and wiped sweat off his forehead with a handkerchief. "I think my hair is melting."

"We'll find more people home at this time of day."

She had wanted to stay with her father that evening, because every minute away was time with him lost. But Francisco went to work despite her pleas and threats. Besides, she couldn't really stay home while María sat alone in jail. She had to help Michael Shaw. The desperation over her father's illness eased, however, whenever she talked with Michael, which unnerved her a bit.

Michael and Toni were going to visit six neighbors whom María and her friend Bonita Ramírez thought might be willing to testify for the defense.

"Here we go. Juan Jiménez." Michael pointed his chin to a house on the other side of the Curry residence. With peeling paint, a slanting porch, cracked windows and green spots of weeds on the brown lawn, the neighbor's place was badly in need of a demolition ball. "Bonita said she saw Juan outside smoking a cigarette when Ben chased María with the butcher knife and another time when he knocked her down."

"And he didn't help?"

"I guess he liked the show."

"Sounds like a great guy," Toni said.

Michael knocked. Sporting a black goatee and a scowl on his round face, Jiménez answered the door but wouldn't let them inside. As Toni told Jiménez in Spanish how they were trying to help María, the man kept his eyes all over her. For that Michael wanted to kick him in the balls. When she finished, Jiménez shook his head and shut the door before Michael could ask any questions.

"That went well," Michael said and checked the next name on his list. "Let's try Virginia Sampson. She lives directly behind María's house."

"Thanks for giving me a ride, Michael. My car died, and I'm waiting for my cousin to fix it. Knowing him, I could be taking the bus for a very long time," Toni said.

"At least your cousins have talent. Mine can barely manage holding a cocktail and chewing gum at the same time. Incidentally, I happen to excel at that."

She put back her head and hooted.

Michael loosened his tie. He liked the abandon of her laugh. When he had picked her up from her house, her lips formed a straight line and her hands were clamped in fists. He didn't have to be a genius to see Toni was hiding something. Now as they walked down Lincoln Street, her arms hung loose at her sides. Her long hair waved along her back. She had submerged her secret, and he foolishly thought of what he might give to learn it.

At the next interview, Virginia Sampson peered at them through thick cat-eyed glasses. She let Michael and Toni in the door but shifted her eyes back and forth at them like they were burglars casing her neat house.

"Did you ever see Ben Curry beat up María?" Michael asked.

"She must have liked it, because she stayed with that man." Mrs. Sampson's tone was clipped as a hedge. Her freckled arms were crossed under her plentiful bosom.

"You didn't answer my question, Mrs. Sampson."

"Everyone in the neighborhood saw them fight."

"María said you work with her at the motel and might testify on her behalf in court."

"I'm not going to say anything nice about that woman. She killed a man. That's a mortal sin." The folds on her neck jostled for emphasis.

"María's husband was going to kill her," Toni spoke up. "She defended herself."

"A sin is still a sin," the woman said.

"Thanks for your time." Michael gently pulled Toni toward the door.

"Holy God." Toni lit up a cigarette as soon as they were outside.

"We definitely don't want her anywhere near court."

Rubén Chacón lived next door to Mrs. Sampson. Whiskered and bent, he met them with a toothless grin and offered a cup of coffee in a tiny kitchen. He spoke no English and listened intently to Toni. Since there was only a chicken-wire fence separating their yards, Chacón could see everything that took place at the Curry house. Yes, he had witnessed Ben knock María to the ground at least three times. Yes, he saw her hold her arm and scream another time.

"It would be a great help to María if you would come to court to testify about what you saw," Michael said.

"I'd like to help, but I can't," Chacón replied. "You see, I am not a citizen. I'm afraid they'll send me back to Mexico.

I've lived in Borden for twenty years. It's my home. My children were born here. If they send me back, I'll have nothing." He apologized with tears in his eyes, which he wiped with a wrinkled handkerchief. "That's why I didn't stop her husband when he beat her up. To my shame, I did nothing. I will pray for María. That is all I can do."

The other neighbors on their list didn't even open the door for Michael and Toni.

"I need a drink," she said after the last rejection.

"I hoped you'd say that."

Toni directed him to drive to Manuel's, a small bar a few blocks away. She had gone there once with Carmen and knew it to be dark and out of the way enough to avoid being seen by anyone. Borden was still a small town, made smaller by the division of Mexican and white.

The jukebox played only Mexican songs, and the bartender made a point of minding his own business. She ordered a beer and Michael, a whiskey, which he downed and then ordered another.

"We didn't do so well today, did we?" she said.

"Our list of defense witnesses is pretty thin. We do have Bonita and the owner of the motel where María worked. He'll at least verify how many times she came to work with black eyes and bruises. We'll also talk with her parish priest. Clergy are the best defense witnesses. They have God on their side."

"You know, when I heard the county had assigned María an attorney, I worried they'd send a lazy one."

He gripped his drink. "This is the hardest I have worked in a while. It's difficult not to get lethargic with the law I usually practice. Divorce decrees and contracts. Legal by the numbers." He swallowed more of the whiskey. "I haven't been this truthful since the third grade, when I admitted killing the classroom's goldfish."

She raised her glass in a salute.

"Now, be honest with me, Toni."

"About what?" She couldn't conceal her suspicion about what he wanted. She didn't want to talk about her father.

"How'd you get to be such a big jazz fan?"

"Jo Littlefoot."

"Who the hell is Jo Littlefoot?"

"My roommate in college. A full-blooded Zuni Indian who played jazz all the time. I grew to love it. We stayed up all night studying, drinking coffee and listening to music. She had the best collection of jokes and made me laugh. We used to compare histories to see who had it worse, the Indians or the Mexicans. She won, but we were a close second."

"What happened to her?"

Toni's mouth dried with the reply. "She killed herself our second year of college. She took a bottle of pills and slept forever. I found her the next morning. In a note, she left me her jazz albums and wrote, 'Toni, you're stronger than me. Don't follow.'"

Michael pushed away his drink.

"I haven't talked about Jo in a long time." *Gotta get out of here*, she told herself. "It's late. We better go. Besides, isn't your wife expecting you?"

"Good ole Jenny."

Sliding out of the booth, Toni smiled. "Yeah, good ole Jenny."

Michael didn't want to leave the bar, but Toni already was out the door. Jo Littlefoot had it right. Toni was stronger.

16

ON THE SMALL BALCONY OF THEIR APARTMENT, Michael sat and sipped a beer. Jenny came through the sliding door wearing a slip taut over her heavy breasts, small waist and hips that grew wider each year. She cuddled up on his lap like a kitten with an agenda.

"What you thinking about, baby?" she asked in a little girl voice she slipped on whenever she wanted to get him into bed. Funny how it didn't work like it used to, she thought.

"About my father."

She kissed his ear. "You two are more alike than different."

Michael started to stand, and she jumped off. "Come on, Jenny."

"You both went to law school and played football." She tried to sound analytical. "That's probably why you don't get along—because you're more alike than not."

"Thank you, Dr. Freud."

"Don't be a sourpuss." Jenny put her arms around him. She took his bottle of beer and placed it on the ground. "Let's go to bed. If we can't have a baby, maybe we can have some fun trying." She pushed one of her legs against his groin.

He stepped back. "I'm a little restless. I'm going to go out for a bit, Jen."

"Please, Michael. You know that cop let you go with only a warning the last time. You better not push your luck."

Michael kissed the top of her head. "They won't catch me. Don't wait up."

After she heard him go through the door, Jenny kicked the beer bottle, hurting her toe. She would show him a lesson. She clicked the deadbolt on the front door and placed a dining room chair under the doorknob to lock Michael out of the apartment. She got under the covers and turned out the light. After a few minutes, she got out of bed, took away the chair and unbolted the door. She was afraid Michael wouldn't even try to get back in.

≈ ≈ ≈

At the Cactus Bar, Michael and Bobby Darin belted out the last chorus of "Splish Splash." Bobby played on the juke-box. Michael sang loudly and badly. A young couple snickered at him as he and Bobby ended the song with a flourish. The couple applauded.

"Thank you, thank you. No autographs, please." Michael's grin widened when he saw Tommy, the obese bartender, heading his way with another double whiskey.

Tommy wheezed whenever he moved. "There you go, Mr. Shaw."

Michael leaned back against the overstuffed booth. "I like this place, Tommy."

"Thanks, Mr. Shaw."

"You know why I like this place?"

"No, but you're going to tell me."

"I'm a damn nobody here, nothing but a drinking customer."

"And a good paying customer at that."

"See, that's why I like it here."

Tommy sat down on a chair near the booth. "You're happy tonight, Mr. Shaw."

"Why shouldn't I be happy? I got a pretty wife, a respectable job and a rich father. I'm jumping with fucking joy. So bring me the goddamn bottle next time."

"Good for you," Tommy wheezed as he got up.

The jukebox kicked up again, and Michael started up "Bird Dog" by the Everly Brothers.

At eleven, Michael stumbled out and searched his pockets for car keys. He beamed with pride at his self-restraint. He didn't shut down the bar, as he had many times. He knew his limit, which was to the point of almost passing out but still with vision enough to drive home through back roads to avoid the cops. He finally located the keys and only dropped them once before opening the car door. After he started the car, Michael peered through the front windshield. The slip of a moon hung like an unanswered question. He watched for what felt like a long time and drove off to find the answer.

≈ ≈ ≈

After reading the same paragraph three times, Toni threw the book across the room. She had read *Jane Eyre* several times because she loved the story of the plain but resilient governess making her way in a remorseless world. That night, however, the romance between the penniless Jane and rich Mr. Rochester troubled her like heartburn. Sleeping on a blue pillow in the corner, Oscar stirred when the book landed on the floor. The dog came over and licked her foot.

"Sorry for waking you." She scratched between his ears. "I bet you miss María, don't you, boy? Don't worry. Michael will get her out of jail. And just because I can't sleep doesn't mean you shouldn't." Picking up the dog, she placed him on the pillow.

She lay back on the bed and closed her eyes, but her nerves pulsated. Getting up again, she washed her face, but it did no good.

Earlier in the day, she and Michael had interviewed Father Hernán Vásquez at Our Lady of the Roses Church on Adams Avenue. When Michael asked him to take the stand at the trial, the priest agreed without hesitation. Father Vásquez described María's soul as troubled, and he glanced at Toni, who felt the priest described her as well.

Drying her face and neck, she peered into the mirror. She had lost weight and found two white hairs.

"Great. Now you're old before your time."

She hadn't slept much after calling her father's doctor. Indeed, he was a nice man who called the illness "progressive and terminal." She cried so hard, her head ached for hours. Her father, however, refused to let her sleep on the couch in the house because she wanted to be near him. She had her own place, and he hadn't done all the work on the garage for nothing, he told her. So between worry about her father and María and the heat, she was getting less than five hours of sleep each night. Her father's health wasn't the only thing keeping her up that particular night.

She wasn't the least bit surprised at the knock on her door.

Michael knocked again and whispered. "Toni, it's Michael Shaw." He tried to focus in the darkness. "God, I hope this is the right house. Toni? Toni? Are you there?"

She opened the door a little. "What are you doing here?" she said harshly but as quietly as she could.

"I know it's late, but I wanted to talk. You know, about María." A stupid excuse, Michael realized, so he kept on smiling.

"Are you crazy? Mrs. Hernández hears everything."

"She won't hear me. I'm the Invisible Man." He covered his mouth to stifle a laugh.

Toni shushed him and opened the door a little wider. "Are you smashed?"

"No. Are you?" He put on a straight face and then cracked up.

"Oh, my God, you *are* smashed."

"Guilty."

"Quiet. You need to go home."

"Home." He stopped smiling and leaned his forehead against the wall. His hair fell into his eyes, "Please, Toni."

"No self-respecting girl would let you in."

Michael held onto the doorknob. "But a nice girl would."

Toni said nothing. Michael blinked rapidly.

"I'm sorry. I'll go," he said.

Toni made the sign of the cross. "Hold on."

She hurried to find a robe. "You must be crazy, girl," she muttered to herself.

The admonishment didn't stop her from opening the door, grabbing his shirt and hauling him in. She kept a peripheral eye out for light from Mrs. Hernández's windows. Not a flicker showed. That didn't mean a thing, however. Toni suspected the old woman spied out her windows when the lights were out.

After three cups of coffee so strong it burned his stomach, Michael held his hand over the top of the cup as they sat at the kitchen table.

"Toni, no more."

"How you feeling?"

"Not too bad, except my head will pay me back tomorrow."

"Good, you deserve it for drinking so much."

"You sound like a judge."

She held up the coffeepot. "You sure you don't want more?"

"Only if you shove the grounds into my veins."

"Believe me. I'm tempted to do that with a plunger. Want something to eat? It might help."

"Believe me, it won't."

"Okay, I won't torture you anymore." She placed the cups in the sink. Turning, she leaned against the counter. "Why do you drink so much?"

"What makes you think I do?"

"Come on, tanked on a weekday. Showing up at a strange house in the middle of the night." She sat across from him. "Are you a drunk, Michael?"

He sat back in his chair, shocked at the air-to-air missile accuracy of the question nobody had ever bothered to ask. "Only when the situation warrants it, which in my case is a lot."

"That's an honest answer."

"Do you make it a habit to let drunken men in your house late at night?"

"Not usually. But I've taken a risk here and there."

"Not me. I've done what's expected of every American boy. College, law school, joining dad's firm."

A slight smile. "Wife."

"That, too," Michael said, though not with satisfaction.

"I get it. You drink because you've gotten everything you've ever wanted."

"It was all so easy, I could have done it in my sleep. And alcohol is my idea of a great anesthetic." He smiled, but his eyes itched with weariness.

"You always do what's expected of you?"

"No."

He took her hand, leaned over the table and kissed Toni with all the uncertainty of a first kiss. For as much as he wanted her, he feared she would reject his all too apparent flaws.

But Toni slipped her hand over his neck and drew him closer. She tasted of peppermint toothpaste and renewal.

Getting up from the table, Toni clicked on the record player and lowered the volume. An unhurried jazz song accompanied her to the door as she locked it. Leading him up from the table, she unbuttoned his shirt and pulled down his pants and shorts, which he stepped out of. Toni slipped off her robe and nightgown. In the middle of the small room, they danced to music tender as an embrace. His fingers brushed over her mouth, along her breasts and around her nipples. Her hands dropped to his sides and then skimmed his chest and his back. He continued to glide his fingers over her face and along her hair. Up her back and down her thighs. His paler hand on her darker skin. His movements resonated on her flesh. Michael's hand went between her legs, where his fingertips lingered. He tapped out his own delicate tune. She pressed his hand down, but didn't moan or writhe. Her breathing scorched his skin.

When Toni switched off the small lamp beside the bed, he gasped at the beauty of the faint moonlight on her. The shadow of the curtain covered their bodies in a pattern of lace. The single bed squeaked with their weight as he slid over and in her. The record had stopped, but still they danced.

17

MARÍA HAD NEVER SEEN two women fight before. She was eating her dinner of rubbery meatloaf and mashed potatoes in the cafeteria when a big blond woman slapped the tray out of the hands of a thin Mexican woman. Food flew. So did rage. The women took steps back from each other. Their lips stretched over clenched teeth before they charged. They kicked and clawed at each other with their nails. Their eyes were slits as they struck out, like hawks tearing at prey. The Mexican dug her nails down the side of the blond's round face. Screaming and bloody, the big blond grabbed a handful of the Mexican's hair and yanked. She bellowed in triumph with the long black trophy in her hand. The women called each other names that María had first heard from Ben.

Cunt. Bitch. Cocksucker. Whore.

María set down her fork. She recognized the vicious faces of the combative women as they were dragged away by the guards. The cafeteria quieted, but María could not finish eating her meatloaf as she remembered the first time Ben had raised his hand to her. It happened the night she lost her virginity.

She had left Puerto Vallarta without packing or saying good-bye to her father or mother, who would only miss her cooking, cleaning and the money she brought home. She did take a handful of sand and put it into her pocket. María breathed in the ocean, not knowing if she would again stand on its beaches. With Ben, she boarded a bus to the United States, carrying nothing but faith in a future.

As a young girl María had dreamed of wearing a lace and embroidered dress to church, of a priest placing a crystal rosary around her neck and that of her betrothed and of humbly placing flowers before the Virgin during the wedding Mass. Of a big dinner with family. Of the wonders of love between a man and woman. As the bus rumbled north, she didn't mind missing out on these rituals. She had a man at her side.

In Nogales, Ben had bought a car and found a place for them to get married—a justice of the peace in a ramshackle office next door to a butcher's shop. She still wore the same clothes she had on when she left Mexico. They were now wrinkled and sweaty from their journey on the hot bus. The justice spoke only English, so Ben had to tell her when to say, "I do." He didn't kiss her when the ceremony ended within minutes.

"Ben, I love you," she had told him as they left the justice of the peace. She didn't lie. He had rescued her from dying alone, and she was grateful. He had shown her kindness and attention.

Ben didn't answer her.

He bought her new clothes, and they ate dinner. Later, at their motel room, María shivered in the bathroom like an innocent girl, although she was almost forty. She combed her hair and rubbed lotion on her body, becoming heady with the smell and anticipation. When she and Ben had strolled the beaches of Puerto Vallarta, he only kissed her. Once in a while and almost with an endearing shyness, he rubbed his big hand over her small chest or wiped it over the front of her panties.

On her wedding night, she envisioned more kisses like the first one on the beach, with his breath filling her.

Ben yelled at her from the other room, "What are you doing in there? Get out here, dammit."

She came out, turned off the light and slipped off her nightgown. She got into bed and waited for love. Ben rolled on top of her. She hadn't realized how much he weighed. He grunted as he entered her, and she cried out with the initial pain as something foreign forced its way inside her and she could not escape, no matter how hard she shoved at him. He pushed and pushed, making the bedsprings squeak and the pain between her legs surge like waves against rocks. His grunts came more quickly, until she thought he was going to pass out. Finally, he rocked off her.

María began to cry as much from the throbbing as the possibility she had made a mistake, despite her love for this man.

Ben stirred, turned toward her and slapped her so hard her teeth shook. "I love you, baby, but shut the hell up. I need to sleep," he said and kissed her cheek.

Naked and bruised from lovemaking, she returned to the bathroom. She stared at the spots of blood on the worn linoleum and wiped a towel between her legs. It came away red.

That had been her life ever since. Pain and love. Blood and kisses.

For seven years, she traveled with him from construction job to job, all over Texas, New Mexico and Arizona. Although she could have no children, she knew contentment. She came to like how he laid on her and even felt pleasure, which was helped considerably when she drank beer. She took care of him when he came home dog tired from work and listened as he complained about all the good-for-nothings who worked with him. He smacked her around only on those occasions when he drank to the point that his smallish eyes disappeared entirely into his face and he fell more than he walked. But even in his drunkenness, his slaps found their target on her face or body.

Then they moved to Borden, and they talked about set-tling there. She found a job, and their life continued. But after Ben severely injured his back on a job, he drank more and began to hurt her more. Like her father, Ben began telling her she was nothing without him and no other man would have her. "You are small and ugly, María," he would say. "Looking at you aches worse than my back." His laugh was full of spit.

"I know I am lucky to have you," she would tell him and believe it.

Unlike her father, who never apologized after slapping her mother, at first Ben would bring her gifts after he hit her. A bracelet. The hard candy she liked. A new nightgown. But those apologies had ended almost as soon as they had started. She began to wonder what she did wrong and tried everything to please him. Surely she must have been the cause of his unhappiness and anger, because most of his ire was directed at her. Each day, she prayed to God to not make him mad and for the old Ben of Mexico to come back to her. But she also recalled what her mother had told her during one of the rare times they did have a conversation. Her mother talked about how her father used to sing under her window and moon with big eyes and love to win her hand. After they married, howev-er, that romantic lover had drowned in the Pacific, and she had been living with his bad spirit ever since. It was the way of men.

María started to drink, which lessened the pain from Ben's hand on her back and legs. The beer also gave her enough bravery to fight back, but not that often, because when she did the beatings only increased. She again felt the solitude of her early years, until God let her find a puppy roaming in the street. She took him home and fed him. Ben had yelled at her to get rid of the mongrel, but she begged him to let her keep the dog. Ben said he liked when she begged, gave in and got drunk. She watched her husband and knew she would go to bed with cuts and welts that night, but it didn't matter. "I will protect you, Oscar," she had whispered to the puppy. And she did.

María glanced down at the tray of jail food, which was now cold. She had never seen two women fight before, but she had seen the ruthlessness warping their faces. She had seen it on her own face, reflected in the blade of the knife she had plunged into Ben's chest.

18

COUNTY ATTORNEY JOE BRENNAN blew cigarette smoke at the three deputy attorneys sitting around the table in the conference room. They had all come from wealthier families than his, were older and more popular in school. But he stood at the head of the table. His name was painted on the glass door to their office. The former Joe "Four Eyes" Brennan was the real law in Mitchell County.

Receiving no help from his destitute parents, he had paid his way through college, working summers in the steel mill alongside Mexicans and Negroes. He never forgave his family for having nothing to give him. After completing law school at the state university, he worked at the county attorney's office and made sure his name got out to the public by shaking what he believed was the hand of every voting Republican in the county. His plan was going as expected and helped immensely by marriage to Sandra Lariat, the pudgy, nondescript daughter of a judge with massive property holdings in the next county.

Yet Brennan didn't want wealth. He wanted more precious commodities: authority and respect. He had developed his own creed: If you can't make people respect you, make them fear you. And that had worked out pretty well.

Thumbing through one of the files before him, Brennan heard updates on cases from the deputies during their weekly meeting. He looked at the tops of their heads as he talked. He reserved eye contact for judges, witnesses and people who could advance his career. He specifically wanted to hear about the María Curry case. He had claimed the lead attorney spot because if the case ended up at trial, murder meant his name in the newspaper. But he left the details and footwork up to his chief deputy.

"Roberts, what do you have for me on the Curry case?"

Chief Deputy Simon Roberts, who was five times more burned out than anyone in the room, consulted his notes. "Lots of evidence showing that Curry and his wife had knock-down, drag-outs. At least two dozen police reports of domestic battery were filed, but no arrests were ever made. They never pressed charges against each other. The bad news: Ben Curry did most of the assault and battery in that relationship. And I'll bet my new Edsel that Shaw's going to use self-defense."

"Naturally." While listening, Brennan intertwined his slim fingers, a gesture he regarded as distinguished.

Sitting across the table, Adam Stevens had one word for Brennan: "asshole." Although "bastard" also fit. Adam crushed out his cigarette. "A jury might feel sorry for the old girl, boss."

"After we get through with her she'll look like Pancho Villa's girlfriend," Brennan said.

The men around the table laughed, even Adam, who was not above kissing a little behind if it made his job easier.

Brennan got up and glanced out the window at the bank building, where Michael Shaw had his office two floors above his own. They had worked together for one year in the county attorney's office, where Shaw had proved fierce in court. That surprised him, because he believed Michael Shaw was going to be all pretty boy and no brains. Brennan came to envy Michael's abilities, connections, fortune and even his face and hair. All the more reason to dislike him.

"Michael Shaw is oh so rusty on criminal matters." Brennan faced the deputies. "He's run after rich man's law too long. Too many divorces and probates. Isn't that right, Stevens?"

"Yes, boss. But my old football buddy can be pretty tough and tenacious. He might come up with trick plays and win."

"You want me to take this one to trial, Mr. Brennan?" the chief deputy asked.

With a confession and the evidence so far, Brennan counted on a high probability for a conviction. Yet Shaw could indeed be tricky. "If it gets that far, I'll be the one to shut down Michael Shaw. But this case is not worth my time. Let's see if he'll play ball."

Brennan closed the file.

≈ ≈ ≈

The regular Sunday game at Borden City Park drew several old football players.

They were men who had worn pads and attitude in high school and college and wanted to remember the glory and youth. During the forty-five minutes or so—the most the older players could stand without too many serious injuries—they trotted out for football and to drink lukewarm beer on an afternoon away from their wives. For the last play of the game, Adam rushed Michael, who tripped and went down hard on his back on the stubble of dried grass.

"Damn, that hurt," Michael growled as he grabbed his leg.

"Be a man." Adam stretched his hand to help him up.

The play continued as Michael led one team and Adam, the other.

Thirty minutes into the game, Adam's muscles protested with only-Sunday use. He could still see himself, however, muscular as a boulder. He loved feeling the slap of the ball in his hands from a pass and then twirling past opponents in a race toward the goal line. Football he aced. Studies were another matter. In high school, Michael could capture the most complex of theories, as well as the prettiest women, who luckily had friends for him.

After the last play, Michael and Adam said good-bye to their teammates. Adam plopped down beside Michael on the grass.

"You're getting to be an old man like your old man."

"You're no spring chicken yourself. Have a beer." Michael reached into a paper bag, pulled out a bottle and grabbed the opener. He took another for himself.

"Those were the days, man. Knocking over the opposition on the field and, after the game, rolling over the cheerleaders. Now I get winded taking the stairs."

Adam often feigned loss of his physical power. He had learned a valuable lesson early on: fool others into thinking he was floored by a tackle, when he in fact had the muscle to push over players like bowling pins.

"Sometimes I really miss school. It's all this grown-up shit I can't stomach." Adam didn't lie about that.

"I know what you mean. All you had to do was stare across the field to see your enemies. These days, you're not quite sure who's going to fuck you over," Michael said.

They drank their beers with soft sucking sounds. Michael was happy the game had ended early. That evening, he planned to take Toni to the drive-in in Milton, a town twenty-five miles away from Borden and anyone who might recognize them. He would tell Jenny he had to work late at the office.

How easy to lie to her, perhaps because he had lied to everyone else for so long, particularly to himself.

"I hear you waived the preliminary hearing." Adam gave him a sideways glance.

"You know very well we waived. What's on your mind, Adam? Or shall I say, what's on Joe Brennan's mind?"

Adam hated when Michael knew what he was thinking. "Okay, then. Here it is. If María Curry pleads guilty to second-degree murder, we'd recommend the court go easy on her."

"How easy?"

"Ten to fifteen."

Michael perked up inwardly but put on his poker face and sipped at the beer.

"Your client confessed. You know that we know they had lots and lots of fights. And Mikey, there's all those stab wounds on Ben Curry's body." Adam clicked his tongue.

"You got shit. Her husband thrashed her every chance he got."

"So your nice lady can plead and get out of prison in ten to fifteen years. Easy time. Otherwise, we go to trial on first-degree, premeditated."

Michael contemplated his beer. "Second, huh?"

Adam stood up and brushed the grass off his pants. "Your client will grease her way through the system. Grease her way through. That's pretty good. Get it?"

Michael didn't laugh.

"Want to get a burger?"

"Not tonight."

"If your client doesn't go for the deal we're offering, she's pretty fucking stupid." Adam suddenly tossed Michael the football. "It's the smart thing to do, Mikey."

19

"TARZAN, THE APE MAN" flashed on the screen like electric moonlight. Teenagers scrambled through the dark, spilling popcorn and pop. Children in pajamas jumped off swings or the free pony rides and ran toward cars. As the opening credits began to roll, mothers ordered youngsters in the back seats to settle down, while fathers worked on the speakers for optimum sound.

Michael and Toni were parked in her car in the last row of the Ranch Drive-in. She had saved enough for a new transmission, which her cousin had installed in no time. She paid him against his will.

The windows were down to let in any evening coolness that might arrive. They had turned off the speakers so the movie became a mere backdrop. The sound did roll along the ground from the other cars.

"Michael, what happens if María doesn't take the offer?"

"It'll be tough. Joe Brennan considers every case a stepping stone toward a senate seat. And he hates my guts. So he's got even more reason to try to obliterate us in court."

"You think María should agree to this?"

He sighed. "We risk losing big time."

Toni took his hand. "You said we'd have a strong case for self-defense. I believe you can convince a jury to set her free."

"Regrettably, you won't be on that jury, Toni. And, while we do have a great shot at an acquittal, with a jury it's always a crapshoot. They could vote guilty."

"Then?"

"The maximum is life in prison. Be thankful the state isn't keen on executing women."

"Oh, God. Could it really come to that?"

"It could. We'll talk to María. It's really her decision, because it's her life."

She leaned against him. At times, Michael had the sense he was defending Toni as well as María. The two women almost became one person when Toni translated for her. But Toni would never have allowed herself to be beaten, and he admired her even more for that. He kissed her. When they pulled away from each other she yawned.

"Toni, I'm really hurt. I thought I was a great kisser. In fact, I was voted best lips in college."

She put her fingers on his mouth. "I'm sure you were."

"So why are you tired?"

"I took another job at a laundry on Pecos Street. I want to help my dad with some bills, and I needed to get my car fixed. This translator job doesn't pay much."

"You should have said something."

"I don't need your money." She scooted back from him. "I can take care of myself."

"I didn't mean anything by it, Toni."

"I know. I told you I have a temper."

He reached out and touched her neck, and she again moved near him. In Toni's older car, with a blanket over the seats, Michael felt sheltered and normal. Their children could be playing on the swings or sleeping in the back. The Michael

Shaw who drank too much and had a rich daddy became as invisible as the light carrying the movie to the screen.

"We really don't know a lot about each other, do we?" Her fingers intertwined with his.

"I want to know."

She had wanted to tell him about her father's illness and cry against his chest for comfort. But she held off. She trusted few people in her life. Even after they slept together, she still could not place all her faith in him, which shamed her. His lips brushed her forehead. Maybe she was the one who had to give her trust first. She had to have faith.

"Michael?"

"What?"

"I belong to you. Even if you don't want me, I belong to you."

Michael blushed. With all his wealth, no one had ever presented him such a profound gift. Before he could answer, she slipped off her panties and unzipped his pants. Hiking up her skirt, she straddled him in a motion that shocked him with its fluidity. He gasped as she drummed her body against his. His longing held her there. At that moment, he knew all he wanted about her as the movie's sound echoed over the drive-in.

≈ ≈ ≈

Michael draped his arm around Deputy Herb Bell at the jail.

"Mr. Shaw, I like and respect you, but this is really breaking the rules." Bell emitted the odor of cheap cigars and onions.

"Herb, you allow the inmates to have family visitors, don't you?"

He wagged a thin finger at the lawyer. "On visiting day, Mr. Shaw, on visiting day."

Although Bell had no intention of saying no, he got a jolt of gratification from making the rich man beg a little. Better than a swallow of cold beer at noon.

"That dog is María Curry's only family. We'll clean up any mess," Michael said.

"See that you do, sir."

A few minutes later, Bell escorted María into the interview room. After the door shut, Michael leaned down and brought Oscar out of a basket.

He had never seen his client happy.

The little dog yipped when he saw María and got so excited he peed. They all laughed, and Michael ran to the men's room to fetch toilet paper to clean up the puddle.

Toni asked María to sit down, and the room became somber.

"Bad news?" María asked.

She petted the dog on her lap as they told her about the prosecutor's offer. She didn't quite understand all that Mr. Shaw said, yet she believed in him. She liked how he had touched her hand when they first met and how his voice held concern and pity for the woman who murdered her man. He defended her although she had no money and had even pulled Ben's brother away from her in the courtroom. Ben had told her white people hated Mexicans, but she had seen no hate in Mr. Shaw.

"Is there a chance I can go home?"

"Yes, María. We'll tell the jury you struck out because you were afraid for your life. We can show how he had hurt you many times before."

"What happens if I don't go along?"

Michael looked at Toni and then engulfed María's tiny hand in his. "You could go to prison for the rest of your life, or worse."

"They could kill me?"

He nodded. Toni's eyes glistened.

María petted Oscar. After a while, she smiled. "Mr. Shaw, I like to play bingo at church. I like to bet a dime in hopes I'll win ten dollars. You're a good lawyer, and I'm an old woman with no man or child. The only thing I have left is chance."

20

LILY ANN STRITCH surveyed her daughter like a piece of real estate, her eyes speculative and exacting. Her daughter had inherited her blue eyes and abundant blond hair, and Lily Ann saw her own once-shapely figure in Jenny. Although hers had spread a little with age, she still could divert a head or two, albeit an old man's head.

"Jenny, you gained a few pounds since I last saw you. Marilyn Monroe curves. Michael must love that."

"I wanted to talk with you about him, Mother."

"I guessed you didn't drive to Phoenix for nothing. And I know how you loathe going anywhere by yourself."

Smacking her lips after sipping a cocktail, Lily Ann smoked and listened. Jenny talked about how Michael still didn't want any children after three years of marriage. And he didn't want to buy the big house she had fallen in love with.

Shaking her ankle, Jenny sat on a blue silk sofa in her mother's well-appointed living room. "How do I convince him to change his mind about a baby, when I can't even convince him to buy a house?"

Lily Ann blew smoke out of one side of her mouth and picked a piece of lint off Jenny's gray suit. Her daughter had traveled more than 200 miles and still didn't ask the right question. Lily Ann would save her the trouble. "Is Michael having an affair?"

Jenny's foot stopped shaking. "Absolutely not, Mother. He's working hard on that trial and his other cases. I'd know if he were fooling around, believe me. He's just scared of starting a family. He and his dad don't get along at all. He's probably afraid of being a father."

"Very insightful, Jenny. You must have got that from *Reader's Digest*."

While her daughter had her looks, she didn't have her guts or initiative. With a less than generous alimony, Lily Ann had gone right to work at Crawford Real Estate. She mastered all the jobs there and sold so many resort properties, she became a partner. Only occasionally did she have to sleep with the senior owner of the company. Jenny, on the other hand, wouldn't last a day out in the world and did well marrying into the Shaw family. She wouldn't be surprised if Michael Shaw was fooling around. The possibility occurred to her as soon as she met him. Those yawning good looks and a father like Martin Shaw, who must have been a philanderer, at least according to the rumors about the old man.

"Why come to me if you know what's wrong?"

"You're my mother."

"Positive there's no pretty secretary he might be seeing on the side?"

Jenny laughed. "His secretary is a little old woman. I've checked her out. I'm not stupid."

"Is he still drinking a lot?"

Jenny looked outside the window. Now she regretted making the trip to Phoenix. Her mother only laid on more criticism about how she should run her marriage and life. "He likes his whiskey, Mother."

She didn't want to tell her mother that Michael had in fact cut back for the past month. It amounted to another indicator of a wobbly marriage. If he didn't stop drinking for her, it could have been for another woman.

Putting out her cigarette in an alabaster ashtray, Lily Ann checked herself in the large mirror on the wall in front of them. She repaired a stray smudge of lipstick with her little finger. "You come here and tell me your husband is staying out late and doesn't want children or a house, and he drinks a lot. That sounds like a cheating man to me." She put fingers in her tight curls. "Believe me, Jenny, I should know the signs. Your father invented them, especially the drinking. Remember?"

Jenny nodded. As a kid, she often witnessed her mother help her father up off the floor, curse at him and then spin around to yell at Jenny to get back to bed. Her mother took charge of everything in her sphere. Jenny's shoulders drooped because she had never taken charge of anything.

Lily Ann smoothed Jenny's hair. "You're probably right. Michael's working too hard on that case. Honey, I hate to tell you, but that's what you get for marrying a lawyer. Although a doctor is the absolute ultimate absentee husband, or so Marcia Crandall told me one day at the golf course. But then Marcia let herself go, gained weight, read too many books and is taking college classes. No wonder her husband doesn't come home. Then there are all those nurses he works with."

"Oh, Mother, be serious."

"I wasted so much of my life and opportunities on your father. It gets me mad even thinking about it."

"Maybe I should just get pregnant, Mother."

"Honey, if you do, he'll come to hate you for it."

Jenny crossed her arms and fell back on the couch.

"Michael Shaw could have had any girl, but he married you, didn't he? For God's sake, don't do anything stupid now.

Hold on. If you do, you'll never have anything to worry about. And don't nag, Jenny. Men hate that."

"You sound like women only live for their men. Without them, we have no other life." Jenny's voice had a sharper tone than she intended. Then again, she only echoed what her mother had raised her to believe.

Lily Ann lit another cigarette and stirred her drink with a varnished nail. "Jenny, men have the upper hand in this world. That's a fact. They have the money and all the jobs. We happen to have a body they want. We also have the ability to tolerate all their bad habits, like drinking, gambling, even other women. In the end, we get everything we want."

Jenny gazed out the window. The Phoenix skyline began to gain radiance in the dusk.

"Jenny?"

"I heard you, Mother."

"So what are you going to do?"

"I'm going to hold on."

"Wonderful. Now I'll go and freshen up, and Max can escort us to dinner."

Lily Ann sauntered into her bedroom and shut the door. The moment she did, Jenny scratched her ankle. She scratched so hard an older scab started to bleed, smearing and tearing another pair of her nylons. The annoying itch had started a few weeks ago, and nothing helped. Not calamine lotion, baking soda or hot baths. She opened her purse for a handkerchief because she didn't want her mother to notice. Scratching was white trash behavior, along with working at a diner and getting knocked up by a man with no money, according to her mother's standards.

Jenny tried to ignore the itch on her ankle and the misery that attacked her like a virus. She scratched and hoped her mother was right about Michael. Her mother had been right about most things. Didn't she predict Michael's proposal?

When they had met at the country club, Jenny hoped to impress Michael by telling him she was signing up for college that fall. She had no intention of following through, however. Careers made women tough and masculine. Her mother was the perfect example. She had finally softened back into a female after marriage to her second and prosperous husband, Max.

Aside from his excessive drinking, Michael had everything Jenny wanted in a man—looks and charm and bountiful prospects. His affluent family was more than a bonus. While he looked like a leading man in a movie, Michael had never been the romantic type and didn't fawn over her with compliments or gifts. Instead, he joked a lot and almost treated her like a buddy. She could live with that. Her expectations for the brightest of marriages, however, started to disintegrate two nights before their wedding. At her apartment she planned to seduce Michael and get pregnant. As her mother often commented about real estate, Jenny wanted to close the deal. In her mother's image, she had come to view the act as a tool to get what she wanted.

After pouring more than a few glasses of his favorite whiskey, she had taken off her clothes and drawn him to her, but Michael stepped back and produced one of those humiliating rubber things from his pocket. "I don't want any kids, Jenny. I'm sorry," he had said. She told him she felt a headache coming on and got dressed.

Their ceremony and reception was glorious, mostly because his father paid for it and Michael didn't pass out from drinking. On the flight to Acapulco for their honeymoon, she convinced herself that marriage would change his mind about kids. In the hotel room, she slipped out of her expensive negligee and into bed, but he again wore the artificial skin. Afterward, he didn't talk about their life together. He went to sleep. Over the years, his lovemaking became less frequently and he approached it like a chore. He would put on the rubber and get on top of her. He couldn't mask his sighs.

For the last month or so, Michael hadn't touched her. Jenny tried to understand his work, but all those papers and writs she found dull. She didn't understand half the stuff he talked about. She didn't understand him.

The front door opened as Jenny poured one of her mother's famous martinis. Her smartly groomed stepfather took a step in and called, "Hello," to no one in particular.

"In here."

"Why, Jenny, it's great to see you." Max, a balding fellow with a winning smile, kissed her cheek. "Where's Lily Ann?"

She pointed to the bedroom, and off he trotted. Jenny wished Michael trotted after her like that. She swallowed her drink and resolved to follow her mother's advice. As far as she knew, her mother had never been wrong when it came to men. Still, Jenny's ankle itched, and she scratched until the wound bled some more.

21

DURING THE DEPOSITION, Michael circled Mrs. Lewis Stratton as if binding her with words. Svelte and elegant, the woman sat upright in a leather chair in the conference room of Smith, Allen & Allen in Tucson. Her styled hair resembled a coiffured spider web.

Michael stood behind her. "Mrs. Stratton, did you have a few cocktails that night?"

Her eyes were fever blisters ready to pop. "Your client caused my injuries, young man."

"Mrs. Stratton, were you drinking that night?"

Eyes focusing on her attorney, George Allen Jr., Mrs. Stratton made a mental note to berate his father for talking her into going with this rubber band of a youth.

"Mrs. Stratton?" Michael said.

"I drank a little."

"What's a little?"

"I don't recall."

"How many drinks did you have?"

"I said I don't recall."

"Is that because you were so inebriated you lost count?"

"See here." She stood up. "Mr. Allen, stop this."

"I can't. I'm sorry, Mrs. Stratton." The young Allen answered as if he had eaten shards of glass. "We'll get our opportunity."

She sat back down.

Michael folded his arms. "How many drinks?"

"Three manhattans."

"Within how much time did you consume these drinks?"

"Two hours, but I ate." She smiled impertinently at her attorney, who had advised her against volunteering anything.

"Any wine with your dinner?" Michael said.

Her smile faded. "Two glasses."

"What did you eat that night?"

"I beg your pardon."

"Did you have a thick steak and a baked potato with lots of sour cream?"

"No, a Waldorf salad."

Michael had her. He sat across from the woman. "Let's tally this up, shall we? Three manhattans and two glasses of wine and an insubstantial dinner before you got in your car an hour later."

Young Mr. Allen pounded a weak fist on the table. "I object to your tone, Shaw."

"I'm done, Mr. Allen. Thank you, Mrs. Stratton. That's all the questions for now. Call me, and we can schedule a deposition of our client." Michael began placing papers in his briefcase. "That is, unless you'd like to talk settlement."

Mrs. Stratton grabbed her purse, and young Allen handed her the cane she had used since her car accident west of Borden. Michael watched her leave and guessed that she probably used the cane to thump the people who worked for her, including her attorney, if she got the chance.

At the other end of the table, Martin studied his son. Michael had become a fine attorney, and he took credit as his mentor. With time, he would become his worthy heir. But not now. Michael bucked at authority like a rodeo horse. His whole attitude smacked of ingratitude. He had everything but appreciated nothing.

"See, Father, you didn't have to come with me," Michael said as the deposition wrapped up. "I'm a big boy. I handled it all myself."

"Your client Harvey Ryan is an old friend of mine, Michael."

"Harvey Ryan is also part owner in the Lucky Hope Copper Mine."

"I have a lot of friends."

"You have a lot of connections."

Martin stood up, but nausea forced him to put his hands on the table for balance. Got up too fast, he reasoned. He drank water to force away the sickness and buttoned his jacket. "I do believe Mrs. Stratton will settle."

"No matter. Our client will still have to pay up."

Michael checked his watch. He wanted to get back to Borden. Jenny had left town to visit her mother for a few days, and that meant one less lie. At times, he wished Jenny would find out about him and Toni, to force a decision out of him. No doubt Jenny would hire his father's firm and sue him for divorce on the grounds of adultery.

Adultery. A dumb word. A legal word. Not one to associate with Toni.

"The Bordereaux for lunch?" Martin stood at the door.

"If you're paying."

"Don't I always?"

The restaurant his father selected amused Michael with its old English decor in the center of such a southwestern city. After a meal of rare roast beef and yorkshire pudding, they sat back in thick padded chairs and quickly reviewed the lawsuit, leaving them not much else to say after that. Martin puffed a cigar, the smoke circling his head like a low cloud.

"I'm happy this murder trial will soon be over, and you can get back to business," Martin said after a time.

"Let's not talk about my case."

"Your time is too valuable for such nonsense. I would have found a way to get you out of that commitment."

"Maybe I wanted to believe in a case instead of just collecting a fee."

Martin took a drink of water, feeling bile rise in his chest. "I'm only trying to say you did a fine job with Mrs. Stratton."

About to take a sip of wine, Michael held the glass in mid-air. "The last time you complimented me was when I threw a winning touchdown against Central High School. Wait a minute, back then you also told me, 'Fine job.'"

"I know I don't praise your work much, but if you weren't a skilled lawyer, I wouldn't have you in the firm."

"Two compliments in one day. My heart may explode."

"Can't we have a nice conversation without an argument?" Martin grimaced as a biting pain sliced through his shoulder.

"What's wrong?"

"Nothing but indigestion. The beef chewed like an old pair of work boots."

"Time to head to the airport anyway."

They didn't talk on the way there or in the plane. Michael checked his watch again. His father dozed against the window, which ruffled his hair. Michael reached out to smooth it, but withdrew his hand. Although they sat next to each other, his father was as distant as another country. Michael couldn't reach that far without getting lost in the void.

The airplane landed in Borden and jarred Martin, who awoke with a snort. "I'm glad we're home," his father said.

"Me, too."

As Michael picked up his briefcase, Martin put a hand on Michael's shoulder. His father never touched him. Not a spank or a hug.

"What is it?" Michael asked.

"A spasm from sitting on the plane. We've got the Hennessey case to discuss tomorrow." Martin stepped in front of his son and took the lead off the plane.

At the bottom of the stairs, he dropped his briefcase, went to his knees and slumped over on his side. Michael emerged from the door and saw his father on the ground, with a stewardess loosening his tie. Rushing past passengers, Michael kneeled beside his father, whose face had become ashen and his mouth gnarled.

"Get him some help!" Michael shouted.

"We're sending for an ambulance," said the stewardess.

"Father, can you hear me? Help is coming."

Sitting down on the asphalt, Michael put his father's head on his lap. His father's eyes barely opened. His expensive suit was wrinkled, and his hair and shirt were wet with perspiration. Michael reached into his pocket for a handkerchief and dried his father's hair and face. He took his hand. "Don't worry. I won't leave you."

When Dr. Ted Sorensen informed Martin Shaw of the diagnosis, the patient did not raise an eyebrow. Under similar circumstances, the doctor had seen patients wail with relief, praise God or thank him for being the best healer in the whole damn world. Old man Shaw seemed to expect the outcome as if entitled to more life.

"Then sign a release so I can go home," the patient said. "The sooner, the better."

Not since his internship had anyone ordered him around. The doctor had detested it then, as he did now. "Mr. Shaw, I'll determine when you can go home."

"I have my own doctor." The old man sat rigid on the bed. "And I'd like a private room."

"I'll consult with your doctor, and the admitting office will have to see to your request about the private room. Your wife and son are waiting. They can visit after I bring them up to speed on your condition."

"I don't want to see anyone right now."

"They're very worried about you, and it might comfort them."

Martin Shaw placed his head back on the pillow and closed his eyes. "Now I'd like to rest."

Dr. Sorensen was stunned by the expert dismissal. "Damn patients," the doctor muttered as he walked down the hall to the glass-enclosed waiting room. Just his luck to draw such an annoying case at the end of an interminable shift. His last duty before he went home would be to tell the family of Martin Shaw that the old man would live.

Martin Shaw's wife saw him coming and pulled a lipstick from her purse. His son sat up from dozing on a firm couch. They rose to meet him as if they were greeting a king. The doctor smiled. At least they showed him respect.

"Mr. Shaw has suffered cardiac angina. Pain caused by an inadequate blood flow through the heart muscle." Dr. Sorensen had lots of practice using layman's terms for patients' families. "The episode was a mild one, and he's quite out of danger."

Michael suddenly kissed Melody on the cheek. He kept thinking about his father on the asphalt, helpless and vulnerable. He almost forgave him.

The doctor looked at his watch. Mentally, he was already out the door. "We gave Mr. Shaw medication to widen the blood vessels. According to test results, the heart wasn't damaged, but we should keep him under observation for a few days."

Melody fluffed her hairdo. "Thank you, Doctor. Can we visit him now?"

"Ah, he's very tired and needs rest, Mrs. Shaw."

"I don't understand."

"He doesn't want any visitors right now."

Michael put his arm around Melody. Her blinking eyes signaled that she had, at last, understood her precarious place in his father's life. The realization probably rolled down to her painted toenails. She was, after all, wife number three.

"Martin will see you tomorrow." Michael's tone mollified her, like a mother reassuring a child she hadn't been adopted. "Anyway, Dad must be feeling better if he's giving orders. Right, Doc?"

The physician shrugged.

Michael held out his hand. "Thanks for everything."

"You're welcome."

Picking up Melody's sweater, Michael gently placed it on her shoulders. "I'll get you a taxi."

Watching the family head to the front entrance, Dr. Sorensen lit a cigarette and inhaled as deeply as he could. He blew out the smoke and wished he had listened to his father and become a stockbroker.

≈ ≈ ≈

At her small house, Toni smoked and paced the floor. Earlier in the evening Michael had called the laundry where she worked and told her about his father's illness. He would get away as soon as possible. Her reply: she'd wait.

Nearing midnight, she still waited and would for as long as it took. She glanced down. Oscar paced with her, making her laugh. Picking up the dog, she snuggled him and felt guilty, as if she had won a prize by default. Toni placed the dog on his pillow and patted his head.

In the darkness, Toni sat down on the bed, hugged her legs and listened. She had left the door open. With every noise, she took in a mouthful of smoke, making her cigarette glow.

From outside came a faint rumble in the alley. A car stopped, a door closed. She put out the cigarette. Oscar growled, and she told him to be quiet.

The next moment, Michael opened the door. "Toni?"

"Here."

He followed her voice. His hand reached out to her outstretched one. He sat down and leaned against her. She undressed him and laid him back on the bed. Slipping off her robe and nightgown, she lay down next to him. They held onto each other until he got up and left at first light.

22

THE PRIEST HELD THE HOST UPWARD. His white and gold vestments pointed the way to salvation. "This is the Christ who takes away the sins of the world."

With the congregation at St. Catherine's, Toni recited the response in Latin, "Only say the word and my soul shall be healed." For more than one month, she hadn't gone to confession. She still took the host at Mass rather than have her father question her about why she didn't. Each Sunday, she also asked for God's pardon for understanding why she slept with a married man. She estimated a penance of about 200 Hail Marys and Our Fathers might absolve such a transgression. Dear God, can this really be a sin? She tapped her closed hand against her chest in time with the altar bells.

≈ ≈ ≈

"*Ándele*, hurry." Francisco led the way down the church aisle, pausing long enough for a touch of holy water in the basin at the foot of the tall statue of Jesus. He wanted to get home to prepare chili. Toni's old childhood friend Juanita, her husband and children were coming to dinner.

Francisco had run into them while entering the church and had extended the invitation: "Come on over and eat. There's going to be plenty. We're celebrating. Carmen is going to have a baby."

Juanita and her husband, Guillermo, agreed, hugged Carmen and shook Víctor's hand. Since Carmen and Víctor had told him the news, Francisco couldn't pass up the opportunity to tell everyone he knew, sometimes even strangers they happened to meet.

"We'll bring beer," Juanita whispered as she rushed her two children ahead of her into the church.

Among friends and relatives, Francisco's green chili was legendary for its kick and flavor and as a reliable cure for hangovers.

When they returned home, Francisco rejected help with the chili from Carmen and Toni in the kitchen. They were responsible for cleaning the house and making tortillas, beans and Spanish rice. Víctor, who had no talent for cooking, went outside to change the oil in his truck. Not even bothering to change from his church clothes, Francisco pulled down a large stainless-steel pot. From Montgomery Ward, it shone like a new cruise liner. After frying cubes of pork, he poured in canned tomatoes, creating a sizzle that made Carmen wet her lips. Wearing a dishcloth around his waist to protect his pants, he sliced onions and jalapeños.

"How many you adding there, Pops?" Toni looked into the pot.

"Enough."

"I remember one time when you added so many jalapeños my eyes watered as soon as I came in the house. I couldn't feel my tongue for two days afterward."

"That was a good batch," he said.

From the cupboard, Francisco brought out a small bag of cumin. He methodically added the spice to the chili as if he was a chemist.

Toni took a big whiff of the bitter but inviting odor. Cumin smelled of home. When she lived in Phoenix, she'd even bought some of the spice to place in a bowl on the counter.

Near dinnertime, Francisco removed from the pot a piece of pork, which shredded with the slightest handling.

Carmen sneaked a small piece of tortilla and dabbed it in the pot. "Wow, Dad. It's great, but hot. I hope the baby doesn't get heartburn."

"My grandbaby will be raised on chili. He'll be sturdy as steel when he grows up."

Toni stole a piece of tortilla away from her sister and dipped it in for a taste. She closed her eyes and smiled. Francisco pronounced the chili ready.

Juanita and her family arrived a little later, and half the pot was emptied in good time. Toni sat next to her old high school friend, who swiped at the last of the chili on her plate. Juanita had filled out with marriage. She and her husband were friendly people who loved to laugh.

Toni used to kid Juanita that an Irishman must have sneaked into her family line somewhere because of the spray of pink freckles on her cheeks, a complexion fairer than those of the other Mexican kids and a red tint to her hair. Juanita would always laugh and say she wished the Irish guy had left her a pot of gold.

"Francisco, you cook the best chili." Juanita blew out a satiated breath.

"It was nothing."

Toni laughed. "That's why you were cooking over a hot stove all day, Pops?"

"Shush, Antonia."

After dinner, Juanita's children sped off to the front yard to find kids to play ball. "Don't get into trouble," she yelled.

Francisco sat in the front room, summoning Víctor and Guillermo. "Come on, *Maverick*'s about to start, then it's *Lawman*."

That left the women in front of the dishes.

"That's okay, we'll wash up," Toni called sarcastically.

"I know you'll clean real good," her father answered with a mischievous grin.

Víctor laughed and picked up his bottle of beer. "Listen, Francisco cooked, and me and Guillermo ate. Ain't that fair?"

"*Sí, el jefe*," Carmen said.

"Women." Víctor shook his head.

"Men," the women replied.

Toni, Carmen and Juanita heard the television start, and they began piling up the dishes.

"Throw me the *estropajo*." Juanita ducked the scouring pad Carmen threw too hard.

Carmen laughed. "Sorry."

Within twenty minutes the kitchen mess disappeared. By that time, Juanita's sons had joined the men, sitting on the floor watching television.

Carmen handed Toni and Juanita each a beer and took a soda for herself. "Let's go to my room and listen to records."

Upstairs, Juanita nudged Toni as they sat on Carmen's bed. "We used to have fun times at our sleepovers."

"Especially when we sneaked up a bottle of beer."

"You guys never let me play with you." Carmen threw a pillow at Toni.

"We did let you play, but you were so obnoxious, Carmen. You came in the middle of the night and tried to fart in my face."

"Quit lying, Toni."

"I remember that," Juanita volunteered.

"Excuse me, ladies, I have to go pee. Again."

"That's the worst part of being pregnant," Juanita said. "The gas is pretty bad, too."

"While I'm downstairs, I'll see if the men want more beer." Carmen left.

"I miss those times we had in high school," Juanita nodded with memories.

"Oh, yeah. Hanging around together and playing Eddie Fisher records. I remember Guillermo showing off for you. His '44 Chevy truck would tear up and down the block." Toni sipped her beer and studied her old friend. "So, Juanita, are you very happy now?"

Juanita's heavy brows blew apart with surprise. "You were always the one for questions. The teachers loved you because you asked such good questions."

"I'm sorry. That was pretty rude. I must have had too many beers."

"*Claro*, I'm happy. I hope you'll be as happy as me someday with your own husband and children, and then you can get fat as me." Juanita grinned, which made her cheeks even broader.

"I look forward to that."

Her friend did appear sanguine. Then again, when they were younger, Juanita had always appeared content with whatever she received or had been offered. She dated whatever boy asked her, no matter how homely he was or how he treated her. Juanita called Toni picky because she wanted more.

"How were those white college boys, Toni?" Juanita asked.

"Let me put it this way. Mexican boys try to charm you out of your panties. The college boys try to talk you out of them."

"No matter what color boys are, they all know what they want." Juanita burped a little and giggled. "My mommy used to say women marry men and turn them into babies."

"That's not much of a leap. I've always thought women were stronger than men, anyway."

Carmen ducked back in. "Who's stronger?"

"Women," Toni said.

Juanita puffed out her sizeable chest. "I may have gained weight, but I can't whip Guillermo."

Toni laughed. "That's not what I meant. Women have babies, clean the house, wash the clothes, tend to their husbands and some of them have paying jobs, too. All men have to do is go out and work."

"And fish," added Carmen.

"And watch westerns on television." Juanita fell back on the bed. "And they have to keep us happy with that little thing between their legs."

"Not too little, I hope." Carmen winked.

"Carmen Marie García Villaseñor! What a mouth." Toni squeezed her sister's arm.

"I'm not two years old anymore, Antonia Cruz García."

"No, you're not. You're a dirty old woman."

Carmen patted her stomach. "If I have a daughter, I'm going to prepare her for being a woman. God bless our mother, but she didn't tell us anything. You'd mentioned the birds and the bees, and she started saying a novena."

Toni sat up. "When I got my first period, I ran to Mamá. Boy, was I scared. She smiled and told me, 'Antonia, you're a woman now.' I started running around the house and yelling, 'No, Mamá, I don't want to be a woman!'"

Juanita hooted, spraying her beer in a mist. "My mom didn't tell me nothing neither. So when I saw Guillermo's thing, I told him, 'Oh no, you're not putting that in me.'"

"You must have gotten used to it," Carmen said.

"What about you, little Miss Pregnant?"

They laughed again. Francisco peeked in. "How you girls doing? It sounds like you're having fun up here."

"We are, Pops," Carmen answered, still laughing.

"What are you talking about?"

"Cooking," Juanita said.

"That's good." He closed the door, and they laughed even harder.

Later that night, Víctor lay in bed as Carmen changed into her nightgown. She traced the roundness of her belly. "God, I'm getting fat."

"No, you're cute." Víctor rolled over in bed. "I saw it again, babe."

"What?"

"That white guy's car. He's driving an older model now, not that flashy sports car. He leaves it down the street. All the neighbors are talking, Carmen."

"So let them talk. They're working on that trial."

"They are working on a lot more than that."

"Shut up, Víctor."

"You can't ignore it, babe."

Carmen folded her clothes and trembled with cold feet on the warm floor. She got into bed and snuggled next to Víctor.

"Maybe you should talk to her, Carmen."

"Toni's a big girl, Víctor."

"Whatever you say, but I wanted to warn you."

She sat up. "I wonder if the neighbors would talk so damn much if he was a Mexican guy."

"Nah. They'd just think she's easy."

"Víctor!"

He gently pulled her back and kissed her lips. "Sorry, but it's true. Let's get some sleep. I got work." He closed his eyes.

Carmen felt gas bubbles rising in her stomach like a soon-to-erupt volcano. She tried to blame her dad's chili. The real cause was the car Víctor had seen parked down the street and the fact that her sister wasn't alone in the little house in the back.

23

THE ENTIRE SHAW LAW FIRM got to its feet when Martin entered.

"Welcome back, Mr. Shaw," gushed his secretary, Mrs. Garrison, a compact woman with rouged, wrinkled cheeks. "We're all so happy you're feeling better. We missed you." She handed him a bouquet of roses.

Four young attorneys, their secretaries and the clerks clapped at the presentation.

Michael stood at the back of the crowd. His own secretary had had to shoo him from his office to the official welcome. Following his release from the hospital, his father had skipped work for five days. Martin stayed away that long only because his longtime physician had threatened him with more tests and treatment if he returned any sooner.

Toni had told him about her father, Francisco. She spoke with such love and as much despair, because the affliction in his lungs would result in his early death. There was nothing to stop it. His father, on the other hand, had escaped death. After Martin had been released from the hospital, Michael went to visit him at home with a gift—a book about Abraham Lincoln's early law career. His father had locked himself in his study, where he slept on a bed set up by the fireplace, Josita told him. She was only allowed in to bring food and change the sheets. With lowered eyes, she also informed Michael his father refused to see him. He wanted no visitors to disturb his recovery. Michael never tried to visit again.

Michael noticed how his father's commanding stride was diminished a notch. His cheeks were hollow, but he still projected a forbidding presence. Accepting the roses and good wishes from the staff, Martin stepped back. His eyes dimmed, and he cleared his throat with discomfort at the simple gesture.

"Thank you," Martin said. "But we have even more work to do. That will do for now. I'd like to talk with you for a moment, Michael." He turned his attention to his secretary. "Mrs. Garrison, please bring your pad into my office in a half an hour. I have a lot to catch up on. "

Mrs. Garrison lost her welcoming smile. "Yes, sir."

The crowd broke up, a few shaking their heads, Michael noted.

"The old man is back, all right," whispered a young attorney to another. He shut up when he noticed Michael listening. They sped back to their cubicles.

Ceiling-to-floor windows covered two walls of his father's office. He kept the blinds closed, which gave the impression of a tasteful dungeon cell. A massive oak desk was bare except for a Tiffany lamp and a tray with a glass pitcher of water and a glass. Martin sat back in his chair and motioned for Michael to sit across from him. The week without his father had been akin to taking a vacation, but all vacations had to end.

"I see you're going to trial soon," Martin said.

"I haven't fallen behind on my work, Father."

"That's admirable." Martin poured a glass of water and sipped carefully.

"I'm glad you're well enough for work," Michael said. How polite they were. His father fidgeted in a way that indicated he had more to say but didn't know how. Michael would help him along, if nothing else to get the hell out of there.

"Anything else you want to tell me, Father?"

Martin shook his head.

Michael left as Martin placed his hands on the clean, shiny desk.

≈ ≈ ≈

Facedown on her small bed, Michael sighed as Toni kneaded his back.

"You have more knots than a rope."

"Yeow," he groaned as Toni rubbed a knot out. "How's your dad?"

"Tired, but he won't slow down. The new medicine his doctor gave him is helping his coughing spells."

"He sounds like a good man. I wish I could meet him."

"One day. How's *your* father?"

"Back to work and recovered enough to boss everyone around. He's a tough old bastard."

"Why don't you like him?"

"He killed my mother."

She stopped massaging. "What do you mean?"

He sat up and faced her. "They argued the day she died. Hell, they argued every day. But that night, I had sneaked out of my room and lain on the carpet in front of my mother's room. I watched their shadows move under the door. He yelled. She screamed.

"I wanted so badly to knock on the door. I wanted to stop him from hurting her, but I was too damn scared to do anything. I fell asleep on the rug."

"You were a little boy. What could you do?"

"I remember my mother carrying me back to my room. 'Mommy loves you,' she said and laid me in bed. She left and took the light with her."

"What happened then?"

"The next morning, they found her body ten miles from the house. Her car had smashed into a telephone pole. All during the funeral, I waited for him to cry. But he never did. That's when I began to hate him." He balled his hands into fists.

"Why don't you talk to your father, Michael? It's not too late."

He relaxed his fingers and put his hands on her face. "I don't know if I can. That resentment's set hard as cement. It's the only real thing between us."

"Were you sorry your father lived?"

"I don't know anymore." An equal amount of animosity and regret weighed on him like a mountain of shale. He put his head on the pillow. Toni took his hand and kissed his fingers. She was crying.

"I hope those aren't for him," he said.

"No, not him."

24

COURT BAILIFF GEORGE ROY carried the red drum up from the basement and placed it on a rickety table across from the judge's bench. With gout invading his legs, he again promised himself to retire but dreaded seeing his wife more than he had to. A decent woman in most every way, Marjorie talked constantly about nothing at all. She clanged pots and clattered dishes like artillery. She chastised the dog for getting hair on the couch or him for not picking up his socks from the floor and leaving up the toilet seat. Give him rotten criminals in court anytime.

George walked past several people in the courthouse hallway, who watched him carry the drum into the courtroom. Only among prospective jurors did the well-off sit next to the not-so. They were all equals when it came time to serve on a jury—that is, unless they were pals with the juror commissioner, who somehow managed to keep their names off the list.

As they waited, the women read books or knitted with yarn stringing out from giant handbags. Two working men in their early twenties played Go Fish on a folding chair between them. They really wanted to play five-card stud with pennies, but they were in a courthouse and didn't want to get arrested for gambling in public. So they played the dullest game of all and tugged at ties. Jerry, a bricklayer with sandpaper fingers, had won his third game from Curt, a carpenter.

Curt glanced over his fanned cards. "Ever get called for jury duty before?"

"Nah. You?"

"Nope. Got any nines?"

Jerry scratched at his neck and the tie he had had to borrow from his father-in-law. "Go Fish. What'd you hear about this trial?"

"A wife killed her husband after a fight."

"Is that all? Got any fives?"

≈ ≈ ≈

Michael again examined the list of prospective jurors. He wanted as many women as possible on the panel. At least the ones who might sympathize with María. If he were County Attorney Joe Brennan, he'd exercise his preemptory challenges and get rid of those women. Brennan would likely want to seat older men who would probably vote guilty to revenge manhood against a woman who had dared to strike back. Michael had no hope for Mexican-American jurors, not that the bailiff might call any. Although they made up almost half of the county's population, they seemed to have vanished during jury selection, which he hadn't really noticed until that morning. So much for a jury of one's peers, at least for María.

Michael's mouth tasted gritty in anticipation of the trial. His nerves also fired up with excitement and challenge. He surveyed the faces of the prospective jurors who would be tasked with judging another human. During voir dire, the people would swear to the judge how much they wanted to do their civic duty and serve. Mostly, they lied. People hated lawyers, feared judges and distrusted the law. They'd rather be home or at work. Despite all that, juries delivered the right verdict, except, of course, when they totally screwed up. Michael couldn't help but admire a system that was great, flawed and terrifying.

Next to him at the defense table, María had her tiny hands folded on her lap. Her long hair went in a braid down her back. She wore a plain dark-blue dress with a cheerless white collar, which he guessed she probably wore to church. No longer the hysterical woman he had first met at the jail, his client sat calm and resigned, as if she knew the outcome of the trial would not be in her favor. Sitting close to María, Toni wore a black suit. Her hair was in a bun, calling attention to her long neck. He couldn't think of her now, not of her body and voice. He took out his handkerchief and patted his forehead. Although the courtroom fans along the ceiling pushed around the air, the temperature was tepid as tap water.

At nine on the dot, Judge Hower pushed through his chamber door, ascended to the bench and asked both sides if they were ready to proceed. They were. The potential jurors were ordered to stand and swear to tell the truth during the questioning.

"Call the first name," Judge Hower boomed.

George Roy reached into the red drum. "Herman Andrews."

With the hesitation of a doomed man, Andrews walked forward. He wiggled in the witness stand as if it was covered in tacks.

"Morning, Mr. Andrews." Michael smiled to put the guy at ease.

The man nodded.

Judge Hower snorted with frustration. "Mr. Andrews, the court cannot record a nod. Please answer out loud."

"Good morning," Andrews replied a little too loudly.

"Mr. Andrews, how do you feel about natives of Mexico?" Michael said.

Andrews chewed the question like tobacco. "You mean wetbacks?"

"That's all the questions I have." Michael crossed Andrews off his list.

"Mr. Brennan?" Judge Hower said.

The county attorney gave a greeting smile and asked only a few questions. He wanted this man, but Michael Shaw would probably toss him from the panel with a preemptory challenge.

"Step down, Mr. Andrews," the judge said after Brennan completed his questions.

"Is that it?" the man asked.

"Probably for you," the judge answered.

Elsie Van Buren, a young woman with broad hips and a high hairdo, answered Michael's questions politely. "I don't have anything against Mexicans. I believe God made us all. Yes, this is what the Bible says."

Michael wrote a question mark beside her name on his pad. If she quoted the Bible, she might also get to the part about "Thou shalt not kill." He took another direction. "Miss Van Buren, if someone attacked you or your family, do you feel you have the right to defend yourself?"

She rubbed her cheek a little. "Sir, is that like an eye for eye? If it is, then yes, I do."

"I don't know about the theology, but as far as I'm concerned you deserve a spot in the jury box."

Michael hid his dismay when Brennan got rid of Elsie with one of his challenges.

Toni didn't like the older woman up next for questioning. She had eyes like a dead cat, and her body was wound as tightly as her thick stockings.

"One Mexican boy stole my car last week." Maggie Billard's words barely passed through her tight lips. "They caught 'm good and sent 'm back across the border, where he belongs. Then, another Mexican kid broke into my neighbor's house. They're thieves, sir. That's how I feel about 'em. They should be thrown back where they came from." Maggie folded her arms with triumph.

As far as Michael was concerned, Maggie Billard could go back where she had come from.

He couldn't believe there could be anybody worse than Maggie until the bailiff called Simon Smith, a farmer of thirty going on sixty-five. Smith believed in capital punishment, not self-defense. He believed Mexicans deserved less than white people. "They rob jobs from respectable 'mericans. A lotta them don't even bother to learn English. If they're gonna live in this country they better learn American."

"Thank you, Mr. Smith." Michael cut in.

"Those Mexicans're drinkers, too."

"That's enough, Mr. Smith."

"Ever see their homes?"

"Your Honor."

"Mr. Smith." Judge Hower's stare was enough to shut the man up.

Michael wanted to get rid of Simon Smith, but he wanted to keep Joshua Kinney, a janitor at the high school. On the stand, Kinney scratched his chin with nervousness but answered with sincerity. "They's hard-workin' folks. I worked with lotsa them down at the mill one summer, and I grew up in North Park."

"The defense will be based on self-defense. How do you feel about that?"

Kinney scratched a little more. "Don't know the legal stuff, but I'd do everything I can to protect myself or my family."

"Thank you, Mr. Kinney."

Jury selection took most of the day and part of the next. By the time Judge Hower brought down his final gavel, they had a seven-woman, five-man jury, including Joshua Kinney. Michael was pleased. Now the work really started: convincing twelve different people of one truth, that María Curry did what she had to do to defend herself.

Deputy Herb Bell arrived from his place in back of the courtroom to fetch María Curry back to the jail after another trial day had ended. "Let's go," he told the woman he considered pathetic. He also stared down at Toni, who was too pretty to be a nice girl, Bell reasoned. That's probably why Mr. Shaw looked her over like she was the main course at a restaurant.

Toni hugged María before she was taken away. "I was sure Ben Curry's brother would be here," Toni told Michael.

"He will. He's going to be a prosecution witness," Michael said. "So we have that to look forward to."

After the courtroom cleared, Michael sat down at the defense table. Toni leaned against the railing across from him. The staid courtroom made her feel how far apart she and Michael really might be. She tapped her heel against the floor for thinking of herself more than María.

"Is it a good jury, Michael?"

"Not bad. We'll have to put them in María's shoes, and I hope to hell I can do that."

≈ ≈ ≈

Michael entered his apartment at five-thirty, carrying law books and a briefcase heavy with notes for the trial. He could have worked at Toni's house, but doubted he would make any progress there. They would have ended up making love. So he went home, if only to stop Jenny's nagging about why he was never home. He planned to see Toni later that night.

Jenny was yelling. A rarity, even after the time he had spilled whiskey on her pale green carpet.

"You did it on purpose! You're so stupid! Are you listening to me?" she shouted.

Michael rushed into the kitchen, where Jenny had a finger pointed at their housekeeper and cook, Lupita Cordova. The remains of a broken serving dish were spread over the floor.

"What the hell is going on, Jenny?"

"She dropped the dish my mother gave us for our wedding. It's an heirloom." Jenny's cheeks fired up with an angry red. Her blond hair had fallen into her eyes.

"I was cleaning and accidently bumped it with my hand. I swear to God, Mr. Michael, that's what happened," said Lupita, who was Josita's daughter and looked just like her mother.

"I know you didn't mean to break the dish, Lupita. Why don't you go home early. Call it a night off." He touched her wide back.

"Mr. Michael, I'll pick up the mess."

"We'll take care of it."

"*Gracias.*" Lupita gathered her purse before Jenny started yelling again.

Michael accompanied Lupita to the door.

"Tell Miss Jenny I'm sorry."

"I don't think she was really yelling at you."

"No?" Lupita's face scrunched with bewilderment.

"Never mind. See you tomorrow."

Back in the kitchen, Jenny kneeled on the floor, picking up what was left of the white ceramic dish decorated with yellow daisies and pink roses along its border. "It's shattered. We'll never fix it." Crying, she held a couple of pieces in her hands.

"Don't worry about it, Jenny. To be honest, I've always thought that dish was really ugly."

"Michael! It was a wedding present."

He kneeled beside her. "I'll buy you a new one. A pretty one."

She stood up. "It's all broken." Jenny threw down the ceramic pieces, ran to their bedroom and slammed the door.

On the way to his small study, Michael poured a drink.

"Son of a bitch."

Jenny knew.

Now that she did, he should march into the bedroom and tell her the rest. Instead, he opened the law books and took another drink.

25

BORDEN FOOD TOWN had opened two months ago. Carmen considered it more of a grocery palace than store. Usually, she went to the corner market in the neighborhood. Mr. Morgan, a fleshy man with a pleasant nature, ran the small store. While the vegetables were sometimes less than fresh, Mr. Morgan made up for it with friendly chat about anything from the weather to who had a new baby. He carried lots of Mexican spices and threw in a candy bar for regular customers who spent more than twenty dollars. Because of that, Carmen felt like a traitor for shopping Food Town, but the girls at work had called it beautiful.

The store featured a new and expanded bakery resembling a stainless steel cathedral. Beautiful glass windows housed hefty loaves of bread, rolls, maple bars, apple fritters, doughnuts and cinnamon rolls. Carmen lingered nearby, enjoying the smell, but they were all too sweet for her. On her way home, she planned to stop at the Sánchez Panadería for Mexican bread. She loved the vague sweetness of the *conchas*, buns with swirled toppings of sugar made to resemble seashells. She put a hand on her stomach, sending a message to the baby: *You'll like Mexican bread.*

Pushing her cart slowly down the aisle, Carmen looked for tomatoes for the salsa to top the chicken tacos they were having for dinner. When she and Toni were kids, they tried to best each other at eating the most tacos. Their dad pulled the tacos from the frying pan, and as soon as they cooled, she and Toni each grabbed one, blowing on their fingers because they were still hot. They'd pile on lettuce, yellow cheese and salsa. Toni held the record for eating six tacos in one sitting.

Placing ten tomatoes in a paper bag, Carmen smiled a little. She was eating for two, so she might break Toni's record.

"Carmen."

Mrs. Hernández and her daughter, Anita, hustled toward her with their cart. Anita looked more like Mrs. Hernández's twin. Anita, however, was nastier than her mom, as Carmen had found out when they were kids. No one dodged Anita's insults or mean tricks.

Carmen wanted to wheel away, but their carts trapped her in the aisle. "Hi."

"Congratulations on your baby." Anita gave Carmen a hug with no feeling behind it.

"Thanks. I'm very happy."

Mrs. Hernández nudged Carmen in the ribs. "You and your husband didn't wait long after the wedding, did you?"

"Víctor and I both wanted children." Carmen's words were clipped; she was annoyed at Mrs. Hernández's suggestion.

The women disregarded the tone. Anita grinned at her mother, who winked back. "And how's Toni these days? I haven't seen her for a long time, not since school."

"I forgot you dropped out to get married before we graduated." Carmen had to rub it in that she and Toni did graduate from high school. "Toni got a college degree and everything."

"Gee, Mom, Toni was always a smart one in school," Anita said.

"I bet she's real busy with the murder case I read about in the paper," Mrs. Hernández said.

Carmen knew where they were headed. She wanted to get the hell out of Food Town.

Anita's brows knitted in nastiness. "Toni and that lawyer fella must be working hard at it. Mom sees him coming and going all times of the night from Toni's house in the back."

Mrs. Hernández smiled with success at making her neighbor squirm. "All the time. Right, Carmen?"

"Mom says he's very handsome and rich, too. Oh, and married." Anita giggled.

Carmen planted her feet. "He's defending a nice Mexican woman."

"Oh, I'm sure it's a very good job for Toni," Anita said. "I wish I could get me some of that nice work."

Carmen tugged her cart. "I've got to go now. I've got to finish dinner."

"'Bye, Carmen. Tell Toni hello for me." Anita and her mom waved as Carmen rushed off.

"See, what'd I tell you, Anita?" Mrs. Hernández said.

"You're right, Mom. It's about time Toni García got what she had coming. She acts like her shit don't stink, with her fancy-ass education. And now, she'd rather go out with white guys who'll spend money on her."

"She'll get everything she deserves." Laughing, Mrs. Hernández put a dozen oranges in a bag.

Carmen peeked around the corner. Mrs. Hernández and her daughter poked each other with joy. Carmen clenched the cart handle until her hands hurt. She should have told them to mind their own damn business. But if she did, it would support what everyone on the block already seemed to know about her sister.

Carmen left the store without buying anything.

≈ ≈ ≈

Francisco sat on a kitchen chair, softly strumming his guitar and singing a ballad in Spanish. He couldn't recall where
he had heard the many songs he knew. Some dated back to the
Mexican Revolution and the days of his hero, Emiliano Zapata. Toni had checked books out of the library and read to him
about Zapata, who looked like he had a lot on his mind in the
old photographs. He was saddened such a hero had been killed
by other Mexicans.

Francisco made up songs about Zapata as well as about own
his life. Musical stories about how he had traveled around
working in the fields. About his mother and his time without
her. His special songs were about Maricela. How his heart
ached without her laughter and love. Part of his soul went into
the grave with her, went one of his songs. He only played it
when he was alone, because he didn't want his daughters to cry.

In the kitchen, Toni and Carmen washed dishes and listened to their father's music. Víctor had gone out to the store
for a pack of cigarettes. Francisco's playing and the dishes clat-
tering in the water filled the silence between the sisters, which
was unusual for them. Carmen was wondering if she should
tell Toni about Mrs. Hernández.

Bumping her sister with a hip, Toni held up a soapy dish.
"You still mad I ate more tacos than you?"

"No. But I'm warning you, I'll break your record someday."

"Dream on."

Carmen dried her hands on a dish towel and kissed the top
of Francisco's head. "Hey, Pops. Tell that story again about
how you met Mamá."

"Ay, you've heard it a hundred times."

"Come on," Toni agreed, although she and her sister had
almost memorized the words he used.

"Okay, okay." It never took much persuasion. Francisco strummed his guitar as he told the story he loved.

His friend had talked him into going to a dance with the promise they'd meet a lot of girls. He was twenty and had a job at the steel mill. In an old hall on the edge of town, a band that had come all the way from Dallas was playing. Admission was only fifteen cents per person. Francisco spent most of the evening staring at Maricela. Wearing a blue dress with a little white collar, she sat with her legs crossed at the ankles. She twisted her hands from nerves. To his happiness, she stared back. They danced, but she kept asking the time. She had sneaked out of the house with a girlfriend and had to be back by eleven, before her dad returned from work at the mill. Following the dance, they met again and again. Each time, Maricela's sweetness eased his rough life.

Two months later, she sneaked out again, and they got married in Bisbee. That night, she snuck back home, too afraid to tell her family. After three weeks, Francisco wanted no more sneaking around. He went to meet her father, José, who could be terrifying when he didn't smile. With as much respect as he could manage, Francisco told José about their marriage.

"'Maricela! Your husband is here,' José yelled." Francisco imitated his late father-in-law's rumbling voice. "Your mother went and hid under the covers in her room. Finally, she came out. José pointed at her and said, 'Your place is with him.'"

"I like that part," Carmen said, which Toni hushed her.

Maricela's mother put her clothes in a paper sack. When Francisco took her to his tiny room in a boardinghouse, he feared she would run back to her father's house. He did what he hated most and borrowed money from as many people as he knew to put a down payment on a house one block away from her parents. Eventually, he and José became friends.

"She was the prettiest thing I ever saw." Their father always concluded with the same line.

"That story gets better every time I hear it." Carmen wiped the table.

Toni kissed her father's cheek. An increased dosage of medicine had helped quiet the coughing, but her father was losing weight. His coloring had become ashen. *Be happy for each day with him,* she told herself. Still, she was tempted to hold on so tight that death would have to take them both.

After her father went to bed, Toni packed the trash in the can behind the house and lit up a cigarette. The night was clean and untroubled. She jumped when the back door opened with a squeak. Carmen came out wringing her hands, a nervous habit she had inherited from their mother.

"Okay, Carmen, spill it." Toni took a long draw. "You've been acting strange all night."

"I was in the store and stupid Mrs. Hernández and her daughter stopped me. You know how nosy they are."

"What's your point?"

"Mrs. Hernández spotted that white guy coming over a lot, and at night." She spoke softly, even though they were alone.

"Michael."

"You mean it's true?"

"For once, Mrs. Hernández is right."

"Holy shit. Does Dad know?"

Toni choked on the smoke. "No, and I'm not going to tell him. Michael is married."

"*Madre de Dios.*" Carmen crossed herself. "I thought you were the smart one in the family."

"Me, too."

"When we were teenagers, we used to say white guys only wanted one thing from Mexican girls."

"He already got that." Toni smiled.

"I'm trying to be serious."

"Sorry."

"I'm worried about you."

"I know."

Toni took her sister's hand and studied the sky. The moon slept somewhere else, making it a night for hiding, for sharing secrets. She let go of her sister's hand and faced her.

"Carmen, you don't have to tell me anything I haven't already told myself. Michael and I . . . well, it's nothing like how Mom and Dad met. But I've never wanted anyone as much."

"Oh no, Toni."

Toni drew a few more puffs of her cigarette. "And that's precisely, my little sister, why it scares the hell out of me."

26

As OFFICER SAM JONES sat in the witness box, his weapon stuck to his side. He concentrated on not sweating into his newly ironed police shirt. How much safer to be on the dark streets arresting crooks instead of up on the stand in front of men in suits. He wished those damn lawyers would hurry up and quit all the legal mumbo jumbo. For more than an hour he had already testified about finding Ben Curry's body and how María Curry had signed a confession, not only in English, but another written in Spanish by one of the detectives, who had lived in Mexico. When the prosecutor submitted the confessions as evidence, Jones thought that should have ended the trial right there. But the lawyers still wanted more from him.

From under a file and with a bit of theatrics, Joe Brennan yanked out a bread knife with a seven-inch blade. "Do you recognize this?"

"Yes, sir. It was stuck in Ben Curry's chest," the police officer said.

Holding out the knife, Brennan walked slowly in front of the panel. Spots of dried blood covered the brown wooden handle. One female juror gasped. María sobbed. The prosecutor continued his questioning, content with the response.

"Officer Jones, before the night of the killing, were you well acquainted with Ben Curry and his Mexican wife?"

"Don't know if 'acquainted' is the right word, sir. Not social like. But we did break up lots of their fights."

"What did you usually find when you answered those calls?"

"Well, Ben and María would be drunk most times. They'd be yelling and throwing things at each other and disturbing the neighbors."

Michael stood up, ready to object. Brennan spoke first. "Your Honor, I know exactly what Mr. Shaw's objection will be. I am prepared to enter into evidence nineteen police reports related to altercations at the Curry residence or at bars they frequented. That should satisfy the defense questions about foundation."

"Take a chair, Mr. Shaw," Judge Hower cut in.

Michael didn't sit back down. "If I can't finish my objection, I hope the prosecution will at least allow me to present the rest of my case instead of trying to read my mind."

"Let's get on with this." The judge tapped a pencil on the bench.

Michael lifted his chin toward Brennan and hoped the prosecutor read the "Fuck you" on his mind.

"Before we were interrupted, Officer Jones, you were telling us how many times you broke up fights involving this Mexican."

Michael stood again. "Your Honor, Mr. Brennan keeps referring to my client as 'that Mexican' or 'this Mexican.' Although Mexico is her native land, Mr. Brennan says it as if it's dirty word, which is prejudicial. My client's name is María Sánchez Curry, and I'll write it down if Mr. Brennan can't remember."

"Mr. Brennan, say her name or call her 'the defendant,'" Judge Hower ordered.

Brennan's back straightened, and the objection rolled right off. "Very well. Officer Jones, tell us what you found at the Curry house on April 13th of last year?"

Slipping on reading glasses, Jones consulted a police report. "I responded to a call from a neighbor about a domestic problem at the Curry house. I found Ben Curry bleeding from a large wound to his head. He said María whacked him with a frying pan. But ole Ben . . . Mr. Curry, I mean, didn't want to press no charges. I told them if I had to come back, they'd both go to jail."

"Thank you, Officer."

As Michael approached, Jones' gut began to churn. From giving testimony at other trials, Jones knew how defense attorneys loved to portray police officers as jackasses and incompetent fools.

"Those many other times you answered calls at the Curry house, wasn't María Curry the one you found beaten and bloody?" Michael asked.

Jones took his time answering.

"Officer . . . ," the judge boomed.

"Yes, I think so."

"It's either yes or no, Officer Jones," Michael said.

"Yes."

"And wasn't it Ben Curry who was drunk most of the time and not his wife?"

"Yes."

Michael asked with a firm tone but took care not to appear to harass the policeman. "How many times did you find María Curry injured, Officer Jones?"

"I'd have to check the reports."

"I checked, Officer. We're talking about ninety-nine percent of the time."

"That much, huh?"

A few people smirked. Jones felt like a jackass and an incompetent fool.

"You even gave María Curry a ride to the hospital for a broken arm after one of those arguments because her husband was too drunk to drive. Do you recall that?"

Jones lowered his head slightly. "Yes."

Michael put his hand to his ear. "I'm a little hard of hearing. What did you say?"

"YES."

"Officer, how tall was Ben Curry?"

Jones swallowed. "About six feet, I'd say."

"A big man?"

"He was hefty."

"Muscular?"

"Yes."

Michael turned. "María, please stand."

After hearing the translation from Toni, María did, but slowly.

"Officer, how tall is María Curry?"

"A little over five feet."

"How much do you think she weighs?"

"Maybe about a hundred pounds," Jones answered and wished he could belt the defense attorney with his baton.

Michael motioned for María to sit and turned back to Jones. "Those times you were called to their house and discovered María Curry hurt and bleeding, did she want to press charges against her husband?"

"No."

"Did you even ask María Curry if she wanted her husband arrested?"

"I don't remember. She don't speak a lot of English, and I ain't so good at Spanish."

More smirking from the audience. Judge Hower glared at the guilty.

"Did you ever arrest Ben Curry for striking his wife?"

"No, sir."

Michael picked up a bunch of papers from his table and flipped through them. "These are all hospital reports about María Curry's injuries that the defense will enter into evidence." He leaned on the witness stand and wanted to shove the papers in the policeman's face. "Was María Curry hurt the night of August 18th?"

"Yes."

"Can you describe the injuries?"

"Her head was cut, and her face was banged up."

"That's all?"

"I couldn't see much more because it was dark and she was covered with blood."

It was what Michael wanted to hear. "I'm finished with this witness."

"Redirect, Mr. Brennan?" Judge Hower said.

Brennan glided out of his chair. "Officer Jones, did María Curry ever attack you?"

Jones raised his head. He knew where the prosecutor was pointing him and gladly followed. "No, but she shook her fists at me and cussed me out lots of times when she was drunk. I don't know a lot of Spanish, but I know the swear words."

"Thank you, Officer."

Judge Hower abruptly stood up. "Court will be in recess until tomorrow."

Officer Jones stepped down, glad to get back to the streets, where he could deal with good, honest criminals instead of a room full of lawyers.

≈ ≈ ≈

Dr. William Nolan prided himself on describing wounds at court proceedings. The county coroner made his explanations precise, visual and alarming enough to hold the jurors' attention. The jury regarded his every word as he talked about what had killed Ben Curry.

"There were three stab wounds in the left side of Ben Curry's stomach, another in the top of his chest and one gash to his right hand, which is what we consider a defense wound," the doctor said.

"Were any of those considered fatal?" Brennan said.

"No. The fatal wound came when the knife entered the body under the sternum. It punctured and caused the collapse of the left lung. The blade also slit the left ventricle of the heart. The cause of death was massive internal bleeding."

"How long before death occurred?" Joe Brennan asked.

"Ten to twenty minutes."

Dr. Nolan leaned back in his chair with satisfaction and smoothed his black serge pants.

Brennan held up two eight-by-ten-inch black-and-white photographs of Ben Curry's body on a metal table in the morgue. One showed the body from the waist up, and the other was a closer shot of his torso. In both, black slits covered the chest and abdomen. At the sight of them, María pressed her hands to her mouth and trembled. Toni put her arm around María's waist to help calm her.

"We wish to submit as evidence State Exhibit No. 25 and State Exhibit No. 26," Brennan said.

Michael had seen the prints and wanted them nowhere near the jury. "Objection. The doctor's testimony is sufficient in this matter. There is no need to show these photographs.

Their sole purpose is to whip up the jurors' emotions like a desert wind." He knew he was going to lose this one.

"Your Honor, the photographs will more clearly illustrate the severity of the wounds," Brennan said.

Judge Hower took a moment, which gave Michael hope. It didn't last.

"Overruled."

Brennan took the prints and handed them to the bailiff, who gave them to the jury. As they examined them, their faces registered exactly what he had wanted: revulsion. He stood on the other side of the witness box. "Dr. Nolan, would it take a strong person to have inflicted the fatal wound?"

"Not necessarily. Not with the right impact and a sharp enough knife, as it was in this case."

Michael stood. "Objection. The doctor's expertise is starting to sound like opinion."

"Overruled."

Brennan smiled at Michael, who smiled back. The prosecutor waved his thin arm at the doctor. "That's all for now."

Michael straightened his jacket and stood in front of the witness. "Dr. Nolan, I got out my family's old anatomy book last night. Very interesting, I must say. I learned the measurement of an average adult heart is about five inches by three inches. Sound about right?"

"Yes."

"That's not big at all." Michael held up a blue piece of paper of those dimensions and showed the jury.

"The heart is not the largest organ in the body, Mr. Shaw." The doctor didn't know what the defense was up to, but he put himself on guard.

"Dr. Nolan, if the heart is that small, wouldn't it be darn near impossible to intentionally pierce it with a kitchen knife?"

"I'm not sure I understand."

"Let's see. In order to damage the heart as you described, a person wielding a knife would have to miss the sternum, which is one hard bone, and bypass the ribs. Then, he or she would have to find the exact location of an organ that is five by three inches. Isn't that right?"

"Yes, but . . . "

"You examined the body . . . Did Ben Curry have an X on his chest?"

"I beg your pardon."

"An X right over his heart." Michael pointed to his chest.

"Objection," Brennan said. "The defense is ridiculing a serious issue."

"Your Honor, I can assure you, I'm making a serious point here."

"Objection overruled."

"So, Dr. Nolan, unless Ben Curry had an X on his chest, this fatal wound might be considered one in a million?"

"I don't know if it's one in a million, but I find it highly unlikely someone deliberately aiming at the heart with a bread knife would successfully find their target. That's usually the purview of skilled surgeons." Dr. Nolan's mouth puckered as he realized what he had just said. He had lost the jurors.

Michael had drawn blood. "Isn't it more than likely, Doctor, that María Curry struck out blindly with a knife while defending herself and unintentionally struck his chest?"

Brennan stood again. "I object. Mr. Shaw is asking the doctor to draw conclusions about María Curry's intent, which is up to the jury to determine."

"I withdraw the question, Your Honor. But it sure sounds like one in a million to me."

People laughed in the audience and jury box. The judge threw a murderous glance. "Mr. Shaw, save your remarks until summation."

≈ ≈ ≈

In an interview room at the jail, María and Toni tried to finish their boxed lunches but only ate half of the dry turkey sandwiches.

"Jail is bad, but jail food is worse." María pinched the white bread. "I don't think even my little Oscar would eat this."

"I wish I could bring you something, but they won't let me. I asked. It's too bad because my dad's chili verde is the best in Borden," Toni said.

"That gets me hungry. All they serve you in jail are runny eggs and gravy with lumps like socks."

Toni laughed and threw the boxes in the trash. When she turned around María was walking the perimeter of the room, her hand brushing the walls as if looking for a secret passage leading outside. Previously, María had showed sadness, hysteria and pain, but the longing she now projected made Toni want to cry.

"I wish I could have visited the ocean one last time," María said.

"Please don't talk like that."

María's lips went up into a smile. The young were ever optimistic, and why not? Life still had possibilities. Toni did. When Mr. Shaw was around, she lit up like sunset sparks over the waves, although she tried to hide her emotions about him. María had felt such hope by the ocean.

"I've never seen an ocean, but I've always wanted to. I think living in a desert gives you a thirst for all that water," Toni said.

María pepped up. "Antonia, there's nothing like where the sea and sky meet. You could keep swimming and could end up in the heavens. The air is full of salt that sits on your tongue. Like tasting Creation. My words can't describe it."

"Your words are perfect." Toni closed her eyes. "I can almost see it."

María told Toni about where she was born and how she had met Ben. How she spent time on the beaches, trying to count the waves as she counted her own heartbeat.

"No wonder you miss it," Toni said.

María's voice was a whisper, as if she had returned from a journey. "Don't worry, Antonia. Someday, you'll get to Mexico and smell the ocean."

Down the street in his office, Michael sat by himself, picking at his lunch. He pushed away his plate of chicken-fried steak and mashed potatoes. Although the food came from Pete's Café, his body rebelled at the smell and at the thought of the next two prosecution witnesses who would take the stand.

27

JOE BRENNAN DREADED THE THOUGHT of having Lorna Dean Richards as a neighbor but loved her as a witness. Her crusty elbows reflected her demeanor. Her mouth resembled a baby bird's squawking for food. As the bailiff swore her in, she claimed the witness stand as her own like a queen taking to a throne. Raising her right hand, the witness swore to God to tell the truth. Her mouth puckered as if God could not hold her back from doing so.

Mrs. Richards adjusted her cat-eye glasses as she spoke. "The Currys were always yelling and fighting. I work very early in the morning at the mill cafeteria, and I could never get any sleep because of all their carrying on. I need my sleep. I'm a widow woman, and I need to work."

"How often did you call the police to complain about their fighting?" Brennan asked.

"Three or four times a month."

Toni glanced over at María as if Mrs. Richards was talking about another woman. María had the fragility of a dried flower, even becoming more so during each day of the trial. Her slight hands were folded on her lap. How much anger and fear she must have swallowed before picking up that knife.

Brennan pointed to the panel. "Mrs. Richards, tell the jurors what happened on the morning of August 16, two days before Ben Curry died."

"I was woken up by their yelling. *Again.* I put on my robe and went into the yard."

"What did you see?"

"María yelled at Ben, 'I'm going to kill you.' I speak Spanish, you know. I've worked for years at the mill, and you have to know the language to deal with all those Mexican workers."

"Don't digress, Mrs. Richards," the judge said.

"Okay. As I was saying, María staggered around, she was so drunk. But she kept telling him, 'I'll kill you, I'll kill you.' And . . . that's what she did."

Michael jumped to his feet. "Objection, move to strike that last comment. The witness is stating her opinion."

"Sustained," the judge ruled.

"What's going on? Do I have to say that all over again, sir?" She looked up at Judge Hower.

"Just answer the question. We don't want your opinion," the judge said.

The woman's face twisted in anger. "Then why am I here?"

"We want to know what you saw, not what you think. Mr. Brennan, continue."

"Now, Mrs. Richards, let's go back to the night of August 18. You were again awakened by the fighting of Ben and María Curry?"

Mrs. Richards talked directly to the jury, as the county attorney had suggested. "I heard shouting and what sounded like furniture being broken. My windows were open because it was so hot. I went outside and heard more ruckus from the Curry house. That mangy dog of María's barked up a storm. Then, all of sudden, it got quiet and stayed real quiet. I guess that's when I got really scared. I called the police and locked my doors."

"Thank you, Mrs. Richards." Brennan sat down.

The woman began to leave.

"Hold on there a minute," Michael said. "The defense would like to ask you some questions."

She sucked on her front teeth and sat back down.

Michael approached with caution. This type of woman had no other life than spying on and judging her neighbors. By watching others do bad, she judged herself good. He would be safer facing down a mountain lion. "Mrs. Richards, during all those times you eavesdropped on your neighbors, did you ever see María Curry crying because she had been hurt?"

The woman hadn't like this lawyer in the expensive suit and his uppity ways before. Now she really didn't like him. "I can't remember."

"You certainly remembered all those other fights in great detail. I repeat, did you ever see María Curry crying?"

"Yes, now that you mention it."

"Did you see Ben Curry hit María?"

"Sometimes."

Michael narrowed his eyes at the woman. "Come on, Mrs. Richards. How about lots of times?"

"Yes, lots of times."

"What did Ben Curry do to her?"

"He slapped her around most of the time."

"Slapped her to the ground?"

"Yes."

"Did you see Ben Curry chase María Curry with a butcher knife?"

"Yeah."

"Did you call the police then?"

She adjusted her glasses. "I probably did. I don't remember. It was all part of their fighting. He'd yell, and she'd cry. He'd punch her. She'd kick him. They both sounded drunk at the time."

"Did Ben Curry ever threaten his wife?"

Mrs. Richards looked ready to spit hammers.

"Mrs. Richards, you must answer," the judge said.

"Yes," she blew out in disgust.

"When?" Michael asked.

"The night she threatened him."

"What did he say?"

"When María said she'd kill him, he told her, 'Not unless I get you first.'"

Michael returned to the defense table. "I'm done with this witness, Your Honor."

Brennan started on redirect. "Mrs. Richards, did Ben Curry express any fear of his wife?"

She shook her head hard. "Yes, sir, he did. On July 4th, I was out watering the lawn. Ben called María a dirty stinkin' Mesican. Then he said, 'You'll be the death of me.' I'll never forget that."

The judge called a break, and Toni sighed with relief. Mrs. Richards strode down the middle of the courtroom, stopping to glower at María. If true justice occupied the world, Mrs. Richards and Mrs. Hernández would move next door to each other. Then again, they might become the best of friends.

≈ ≈ ≈

Daniel Curry wore animosity like his ten-year-old suit. Both were well lived in. When he was sworn in as a witness, his eyes didn't leave María, who put her head down so as not to look at him.

"WHAT'S HE GOING TO SAY?" Toni wrote on a note she passed to Michael.

"IT WON'T BE GOOD," Michael wrote back.

"Mr. Curry, when was the last time you heard from your brother?" Joe Brennan stayed seated. He didn't want to get in the way of the witness's vehemence toward the defendant.

"In late April of last year."

"What was the circumstance?"

"Ben came up to Prescott. He had lost a job and wanted to borrow some money."

"During your brother's visit, did he say anything about his marriage?"

"Objection." Michael stood up. "This is not relevant. How is this line of questioning material to this proceeding?"

"Your Honor, I can assure you this query will pertain to the state of Ben Curry's mind before his death," Brennan said.

Michael could almost see Hower weighing the arguments.

"Overruled. But don't take advantage of this, Mr. Brennan," Hower waved.

"Never, Your Honor. Mr. Curry, now tell us about your brother's feelings for his wife." Michael got to his feet again. "Objection. Daniel Curry wouldn't know what his brother felt."

"Sustained."

Brennan wiped down his glasses. "Let me put it another way. Mr. Curry, what did your brother Ben say to you about his marriage?"

"He said he needed the money because his wife was always drinking and playing bingo at the church hall." Curry spoke with the deliberation of the hunter.

María shook her head no as Toni translated.

"But María Curry worked, didn't she?" Brennan said.

"Yes, cleaning at some motel. But Ben said she went through her money quick and then went through his."

"Did he express any fear of his wife?" the county attorney asked.

"My brother said he worried about her temper. She cracked his head with a frying pan, and he showed me the scar. It was a nasty one. Right here." He pointed to the place on his own head. "My brother also said he kept one eye open at night because she kept telling him she'd kill him one day while he slept."

"Your brother was a big man, and he was still afraid?" Brennan asked.

"He said María had a mean streak. She was small but fast and spiteful when she had a few beers in her. You know those Mexicans."

"Objection," Michael said.

"No opinions, Mr. Curry," the judge said.

"Did you talk to your brother after his visit?" Brennan went on.

"No. I never saw him alive after that."

"No more questions." The prosecutor sat.

Michael wasted no time. "Did your brother say why his wife hit him with a frying pan?"

"No." Daniel Curry gripped both sides of the stand.

"Let's go on for the moment. When your brother visited you in Prescott, did you two go out drinking?"

Michael had recognized a man with a thirst like his own. During their first encounter in court, Curry's red face wasn't due to the emotion of the moment. He had the broken veins of an alcoholic and smelled like stale foam.

Curry licked dry lips. "I think we went out for a beer or two."

"Only two?" Michael said, and people snorted in laughter.

Curry gave Michael a lethal glare.

Brennan rose. "Objection. What does this have to do with anything?"

"You opened the door, I just stepped through," Michael said.

"Enough," Judge Hower ruled. "Mr. Shaw, get to the point soon."

"Immediately, Your Honor. Mr. Curry, when I saw your name on the witness list, I called the Prescott Police Department. They sent me a report about how you and your brother got into a fistfight with four guys at a place called Max's Bar and Grill. Your brother was arrested for clobbering one of the men with a barstool. Remember that?"

"Kinda."

"Too drunk to remember?"

"No."

Daniel Curry appeared ready to leap off the stand at Michael, who hoped he would just to demonstrate the family's love of aggression.

"In fact, didn't you and your brother spend the night in jail for that brawl?" Michael asked.

"Those guys started it."

"And you certainly finished it."

"Mr. Shaw . . . ," the judge said.

"Sorry, Your Honor. Mr. Curry, María says her husband never mentioned you. Why do think that is?"

"Ben was ashamed he married a Mexican."

"Did your brother say that, or are you guessing?"

Curry crossed his arms. "I'm guessing. But I'm right."

Michael saw an opening and took it. "Before that April visit, when was the last time you had seen your brother?"

Daniel Curry closed his eyes in memory and then opened them. "Maybe twelve years."

"So you two weren't exactly close?"

"He was my brother."

"That doesn't answer the question. Did you and your brother have a disagreement?"

"Yeah."

"About what?"

"'Cause Ben married a Mexican." Daniel Curry looked at María as he spoke.

"One last question. Did you lend your brother any money?" Michael said.

"No."

"I'm done with this man." Michael threw up his arms to show the jury he hadn't taken Daniel Curry seriously. He hoped they wouldn't either.

"Redirect, Mr. Brennan?" the judge asked.

The county attorney approached the witness. "Did you love your brother, Mr. Curry?"

"We were blood. He was my only brother."

28

ON THE WAY TO TONI'S HOUSE, Michael tripped on a hole in the alley he didn't see in the darkness. He fell to one knee. Cursing through clenched teeth, he watched for Mrs. Hernández peeping out of her curtains. But if Michael couldn't see the rut, he certainly couldn't see Deputy Herb Bell in his parked car farther down the alley.

After court ended for the day, Bell had gripped María Curry's forearm and hauled her back to the jail, but a little claw raked at his stomach. He had learned to listen to that inner signal. He heeded it when he decided not to go hunting with his father-in-law. It was the right decision, because the old man got shot in the back by some fool who took him for a deer. He listened to his innards when he decided to go into the county sheriff's business, instead of staying a clerk at J. C. Penney. Even though the job offered a manager's spot in six months, something told him far better things waited for him at the courthouse. Some people may have called it intuition. Bell called it his ulcer to the human soul.

Bell had backtracked to the darkened courtroom. The doors were shut, but he opened a side door slightly and put his face smack against the opening. He made sure no one else was watching him. "Well, well," he muttered. "Ain't that touching."

Inside the empty courtroom, in the corner near the jury box, Michael Shaw pressed the Mexican woman to the wall. Their arms intertwined like obscene vines. Later, he got the Mexican's address from a county clerk and sat in his car in the dismal neighborhood. His ma used to say the Lord punished people by making them poor. By that account, these North Park people had all sinned and were doomed to lives of low wages at jobs white men didn't want. However, his ma never did answer his question about why they were punished.

As soon as it got dark, Bell waited for Michael Shaw in the alley. He half hoped the lawyer would stay home, but there he was, slipping into the brown whore's house.

"My, my, counselor." Herb Bell now had one more duty to perform.

≈ ≈ ≈

Michael and Toni sat drinking strong coffee at the kitchen table.

"Michael, you're worried. Now I'm worried."

"Let's just say the nosy neighbor and Ben Curry's brother didn't help our case."

She didn't respond.

"God, Toni. What if I muff it?"

She placed her hand on Michael's. "You won't."

"Brennan's working hard to portray María as a vengeful woman capable of killing. The jury might start doubting our self-defense argument."

"You'll remind them how her husband hurt her over and over again. When she tells her story, the jury won't be able to do anything else but set her free. I know this world is crazy, but María deserves justice, doesn't she, Michael?"

"My dear Toni, you know better than me that Lady Justice can't see beyond her nose sometimes, with or without the blindfold." He took her hands and kissed their palms. "Quit trying to cheer me up with all that damn encouragement. I want to wallow in self-pity and uncertainty. It's what I do best, especially with a drink . . . or five."

"A waste of time. Besides, I do have something to pep you up."

She walked to the record player and a stack of albums.

"Toni, your jazz records are not cheery."

Thumbing through her collection, she found a record and smiled as she put it on the turntable. An infectious, scratchy Mexican song played. Oscar woke up from where he napped on his pillow in the corner. Toni danced over to Michael. Her arms out. Her hips calling.

"I'll teach you real dancing." She tried to tug him out of the chair.

"My feet hurt."

"What? I can't hear you. Music's in my ears."

She pulled at his arms until he got to his feet. Dancing energetically around him, she took off his tie. He resisted. She swung his tie around and tossed it on the floor next to Oscar, who began to chew on it.

"We'll forget our troubles," she said.

"We'll get exhausted."

She took his hands. "Follow me."

"I'm no Gene Kelly. I can't even waltz."

She jerked him to her. "This is sort of like a polka. Can you polka?"

"No."

"Everybody can polka. How come you white people never learned to have fun?"

"Now, don't be insulting."

She grinned. "I think you can't have fun because you don't have enough trouble in your lives."

He smiled now. "What? My life *is* nothing but trouble, Toni, especially since I met you."

"That's ridiculous. You don't have any spice in your lives, no change, no challenge, no chili. We have to live with all that, so we have to keep moving." She bumped her hip against his.

Michael began to follow her. "You could be right."

"You bet I am."

Michael followed clumsily at first. She put her hands on his hips.

"That's it. I'll make a Mexican out of you yet."

Soon they were dancing around the room. Michael laughed. He tripped and grimaced when he stepped on her toes. But her eyes were splendid. The feeling made him almost dizzy, like being on a merry-go-round.

He led her over to the bed. "These steps I know."

They slid off their clothes, hips touching and moving, even though the song had ended.

They descended onto the bed and made another type of music. Afterward, they lay on their backs. Their bodies were silvery with sweat. Michael dozed. Toni knew she had to wake him soon and send him home. While she watched him, it occurred to her that nothing else mattered outside the small space they shared. Her hand went between her legs to the wetness of their lovemaking. She smelled the saltiness.

She smelled the ocean.

29

LAYING ON THE BUNK IN HER JAIL CELL, María wished she had cotton to stuff in her ears. Her cellmate, a squat Mexican woman named Dede who had robbed a jewelry store with her boyfriend, never stopped talking about her rotten life. María welcomed lights out, when Dede would finally shut up and start snoring. In those tranquil times, María shut her eyes tightly, clasped her hands together and prayed to Jesus. Not to the Jesus whose face appeared painted on votive candles or on statues at church. She prayed to the Jesus of New Mexico.

Years before, she and Ben were driving to one of his construction jobs in Albuquerque when she begged him to take a side trip to the Santuario de Chimayo, south of Taos. The shrine was famous for its statue of the Santo Niño de Atocha, which people claimed walked at night and brought about healing. The faithful even brought the statue baby shoes, the soles of which were dirty the next morning.

As they neared the Santuario, María was convinced of its holiness because pilgrims crept on knees up to the chapel with the statue of the young Jesus dressed in a blue frock, wearing a cavalier hat and holding a shepherd's crook. Their faces glowed with devotion. She had urged Ben to come see the statue, but Ben refused to go inside. He had been raised a

Baptist and never forgave his parents for taking all the joy out of living, he had told her. He had no use for them or God. It was the only time he had ever mentioned his family. Glancing at his watch, he told her, "I'll wait in the car. You got an hour for your miracles."

At the front of the church, a carved wooden Jesus on the cross dominated the sanctuary. Even the flames of the candles bent toward him. He was not the blue-eyed, pink-skinned Jesus she had seen in pictures. This Jesus had skin dark as hers. Painted blood from a crown of thorns flowed thickly over his black hair. Real nails had been pounded into his wooden hands. María was seized by the agony on Jesus' face. Here was a man who knew suffering as she had known it at Ben's hands.

After the visit, María no longer prayed to the golden Jesus found in so many churches. She prayed to the Jesus of wood and sorrow she had seen in the church in New Mexico.

30

BEFORE THE NEXT TRIAL SESSION, Michael sat at the defense table studying his notes. He expected the prosecution to wrap up that day, since Brennan had no more witnesses.

He turned to inspect the gallery. Few people had shown an interest in the proceeding. Only one or two courtroom workers slipped in during their break for the chance to hear juicy testimony. Unfortunately, Kent Wyman, the reporter from the *Daily Sun*, sat in the front row every day, wearing a cheery polka-dot tie as he scribbled in his notebook. Wyman had once confessed to Michael that he loved covering trials because they were true life, not the births or society news. Crime revealed the meat of humanity, albeit rotten meat. Michael thought Wyman had the substance of wet newsprint.

Michael turned back to his notes and could smell Toni's perfume. He wondered what would happen after the trial ended, as if it and his relationship to Toni were fused together.

Judge Hower entered, and the trial day began.

Joe Brennan cleared his throat. "The State calls Isabel Ontiveros."

Who the hell was that? Michael held onto his trial poker face. He turned to María, whose face scrunched up with worry, and that made him worry.

With a cue from the bailiff, a slender young woman peeked through the open door. With two fingers, Judge Hower waved her forward and pointed to the witness stand.

Michael leaned over and whispered to Toni, who sat next to him. "Ask María how she knows her." He stood up with an objection to gain some time. "Your Honor, this woman's name wasn't on the list of prosecution witnesses."

"Miss Ontiveros came forward only a day ago with pertinent information in this case," Brennan said.

"So convenient," Michael said.

"Mr. Shaw, it's too early in the morning for your sarcasm. I'm going to allow her testimony," Judge Hower responded.

"Then the defense seeks a postponement of a day to prepare," Michael said. So-called surprise witnesses were more the devices of television shows and the movies, but they did happen, and the surprise usually worked against the defense. He knew this because he had called a few himself when he had sat at the other table as a deputy county attorney. The testimony of last-minute witnesses seemed to carry a sense of urgency, as if they were a burning bush of justice. Besides, it would be damn hard to prove that the surprise witness was no surprise at all to Brennan.

"Motion denied," Judge Hower said. "Let's get on with this, but Mr. Brennan, you had better come to the point."

Michael sat and listened to what María said via Toni. "Isabel used to work with her at the motel. María says the woman doesn't like her."

"Why?" Michael said.

"She thought María got her fired."

Judge Hower cleared his throat. Michael didn't have more time to listen because Brennan had started his questioning. Michael did know one thing about the witness. She was probably going to be dangerous.

Isabel Ontiveros had shiny raven hair and wore a white blouse, black skirt and glossy new pumps. Michael guessed she was in her early twenties. She would have been a pretty girl except for the hawkish squint of malice on her face.

"How do you know María Curry?" Brennan asked the witness.

"We used to work as housekeepers at the Santa Fe Motel on Tobin Street." Her voice lifted in an exaggerated gentility that put Michael further on edge.

"How long did you work together?" the prosecutor said.

"From December of last year to July of this year."

"Was María Curry a good worker?"

Isabel Ontiveros shook her shiny hair. "Oh, no, sir. She was lazy, and she steals."

"Objection," Michael stood up. Here was one more person victimizing María. One more beating. "Without any foundation, I call this prejudicial to my client."

"This is the witness' firsthand observation of the defendant's behavior," Brennan said, nonplussed.

"Is that what they call character assassination these days, Joe?" Michael's voice was harsher than it should have ever been in a courtroom.

"Objection sustained," the judge said. "And Mr. Shaw, you would do best to control yourself, or you might be facing contempt."

Michael sat back down.

"What did María Curry steal?" Brennan continued.

"She stole some soaps and shampoos from our cart. María even took a camera that had been left in one of the rooms. I told her we should turn it in, but she said she'd sell it so she could buy beer."

Isabel batted her eyes at the jury when she talked. Michael thought that with very little training, she could have been a fine actress. She was giving a first-rate performance now. He looked at María, who listened to Toni's translation and then shook her head at the accusations.

"Did María Curry ever talk to you about her husband, Ben Curry?" Brennan rolled on with confidence.

"Oh, yes. More than once she called him a son of a bitch and said that she'd like to kill him. She told me this in Spanish."

"Did she say why she wanted to kill him?"

"Yes, because her husband was a smelly tightwad who didn't give her any money and treated her like a slave."

"Objection. I move to strike all of this woman's testimony as prejudicial and inflammatory. There is no evidence to prove any of this happened, other than inside her pretty little head." Michael stared at the young woman on the stand. "Why don't you just admit you're lying and save us time?"

"Your Honor, Mr. Shaw is bullying my witness, and it's not even his turn to question her," Brennan said.

"She should be bullied. I've never heard such blatant defamation," Michael shouted and at once knew he had messed up. He was angry with himself because he hadn't anticipated Isabel Ontiveros. He should have known about her. He should have asked María if she had any enemies and done more investigation, but he didn't because of his increased attachment to María and Toni.

"Mr. Shaw!" Judge Hower said. The courtroom froze. The Zeus-like judge was about to throw a thunderbolt. "I've warned you about your displays of disrespect for this court. I hold you in contempt and order a fine of 200 dollars."

Michael gritted his teeth. In all his years in court, he had never lost his temper. Worse, he probably ended up giving more credence to the woman's miserable testimony. He couldn't look at María and Toni, dreading their disappointment.

Maybe with damn luck, the jurors would think he was being overzealous because of his client's innocence. Logically, the next best thing to do was grovel. He could do that. "I deeply apologize for my conduct, Your Honor."

Judge Hower's face slackened but only a bit. "Proceed, Mr. Brennan."

"Miss Ontiveros, why did you come forward to testify?" said the county attorney, who was delighted at the great Michael Shaw's goof.

"Well, I read in the newspaper about the trial, and I thought people should know what kind of person María Curry really is." Triumph glazed over her face.

"Thank you, Miss Ontiveros." Brennan sat down.

"Cross, Mr. Shaw?" the judge said.

Michael walked toward the witness stand. "Why did you leave your job at the Santa Fe Motel?"

Her hawkish eyes reappeared. "I quit."

"Really? You weren't fired?"

Isabel Ontiveros' stare shot to María. "Did she say that? Well, she's lying."

"That's easy to prove, unlike your testimony."

"Your Honor," Brennan rose.

The judge's eyes closed ever so slightly.

"Let me rephrase. One of the defense witnesses that we will call includes the owner of the Santa Fe Motel. Will he say that you quit or were fired?"

"We had a difference of opinion," Isabel Ontiveros said.

"That means you were fired?"

"Yes."

"What was the disagreement about?"

"Objection. I don't see the relevance," Brennan said.

Judge Hower took a drink of water and then replied, "Mr. Brennan, I gave you latitude with your questioning, which we should extend to the defense."

Michael breathed out. Even though the man had just fined him, thank God for judges.

"Please answer," the judge told the witness.

"The owner thought that I was the one taking the soaps and shampoos and the camera." Her boldness returned.

Michael surveyed the jurors again. A few tilted their heads as if forming a new opinion of the witness. He had to keep at it, but with caution. "Miss Ontiveros, why didn't you tell your boss that María Curry took the items, as you claim?"

"He'd just think that I lied."

At last, Isabel Ontiveros had given Michael something with which to work. He had to destroy this woman to save María. "Why would he think that?"

"I don't know."

"Have you ever lied to him before. And remember, we'll be talking with him."

She shifted in the seat. "Well, María had told him the soaps were gone, and he thought I did it, so he fired me."

"But you didn't answer the question. Have you ever lied to him?"

She ran her hand down her hair. "Yes."

"About what?"

"I can't remember."

"You remembered all those other items involving María. When did you lie?"

"I don't remember."

Michael let her evasiveness sink in with the jury and then asked, "Did you steal the soaps and shampoo and camera?"

"No, María did."

"Then why did María report them missing, if she stole them? If I took something, I sure as heck wouldn't tell anybody." Michael gathered as much charm as he could generate for the jury. The calmer he appeared, the more agitated she would appear.

The woman's lips came together hard.

"Miss Ontiveros, please answer," Michael prodded.

"I don't know."

"Do you blame María for getting you fired?" Michael said.

"It was her fault." The gentility in her voice transformed into shrewishness.

"When you claimed María talked to you about her husband, was anybody else around?"

"It was just us." One side of her mouth implied a smile. "One girl to another."

To Michael, Isabel Ontiveros didn't act like a model citizen testifying out of civic pride. She was tough as a boxer and definitely wanted something, and he had guessed what it was. "Ever been arrested, Miss Ontiveros?"

The woman stopped smiling, and her eyes raced to Brennan, whose face did not change.

"Well?" Michael said. "Have you been arrested?"

"Yes."

"What did you do?"

"I got picked up for helping my boyfriend steal cars."

"What's wrong, soaps not enough?" Michael said.

"Mr. Shaw, how would you like to pay a 300-dollar fine?" Judge Hower said.

"I will if you order it, Your Honor."

Judge Hower rolled his eyes. "Get on with this."

"Did you ask the prosecutor for anything in exchange for your testimony?" Michael said, a little more sure of himself.

"I asked him if he could do anything about the charges against me."

"What did Mr. Brennan say?"

Her eyes constricted at the prosecutor. "He said he would take another look at my case and see if his office might be able to make a deal with my lawyer. But he made no promises."

"How many cars were stolen?"

If Isabel Ontiveros could, she would have spit poison. "Eleven."

Michael was satisfied. "I've got no more questions for this woman."

On redirect, Brennan again asked, "Did you lie today, Miss Ontiveros?"

She sat up. "No."

The gavel came down at four, and Michael was exhausted. Before they took María back to the jail, he lightly touched her shoulder. "I'm sorry about my outburst today. I hope it won't hurt our case."

As María talked to Toni, she smiled.

"What did she say, Toni?" he asked.

"She said no one has ever fought for her like that. It made her feel good," Toni said.

Later that night, Michael lay across the bed at home. His tie looked like a crinkled silk snake hanging down from the chenille bedspread. He didn't have the strength to wipe the crust off the side of his mouth. The back of his head felt squeezed, and it throbbed.

He didn't know how long he had lain there. He did remember Jenny shaking his shoulders to try to rouse him for dinner, but his eyes wouldn't open. The bedroom was dark. He turned over with a groan.

From the living room, he heard the television. He undressed and got under the covers and wished he was drunk enough to forget that day of testimony. Failure crushed his chest. He wanted Toni lying down beside him.

Thankfully, the prosecution had ended its case. Now the defense would have its turn, and María's story would be told. As much as he looked forward to that, he wished to hell that Isabel Ontiveros hadn't wanted to make a deal for stealing cars. He wished the jurors would see her as a liar and opportunist. He wished he had kept his mouth shut and avoided the contempt ruling.

But after all his years before juries, he accepted the fact that Miss Ontiveros had hurt the defense, and over what?

Goddamn motel soap.

31

ALL DURING THE TRIAL, contrition wrapped María's heart as
the police, neighbors and Ben's brother talked out loud about
her great sin. Without Toni and Mr. Shaw there, María
believed her heart would have dried to ashes. But for the past
few days, Mr. Shaw called to take the stand people who were
on her side. The Negro bartender described how Ben turned
mean when he was drunk, picked fights with everyone in his
bar and batted her around. Her friend Bonita also told everyone that she saw Ben raise his hand against her more than
once and even chase her with a butcher knife. When Mr.
Shaw asked Bonita if her friend had spent lots of money on
bingo, Bonita swore to God and the judge the most María had
ever paid was one dollar a week for six cards.

Comforted as she felt about their support, María was sick
to her stomach for letting those people bad-mouth her dead
husband. That day, Nick Greene, her boss at the motel where
she cleaned, was on the witness stand.

"What kind of worker is María Curry?" Michael asked.

"One of my best. Always on time, reliable and thorough,"
said Greene, who was a thin man with a thin mustache.

"And what if she were free today?" Michael asked.

"She could have her job back anytime."

Michael gave him a smile. "Can you describe María Curry's personality?"

"Sir?"

"Was she loud?"

Now Greene smiled. "No, sir. She is a quiet woman, but she loves to laugh."

"Did she get along with your other employees?"

"Yes, sir. Every Christmas, she would bring us all tamales that she had made."

"Mr. Greene, ever notice anything about María's appearance when she came to work?"

"Yes, she often had bruises on her arms and legs, and on more than one occasion, she had a black eye. One time she came to work with a broken arm, but insisted she still could clean."

"Did you ask what had happened to her?"

"She would only say she had fallen down the stairs at her house."

"Did she ever complain about her husband?"

"No, sir."

"Ever meet Ben Curry?"

Greene gripped the front of the witness stand. "I met him."

"Tell the jury about that."

Greene turned to look at the panel. "About one month before he died, María had begged me to hire Ben for a maintenance job that opened up at the motel. I hired him but mostly out of a favor to her."

"What happened?"

"Ben came to work drunk after the second day on the job. He started yelling at me when I told him to go home. Then he cursed me and pushed me down before he left."

"Mr. Greene, let's talk about Isabel Ontiveros," Michael asked him. "Did you fire her?"

"Yes, she was stealing items from the cleaning cart," Greene said. "I count the items every night, and they were gone after her shifts. She made excuses like the guests were taking them, but it kept happening."

"Did she steal anything else?"

"My wife caught her in the office with the money box open."

"How do you know she was stealing?"

"She had her fist around some money. My wife told her to drop it and get out or we'd call the cops."

"Did María Curry ever steal from you?" Michael said.

"No. She was the one who told me about Isabel. I trust María."

María cried at his testimony.

"If Miss Ontiveros was stealing from you, as you say, why didn't you call the police?" Brennan said when it was his turn to ask questions of Nick Greene.

"Because she threatened to sic her boyfriend on us if we did. I saw him once when he picked her up. He was big as a house," Greene said. "I'm ashamed to admit this, but I was scared."

To that answer, the prosecutor swallowed like he had a chicken bone stuck in his throat, which pleased María. It was wrong to hate people, but she felt like a corrupt shadow anytime Mr. Brennan looked her way.

Michael's next witness was Clarence Whitfield, Ben's old construction boss. It had taken a bit of persuasion to get Whitfield to testify. When Michael had tracked him down at his office, Whitfield said he didn't have the time and didn't want to get mixed up with "court stuff," but Michael had flattered and pleaded in the name of justice. Whitfield finally agreed, but Michael suspected he did so only because of the Shaw name and any connection Whitfield hoped it might bring to his business. While Michael risked a defense witness with an uncooperative attitude, he wanted Whitfield on the record. A muscular man in working clothes and with a face full of bad skin, Whitfield glared at everyone as he was sworn in. Michael didn't flinch. He had gotten used to people despising attorneys ever since he passed the bar. He didn't blame them, because lawyers usually became wealthy off their woes. Michael buttoned his jacket as he approached the stand. "When did you first meet Ben Curry?"

"About eight years ago. He had moved to Borden and came looking for a job. He had a lot of construction experience, so I hired him."

"How long did he work for you?"

"A little over three years."

"What kind of worker was he?"

"Good. Never late. Strong as a damn ox."

"We don't use cuss words in my courtroom." The judge scowled.

Whitfield bit his lip as if keeping in more curses.

"Mr. Whitfield, did Ben Curry get along with the other workers?" Michael continued.

"Yes, most of the time. The others did grouse because Ben would tell them how to do their job. He wasn't popular, but I don't run no girl's school."

"Why wasn't he popular?"

"Well, he had a temper and once in a while got in arguments with the other men."

"Was Ben Curry ever seriously injured on the job?"

Whitfield scratched at his heavy shadow of a beard. "About five years ago, he was carrying two-by-fours when he fell into a ditch. Ben twisted his back real bad. He was gone from the job, let's see, about three weeks."

"When Ben Curry returned to work after he had fallen, did he change?"

Whitfield fidgeted. "Yes."

"How?"

"He began to get into even more fights with the other workers."

"Verbal?"

"No, sir. I had to break up some fistfights. I warned him he had better quit making trouble."

"Did Ben Curry drink on the job after his return?"

"I caught him a few times."

"Did he become abusive?"

Whitfield shook his head. "Ben got into it with my foreman. He punched him and knocked him to the ground, so I fired Ben."

Michael sat down, and Whitfield turned his sneer to Joe Brennan, who started in on his questions.

"What was the cause of the disagreement with the foreman?" the prosecutor asked.

"The man called Ben's wife a dirty Mexican. He didn't let nobody talk shit about his wife."

"Mr. Whitfield, don't curse," the judge said, pointing his gavel at the witness.

"What kind of worker was Mr. Curry when he didn't drink?"

Whitfield fidgeted more. "Didn't you hear? I already answered that one. Are you done with me yet?"

The judge looked at the witness and ordered, "Behave, Mr. Whitfield, and answer the questions civilly."

"That's all anyway, Your Honor," Brennan said.

"Redirect, Mr. Shaw?"

María remembered the foreman's blood had covered Ben's work clothes after the fight that got him fired. She told Toni, who passed the information to Michael.

"Mr. Shaw, the witness and I are not getting any younger." Judge Hower pointed at his watch.

"Excuse me, Your Honor. Mr. Whitfield, Ben Curry didn't just knock down your foreman, did he?"

"No, sir."

"What did he do?" Michael needed a crowbar to pry the information out of the man.

"Ben broke the foreman's nose and blackened both of his eyes. The foreman also lost a front tooth. A terrible mess, you bet."

"Thanks, Mr. Whitfield."

Whitfield readied to leave but peeked first at the judge.

"Okay, you're done." The judge waved him on.

≈ ≈ ≈

Peering over thick glasses, Father Vásquez raised his hand to tell the truth, and María wondered why he even had to be sworn in.

"I've known María for about eight years. Ever since she and her husband came to town she's attended my church, Our Lady of the Roses."

"Was she an active member of your congregation?" Michael asked.

"She came to Mass every Sunday and volunteered to clean the church every week, along with other women in the parish. When she wasn't working, she would also help cook funeral dinners. María is a wonderful woman who helps anyone in need."

"Please elaborate, Father."

"When a family from our parish got burned out of their home, María cooked for them and gave them some of her blankets, though she's not a wealthy person."

"Did María ever come to church with injuries?"

"I noticed bruises and cuts on her legs and face. She even showed up one Sunday with a broken arm."

"Did she tell you how they happened?"

"She didn't want to talk about it. One evening, however, I saw her cleaning the pews, and she was crying. She finally admitted her husband had beaten her."

"What did you do when you she told you?"

"I offered to talk with him. But she begged me not to go talk to him. She was afraid he would hurt me, too."

"Father, you were born in Mexico and later became an American citizen, is that correct?"

"Yes. I love this country, but I am also very proud of my people and my heritage."

"Are there aspects of your native culture you don't like?"

"Yes, Mr. Shaw."

"Like what?"

"I dislike the attitudes of some men towards women."

"Tell us more, please."

The priest took off his glasses. Dark curly hair surrounded a face forged out of compassion. "Of course, not all men hold such beliefs, but there are those who think that women are only on Earth to clean, cook, have their children and give men their pleasures. For many, it's a sign of manhood when they have total control over their women."

"How do the women usually accept this treatment?"

Father Vásquez talked to the jurors. "Many of the women from Mexico or who are of Mexican descent accept it without question. They view a slap as another part of life with a man, just as that man might caress them with the other hand."

Michael spotted one of the female jurors nodding in agreement. Her response sent a charge through his body. "Would it be unusual for a woman raised in Mexico not to summon the police for help?"

"Not at all. Mexican people tend not to trust the police in this country or theirs. They will first seek out their own people for help or the church. They don't believe white policemen will help them, and unfortunately, those beliefs are often justified, Mr. Shaw."

Michael smiled at the priest. "Thank you, Father."

Joe Brennan hated to cross-examine clergy, especially those testifying for the defense, because they seemed to have God on their side. He had to proceed with diplomacy. He greeted the priest with respect and then asked, "Would you consider María Curry a good Christian?"

"I would say so."

Brennan picked up a pile of papers from the prosecution table. "But you are here today because María Curry is charged with stabbing her husband to death."

"I know."

Brennan hoped to use religion to his benefit. "Father, is it not only against the state's law but God's law to kill?"

"Yes, sir, it is."

"And wasn't it in the Book of Matthew that Jesus advised, 'Whoever slaps you on your right cheek, turn the other to him also?'"

"That is correct, Mr. Brennan."

"María Curry didn't turn her cheek that night, did she?"

"No, but I also believe María had turned her cheek for many years to the violence done to her."

"Didn't María Curry sin?"

"If she did, Jesus is in the forgiving business."

"That will be all."

Brennan sat back down at his table. Forgiveness, his ass. If he never had to cross-examine another religious man, it'd be way too soon.

32

MARTIN SHAW MASSAGED HIS TEMPLES and eyes. He sighed at the enormous file on his desk. Another attorney in the firm had taken over Clark versus Rochester, which was his case before he took time off. But he prided himself on checking the work of every attorney there, even his own son's. The letter-head carried his name, and any shoddy job reflected on him.

Martin felt foolish after the incident at the airport. Sprawled out on the tarmac, perspiring and laboring for air like a newborn, he had lost command of his own body. He did-n't fear death as much as loss of control. He didn't recall much after he had fallen, except for everyone's eyes upon him, all full of concern and pity. Michael had held him like a baby, and he winced from the indignity caused by his betraying heart. In a life where he had dominated most everything, something had slipped past him that day at the airport.

Mrs. Garrison, his secretary, knocked and entered only after Martin allowed it. "Your wife called and reminded me to send you home. She said she doesn't want you working any more hours this week."

Martin sighed again at the nagging he endured at the office and at home. Normally, he would have berated his wife and secretary for it. But he was tired. "I'm just finishing up."

"Mr. Shaw. There's also a sheriff's deputy in the waiting room who insists on seeing you. He says it's of a personal nature, and I quote, 'It will be worth your while.' Shall I set an appointment for him?"

Martin picked up the file. "I'm really busy now, Mrs. Garrison, as you can see."

"I know, sir. But he says he has some important information about your son."

Martin put down the file. "Wait ten minutes before you bring him in, and then you can go home."

She nodded and shut the door.

From a shelf across from his desk, Martin picked up a photo of Michael in all his football glory, his arm drawn back for a forward pass. With his handkerchief, Martin rubbed out a thumbprint on the glass and reminded himself to reprimand the cleaning staff for a sloppy job of dusting. Replacing the photograph, he sat down. This deputy had better not waste his time, or he would ensure the man ended up patrolling school crossings for the rest of his life.

Mrs. Garrison opened the door for the man.

Deputy Herb Bell held back his shoulders. Everyone in town knew Martin Shaw could run men out of town, put them out of business or ruin them in some other way if they got on his bad side. Bell had seen him at the courthouse but never talked with him. Martin Shaw had money and power, so Bell had planned carefully what he would say. The deputy swallowed, but he had to show the rich man he was serious minded.

He stuck out his hand. "Mr. Shaw, I only have the highest respect and regard for you and your son. That's why I am here today."

Martin didn't offer a seat or his hand.

Bell stood in front of the sizeable desk. "You may not know it, but I have worked for the county for six years."

"That's not why you're here, is it? What's your name again?" Martin asked dryly and inspected his nails.

"Deputy Herb Bell. I work at the jail. I see lots of stuff. I hear lots of stuff. You might call me the Walter Winchell of the lockup. Well, sir, it's about your son."

"What about him, Deputy?"

Bell dared to take a closer step to the desk. "He's involved with a Mexican woman. Everybody's talking about it. I've even seen the two of them together myself."

"What Mexican woman?"

"Some gal from North Park who's working with your son on that murder case. She's the interpreter for the Mexican who killed her husband."

Martin contemplated the file on his desk. Although his first instinct was to crush Herb Bell with one fist, he said, "Go on."

"See, Mr. Shaw. You got a quality job and a beautiful office like a king and probably a beautiful home. But I work hard there among the criminals and undesirables. I don't get much pay, but I'm a public servant and I felt it was my duty to come here today."

Martin clasped his hands together on the desk and finally faced the informer. Like all those who had something to sell, the deputy's eyes were dusky with want. "Tell me what you've seen and heard, and you may be rewarded for your public service."

"Yes, sir, Mr. Shaw. You are my kind of people. And whatever I tell you, believe me, sir, it will stay strictly between the two of us."

Though he wasn't invited to, Bell sat down in the chair as if it were made of gold.

≈ ≈ ≈

Tommy, the bartender, brought two more beers to Michael and Adam, who sat in a corner booth talking and laughing more loudly with each drink. He shook his head at grown men acting like kids, but he wouldn't be in the bar business if he judged them too harshly. And these boys were first-class pay-ing customers at eight bottles apiece and counting.

"Thanks, Tommy," Michael said.

"Sure thing, Mr. Shaw."

Michael hadn't been with Toni for the past few nights because she was caring for her father, who had suffered anoth-er attack from his besieged lungs. Michael loved to be with her but was also wearied each time, not only because of their urgent lovemaking, but also because of the will it took to leave her and go home. He more than welcomed Adam's invitation to get out of the apartment. Jenny had pouted and sung Broad-way tunes out of key because he refused to buy the ostentatious house with the flamingos. When she had asked why, he shout-ed at her to leave him alone and quit pestering him about the goddamn house. The next night, he took her to an early movie and dinner as an apology. Afterward, Jenny looked at him like he had killed her dreams, which he had. But they were her dreams, not his.

He and Adam hadn't talked much during the trial. Occa-sionally, Adam dropped by the courtroom, listened to a few minutes of testimony and left. To save his nights for Toni, Michael missed several Sunday games so he could work on María's trial and catch up on his other cases. So when Adam called to go out for a beer, Michael declared war on sobriety. He hadn't gotten smashed since he and Toni first slept togeth-er. But as Michael got drunk at Tommy's place, he had the uneasy feeling he was cheating on Toni.

After finishing the last bottle of beer, Adam stared at Michael, grinning and touching the top of his crew cut.

"What is it, Adam?"

"I'll bet you'll be sorry when this case is over." Adam sputtered like a pot boiling over. "You know." With his elbow, he poked Michael hard in the ribs.

"What?"

"You're doing that little interpreter of yours. I've seen her." Adam wolf whistled so sharply the other bar patrons shifted in their seats.

Michael said nothing. Drunk as he was, it was safer to buy a front-page ad in the newspaper than tell Adam, who deemed tact as something involving horses.

Adam no longer grinned. "Mike, buddy, I'm really hurt you didn't tell me. We're old friends, but I had to hear about your little affair from courtroom cafeteria gossip. I want all the nasty details, man. They might improve my dull married life. Fess up." He poked him again.

"No, Adam." Michael set down the bottle of beer he was about to drink.

"I never held out on you. I told you about the teenage whore I had in Tijuana."

"I never asked you to tell me anything."

Adam's eyes went yellow from the beer and spotting weakness in Michael. "Then tell me this, my old friend. Is it true love or just screwing around?"

Michael dragged himself out of the booth. "I'm going home."

Adam followed. "Don't ignore me."

"I'm going to bed."

"Which one? Your wife's or that Mexican tart's?"

Michael lunged at Adam. They knocked over two tables. Glasses crashed as they scuffled, a fight of drunken men, one of clumsy swagger.

Lawyers or not, Tommy wasn't going to let them wreck his bar. He picked up each man by the collar of his nice shirt and hauled them to the back door. "I like you, Mr. Shaw. But it's time to say good night. I'll put the beer and the broken glasses on your tab."

With efficient ease, Tommy threw them out the door and into the alley. Michael stumbled to the ground. Adam landed on his feet, twisted around and pinned Michael to the ground. "What's wrong? Tap a nerve, did I, buddy?" Adam said.

"Get off me, you fucking gorilla."

"Let's go down memory lane to those old days in high school when we got tanked and drove to North Park. Remember, we threw paper bags of cow shit at the Mexicans? Or how about the nights we hunted down the greasers in our car to see how fast they could run?"

Michael quit struggling.

"See, you remember. I bet you haven't told your spic sweetie about those good times." Adam let Michael go and stood up.

Luxuriating in the brief payback, Adam understood even through the drunkenness that he would ultimately be the one to pay for his actions. As he did playing football, the only thing he knew was to charge ahead.

"Think on it, Mikey. All those years, your old man screwed over those Mexicans at his ranch with dirt pay and backbreaking work. Now, you're screwing one. Damn, it's a Shaw family tradition."

Brushing dirt off his pants, Adam felt his pockets for keys. "Whew, I've had enough fun. Be sure to lay a kiss on your little gal for this gringo."

Michael sat there on the gravel in the alley. Adam had gone but left the truth behind.

≈   ≈   ≈

Toni waved at the cigarette smoke as she sat on the bed in her little house. Her skin felt tightened around her bones, and her eyes itched with dryness. Five days ago, her father's cough had intensified to the point he did the unthinkable, at least for him. He called in sick for work and asked her to drive him to the doctor. A tall man with sympathetic eyes, Dr. John Custer asked her into his office while her father got dressed in the examining room. Francisco had bruised a rib from the coughing and should rest in bed for three days, the doctor advised. He also increased the medicine to ease the cough. She again asked if her father could be healed. He answered there was nothing to be done and put a large hand on her shoulder. She had called Michael at his office to tell him about her father and that he shouldn't come over for the next few nights. As they had prearranged, Toni identified herself as the secretary of a lawyer in Phoenix who needed to talk with Michael about the Sullivan case.

While Francisco stayed home, Toni ordered him back into bed whenever he tried to mow the lawn or cook. He asked if it was okay to lift his fingers to play the guitar, and she said yes, but warned him not to be a smart aleck.

After his sick days had passed, her father insisted on going back to the mill that very morning. She and Carmen tried to talk him into quitting, but he refused. Staying at home wouldn't heal him, he said. The sisters finally agreed to let him go if he promised to ask for easier duties. So Toni made his lunch and watched him drive off. She called Michael at his office and asked him to come to her house. The nights without him had left her disjointed and aching.

Nearing eleven, she finally heard his footsteps outside her little house. Oscar growled. "*Cállate*, little one." She petted his ears and stubbed out her cigarette. "We don't want to scare this one away."

Michael opened the door of the dark room and stood in the doorway. His eyes focused on her in the shadows. They met in the middle of the room, crushing their bodies together with need. Something crashed through the window near the door and landed on the floor with a thud. Michael put his arms around Toni to protect her. Oscar barked and jumped on the bed. Dogs around the neighborhood answered Oscar.

"Are you all right?"

"Yes."

"What the hell was that?" Michael picked her up and placed her on the bed. He grabbed the brick that had been thrown through the window. "I'm going to catch the son of a bitch."

He dashed outside. "Damn him," he hissed and couldn't wait to pound Adam, whom he expected to be waiting for him. But there was no Adam or anyone else he could see in the moonless night.

The lights flashed on in Mrs. Hernández's windows. Michael ducked into a shadow. He didn't want to cause more trouble for Toni. He crept back to the little house.

"Goddammit." He gripped the brick more tightly.

"Oscar, quiet," Toni shushed the dog as Michael came in the door. "Let me see it, Michael."

"No."

She held out her hand. He gave the brick to her. "GREASER BITCH" was written in red paint.

"Oh, God."

He sat down next to her on the bed.

Carmen rushed in through the door. "Toni, what happened?" She didn't acknowledge Michael. Whatever had happened, it was his fault.

He hurried to his feet from the bed, a look of guilt on his face.

"Nothing, Carmen. A stupid kid threw something in the window. Please, go back to bed. I want to clean up the glass. I'll sleep in the house tonight."

"But Toni."

"Carmen, now go in, please." She repeated it in Spanish and touched her sister's arm.

Carmen nodded. She couldn't look at the man who had caused Toni these problems.

"What's going on over there?" Mrs. Hernández yelled from next door to no one in particular.

"Don't say anything." Toni squeezed Carmen's hand.

Carmen gave a sharp nod and walked to the fence to tell Mrs. Hernández that kids had broken a window.

The older woman listened to Carmen's excuse but could not get anything more out of her. Yet Mrs. Hernández's radar told her Toni wasn't alone in the little house.

While Michael found her slippers, Toni held onto to Oscar. "Here, or you'll cut your feet." He put them on her.

"Who did this, Michael?"

"I don't know. When I find out, I'm going to shove that brick up his ass. You sure you're all right? Shit, your cheek is bleeding."

He got a towel from her bathroom, wet it and gently dabbed at her face. "There's a piece of glass." He pulled it out. She grimaced. "I'm so sorry, Toni."

"Why? You didn't throw that brick. But you better go."

"I don't want to leave you."

"I'll be fine. That ass won't come back tonight. Go, Michael."

He kissed her. On the way to his car, the brick felt heavy as a boulder. His arm hurt, as if somehow he had helped heave the thing through the window.

Toni swept up the glass while Oscar watched from his little pillow. One of her album covers fit nicely in the window and covered the break. Satisfied with the job, she picked up the dog and went to her father's house.

Carmen sat at the kitchen table, a cup of coffee in her hand. While holding Oscar, Toni poured herself a cup and warmed up her sister's. Toni shook a little, put Oscar down and steadied the cup. Carmen wasn't angry or frightened. Her sister was disappointed, and that hurt Toni more than anything.

"I'm glad Dad and Víctor were working. I don't know what would have happened if they'd been home," Carmen said.

"You and me both."

They drank their coffee.

Carmen reached out for her sister's hand, which was cold. "What if you end up getting hurt, Toni?"

"Carmen, it's inevitable."

"What's that mean?"

"That it's going to happen sooner or later."

By the time the sisters had finished their coffee, Deputy Herb Bell had reached his house on the south side of Borden. His duty had dictated he tell Martin Shaw about his son and the Mexican tramp. Chucking the brick into the window was all his idea.

33

NURSE JANE FARROW sat outside the courtroom in her nicest black suit and high heels, but she always felt more comfortable wearing her whites. At the hospital, she was just one of many people in white going about their persistent business of helping patients. She loved the calm of hospitals and especially the evening shift, when most of the moans had been subdued by pain medications and assurances. Occasional emergencies generated excitement and rush, but then all quieted again with treatment or death. Growing up a middle child, she had become used to moving unobtrusively through life. She disliked being singled out for anything. A decent and unremarkable life had brought her contentment. At the courthouse, however, people walking down the hall stared at her as if she had committed a crime.

She picked a piece of lint off her skirt and flicked it away. The courthouse smelled of body odor and shoe leather. She had grown accustomed to the antiseptic odor of the hospital, although at times she wondered if it had ruined her sense of smell. Whenever she cooked her favorites of turkey and ham at home, the aroma sometimes carried a tinge of disinfectant.

Jane Farrow looked at her watch and wondered when she would be called into the courtroom. Her supervisor had urged her to refuse to testify. If the defense lawyer had to subpoena her, he probably wouldn't even summon Jane because he didn't want a hostile witness on the stand, said the supervisor who had seen that very thing happen on an episode of *Perry Mason*. Besides, Jane shouldn't get involved in "that Mexican's troubles." "She put up with the whippings all those years. She must like it," the supervisor had said. "She only made more work for us."

Even Jane's husband, who was as quiet as she, wondered if she should take time off to appear in court on behalf of a complete stranger. But Jane had told him and her supervisor that she had agreed to testify and wouldn't change her mind. They both shook their heads at her decision, but they hadn't seen that woman's blood, so much blood it stained her best white shoes.

≈ ≈ ≈

Michael had found the nurse by examining the hospital emergency room records of María's treatment. The name of nurse Jane Farrow was listed on three of those reports. That included the night of August 18—the night Ben Curry died. It didn't take much encouragement to get her to come to court, and for that Michael was grateful. Jane Farrow was one of those plain, unassuming women who waited on people, either at restaurants or at stores or in hospitals. Someone just doing her job. But when he first talked with the nurse, he noticed her green eyes were among the kindest he had ever looked into. If she had tended to a wound or illness of his, he would have immediately felt better. He needed to feel better that day, especially after what had happened to Toni. But the trial needed all his attention, and he had to repress his anger at the bastard who had thrown the brick.

Michael smiled and greeted the nurse after she had been sworn in. "How long have you worked as a nurse at St. John's Hospital?"

"Seven years." Her voice could barely be heard above the ceiling fan's whir.

"Please speak up so the jury and the court reporter can hear you, Mrs. Farrow," the judge said.

"So you've worked as a nurse for seven years?" Michael restated the question.

Jane Farrow sat up. If she was going to do this, she would do it right. "Yes, sir." Her voice was stronger than she imagined it could be.

"Do you recognize María Curry?"

"Yes, sir."

"In what capacity?"

"She was brought into the emergency room three times, sir."

Michael presented her with copies of the medical records that he would also enter into evidence. After reading them, he still had a difficult time accepting how much abuse his client had lived with. "Let's talk about the night of February 3rd, 1957," he said. "What were her injuries?"

The nurse peered down past her glasses to the paper, but she would have remembered without it. She looked up. "Mrs. Curry had three cracked ribs."

"Did she appear to be in much discomfort?"

"Oh, yes, sir. I had to help the woman undress to get into a gown for the examination. The patient flinched and moaned every time she moved," the nurse said. She also recalled that the arrogant intern, who was a young man on whom she had smelled whiskey more than once, didn't even care what happened to the patient. He just treated her and left.

"Besides the cracked ribs, was she hurt in other ways?" Michael said.

"Yes, there appeared to be severe welt marks on her back and on her legs, and her right eye was blackened."

Michael approached the witness. "I understand you speak Spanish. Did you ask her what happened?"

"She said she had fallen."

"Those welts, did it appear she had been struck with an object?"

"Objection," Brennan said. "He's asking this witness to speculate."

Michael shot back, "Your Honor, Jane Farrow is an experienced nurse in an emergency room who has seen many kinds of injuries. She knows her business."

Judge Hower tapped a finger against his jaw. "I'm going to allow it."

Michael nodded. "Mrs. Farrow, once again, did it appear as if María Curry had been struck with an object."

"Yes." The nurse was pleased she could speak out.

"Now, let's go to the day after Thanksgiving, 1958. Did you again help treat María Curry at the hospital?" Michael said.

"Yes, sir."

"Can you describe her injuries?"

Jane Farrow glanced at the records from that visit, but again remembered the woman.

"She came in with a broken left arm."

"Any unusual bruising, Mrs. Farrow?"

"Yes, there appeared to be handprint-shaped bruises above and below the break."

"Did María Curry say how her arm had been broken?"

"She told me it was an accident. That she had slipped down some stairs."

"On those two occasions when you treated her, did you believe María when she said she had fallen?"

"No, sir. It looked like she had been beaten, and badly."

Michael surveyed the faces of the female jurors and was gratified to see doubt pass across them.

"Objection. Conjecture," Brennan said.

"Overruled," the judge pronounced.

Michael went on. "Lastly, Mrs. Farrow, let's discuss the night of August 18th, when María Curry was again treated at the hospital. Please describe her wounds."

In a town where most victims' injuries were from car crashes, industrial accidents and sometimes knife fights, Jane Farrow had been stunned by all the blood covering María Curry. When the police brought her in, she didn't even recognize her as the same person she had previously treated. Only when Jane began cleaning off the blood did she realize this was the same woman.

"Mrs. Curry suffered a four-inch cut on the left side of the head, and her nose had been bloodied. She also had blackened eyes and bruises to her torso. There were also bruises around her neck, as if she had been choked."

"Objection, speculation." Brennan said.

"Overruled," Hower said.

Michael removed two photos from under his notes. "I would like to enter these as evidence, marked Defense Exhibits Nos. 16 and 17." He displayed ten-by-twelve-inch black-and-white blowups of the front and side mug shots taken by the Borden police on the night María was arrested. After all the testimony about how María had been hurt by Ben, the panel hadn't really seen a clear image of the damage to her. In the photo, both of María's eyes were blacked and puffy. The wound on her head was stitched and angry looking, and clear handprints appeared on both sides of her neck. Her dress was ripped and black with blood. Since Brennan's photos of the deceased Ben Curry had been allowed, Michael didn't expect an objection from the county attorney, and he was right. Brennan remained silent.

Michael handed one of the prints to the bailiff for the jury. The other one, he gave to the nurse. "Mrs. Farrow, was this what María Curry looked like on August 18th?"

"No, sir."

Michael stiffened with doubt. "What?"

"When I saw her, Mr. Shaw, she was covered in blood, literally from head to foot."

"Thank you, that's all," said Michael, who wanted to kiss Jane Farrow.

"Mr. Brennan," the judge said, but the prosecutor already was walking toward the witness stand.

"Didn't you also treat Ben Curry for an injury?" He handed her another record.

The paper work prompted the nurse's memory. She recalled a belligerent man who smelled like an old brewery and swore at her and the doctors as they were trying to help him.

"Yes, sir. He had a three-inch gash near the middle of his scalp and required several stitches."

"Did he say how he got that wound?" Brennan said.

"He said his wife smacked him with a frying pan."

"You said you speak Spanish. The night of August 18th, did you ask María Curry what happened?"

Jane Farrow bowed her head slightly. "Yes, sir."

"What did the defendant say?"

"She said her husband was going to kill her, but she killed him first."

"No more questions," Brennan said.

"Redirect?" Judge Hower asked Michael.

"Oh, yes," he replied and stood up. "When María told you she had killed her husband, was she happy about it?"

"No, sir. She was crying and hysterical."

"Mrs. Farrow, why did you come today to testify for the defense?"

The nurse appeared a bit bewildered at the question. "You asked me to, sir?"

Michael smiled. "So I did. But I didn't have to threaten you with a subpoena, did I?"

"No."

"Then why? Surely you are a busy woman."

"It was my duty to tell what happened to the patient."

"What do you mean, 'duty'?" Michael said as those green eyes widened.

"I'm not sure how to explain it, Mr. Shaw."

"Just try your best."

"Well, if I didn't come here to tell you what I had seen, then it would be like María Curry had never been hurt. And she was." Jane Farrow had never been so sure of anything.

34

MICHAEL TOOK IN A MOUTHFUL OF AIR. He wasn't quite sure how his request was going to go over. He already had been held in contempt and didn't want to chance another citation. "Your Honor, before the jury returns, the defense has a request that may sound unusual, but we believe it will help these proceedings."

Judge Hower's eyes compressed to slots. "I can hardly wait to hear it."

"Mrs. Curry is a very frightened woman, and she needs a little help getting through her testimony today. So we request she be allowed to testify with her little dog sitting on the floor beside her."

Judge Hower shifted his jaw. "You did say a dog?"

"Yes, Your Honor."

"That's what I thought you said."

"The jurors will never know the animal is there. The dog is well behaved and will put my client at ease so she can concentrate on her testimony. If she becomes too emotional or overwrought, we may be forced to stop and start the hearing."

Judge Hower leaned over the bench. "Mr. Shaw, we've heard almost everything in this courtroom, but this certainly takes the cake. This in fact may go down in the annals of Mitchell County jurisprudence."

"I certainly hope so, Your Honor."

"Mr. Brennan, your comments."

Brennan took a spot beside Michael in front of the bench. "We object vigorously. Mr. Shaw is hoping to tug at the heart strings of the jurors. He'll be asking for violins next. Worse, allowing a dog will insult the dignity of your courtroom."

"The dog is very small, and we're talking about extending my client every right to which she is entitled, although it may not include a dog to help calm her. María Curry faces long-term incarceration or even a death sentence. We must allow her every opportunity to tell her side of the story."

Judge Hower leaned back in his chair. For most of the proceedings the defendant had been apprehensive and edging near hysterics. He cleared his throat. "Mr. Shaw, I will allow the dog in this courtroom, but if I hear so much as a whimper or yap, or if the animal so much as scratches his ear, you know very well who'll be in the doghouse."

"Thank you, Your Honor."

"We'll take a fifteen-minute break. When we come back in session, have your client and the interpreter take the stand, bring in the dog, and then we'll bring in the jury." The judge rose and exited the courtroom, mumbling, "A goddamn dog. What'd you know?"

Toni hugged María but still prayed for all of them to get through this day. Ever since the brick had smashed through her window, her stomach burned and the whole world felt off-balance. Maintaining the vandalism lie to her father dismayed her. One more lie on top of so many others, and she feared the weight of them toppling her over.

Toni poured water from the pitcher and drank.

María's eyes followed her friend. "How are you today?"

"I'm fine. Are you ready?"

"I'm not sure I can go up there. I'm so frightened. My heart is banging in my chest. Can you see it?"

"Don't worry, Oscar and I will be right beside you."

Michael walked in the door and smiled at them. He placed his large hand on María's shoulder. "It's time."

Nodding at Toni's translation, María wanted to escape through the doors. No matter if the deputies took aim at her back with their big guns. Maybe today was going to be her real punishment—confessing, not to a priest, but to strangers with darkness in their eyes.

Bailiff George Roy carried Oscar in. When the dog spotted María, he jumped out of George's arms and ran around the witness stand trying to reach her. Finding no other way, the dog bounced onto the lap of hefty female court reporter, who cried out as Oscar bounded from there into María's arms. María kissed the dog, placed Oscar on the floor beside her and told him to lie down. Toni moved a chair next to María.

"Sorry, Your Honor," Michael said.

Judge Hower only rolled his eyes at the scene. "Bring in the jury."

The bailiff opened the door to the jury room and shouted, "All rise," as the panel shuffled in.

"Swear in the interpreter, then the witness," Judge Hower directed.

George Roy took a worn Bible over to Toni. "Do you solemnly swear to accurately interpret the testimony you hear today, so help you God?"

"I do."

George held out the Bible to María. "Do you solemnly swear the testimony you give here today will be the truth, the whole truth and nothing but the truth, so help you God?"

María bent her head a little to listen to Toni's translation.

"*Sí*. Yes," she said.

Oscar placed his head on her right shoe and closed his eyes. María sighed.

"María, tell us about your life with Ben Curry. Were you and he happy?" Michael began his questioning.

"For many days we were, Mr. Shaw." Toni translated for María. "When Ben had a job, he was a contented man. I used to travel around with him to his construction jobs."

"When did you settle in Borden?"

"Eight years ago."

"Did your husband get drunk over the years you were married?"

"Yes."

"How often?"

"Every weekend. He said he liked the taste of beer better than anything in the world."

Judge Hower's glare quelled a flicker of laughter from a few people watching the trial.

Michael cleared his throat and then continued. "Did he drink more after his injury at the construction site?"

María nodded. "Yes, sir. But he told me he had to get drunk because his back hurt him. He was in much pain."

Despite how Ben had treated her through the last years, she often was sorry for him. How he would double up and moan or lay flat on the floor because any movement caused him agony. When she saw that, her own injuries felt small. Beer made him feel better, but it also drew out the meaner version of her husband. At times, she'd watch him as if he had become a stranger who lived with her.

"After your husband was fired from the construction job by Clarence Whitfield, did he find another steady job?"

"No, Mr. Shaw. He worked a lot of jobs."

"Like what?"

"He was a night watchman and a mechanic and a janitor at a few places. He always wanted to work, Mr. Shaw. He was a proud man."

"Did he keep those jobs for long?"

She shook her head. "Only for a few months at a time."

"Why?"

"He told me the bosses were stupid, and they fired him for nothing."

"María, did Ben ever strike you when he drank?"

Her eyes fluttered.

"María, you must answer."

"When we first got married, he might slap me if he was real drunk or if I made him mad. It was nothing. After he got hurt, he drank a lot and beat me more often. I kept asking, 'What's wrong, Ben? Tell me, and I won't do it again.' Most times, he didn't say nothing and kept hitting me."

"With his fists?"

"Yes."

"Did he ever strike you with an object?"

She lowered her head. "His belt buckle."

"When did this take place?"

"About two years ago, in February."

"Tell us what happened."

"Do I really have to, Mr. Shaw?"

"Yes, María."

She never liked to think about that day. Not only because of the physical hurt she went through, but it was the day she almost came to hate Ben.

"María, please answer," Michael said.

"I was taking a box out to the shed, and I accidently spilled a big jar of motor oil all over the floor. I was cleaning it up when he came home. He started yelling and calling me a stupid woman. I didn't think he'd get so mad."

"Was he drunk, María?" Michael asked.

"Yes, sir."

"Then what happened?"

"He grabbed me by my hair and arms and dragged me into the basement of our house. Then he took off his belt." Ashamed of herself and for her husband, María kept her head down as she talked, but Toni looked right at the jury.

"Ben sat in an old rocker, watching me and slapping the belt against his palm. He told me to take off all my clothes." Her voice vanished into nothing.

"Please, María," Michael said.

"I took off my dress and underclothing. I begged him not to hurt me, but he didn't answer. Then, then, he whipped me with the belt."

Several of the female jurors held hands to their mouths. A male juror gnashed his teeth.

"Where did he strike you?"

"On my legs and back. I asked him to stop please, please stop. He kept whipping me and saying, 'María, you belong to me, and I can do anything I want. Even kill you. You're so worthless.' And I said, 'Yes, Ben, you are right.' I think I passed out after that."

"When you came around, what happened?"

"I could hardly move. Ben drove me to the hospital."

"What did he say when he dropped you off?"

"He said if I told anybody what he did that he would kill me. So I told the doctor and nurse that I had fallen."

"María, why didn't you call the police when he beat you?"

"Ben told me the police would ship me back to Mexico in a cattle truck."

"Is that why you stayed?"

"I loved him, Mr. Shaw. When we got married, I promised to stay with him in sickness and in health. We had fights, yes, but sometimes he would bring me presents afterward. Sometimes, he even cried. Imagine a big man crying so I wouldn't leave him?"

"Did you threaten to kill Ben the night of August 16?" Michael had to address the issue but let María explain why.

"Yes, sir." Shame slowed her heartbeat.

"What led up that?"

"It was our anniversary. We both celebrated, and I had too much beer that night. But so did Ben, and he began punching me for no reason. He knocked me down and kicked me."

"Why did you threaten him?" Michael's voice lowered.

"Because he told me he would kill me and dump my body in the desert. He told me no one would miss me, not even him. I felt . . . " Her head stayed down.

"What, María?"

She raised her head. "Hopeless, sir. I thought I could scare him, but he wasn't scared of me."

"Now I want to talk about the night of August 18th."

María feared the question and reached for Toni's hand beneath the railing.

≈ ≈ ≈

The whole thing had started over a chicken dinner and a paycheck.

Ben had tired of sitting around waiting for María to come home. His back ached throughout the day. No position gave him comfort, not in bed, not in a chair. All he had anymore was the damn pain. Like a rusty saw cutting him in half. The medicine the doctor prescribed didn't do much for his back but made him constipated and useless in bed. He couldn't sleep and couldn't remember the last time he had had a satisfactory shit. He wanted to die, but not without a drink first.

Beer suppressed the misery. He drank until he passed out and started again in the morning. He wondered why his idiot doctor didn't prescribe pure grain alcohol.

All he did was wait. Wait for María and her paycheck. Wait for relief from the booze her paycheck would buy. The minute hand advanced, and the teeth of the rusty saw deepened into his mid-back.

He heard the porch creak.

María stepped cautiously into the house, praying for a restful night, one where Ben had already drunk himself to sleep without touching her. As usual, he was sitting in his big chair, watching television. For the past month, the house had grown even hotter with his temper. He had lost another job, this one at the motel where she worked. He hadn't looked for another job since. He constantly complained about his back and drank every day until he passed out in his chair or in the bed. Whenever he talked to her, there was accusation in his voice, as if she was responsible for his pain.

As María shook off her tennis shoes and got into her cozy but worn pink slippers, his eyes followed her. His heavy gray brows drew into his eyes. A familiar signal of a storm forming inside him.

"Where's your paycheck, María? I want to buy some beer. There's nothing in this house to drink."

"Ben, we have to pay the rent. Mr. Lowell says he'll kick us out in the street."

His silence frightened her.

"I'll cook chicken tonight, the way you like it."

"I fucking hate chicken. That's all we eat."

"I'll fix it special, with onions and chilies."

With a large knife, she split the chicken at the breast and placed the pieces in a pan with the onions. A splash of hot oil stung her hand, and she rubbed it. She peeked back at Ben,

who still sat in front of the television. "I'll pay Mr. Lowell, and
we can go out to Willy's on what's left over. We'll have a fun
time."

"That chicken stinks. I can't eat it."

"Ben, you need to eat. You'll find a better job soon."

"A man ain't nothing without work."

"You're still a man."

She heard him get out of the chair as it cracked against the
wall. His footsteps coming toward her. Please God, no more.
She leaned over the counter. No more.

"I said I don't want no chicken. I want that paycheck."

Slapping the right side of her face, Ben knocked María to
her knees and out of her pink slippers. Her forehead banged
the corner of the counter. The knife she held flew onto the
floor.

"You can have the check. It's in my purse." The blood from
the cut streamed into her eyes.

María didn't smell beer on him. His eyes were clear and
dense with hate. Ben bent over, and one hand went around
her throat, and then his other hand. He began to squeeze.
María made the sign of the cross. She was going to die. Oscar
began to bark from his round pillow in the corner of the room.

"Ben, I love you," she croaked.

"Then you're stupid."

She started kicking hard. He released his grip and straightened up, putting his hands immediately to his back. His face
contorted. "Dammit. Dammit."

The dog charged Ben and nipped his back heel.

"Shut that goddamn dog up, or I'll do it for you."

Through all their fights, the dog always slept miraculously,
and Ben paid Oscar no mind. Tonight was different.

"Don't hurt him, I beg you." María stood, rubbing her
hand across her bleeding head.

"Ever since you found that mutt wandering in the street, you've treated it better than me."

He backhanded her, and she again folded.

"Know what? I'm going to put the dog out of its misery. Then you, María, and finally, me."

Ben stepped toward Oscar, who continued barking and nipping at Ben's leg.

"Leave him alone." María rushed to her feet and grabbed another, longer knife on the counter.

Ben chortled and grabbed Oscar by the scuff of the neck. The dog yelped. "One twist and doggie heaven."

María swung.

The knife made a slight *flittt* sound as she jabbed it into his stomach. Ben gasped and dropped Oscar, who yelped and ran into a corner. A spot of red appeared on Ben's T-shirt.

"Ungrateful fucking bitch. I got you out of Mexico and made you a goddamn American." He reverted to English, which she didn't understand. "This is how you treat me for all I've done for you?"

Ben took another step and swung his massive fist, but she put up the knife, and the blade sliced the meat of his hand.

"No more, Ben. I've hurt you."

"I'll say when it's enough."

With his other hand, he pushed her chest. She fell on her back, and the knife skidded out of her hand. María scrambled, picked up the knife and stabbed his stomach and chest so fast she wasn't really aware of what she was doing. He looked down at his T-shirt, now soaking with blood.

"Bitch. Now you've really done it." He came after her again.

"No!" She swung hard with both hands. The knife went into his chest up to the handle. She let go of it.

Ben stared down at the knife. "I didn't mean nothing by it," he whispered in Spanish, like a boy who had stolen money from his mother. Stepping backward, Ben slid down the wall.

Blind with tears and blood, María scooped up Oscar. She sat across from Ben until his chest stopped moving, because she didn't want to leave him alone as he died. His face had a restfulness she had not seen since they met. María smiled.

≈ ≈ ≈

The overhead fans whirred. No one made a noise or moved.

"Were you afraid for your life that night?" Michael said.

"Yes, Mr. Shaw. I had never seen Ben so crazy. He had threatened to kill me before. But that night I knew he was really going to do it."

"So you defended yourself?"

"Yes. I tried."

"María, did you intend to kill your husband?" Michael said.

"No, I didn't." She sobbed into a handkerchief that Toni handed to her.

"Thank you, María." Michael gave her a small nod that said, "You did well."

The judge motioned to Brennan, who had watched the jurors' faces for signs of sympathy. Chagrined, he found a few. He wanted to lose no time changing the jury's minds about this killer.

"Before the night Ben Curry died, did you ever strike him?"

The question jolted María and Toni, even though Michael had warned them the prosecutor would ask that.

"Yes, sir. With the frying pan."

"Did he bleed?"

"Yes, sir."

"Did you ever hit your husband with anything else?"

"Yes, sir."

"What?"

"A stick and some plates."

"Did you draw blood from him in those attacks?"

"Yes, sir." This was part of her punishment, María thought. Telling her sins.

"When you threatened to kill your husband on August 16th, how were you going to do it?"

María looked at Toni with befuddlement on her face. "I don't understand, sir."

Michael was not confused. He knew how the question would be answered, and it would do María no good.

"Did you tell him you were going to shoot him?" Brennan asked

"No, sir."

"What did you tell your husband you would do to him?"

María closed her eyes. "That I would get a knife and slit his throat."

Brennan glanced at the jury. Some of the sympathy began to dissipate, and he promised himself a gin and tonic.

"Mrs. Curry, you testified you were afraid of the police and that's why you didn't call for help. Were you also afraid of an ambulance?"

She opened her eyes. "I don't understand."

"On the night of August 18th, why didn't you call for an ambulance to help your husband?"

"Ben died, sir."

"Did you watch him die?"

A distressed nod. "There was nothing I could do."

"Oh, I see. You're a doctor."

"No, sir."

"How long between the time you stabbed him and when he died?"

"I don't know."

"Ten minutes?"

"I don't know."

"Twenty?"

Michael stood. "Objection. She answered the question. She didn't know."

"Sustained," Judge Hower said.

Brennan shrugged ever so slightly and turned to María. "On the night of August 18th, did you intend to kill your husband?"

"I wanted him to stop hurting me."

"Did you intend to kill him?"

"I wanted him to stop."

"Did you kill Ben Curry?"

"Yes."

Brennan let the statement sink through to the jury and then took his place at the prosecution table.

Michael immediately stood up. "María, those few times you fought back against Ben Curry, what happened afterward?"

"He beat me worse."

"After the incident with the frying pan, did you ever touch your husband again?"

"No, sir."

"Why not?"

"Because the next night, Ben woke me up and was holding a knife against my throat. He told me if I ever touched him again, he'd slice my neck like a deer."

"María, up until the moment he died, did you love your husband?"

"Yes."

"Was he a good man?"

"Good or bad, he was my husband."

"Thank you. Your Honor, the defense rests."

Judge Hower cleared phlegm from his chest. "Let's call it quits for today. We'll take the weekend and start with closing arguments on Monday. All rise for the jury." The judge stood and sighed at too much death, too many human frailties.

The courtroom began to clear. María still sat at the witness stand. She picked up Oscar and put him on her lap. Toni hugged her.

Michael walked over. "María, I'm very proud of you, very proud," he said in halting Spanish he had asked Toni to teach him.

"*Gracias*," María said.

They petted Oscar, whose tail went wild because of all the attention.

35

MICHAEL RODE THE ELEVATOR to his office to finish the notes for his closing argument. In the evening, the building settled into silence. He whistled a made-up song, thinking that an acquittal was a real possibility. Goddammit, a great possibility. Still, the optimism and his song didn't last past the third floor. He and Toni hadn't spent any time together since the brick through the window, and he had lost his best suspect. Adam had been in Phoenix for a meeting, so that meant someone else knew about them.

Opening the door of his office, he stopped at the threshold. His father sat behind Michael's desk. The inside of Michael's mouth suddenly felt dry. Michael attempted to hide his anxiety. Martin Shaw was there for a reason. Maybe a little sarcasm would get rid of him.

"What a surprise. I don't think you've visited my office since you ordered me to rip down the Marilyn Monroe photo from the wall."

"Where's your translator? I hear you two are inseparable," Martin said.

Michael walked over to the credenza on the opposite wall and pulled out a bottle and glass. Here it comes, he thought, another brick through the window. Michael hadn't planned on drinking that night, but seeing his father dehydrated his soul. Pouring a short one, he sat down on the chair in front of his desk. "The interpreter is visiting María Curry. I hate to sound rude, but I've got lots of work to do, and what the hell do you care anyway."

"I've heard that woman is helping you in ways you can't discuss in court."

"You heard wrong." Michael swigged some of his drink.

Martin leaned over his son's desk. "Exactly what is your relationship with this woman?"

"None of your goddamn business." Michael got up and paced in front of the window. He got mad at himself for acting like a guilty man, which he was.

"This sleazy affair is causing our family ridicule."

Michael gave a laugh, albeit a shallow one. "Sleazy? Come on, Martin. You sound like a Fannie Hurst novel."

"Sit down!" Martin boomed.

At last, the great Martin Shaw had lost his cool. Michael almost refused, but he reluctantly obeyed his father and sat back down.

Martin adjusted his silk tie. His voice quieted. "You have a brilliant future ahead of you, Michael. If you take control of your drinking, you can go as high and as far as you want. This woman only wants to trap you."

Michael took another sip of his drink, although the whiskey burned his stomach more than usual. "You're summing up for the jury. You even used your sincere voice."

"Have you given her money? Presents?"

Michael set down his glass. "Not a thing. And she hasn't asked. But I'll tell you something, she can have anything she wants." He should have told that to Toni. He was a damn fool.

"It's embarrassing to me personally. I walked into the barbershop the other day, and two men from the bank stopped talking, and you know exactly what they were talking about."

"What about all those times I was drunk on my ass? I suppose such behavior was acceptable. What hypocritical horseshit, even from you." Michael could do nothing but grin.

"I've worked too hard for you to ruin us in this town and in this state." Martin stood up and walked around the desk.

Not wanting his father standing over him, Michael stood up uneasily and pointed at his father with his empty glass. "Son of a bitch. I finally get it. This sticks in your craw because she's a Mexican. But if her first name was Peggy or Suzy or Janie, now, those are appropriate mistresses. Then again, Martin, you're the expert there."

Martin slapped the glass out of Michael's hand. Michael's mouth opened with surprise. His father had never raised his voice or shown such physical anger. He was the king of contained vitriol.

Michael recovered quickly. "I've never seen you so emotional. How does it feel?"

"You leave me no alternative."

Michael took another glass out of the credenza. "What are you going to do? Banish me from the country club? I can do what I want."

"This involvement demonstrates a clear lack of judgment and a disregard for any of today's moral standards."

"Christ. You should be choking on the word 'moral' after what you pulled with my mother."

Martin disregarded Michael's comments and talked as if dictating the terms of a contract. "Unless you stop this affair, consider your employment terminated at this firm. I want you out of this office tonight. You will also be cut off from any of the family money, investments or inheritance." He paused.

"Let's see how many drinks you can buy working from a store-front office."

"You'd do that to me?"

"I'm doing it for your own good."

Not wanting his father to see his hands tremble, Michael shoved them in his pockets.

"What, no more jokes, son? I want to be proud of you again for one goddamn moment. You had your fun, now it's over."

Michael slumped into the chair. "Why do you hate her?"

Martin blinked at the question. "I don't hate her. She's just inconsequential. Now, do you start packing, or are you staying with the firm?"

Dropping the glass, Michael closed his eyes. He couldn't move his fingers. He couldn't move from the chair. He couldn't move from his life. He was yellow as the moon over town. When he opened his eyes, his father had started puffing on a cigar.

"The doctor said I shouldn't have these, but we can't ignore the joys of life." Martin knew a victory when he saw one. "You've made the right choice, Michael."

Michael looked at his father. "Do you realize this is the longest conservation we've had in a long time? Don't you think that's sad?"

Martin left.

"I think that's sad," Michael said.

For an hour afterward, Michael did not glance at the notes for his closing.

"*Jus vitae necisque*," he said to himself. The power over life and death. The power of his father over his life. Michael couldn't think of the appropriate Latin legal term to describe himself, but several English ones came to mind, and none of them involved the word "bravery."

Packing notes in his briefcase, Michael left for the court-house like a man on the way to a gallows of his own construc-tion. When he got there, he entered the side door nearest the jail, where Toni still visited María. He would wait and talk with her. Maybe she'd pass on to him the determination to tell his old man to go to hell. But when he saw Toni coming from the jail, he ducked behind a marble column. She was putting on a thin coat when a large deputy walked over to her and started to help.

"Thank you."

"You're welcome," said the big man.

Michael recognized Nick Conrad as a tackle who had been in high school two years behind him.

Nick grinned at Toni. "Where you going, señorita?"

Toni recognized the grin. "Home."

The deputy stepped closer to her. "How about going for a drink? There's a real nice place down the street. I get off in a half hour. You can meet me there. We can talk about the law."

"No, thank you." Toni tried to step around him.

The deputy held out an arm to stop her. "You're so pretty and so polite. Very polite to white guys." His voice lowered to sludge.

Michael clung to the column. If he didn't, he would fall off the earth.

"Get out of my way," Toni ordered the deputy.

"What's the matter? Not like us poor working men? I'll prove to you I'm better than any old lawyer. Much better." The deputy hiked up his pants. Toni pushed past while he laughed snippily. "See you around, señorita."

The deputy's heavy footsteps faded in the other direction. Michael waited for the silence before he struck his head against the column until the ever so cool marble became streaked with blood.

36

THE PLACE EXHALED LYE AND BLEACH. Bags of soiled clothing suspended in bags from the ceiling looked like organs of a giant creature. Clean clothing on hangers traveled along conveyors running along the wall, while large tubular washers churned and sputtered. Sweat gleamed on the faces of the Mexican women at the Borden Laundry Company. Feeding clothes into machines, they chatted in Spanish about children and husbands. Everyone knew everyone else's business because the workers had to shout to be heard above the thrumming machinery.

Toni respected their simple gratitude for jobs and food on the table. They were content enough with keeping clean homes and having children who loved God. She folded the sheets emerging from the rollers of the ironing machine. Her partner, Rosie Rojas, an older woman with large arms and a tiny face, chatted like the motors running the washers. Within a few days of working there, Toni knew much more than she wanted to know about the Rojas family, including how Rosie's son had earned a prison term for slicing up a neighbor who slept with his wife. She and Rosie simultaneously grabbed one end of the cloth as it rolled out of the pressing machine, folded it down the middle, met their hands and folded it again.

They repeated the maneuver in perfect teamwork, creating stacks of sheets ready to tie with white string. All the while, Rosie gabbed.

"But my boy, you know, he meant no harm, Antonia."

"I'm sure he didn't, Rosie."

"In Mexico, he would have been a good boy, but in this country there's too much freedom. The young people go crazy here. Oh, not you. You're a good girl."

Toni was about to change the subject when she saw Carmen wave at the back door. She glanced at the clock.

"Rosie, I'd like to take my break now, if that's okay with you. My sister is out there."

"Sure. My feet are killing me, anyway."

Toni headed for the back door.

Carmen held out a paper bag and swung it enticingly. "Dad sent potato and chorizo burritos."

The sisters sat close together on the back steps. Toni had grabbed a clean rug and placed it down, figuring she would wash it again later. The warmth of the room heated their backs.

Toni gently nudged her sister. "It's late. You and the baby need rest."

Carmen patted her bulging stomach. "I feel good. Besides, Dad was tired, so I told him I'd bring you some food."

For a while, they sat and watched the steam rush out the big vents on the side of the building.

"The trial is almost over, Toni. What happens then?"

"I don't know, I really don't."

Carmen raised her head. "Hey, the baby kicked. Feel." She placed Toni's hand over the spot on her round belly. After another kick, Toni smiled and withdrew her hand.

"What does it feel like?" Toni asked.

"Like your insides are moving on their own, but it doesn't hurt. It's nice, like the baby is ready to come out and meet me. This may sound funny, Toni, but I feel like a real woman, being pregnant." Carmen's eyes were glassy with tears.

"It's not funny at all. It's beautiful."

"If it's a girl, I'm going to name the baby after Mamá."

"She would have loved that."

"I want you to baptize the baby."

"I hoped you'd ask."

"*Comadre* Toni."

"*Comadre* Carmen. I like the sound of that." Toni huddled closer to her sister. "The nights are getting cooler. Maybe I'm getting old, like Mrs. Hernández. Pretty soon my bones will dry up like flour. My blood will be thick as lard, and I'll start having heart attacks."

"Not you. You're too ornery. Besides, I want the kid to be like his aunt and go to college."

Toni laughed. "What do you want the baby to be?"

"Happy."

Toni hugged her sister. "I'll split these with you."

They dug into the bag.

≈ ≈ ≈

After her shift, Toni sat in her little house. Carmen was right. She was dumb as a doorknob. She went outside. Clouds covered the stars, making the darkness complete. Growing up, she believed her life was blessed because of the people she loved. They had each other, never had to go without food and lived in a nice home. But her mother had died, and the blessings became illusory. They could be taken away so easily.

There was Michael, whom she counted as a blessing. There were also the obstacles for both of them, which placed their relationship in a night without the moon.

The porch light went on across the yard. "Antonia," her father called. "*Teléfono, m'ijita.*"

"Coming."

Francisco left the room as soon as Toni said, "Michael" into the phone. He had heard the name before, when he caught other men at the mill talking in the cafeteria. They always shut up when he entered. He stirred at Toni's loud voice but didn't leave his bedroom, where he sat on the bed with his hands clasped together. Carmen and Víctor had gone out. A fortunate thing, because her sister would have grabbed the phone from Toni and started cursing at the man on the other end.

Toni's hand was tight on the telephone. "What did you say?"

On the line, Michael repeated the words, which carried a hollow and faraway echo. Toni huffed into the phone. She tasted blood in her mouth. Her eyes stung, but she was too mad to cry. "You didn't have the guts to tell me to my face, did you?"

Michael sighed into the phone, the air brushing into her ear with betrayal.

She listened as Michael stammered with the words. For a man who lived by knowing what to say, he was hardly able to speak.

"What about María?" she asked.

Michael had apparently forgotten about his client. He mentioned something about another translator.

"I can't desert her. You don't need anyone else. María counts on me and trusts me. I can't let her down," Toni said.

Michael breathed out as if he had no more air in his body. Music played in the background. He was at a bar, which made her angrier. He had no explanation, and she wasn't going to ask for one. Michael only called it "over." Toni willed herself to think, to find a reason. Discarding the obvious ones, including his marriage, she tried to find answers in what he told her in the darkness, in bed. It was all shit, and she was stupid.

My God.

"Wait, wait. No more," Toni interrupted his stammering. "I won't make any trouble for you. Tell your father he's got nothing to worry about."

She hung up, still holding the receiver.

Standing outside his room, Francisco coughed quietly. Toni threw down the phone, rushed to him and sobbed, putting her hands over her face.

"Don't cry, *hijita*." He patted her back. "No man is worth it."

≈ ≈ ≈

"Hey, you done in there?" A man with a red Adam's apple tapped on the glass of the booth. "I gotta use the phone."

Michael opened the door, and the man rushed by him into the booth. Michael went to his table in the corner. Tommy had left him a glass of whiskey. He hadn't tasted it yet. His arms and legs were numb. Like the night his mother died. Like the day he quit the prosecutor's office. Since those times, he had lived with aimlessness. Nothing had given him purpose until Toni. Now, he had let her go.

Michael picked the drink up and threw the glass against the nearest wall. Spilling several bills on the table, he walked out of the place.

Unfettered, Tommy brought over his broom as Michael left the bar. "That is one fucked-up lawyer." The bartender whistled through his teeth.

37

ACROSS THE STREET FROM THE LAUNDRY, Herb Bell watched the rest of the shift leave but didn't see the girl. A couple of things kept him from visiting her house with the warning he carried from old man Shaw. Her damn little dog would probably bark its head off. Plus her old dad might have a shotgun. So he'd deliver his message at the job she deserved—cleaning up after white people.

Greaser whore. He wanted to call her that, but she might recognize his voice from the courthouse. Then again, what did he care if she knew his identity? What could she do to him? He was a deputy, for fuck's sake.

He grinned because the girl had parked well away from the lights of the laundry. The dark hid his face. He had also changed into jeans and a dark shirt. No one would see him coming.

The mill blasted twice. Midnight. She walked to her car like she was bucking a windstorm. Michael Shaw must have already told her to get lost. Still, old man Shaw wanted insurance the girl didn't bother his son again or stir up problems for the family with any false accusations. The old man had appreciated Bell's suggestion.

The deputy ducked into the back seat of her car. The girl got in, but she didn't start up the motor. She just sat there. Bell leaned forward behind the driver's seat and placed his right hand over her mouth, yanking her head backward. She fought against him, attempting to reach the horn. But he grabbed her left arm and pulled back even harder on her head. She was helpless.

"No, you don't. Now, stay away from Michael Shaw, bitch. Or you and your family will be knee-high in shit." He had intensified and deepened his voice to disguise it.

Her thrashing continued. He had power over this woman, like he had power over Michael Shaw. He could do anything he wanted to her and grew hard at the opportunity. Bell slid his left hand under the girl's blouse and bra to her right breast. He squeezed hard. His rough fingers pulled at her nipple with malevolency and lust. She inhaled and stopped squirming. He eased his grip with what he believed was her invitation. But the girl opened her mouth wide and bit hard into the palm of his hand. Bell cursed, drew back his hand and then slugged her on her right cheek.

She pulled free, bolted out the door and ran. By the time Bell climbed out of her car, the girl had disappeared back in the laundry. Bell ran to his truck, parked on the next street over. His hand throbbed and bled.

"Fucking bitch!" Still, the fact the powerful Martin Shaw owed him for his services did lessen the sting.

38

FOR THE PAST MONTH, María had rubbed tiny circles on the middle of her chest. She had begun to feel a piercing in the exact place where she had plunged the knife into Ben. Nighttime was when the unseen gash throbbed. Other times, it just burned. In the early morning hours, she would often wake from the pain and check herself in the metal mirror on the wall of her cell. She truly expected to see the eye of a knife wound looking back at her. An open cut, raw and red as new meat. Although she couldn't see the wound, she knew it was there under her skin, tainting her soul with guilt. Her friend Bonita had come to see her and asked if the priest had heard her confession yet. But María hadn't invited him to the jail. No matter what the church taught, she feared God would not forgive her.

That Saturday, Toni visited. Mr. Shaw had arranged for them to meet in one of the interview rooms, while other inmates had to talk with their families through metal mesh in the jail visiting area.

As soon as María was brought into the room, Toni said, "Come here, please. I want a look at you."

But María was the one who took Toni's face in her hands. Bruises marked the left side. The skin under Toni's right eye had darkened. "*Madre mía.* Who did that to you?"

"No one. A bag of laundry fell, and I didn't duck in time."

"Little girl, I know the signs. Tell me what happened."

Toni lit a cigarette. The smoke weaved a white airy border back and forth as she paced the room, keeping her head down.

"I didn't see his face. He was in the back seat of my car." She shivered. "He touched me . . . I bit his hand. That's when he punched me, and I ran away." Toni didn't mention the rest. The threat to stay away from the Shaw family. María had enough to worry about.

The night Toni was attacked, she had called her sister to come get her from the laundry. Toni had also lied to Carmen and her father about her injuries. If she told them what really took place, she was positive they would have gone after Michael, who had nothing to do with the assault. She was sure of that. Thankfully, her sister and father believed her story and didn't think anything of it when she started to sleep on the couch. She told them it was too hot in her little house.

"You didn't call the police?" María said.

"They'd only think I asked for it. I'm okay, really." Toni stubbed out the cigarette and sat down by María. "Let's talk about how you're doing."

María studied her. "Antonia, what else is wrong?"

"Nothing. The laundry is a lot harder than I imagined."

"You're lying again."

"María, please."

"It's about you and Mr. Shaw."

Toni opened her mouth to speak, but then closed it.

"You don't have to hide with me, Antonia."

"Michael will still help you. It's his job. Maybe we should find someone else to translate for you. I don't want anything to hurt your chances in court. It might be best if I went away."

María kissed her cheek. "You are my friend. I want you with me."

"You're my friend, too."

"You love him."

Toni took María's hands. They were cool and small. "I can handle this. I've had disappointments before."

Both of them couldn't help but smile.

"We know disappointment very well. It's like a relative standing on your doorstep," María said.

"Only this time, I hoped it would be different."

"Men are such mysterious creatures, Antonia. They can bring so much pleasure and suffering. Remember that old Bible story about how God took a rib from man while he was sleeping and He made a woman? I believe men remember the misery woman caused when God took the rib. And men want revenge. I realize now men pay us back with love."

Toni started to cry. María held her close and rocked the young woman. Toni's tears on her chest felt like absolution.

"M'ija." María spoke in her ear. "Do me a favor?"

"Anything," Toni replied.

"Will you ask Father Vásquez to come and hear my confession?"

Toni nodded. Neither of them had a handkerchief, so María dried Toni's face with the hem of her jail dress.

39

JENNY HAD LEARNED FROM HER MOTHER to spend money, and lots of it, on herself. Spending cured most problems in life. So before her lunch with Martin Shaw, she went shopping. But Jenny could not concentrate enough to enjoy the racks of dresses or rows of shoes. Her mother's remedy was ultimately pointless. Who was going to notice her new outfits, anyway? During trials, Michael had always worked long hours and gotten irritable, which was why she hated the law. But now, he worked even longer hours. He wasn't ill-tempered, but courteous and indifferent to her, and he had been sleeping on the sofa in his office. He said he was too busy with work and didn't want to wake her.

Her last stop before lunch was the Modern Woman Shop on Clarence Avenue to check if any new styles had arrived. Angie Harriman caught up with her near the blouses. She smelled Angie before she saw her. An overwhelming floral perfume that gave anyone a headache if they stood near longer than five minutes.

"Why, Jenny Shaw, I haven't seen you since your father-in-law's wonderful birthday party."

"How nice to see you again, Angie."

They were the same age. Yet Angie already had three children, all with no chins, like her husband.

Angie stepped closer to feel the fabric of a blouse. "How is your handsome husband?"

"He's fine, but really busy."

"Oh, yes, that murder trial."

Jenny began to perspire. She suspected that everyone who was anyone knew about Michael's affair. Two weeks ago, at her weekly bridge game at the country club, she was sitting in one of the stalls when two women came into the bathroom cackling about how Michael Shaw was sleeping with a Mexican from North Park. A Mexican, of all women, they said. How humiliating. Poor Jenny, poor, poor Jenny. She stayed in the bathroom for fifteen minutes and then sneaked out the back door.

Angie patted Jenny's shoulder. "You know you can call me if you want to talk."

Holding her purse tightly, Jenny pointed to a gaudy blouse on the rack. "Look at this one. It's your style, Angie. Please excuse me. I have an appointment." But all the way out of the store, her high heels clicked out, "Poor Jenny." Poor, poor Jenny.

At Louie's Restaurant, Jenny asked for a table in the back. She scolded herself for not knowing what she should have known. She ordered a gin and tonic, double. Perhaps Michael knew what he was doing. How nice to become deadened. She scratched her ankle.

Martin stood beside her, startling her. "How's my girl? I'm so glad you could meet me today." He kissed her cheek and sat down. His face had thinned since his illness, which he chose to call an "incident."

"How's Melody?" she asked.

"Shopping."

"I'm doing more of it lately myself."

"Why not? Women deserve nice things."

An older waiter came by with menus.

Martin took them. "We'll order in a minute." The waiter left. "Jenny, you know I consider you almost a daughter, more than an in-law."

"Thank you, Dad."

From his inside pocket, he took out the cigar he had waited to smoke all day. "Jenny, you must have noticed Michael's preoccupation lately."

She bit her lip at what he might say next. "Yes."

"I want to assure you he'll be back to normal very soon."

Which normal, she wanted to ask. His drinking, his refusing to have a baby or buy a house? "That's reassuring. I have been worrying about him."

"Michael may not believe this, but I want to help you both have a prosperous life. Melody told me you liked a vacant house on Byrd Avenue."

"I don't think it's still for sale."

"Someone had made an offer, but never mind that—it gets complicated. Let's say I checked into the matter, and I have put money down on the house. Consider it an early anniversary present. And this is not negotiable." He smiled.

"Oh, Dad. This is too much." She got up and hugged him.

The kitchen door opened. A young, pretty Mexican woman was scrubbing the dishes. Jenny frowned slightly at the reminder of who could stand in the way of her dream house and life. Martin sat back and smoked. If nothing bothered him, perhaps she shouldn't be bothered, either. The Mexican girl was staring right at her when the kitchen door swung closed. Jenny returned to her seat. "I don't know if Michael will let you do all that."

"Don't worry about him, dear. He'll come around. Now, let me order for you. And I promise to tell Michael about the house. You don't have to bother your pretty head with the business details."

Jenny did not argue.

After lunch, she said good-bye to Martin and drove alone to the house she wanted so badly. One of the flamingos had fallen over, and she got out of the car and picked it up. The trees were overgrown. She went to the backyard and sat on the wood bench underneath one of the large trees. Her life would come to pass, as her mother had predicted, with fashionable parties in her own house. She envisioned windows warm with light from Thanksgiving candles. An opulent Christmas tree with each ornament personally selected by her. In the study, her husband held a glass of brandy and read a book. She shook her head. Wait, scratch the brandy. And, best of all, there was a baby napping in her arms. All her plans lay before her like a new dawn.

Still, the only thing Jenny could do was sob.

≈ ≈ ≈

The moon held him in its light, like one of those movies where hard-boiled detectives sweated a suspect for a confession. Michael sat on the balcony, rocking back and forth, propelled by doubt. The next morning he had to argue for María's life. In a strange way, he was defending his own.

Wearing a new pink sheer nightgown, Jenny slid open the glass door. "Michael, what are you doing out here? It's chilly." She closed the door and ran back under the covers.

When he came in, she was reading a magazine in bed. She bounced her legs under the covers, like a kid needing to go the bathroom. "I got chilled in my little nightgown," she whimpered in a sexy intonation. She fingered the silk straps and slid a finger along the lace over her breasts. "Come to bed and warm me up?"

Instead, Michael sat down on the stuffed chair in the corner. "You go to sleep. I still have work to do."

Putting down the magazine, she sat up. "You're not going out, are you?" A warning more than anything.

"I'm not going out."

She smiled and fell back on the pillow. "We need more time together. We can go out to dinner and dancing at the club after this case is over. Or maybe on a vacation to Palm Springs."

"That won't help."

"I had lunch with your father." She tried to make it sound nonchalant.

"Why, for fuck's sake?"

She pulled up the covers to her chin. "You know I don't like it when you talk like that. It's common."

"I guess I'm fucking common."

Jenny pouted, but it didn't last. She got out of bed and knelt in front of his chair. "He wanted to tell you first, but I can't wait. He put money down on the house I love. He wants us to be happy."

Michael put his head in his hands. "God, Jenny."

"We deserve it."

"Deserve what? Pink flamingos?"

"Why not?"

"Life isn't like one of those Broadway numbers you keep singing. It's not 'Oh, What a Beautiful Mornin' or 'Some Enchanted Evening,' goddammit."

He clutched her arms and pulled her up from the bed. "There's death and murder and lies out there. You've got to see the truth of it. If you don't, Jenny, you're going to wind up like those women at the country club who play cards all day and drink a fifth of whiskey at night waiting for their husbands to come home."

Michael released her. Jenny's shock gave way to tears, and she fell against the headboard.

"I love you and want us to be happy more than anything in the world," she cried.

He stood over her. Such a simple thing she wanted. "Sorry I grabbed your arms." Staggering a bit, he pulled her forward again. "Come on, now. Go to sleep, Jenny. Dream of pink birds and green lawns and swimming pools over bomb shelters. Why the fuck not?"

40

As Toni entered the courtroom, she rubbed her hands to warm them. Michael sat at the defense table, wearing the impeccable three-piece gray suit she liked. Inside, people chatted or shuffled feet and papers. She only heard a gurgling in her ears, as if her blood was draining away. For once the courtroom was cool, but she perspired at the prospect of seeing Michael. *God, let me be brave*, she prayed. As she was about to sit at the defense table, he looked up at her. His eyes were bloodshot. A stitched two-inch slash marked his forehead. He appeared to be a sleepwalker who had just awakened. Generally, he looked like hell. But his face went even grimmer with concern at the sight of her. He got up, took her arm and led her to the empty courtroom next door. She was too tired to resist and let herself go with him.

"What the hell happened to you?" he said after shutting the door.

Shaking off his hand, she repeated the fiction about the laundry bag. It took all her will to keep her voice flat and perfunctory. She couldn't spare him any more of her emotions. He had taken too much already.

"Toni, please." Michael reached out to her, and Toni pushed his hand away.

She stepped to the door. "We've got to get back." She left him in the room.

Michael swallowed so hard his throat ached. He had hoped she would act childish and call him names, so he could be vindicated in breaking off the affair. Instead, she demonstrated poise when meeting the heel who had dumped her.

Back in the courtroom, Toni waited for María. She swiveled at the sound of the clicking handcuffs on Deputy Herb Bell's belt as he brought in María. She hugged Toni.

As Toni held María, she noticed the deputy leered at her, as if he could see underneath her clothes. His right hand was bandaged. It was him. In her car. Threatening her. Assaulting her. Toni's mouth and eyes watered, and she wanted to throw up. She couldn't leave for the bathroom because court was about to start. So she covered her mouth.

"Something wrong?" María said.

Toni took away her hand and sipped water. "*Nada.*" She wiped at her eyes with her handkerchief.

"Toni?" Michael had sat down.

"I'm nervous. I'll be fine."

María pointed at Michael and said something in Spanish to Toni.

"What did she say?" he asked Toni.

"She's not scared anymore because you're on her side. She wishes you good luck today. You have my best wishes, too." Toni gave a small smile, which she meant.

"Thank you." His voice cracked.

Joe Brennan watched with satisfaction from the prosecution table. The rumors about Shaw and the woman were true. The stupid son of a bitch. The freshest gossip hinted at how old man Shaw had made Michael dump the Mexican mistress with threats of being kicked out of his fancy office. The intrigues made Michael Shaw vulnerable and ready to lose.

Brennan considered sending the interpreter a bottle of tequila after the trial.

Before Bailiff George Roy had barely finished saying, "All rise," Judge Hower entered the courtroom.

The judge took his seat at the bench. "Are you ready for closing arguments?" he asked the attorneys, who both indicated they were.

First, Brennan carefully outlined the state's case against María Curry, from the police reports to the physical and medical evidence. With the dry facts out of the way, he made his real case for a guilty plea.

"Ladies and gentlemen, don't let María Curry fool you. Yes, she's a woman who appears cowering and powerless. Why, she even needs a translator to speak for her." He smiled like it was a private joke between them. "Please, do not be misled. This woman took the law into her own hands, small as they may be, weak as they may be. Yet those hands were strong enough to drive a knife deep into the chest of Ben Curry on the night of August 18. She found the strength to kill."

The county attorney took measured steps back and forth in front of the jury. "This murder was no heat of the moment incident, as the defense will lead you to believe. On August 16th, only two days before his death, María Curry had warned her husband that she was going to kill him. And with what weapon did she threaten her husband? A knife. A knife, ladies and gentlemen. What we have is premeditation. I know that is a legal word. But in this case, it means she knew what she was doing and carried out her intentions on the night of August 18th."

Brennan pointed to Michael. "Now, Mr. Shaw will ask you to consider the color of her skin and her culture as if they were pieces of evidence, like the bread knife she plunged into her husband's chest. He'll even describe her as the victim who was trying to protect herself and her little dog. The defense is literally trying to color-blind you. But color and culture are no excuses for murder."

Brennan again walked to the jury box but directed his gaze at María, who bent her head to hear Toni's translation. "But this woman is no victim. During all those years when Ben Curry allegedly hurt his wife, she could have run away. But she didn't. She could have asked for help. She didn't. María Curry herself victimized a victim. By her own admission, her husband was practically an invalid who lived with tremendous pain because of his back injury. How could someone like that defend himself against an enraged woman with a knife? The answer is he didn't. You saw the photographs of the deceased. María Curry did not stab him once, but many times."

The county attorney's voice gained ferocity. He pounded on the jury's box. His eyes grew large with vehemence. He had practiced the actions the previous evening at home. "On that fatal night, María Curry could have called an ambulance to save her husband, but again, she didn't. A few minutes could have saved Ben Curry's life. What did she do instead? She sat and watched his life's blood flow out of him."

María nodded her head in agreement.

"I'll admit Ben Curry was probably not the best husband in the world, but that was no reason for him to die. In truth, María Curry wanted her husband dead, and she made it happen. The only verdict possible is guilty of murder in the first degree."

He stood there a while and then sat down.

"Mr. Shaw," Judge Hower invited.

At the back, Jenny had entered a few minutes earlier and sat down, but Michael hadn't noticed. She never had visited the courthouse, and the place made her feel ignorant. Now, the only reason she had come was to see the woman. She wanted to put a face on her fears. Jenny tilted her head for a better view. The young Mexican woman sitting at the front table concentrated on Michael as she translated for the older woman sitting next to her. Jenny frowned. The Mexican was very pretty.

After thanking the jury for their patience and hard work, Michael also reviewed the specific testimony of the witnesses about María's many injuries at her husband's hands. Before he continued and for the first time ever in a courtroom, he silently prayed he would win. His best argument was going to be María's life.

Michael faced the jury. "María Curry is the first to admit she is no saint. She is just a human, with all our faults and fears. She is also a woman who endured hell.

"María fell in love with Ben Curry and married him and had the highest hopes for a good life. For years, he worked hard and supported her, but he also drank, and when he drank, he abused his wife. A slap here. A slug there. Then came the accident at the construction site, and the injury intensified his cruelty toward her and others. Her husband even whipped her like an animal with a belt in a darkened basement.

"Now, María is a native of Mexico and was raised to believe, rightly or wrongly, that men were rulers of the household. So she accepted this as her lot, and the beatings and degradation became a part of her life. Yet because of her marriage vows, and more importantly because she loved Ben Curry, María did not leave.

"Her neighbors, her employer at the Santa Fe Motel and Father Vásquez all describe a woman who is meek, generous, honest and hardworking. That is María Curry. Yes, she drank occasionally, but who could blame her after living with such mistreatment at the hands of her husband?

"There is no denying that she and her husband had not arguments. They did, and loud ones. Yet, according to the officers' testimony and hospital records, it was mostly María who suffered. You saw photographic evidence of how she had been savagely beaten, and that was only one time among many. She nursed not only broken bones but a broken spirit and lived without hope. And the single time María fought back with a frying pan, she paid for it with a knife against her throat and more threats against her life." As Michael talked, he looked at each and every juror's face, hoping to connect. They were listening intently. He had to convince them.

"While the prosecution tries to portray Ben Curry as a defenseless man, witnesses testified again and again about his violent nature. Even in pain, he still had power enough to hit and terrorize his wife. It is true for humans as well as animals that when wounded, they are the most dangerous, and so it was with him.

"On the evening of August 18, Ben Curry again played out his ritual of brutality. As he choked her, María believed she was really going to die. In desperation, she fought back and attacked with the only weapon within reach. But this was out of pure instinct. An act of self-preservation."

Michael held onto the rail enclosing the jury box. "And wouldn't any one of you do the same in such a situation? If someone had battered and knocked you down and finally started squeezing the life right out of you, would you just lay back and die? I think not. You would protect yourself. You would have the right to defend yourself. And that's what María did. She wasn't trying to kill. She was trying not to be killed."

Michael paused, his voice ragged with emotion. He held onto the jury box, hoping to send his certainty through the wood to the jurors. "María took her husband's life, but there is no integrity in taking hers or in putting her in prison for life. She's lived with injustice for so many years. Please, please, do justice by her now."

Several minutes before Michael finished his summation, Jenny had left the courtroom. She had seen more than she wanted. The young Mexican woman watched her husband with the eyes of a lover.

41

ON A NAPKIN, Cyrus Graham wiped chicken grease off his fingers and called for another count. The postman had been elected foreman after telling the others he was an Elk and Mason and knew how to run a meeting. Besides, he was the only person who wanted the job.

When the judge first handed the jurors the case for deliberation, they held a count. Nine for guilty and three not guilty on the first-degree charge. After four hours of discussion and reviewing the evidence, they conducted another count. Now eight for guilty, four for not guilty. They had broken for a chicken dinner, which was sent into the jury room. They did agree, the more quickly they reached a verdict, the sooner they'd all go home. But the arguments again went round like a wheel.

While eating their fried chicken meal, they talked of death.

"She confessed, and her prints were the only ones on that knife." Graham picked up a wing.

"I know she did, but she was afraid her husband was going to kill her. If a big man came after me, I'd defend myself," said Lucille Cunningham, a spindly schoolteacher who spooned out more coleslaw.

The not-guilty holdouts included one man, Joshua Kinney, which surprised Graham.

"That fatal wound really bothers me. Even if she had wanted to, I don't think she could have aimed the knife right at his heart." Kinney shyly took another chicken breast. "To me that says she had no intention of killing the man. She only lashed out trying to fend him off."

Roxy Barton, a young, antsy woman who worked at Pete's, shook salt on her potatoes. "Yes, but she wanted him dead, and she stabbed him something like four or five times. That's premedication."

"Premeditation," Graham corrected her.

"Well, she knew she wanted to kill him." She stuffed a spoonful in her mouth.

"But those awful beatings," answered Georgia Fletcher, a housewife. "She lived in fear, like Mr. Shaw said."

"She sure was handy with that frying pan," Graham added. "Mexicans do have tempers, and she sure bared hers."

"That's hooey." Kinney pushed his half-eaten plate aside. "All I know is this: if we send her to prison or set her free, a man is dead. No matter which way we decide, there's nothing here but losers."

The jurors all chewed, digesting more than chicken.

≈ ≈ ≈

Slap. Slap. Slap.

Oscar ran with the red ball so fast, his small legs were a furry blur. María threw the ball on the floor. Oscar caught it on the rebound and put it on her lap. "I missed you, my Oscar." She threw him a bit of hot dog that Toni had brought.

Panting madly, Oscar bounced for another chance at the ball.

Toni leaned against the wall. The room where she and María waited on the third floor of the courthouse had no window and was stuffy, even though it was larger than the one where they usually met in the jail. While they waited, Toni talked to María about what she had planned for her when the jury set her free. First, dinner with her father, Carmen and Víctor so María could understand family meant calm evenings and laughter. She had also invited María to live with her in the small house. Toni tried to sound optimistic, but her head ached. Standing on the other side of the door was the man who would have raped her if she hadn't bitten him. More troubling was the uncertainty over María's fate.

"You can have a good life with us," Toni said.

"We'll see, Antonia," María replied as if talking to a child.

"Okay. We'll see."

Toni's hands gripped together so tightly her nails bit into flesh as she pleaded to God, *This woman has suffered in a world full of suffering. Help her.*

≈ ≈ ≈

"Mr. Shaw, you okay?" Pete leaned over the table. "You're pale as a dry creek, man. You could use some of my biscuits."

"I'm waiting for a verdict. We're talking life and death here, so I'm nervous as hell."

"I'll bet. I don't want your job."

"At times like these, I don't want it either."

"We could use another cook."

Michael laughed. "If I cooked, you'd have plenty of lawsuits on your hands."

Mrs. Pete came out with two paper bags.

"There you go, Mr. Shaw. Three coffees and three chicken dinners."

"Thanks." He pulled out money and took the bags.

"Good luck, Mr. Shaw," Pete called. "Don't forget about that cook's job."

"I'll let you know tomorrow."

Michael hurried to the courthouse, which had cleared for the lunch hour. He could have had the food delivered to Toni and María in the courthouse and worked on the new case on his desk back at the bank office. But he wanted to be near Toni, even if she barely spoke to him. He was most hurt by her eyes, which had darkened with contempt.

If the jury didn't reach a decision by the evening, Michael knew the judge would sequester them for the night in a hotel by the state highway. But the judge also hated to spend money, so he'd give the jurors every opportunity to come up with a verdict. Michael tripped on the top step to the courthouse. Once they made the decision, he'd never see Toni again.

"Mike," Adam called to Michael.

Since their scuffle at the bar, Michael had avoided Adam. Their meeting, however, was unavoidable. The courthouse was a small place.

Adam scratched his cheek. "I sat in on the trial here and there. You did a good job."

"We'll see how good." Michael held up the bags. "I've got food, I better be off."

"Right. I'll be seeing you around."

"Sure." Michael took a few steps.

Adam's large face softened to butter. "I'm sorry about what I said. I don't even know why. I can be a fucking asshole sometimes."

"You won't get an argument from me."

"You got guts, Mikey. That's all I can say."

"I got nothing." He walked off.

≈ ≈ ≈

As the hours continued, Michael swore he saw the rolls harden from their half-eaten dinners. María played with her scrubby dog, tossing the sticky ball to Oscar over and over. Toni glanced up from her book, but not at him. She occasionally took Oscar outside to pee. Michael sipped at lukewarm coffee and tried to read notes on another divorce case, which had become as rote as the multiplication table. His eyes couldn't hold onto two words in a row. There was a sudden rap on the door, and he spilled his coffee.

"Son of a bitch." He wiped drops off his tie. He looked at his watch. Six fifteen.

George Roy stuck his head in the door. "Mr. Shaw, the jury's coming back."

Herb Bell waited at the door. María kissed the dog and gave him to Michael, who handed him off to a clerk he had paid to watch the dog that day.

As Herb Bell led María away, he peeked back to see if Shaw and the young Mexican woman would keep their hands off each other. Although he was still angry about the bite on his hand, he grinned at their distance. Mr. Shaw gathered his papers. The woman picked up a book and her purse. Their mouths were both pinned down by unhappiness. Content he had done his duty, Bell left with María.

As they were going out the door, Toni stopped, and Michael bumped into her. She turned to face him. "Michael." Her voice was as intimate as their nights together. "No matter what happens now, you should be proud of what you did for María. Never forget that."

She rushed out before he could speak. Michael picked up his briefcase and slowly shut the door behind him.

42

THE TRIAL HAD MADE PAGE ONE for the first week, but in the proceeding days, the editor relegated the coverage to the inside pages of the local section. Reporter Kent Wyman enjoyed the prospect that any verdict would land him on page A-1 again. He sketched the face of smiling woman on one side of his pad and a woman hanging from a tree on another. Murder trials sold newspapers, like other crimes and tax hikes. This trial had started slowly but turned spicy with the defendant's stories of beatings and all. Readers loved details of someone else's misery so they could feel better about their own lives.

"All rise," the bailiff's voice boomed.

Judge Hower took five large steps into the room and ascended to the bench. "We're back in session in the case of the State of Arizona versus María Curry. Ladies and gentlemen of the jury, have you reached a verdict?"

Foreman Cyrus Graham stood. "We have."

Holding out his hand, Judge Hower waited for George Roy to retrieve the written verdict from Graham. The judge read the paper and handed it back to the bailiff.

Each action tapped along Toni's spine.

"The defendant will please rise and face the jury," the judge said.

Toni whispered to María, who stood straight. They held hands. Michael rose. His knees had the consistency of apple butter.

Graham had memorized his speech. "We, the jury, find María Curry guilty of first-degree murder."

María didn't need a translation. A tear slid down Toni's cheek as María gripped her hand more tightly. Michael's mouth warped with disbelief. He put his hand on the table to steady himself.

Judge Hower tapped his gavel to hush up the people in the gallery, whose murmurs were split between agreement and disagreement. He peeked over his glasses at the defense table.

"María Curry, you are judged guilty of murder in the first degree. Do you have anything to say before sentence is pronounced?"

"I am sorry for what I did. I have made peace with God and asked forgiveness for my sin." Although María spoke true, Toni translated in a shaking voice.

"Very well. I don't believe hanging is warranted. You have no prior criminal convictions and were the victim of many crimes committed against you. In the end, however, you became the criminal by killing Ben Curry, and in a most brutal way. Therefore, I sentence you to life behind bars. You shall be transported immediately to the women's state correctional institution."

María watched the judge's eyes, which were lifeless as the wood in the room. She didn't react as Toni translated in a quivering voice.

Judge Hower turned to the jury. "You are dismissed with the thanks of the court."

"All rise," the bailiff shouted.

The courtroom cleared. Wyman readied his pencil and paper to catch a printable quote. Emotions were hottest right after a verdict. "Mr. Shaw, any comment?"

"No."

"Plan to appeal?"

"Get out of my face. And you can fucking quote me."

Wyman quit writing. With a shrug, he switched his attention to Brennan.

"The jury and judge served justice today." Brennan used his best voice. "The verdict confirms the fact no one is above the law. Murder is murder, no matter the motive."

At the verdict, the county attorney had maintained a professional face and promised to save his smile for a more private time, along with a cocktail. Joe Brennan had finally bested the great Michael Shaw, who appeared ready to topple over. Not one person congratulated the county attorney as he gathered his files and walked out of the courtroom, but he didn't mind. He didn't mind at all.

Deputy Herb Bell did not conceal his pleasure when the verdict was read and grinned so hard his mouth muscles protested. He put on his deputy's somber face when he fetched the murderer. "She's got to go, Mr. Shaw."

Michael motioned for him to stay back.

María kissed Toni's cheek. "Antonia, you keep Oscar. He likes you, and I'll be happy knowing he's with you."

"I'll come see you. I promise, María."

Michael put his hand on María's shoulder. Underneath her fragility was the stamina of a survivor. Hell, she had lived all those years with Ben Curry. "Toni, please tell her we'll appeal this to a higher court. We can beat this sentence and probably get her a new trial. I know I can win it for her."

Michael added, "María, they only convicted you because Ben was white and you're Mexican."

As Toni interpreted his words, María shook her head and said something in Spanish.

"María says not to bother. Nothing will change. It's all she can expect from life."

María took Michael's hand in both of hers. "Thank you, Mr. Shaw, for your kindness to me. God bless you." Her English was as halting as it was endearing.

The deputy took María away. Toni watched her friend go. Nothing will change, María had said. The veracity of it spread in her. She left without a word to Michael.

After Toni had gone, Michael sat in María's chair and prepared to serve his own sentence.

43

WHILE JIM, THE COOK, dished out stuffing, Josita put another sprig of parsley alongside the huge turkey she had prepared to serve to the Shaw family.

"This bird could serve ten people with enough left over for turkey enchiladas. And Mr. Martin hates leftovers," she said.

"White people waste everything. Food, money, their lives. They must think they get more when they die." Pablo leaned against a broom.

Jim laughed. "You said a mouthful, boy."

"Besides, what've they got to be thankful for? They got it all."

"You sound jealous, Pablo," Michelle said as she cut the pumpkin pie.

"Not me. I'm thankful for what I can get. I'd be thankful for a date, Michelle."

"Then you're going to be disappointed."

"Josita, when are you celebrating Thanksgiving?" Jim asked.

"Tomorrow. My daughter and her husband and children came in from San Antonio. They can't be here for Christmas, so this will be our big celebration."

"That sounds nice."

"What about you?"

"Oh, me and the wife will go out to eat."

Josita lifted the platter. "No, you aren't. You and your wife are coming to my house. We have plenty. No one should be without family."

The cook blinked. "I'd like that."

"I better get this turkey in there, or we'll all be looking for another job."

"That's something to be thankful for," Jim said.

≈ ≈ ≈

Martin bowed his head over the turkey and glanced up at Michael. "You say the prayer, son." The request was really a command.

"Dear Lord, thank you for all the bounty before us and our family. Amen." The hypocrisy tasted like burnt yams in his mouth.

"How eloquent," Melody scoffed.

Michael unfolded his napkin. "You know us Shaw men. We have a way with words."

Through the first and second courses, Jenny chatted about their new house. Melody suggested a decorator. Martin talked about the pride of ownership, while Michael asked Josita for an aspirin. Jenny was driving him insane. He had told her he'd never step foot in the house until she had all that pink painted over. She pouted for a full week but finally relented. She was so pleased with the house, she hadn't protested when he asked for a separate bedroom.

"Going through the motions," Michael said out loud.

"What?" Jenny's fork was poised with turkey.

"I said, 'Gravy for the turkey.'"

The chat stayed small through the pumpkin pie, until Martin shoved away his dish. He stirred cream into his coffee with his spoon, tapping the side as if calling court to order. "Michael, Elias Smith is retiring from the state senate after this session."

"I heard," Michael answered flatly.

"The boys at the central committee mentioned you. They said, 'Michael Shaw will be a great candidate.' They could see your name on the ballot."

"That's better than on a wanted poster."

"A legislative stint is only a hop away from the governorship. This is even a better opportunity than a judicial post."

As much as she would hate to leave her new house, Jenny smiled at the image of herself in the governor's mansion. "Martin, why didn't you ever run for public office? I'm sure lots of people must have wanted you to."

Michael perked up at last. "That's a very good question."

Annoyance floated briefly across Martin's face. "My talents were more valuable behind the scenes."

"Like giving candidates money and direction?" Michael said.

"I meant strategies. Sometimes, politicians get lost in all that power and need to be reminded of why they were elected. Consider the possibility, Michael."

"If I must."

After dinner, Jenny and Melody went to the dayroom to discuss curtains and carpets for the new house. Martin went to his study. Michael sat alone at the table, staring at his half-eaten pie. Suddenly, Josita stood beside him. He hadn't heard her enter the room.

"Excuse me, Mr. Michael, can we start to clean up now?"

"What? Sure."

Michael watched her gather the dishes and place them on a large tray. He started to help.

Confusion slowed Josita. "Mr. Michael, I can handle this."

Michael laughed. "I know you can. You've handled everything else in this house for years."

Her gold tooth shone in her smile. "Yes, sir, I have."

"Josita, you have five children, right?"

"You remembered. They're all grown up now."

"And Diego, how is he?"

"Very well, Mr. Michael. Getting older but still strong."

"A great cowboy and a nice man."

"He likes you, too."

"Does he?"

"He said you had a dirty face and fire in your eyes when you were a kid."

"Those were the days."

Putting her apron to her face, she giggled. Michael picked up the tray and carried it into the kitchen for her. The cook, Michelle and Pablo froze. Michael placed the tray of dishes onto the counter.

"Thank you, Mr. Shaw," Josita said.

"*De nada.*" Michael smiled at everyone. "Happy Thanksgiving to all of you."

"And you, sir," Jim said.

Michael left the kitchen.

"I'll be a son of a bitch," Jim proclaimed.

"It must be true what they say," Josita said.

"What?" Michelle asked.

"About Mr. Shaw and the Mexican woman."

Pablo continued mopping the floor. "And I heard he treated her real dirty. He's being nice to us out of guilt."

"Pablo, shut your mouth," Josita said. "At least it's a start."

Upstairs, Michael opened the door to what used to be his mother's bedroom. He hadn't visited the place for years and didn't know why he ended up there. All signs of his mother had been removed, as if he had dreamed her all along. A large pool table replaced his mother's fine brass bed and pine furniture. Thick brown carpet and gold brocade replaced the white carpet and flouncy cream curtains. One year after his mother died, his father had married Lucille, ten years his junior and a former Miss Arizona. She redecorated the bedroom. After eight years, however, his father paid her off when the curvaceous beauty went as stale as lipstick left out in the sun—not to mention the rumors he'd heard of her affair with the country club golf pro. All Michael remembered of Lucille was her undying love for cigarettes and Hershey bars. She patronized Michael in the sight of Martin and ignored him the rest of the time. In retribution, he stole her supply of candy bars and fed them to the horses on the ranch. When she found out, she slapped him.

Michael shut off the light and went down the hall to his old room, which had not changed since the day he went away to Harvard. A flag of the Borden Panthers signed by his former teammates hung on the wall above his desk. On shelves were trophies for track, debate, golf and tennis. He couldn't believe all the shit he had collected to prove what he had achieved. In the closet hung his letterman's sweater, and a deflated football was stuffed in the corner. He grabbed the ball, put on the sweater and went outside.

≈ ≈ ≈

Not wanting to hear the decorating tête-à-tête of Jenny and Melody, Martin kept to his study to smoke a cigar. He stood before the large window, the smoke curling against the glass. Under the porch lights in the backyard, Michael tossed a flattened football up and down. Martin put on his glasses. Michael wore his old letterman's sweater. He smiled. The boy came around. He didn't put up much of a fight about anything these days, not the house or a political run. Martin wondered if he had forced the nerve out of Michael after the business with the Mexican woman. Nonsense. Michael had simply become more flexible. His law work hadn't suffered at all. His son worked harder than the younger attorneys fresh out of law school who wanted to prove themselves in the firm.

Martin studied a framed photo of his father, Monroe Shaw, sitting at the very desk that was now in Martin's study. From the date in the corner of the photo, he figured his father was thirty. But hard work had aged his appearance to sixty.

"Hard work." That phrase had been repeated to him so often by his father, it could have stood in for his middle name: Martin "Hard Work" Shaw. With a little money from his parents, his father had set off to Tombstone to make his fortune, as people did in those days. Monroe chose not to work in the mines that paid little and readily broke backs, but rather made money selling goods to the miners, gamblers, saloon owners and other inhabitants of the notorious town. With enough money in his pockets and enough smarts to leave before the silver ran out, Monroe settled in Borden. He bought land and started a ranch, which he expanded to one of the largest operations in the state, with forty thousand head. Though a drought crippled everyone for miles around, he survived by determination and by having the wisdom to fence everything he owned to keep people and free rangers out. Monroe garnered enough influence to persuade the railroad to run a line near enough to his ranch to ship his cattle. He used profits from the ranch to buy more land, grow cotton and invest in businesses and property in Borden and beyond, as well as purchase the services of men who would kill intruding wolves, bears, Apaches and an occasional sheepherder. Climbing up was all Monroe knew how to do. He had seen what lay below wealth.

Martin's father did not have time for a family until his late twenties. His mother, Sarah, was the spinster daughter of a prominent banker who understood her place was building a home, just as her husband was building his empire. Martin remembered a slight, timid woman who asked for nothing. His ex-wives could have learned a thing or two from her.

Of course, Martin had disliked his father tremendously. Monroe never had a kind word to say about anybody and was miserly, preferring to spend his wealth on impressing guests instead of on his family. His father would be gone for months on end and treated his home like another business. He crept over household ledgers and acted the despot to his wife, son and servants. Whenever his father spoke to him, it was always in short bits of advice. Save your money. Don't lend money. Buy land. Invest wisely. Trust no one.

His parents died in their late fifties—Sarah from an asthmatic attack and his father from a busted heart while touring a cotton gin he was preparing to buy. At Monroe's funeral, Martin finally comprehended his father's death was just one more sacrifice to their family's legacy. He had left the tenth largest fortune in the state.

Martin conceded he might not have toiled as hard as his father, but his own kind of labor had increased the Shaw holdings more than twofold. Monroe Shaw would have been proud.

In his study, Martin drew in the cigar smoke, which now tasted bitter. For all his success, he wondered why he couldn't get Michael to understand the imperative of ambition. Martin sat at his father's desk and opened a file to a new case.

Outside, Michael glanced at the light in his father's study. He took off the letterman sweater and placed it and the football in a trash can. He walked to the edge of the garden and to the brick wall separating his father's yard from the desert. He opened an iron gate and stepped out a few yards, not even watching for the stubby cactus brushing his pant legs. The silence buzzed in his head like a mass of flies.

He cursed himself for not having taken the steps sooner.

44

CARMEN PUSHED HER WAY through the crowd at the Azteca Bar. Since their waitress spent more time arguing with her boyfriend than serving people, Carmen took the initiative and ordered beers for Víctor and Toni and a soda for herself. Toni had finally come out with them, even though she had had to bully her sister to leave the house. Toni had quit the county job, worked at the laundry, cooked, cleaned the house and read books. She didn't want to talk about the lawyer. All their lives they had shared secrets, worries and dreams. Even when their mother died, they had talked into the night about how they were dead inside, as if they had followed her into the grave. Now her sister had sealed herself off.

Damn that Michael Shaw. Carmen vowed if she ever saw him again, she'd spit in his blue eyes.

They sat at a table in a corner. Carmen had made sure they left home early to get a spot because the band playing was popular and the place filled quickly.

"Here you go." Carmen spoke loudly over the music and the talking of the people packed into the bar.

Víctor took a beer. "Thanks, babe. Aren't you glad you came out, Toni?"

"Yes, thank you." Toni hoped her lie sounded convincing.

294

The lively music could shoo away any grief, at least for the couples dancing with verve and abandon. Those who already had had too much liquor weaved their way to the bathrooms and back again for another round.

Carmen held up her soda bottle. "You two, drink up, 'cause I'm driving."

Toni glanced around the bar. "Nothing's changed."

Carmen was encouraged. Toni appeared to relax. "See, *mujer*, people are having a good time."

"So that's what it looks like."

Carmen bought another round for her husband and sister. The beer settled in Toni, heating her stomach. She fought the respite. If she made herself like the steel her father forged, nothing could damage her again.

"Toni, how you doing?" Jesús approached at the table. He wore a blue cowboy shirt and dark pants pressed crisp as a fresh-minted bill.

"Hi, Jesús."

Víctor reached out his hand to Jesús. "Sit down, bro."

Jesús took a seat. "Congratulations on your baby, Víctor."

"Thanks, man."

Carmen punched Jesús in the arm and pointed to her rounded stomach. "How about me? He didn't do it all himself, *tonto*."

"Carmen, all women have to do is have the babies. Men have to pay for them."

"Listen here, Jesús, I remember when you had *mocos* running down your face and we had to tell you to wipe your nose."

"Víctor will have to live with all those stretch marks and *chichis* out to here." Jesús extended his arms out as far as they could go.

Toni and Víctor laughed.

Carmen wanted the last word. "Go to hell, Jesús."

"Probably. First, I want to talk to your pretty sister."

"*Pendejo*," Carmen said.

"*Gordita.*"

"*Moco* face."

"Big *chichis.*"

Jesús scooted his chair closer to Toni. "Now we can go out, right?"

"She's nursing a broken heart," Víctor said, slurring his words.

Carmen glared at Víctor.

Víctor put his hand up in defense. "What'd I say? What'd I say?"

"A broken heart?" Jesús said as he gestured for Toni to join him on the dance floor.

The band started up a ballad.

"You'll forget everything in my hands," Jesús said, pulling Toni to the middle of the dance floor.

"That I'd like to see."

He held her closer than she wanted. His hands were rough as her father's. He smelled of a fresh shave.

"You know, Toni, we could try it again. We were pretty good for a while there."

"For a while."

"Your dad likes me."

"My dad likes everybody."

"Toni, I don't know why you don't want to talk about it. Everybody knows that white guy dropped you as quick as he picked you up. You should have kept with your own," he said into her ear as if sharing a secret.

"Christ, this is a small town. I'm surprised somebody didn't put it in the church bulletin." She pulled away a little, though he held her and continued dancing. "It's nobody's business. You can put that in next week's bulletin."

"I'll bet your old man even knows what happened."

Toni's hands grew hot. "Leave my father out of this."

Jesús whispered seductively, "If we start seeing each other, everybody will know you haven't gone gringo on us."

Her feet stopping moving.

"You don't want to be called a coconut, do you, Toni? All brown on the outside and white on the inside. Fess up. Since you came back to town, you've changed, girl. Then you go out with that rich white lawyer. ¡Híjole!"

"I went to college to be a teacher," she told him in Spanish, evenly, deadly. "And as for . . . " She didn't want to say Michael's name, although she didn't know why she should protect him. "My God, Jesús. If that's what you think of me, why do you want to go out. Unless you just want to screw me."

By that time, couples around them were listening more than dancing, including Carmen and Víctor, who had joined them on the dance floor.

"You're making a damn fool of yourself," Jesús said.

"You're like all those people who can only see I'm brown. And who the hell are you or anyone to tell me what's Mexican and what's not?"

Toni stalked off. Jesús took off in the other direction.

"Toni, wait," Carmen yelled. Her sister had already reached the door of the bar and pushed through.

Couples shook heads, whispered and started dancing again.

Carmen and Víctor went back to their table and gathered their coats.

Víctor helped Carmen on with her jacket. "What did I tell you, babe? Hanging with white people will make you crazy every time."

45
Winter 1959–60

AT FIRST, Francisco decided his stomach was on fire because of the bean burritos he had had for lunch. The heat spread out through his body. In the dirty mirror in the locker room at the mill, he saw an old man fighting for life. He wet his face in the sink. Sluggish footsteps sounded behind him. He straightened with effort. Ricky Villanueva, a young, muscular worker, had already unbuttoned his pants as he entered the bathroom. "Francisco, you feeling okay, man?"

"Only heartburn."

"I hear that. Like farting fire." Ricky entered a stall.

Agony seized Francisco's chest. He gripped the sink.

Ricky emerged after a long pee. "See you back in hell," he said on his way out, not noticing Francisco's face.

The anguish faded, although Francisco's breathing was as shallow as a footprint in the desert. *Señor*, he prayed, *let me not be afraid of what waits for all of us. Wipe away my sins so I can stand tall at your feet and be united with my Maricela and my mamá. May I act like a man in the face of death and not stumble before heaven.*

He had started reciting that prayer as soon as the doctor told him his lungs had been shredded. He realized he was set to die, and soon. He had seen the sickness in other mill workers, among them his late foreman, Jimmy Ralston. The red-headed man was said to have cursed the mill with his final words.

Francisco refused to spend what time he had left in anger. He counted himself lucky to have lived at all and to have a family he loved and who loved him, which should make any man thankful. He blessed God for each day he had seen the morning light sweep past the curtains and light the faces of Antonia and Carmen.

Walking out of the bathroom, Francisco put on his work glasses and entered the open hearth. He didn't get a chance to repeat his prayer before he collapsed in the shining crimson air of the mill.

≈ ≈ ≈

Through the laundry, Víctor searched for Toni. Sweat soaked his shirt as he hurried. She panicked when she saw the worry on his face.

"Come with me, Toni. It's Francisco." He shouted to be heard above the din of the machinery. "He's in the hospital. Carmen's there already."

Toni dropped the pile of clothes she carried.

Her supervisor, a big woman with yellow curls like soap bubbles, came up to her. She touched Toni's back. "Go ahead, now, sweetie. Your brother-in-law explained everything. I'm sorry about your dad."

As she and Víctor drove up to St. John's Hospital, Toni took out a compact and handkerchief and dabbed powder on her red nose, but her eyes remained puffed. She didn't want her father to see her so despairing.

The hospital's gigantic cross threw a shadow over the front entrance.

"I hoped I'd never have to come back here," she said.

"Don't talk like that. Your old man is strong," Víctor said as he parked his truck.

They ran to the third floor. Francisco lay in the last bed by the window in a ward of six patients. Carmen sat by their father, holding his hand.

"Toni," she cried out, "I'm so scared."

Their father slept, but his respiration came from a buried place and had to struggle to be free.

A thin nurse shoved in between them to put a thermometer into Francisco's mouth. "Dr. Custer is finishing up his rounds. He'll talk to you about your father in the waiting room down the hall."

Later, the doctor's voice sounded of sympathy but was eroded by exhaustion at the end of long day. Dr. John Custer fell back into a pale green chair and lit a cigarette. The smoke made Toni want to join him, if only to postpone what he had to say. "Your father is suffering from a type of pneumonia due to his damaged lungs."

Carmen grabbed Víctor's hand. Toni put her own hands to her mouth to stop from crying out.

The doctor let the cigarette dangle from his thick fingers. "We've seen a lot of this condition in men who work at the mill and in the mines."

"Can he come home?" Carmen asked.

"Not right away. He needs oxygen and rest. I want to watch for infection."

Carmen buried her face in Víctor's chest.

The doctor stood up. "Your father will be comfortable here, and you can visit him anytime." He put out the cigarette in an already full standing ashtray and placed a hand on Carmen's shoulder. "If you have any questions, the nurses know how to get a hold of me."

They thanked him. But Toni wanted to ask how long. The question stayed inside her.

Dr. Custer knew what she wanted. "Miss García, your father's heart is strong, and so is his will, so let's wait and see."

Toni and Carmen hugged each other for a long time while Víctor placed his hand on Carmen's back. Toni pleaded to God to strike her down instead of her father but was too educated to really believe in miraculous bargains. She prayed for another miracle that had even less hope of coming true.

Michael.

≈ ≈ ≈

"What time is it, *hija?*" Francisco whispered.

Toni leaped up from her chair. "How are you, Pops?"

"What time is it?"

"About eight at night."

"So late," he said in Spanish. He tried to sit up but coughed and perspired. "Where's Carmen?"

"She was exhausted, so I sent her home."

"Good. Her and my grandbaby need some sleep."

"She'll be here first thing in the morning."

He tried to raise his head. "I want to sit up, *hija.*"

Putting her hand on his moist back, she helped him.

"When can I go home?"

"You're going to have to stay here for a while, Pops."

"I hate hospitals." His chest moved slightly. "*Madre de Dios*, they wake you up at all hours to make sure you're still alive. Then, *ay*, all the food tastes like mashed potatoes."

Toni smiled a little and sat down at the edge of the bed. "I'll have to sneak in something better."

"What about the nurses? They smell like medicine and could probably crush me with one hand."

"Then you better behave."

Toni wiped the perspiration away from his face with a washcloth.

"Sleep now. I'll read to you. I brought a book from the library about Benito Juárez."

Francisco closed his eyes. "The best president Mexico ever had. Did you know he was a full-blooded Indian?"

"Yes, I did."

"His armies kicked the French out of Mexico."

She opened the book. "I know. Old Benito was a fighter, just like you. Now close your eyes."

He opened one eye. "I forgot you were a teacher."

"Shhhh." She began to read.

≋ ≋ ≋

At the Borden Country Club across town, big Howard Hansen puffed on a cigar and sized up Michael as if he were a blond with a big chest. The fat man filled the chair in the upstairs lounge as he considered Michael's political future. An *HH* was embroidered on his tie in elegant script. Sitting next to Hansen, Martin also smoked a cigar.

"State senator, huh?" Hansen said.

Despite his weight, Hansen's voice sounded like Brenda Lee's. Michael and almost everyone who knew him laughed about Hansen's voice behind his back. They didn't want to make him mad, because the big man hoarded grudges. The owner of a chain of department stores, Hansen had a vicious way of doing business that was legendary in the chambers of commerce across Arizona.

Ice tinkled as Martin shook his glass. "Michael is a superb choice for a candidate. He served the people in the county attorney's office and demonstrated a range of excellent skills in my firm."

Michael exhaled. Maybe he should have reminded his father how only a few months ago he had threatened to kick him out.

"The Shaw name goes a long way in this state, and your money goes a long way, too, Howard," Martin said.

"A looonnnngggg way," Hansen agreed and faced Michael, his double chin catching up with a wiggle. "This country is on the brink, son. We got the Russians beating us into space and threatening to bury us under a nuclear cloud. We got nigger music and Hula-Hoops. And we've lost strong, true Americans like Joe McCarthy."

"The U.S. Senate condemned McCarthy," Michael said.

"He was getting too close to the truth."

"What truth? That he was a vindictive asshole?"

Martin cleared his voice. "You can see Michael is passionate. With your help, Howard, he can be the next senator headed to Washington."

Howard took the smoke in and out of his mouth a few times. "Martin, we've known each other for more than thirty years. Before we throw this boy's hat in the ring, I want to know something." He glanced around the room to see if anyone else was listening. "You know to what I refer, Martin."

Martin studied his club soda. "I don't know what you mean."

Hansen gave a lilting Brenda Lee laugh. "You're so full of shit, Marty." His voice lowered. "We're all friends here. Word around town is your boy messed around with a Mexican dame from the president streets."

His face unchanged, Martin took a drink of his soda and then said, "Unfounded gossip."

Michael sat back and smiled. He had promised his father to let him handle the question should it arise. He had easily made a pact with the devil because he didn't care about the life his father wanted to create for him. He had convinced himself they couldn't touch him on the inside, at least not yet.

"Michael, what about that?" Hansen said.

"Well, Father?" Michael said.

Martin put the drink down. "My son is a family man and a skillful lawyer. He will be a great senator. He is the future of this country. If the Mitchell County Republican Party throws its support behind him, he won't let you down."

"Let the boy speak for himself. What about it, young Shaw? What about those rumors?"

No way was he going to let this blubber of a man even think about Toni. "I plead the Fifth."

Howard blasted out air and smoke. His eyes teared from laughing. "Martin, your son here is as impressive a liar as you are. He may very well end up the next Joe McCarthy."

Slapping Michael on the knee, Hansen winked before leaning back in the chair. "Hell, the fact you're screwing women at all will probably even earn you a few extra votes." He heaved back and laughed spit and arrogance.

46

EVEN WHEN HE WORKED as a deputy county attorney, Michael never visited a prison. He wondered now if he would have acted less strident in his prosecution if he had actually seen where criminals were incarcerated. Located 200 miles north of Borden, the state women's prison lay smack in the middle of the desert. Then again, in a state like Arizona, there was a lot of desert, and most everything rested smack in the middle of it. Unlike the arid landscape he had admired from his tree house, the ground leading to the prison appeared deadly enough to swallow him whole if he dared leave the road. He pressed the gas pedal to speed past it.

Still, the drive constituted a nice escape. Jenny's mother had visited for the past week. Having to be around Lily Ann's fake glamour, snobbishness and pearl earrings made the large house shrink around him to the size of a closet. When he told Jenny he was off to see María Curry in prison, Lily Ann's eyebrows raised so high, he believed they might stick to her stiff hairdo. "Something wrong?" he had asked sweetly.

"Nothing at all, Michael. What an attentive lawyer you are to visit clients already sent to prison," Lily Ann had said and then sipped her cocktail.

He had opened his mouth to say something but closed it
again when he recalled his promise to Jenny to be nice to her
mother. Throughout her visit, he smiled vacantly during the
inane discussions of window treatments, or else he sneaked off
to sit in the study Jenny had created for him, with its sappy
paintings of ducks and silly plaid wallpaper.

If he hadn't gotten out of there, he would have been
tempted to burn the place down.

≈ ≈ ≈

Behind the fences topped with razor wire, the prison buildings made up a city of dejection. As Michael stepped through
the gravel parking lot, his footsteps sounded forlorn. Inside,
guards manhandled him in search of contraband. They were
bigger than any player he had ever met on the football field.
Painted in rotted cream colors, the halls seemed to go
nowhere via shiny linoleum floors. Michael tried to judge the
most pungent smell in the place—piss, antiseptic or body
odor. He gave antiseptic the lead, with piss a close second.
When the guard stopped in front of a metal door to the visiting room, Michael actually was surprised there was a destina-
tion to all the uniformity.

Removing his tie, Michael placed it in his pocket. On the
banged-up table in the visitors' room was a bag containing
Baby Ruths, Hershey bars, toothpaste, a hairbrush, handker-
chiefs and several books and magazines in Spanish he had
asked Josita to find for him. He had also placed 200 dollars in
María's prison account so she could buy other items at the
prison store. He asked the guards not to mention his name as
her benefactor. How small a gesture for his failure. He had
appealed the trial verdict to the Arizona Supreme Court,
claiming rampant prejudice had violated his client's civil

rights. The justices denied his request for a review of María's case and would not even look at the court record. María didn't have to know about the second loss.

The door squeaked open, and a blond matron entered. She could have played tackle on any men's team.

"Mr. Shaw?" The woman spoke as gruffly as a car refusing to start. "I'm Guard Williamson. I'll be your translator for the visit." The woman took a seat. "The inmate will be here soon."

"Where'd you learn Spanish, Guard Williamson?"

She stared straight ahead and put her hands in her wide lap. "My parents had a farm in Texas. You had to know how to speak Mexican to order around the workers."

"I'll bet you did."

"Comes in handy. We have lots of Mexicans incarcerated here."

Michael sat back in his chair. "Maybe because they're the ones who can't afford good lawyers."

Guard Williamson wrinkled her nose as if she smelled something worse than piss in the air. Within a few minutes, the door squeaked open again. María came out from behind the shadow of another sizeable matron.

"Mr. Shaw." She displayed a smile of surprise and a little apprehension.

"Hello, María."

He wanted to hug her but was afraid he would offend. He held out his hand for her to shake. Her cheeks were fuller, albeit paler. Her hair had whitened and was clipped short in a ragged haircut.

The matron who brought her in stood by the door. María sat down across from him.

"Anything wrong, Mr. Shaw?" guard Williamson translated.

"I wanted to see you and make sure you're all right." Michael presented her the bag.

Needing no translation, María picked up each item and examined it, grateful for the gifts. "Mr. Shaw, you're very kind." She used English words here and there. "See, I've learned."

"I talked to the warden, and he said you are doing well. You might be eligible for an early parole. We'll work on that."

"Thank you, but whatever happens is God's will." She crossed herself.

"How are they treating you?"

"Good, Mr. Shaw. I work in the garden and sometimes in the kitchen. I talk to other women here and eat good."

"Then how come you're pale, María?"

She became embarrassed. "I caught a little cold, that's all, and it took a long time to get over it. Excuse me, Mr. Shaw, but you don't look so good, too. Are you sick?"

"A little under the weather."

She took a piece of paper from her pocket and patted it affectionately. "Antonia wrote me a letter."

"How is she?"

"Her father is very sick in the hospital. That's why she couldn't visit me."

"I didn't know," he said quietly.

"He may never come out again."

"Toni and I, we haven't . . . talked." His voice dropped off.

"I know, Mr. Shaw. She wrote me."

He suddenly recognized the English words were coming out of Guard Williamson, who sat up with attention during their conversation. He didn't give a shit. "Did Toni say anything else about me?"

"I don't know." María refolded the letter.

"*Por favor*, María."

"She wished you had been stronger."

The words slammed into his chest like a cannonball.

"I'm sorry." María reached for his hand. "I shouldn't have told you. I don't want to hurt you, after you've treated me so well."

The other matron glanced down at her watch. "Two more minutes."

"Thank you for coming to see me and for the gifts," María said in English.

"I'll come back again, if that's all right."

María's small face lifted with a smile. "I'd like that, Mr. Shaw."

"Then I'll see you soon."

María stood but didn't leave. "You know, I did write back to Antonia."

"That's good, María."

"I told her she was wrong about you."

The matron guided María out the door.

47

TAKING PLEASURE IN KEEPING at least one secret, Jenny never told her mother about the young Mexican woman. Besides, Lily Ann would only have heaped more advice on her, which implied Jenny couldn't think for herself. Then again, she hadn't for a long time.

"Michael is coming along nicely." Her mother arranged a fur piece about her neck as they waited for her flight. "That boy could become a reliable husband yet."

"Mother!"

"Well, congratulations again on your new home. It is beautiful, and I hope you'll follow my decorating tips. If you do, your home will become a showplace."

Jenny slumped.

"What's wrong with you? Are you pregnant?"

"No."

"Don't worry. That'll be next. If he changed his mind about the house, children won't be far behind."

People began to board the airplane. Her mother kissed Jenny. "I'm sorry again we won't see you for Christmas, but Maxwell promised me the holidays in France."

"Have a wonderful trip."

She hugged her daughter and whispered, "Children will keep a man around."

"Thanks for your confidence." Afterward, Jenny wasn't sorry to see the plane climb into the sky.

Moving into and decorating the new house left little time for Jenny to worry about the woman from the courtroom. Michael never confessed to anything, and she never asked. He had stayed home since the trial ended, which told her the affair was over. Like his father, Michael ate dinner and then spent most of the time in his study. The intruder was out of their lives. Still, each time Jenny stopped in a store or walked down the street, she kept an eye out for the woman. As for her mother's predictions of her pregnancy, fat chance, since Michael slept in another bedroom. But she would work on enticing him back to her bed, and it would only take one time to get pregnant. To heck with that hussy.

On her way back home from the airport, a rush of what felt like bathwater went through her, and Jenny dared to sing "Younger Than Springtime." She—Jenny Anderson Shaw—finally had the upper hand. She had Michael.

≈ ≈ ≈

When the phone rang, Toni had just stepped into her father's house with a bag of groceries. She rushed, even though she feared it might be the hospital with bad news.

"Toni?"

She paused for a moment in surprise. "Hello, Michael."

"María told me your father was hospitalized. How's he doing?"

Because she wanted to tell him everything, she decided to tell him nothing. "He's holding on. Thank you for asking.

María wrote that you visited and brought her gifts. She really appreciated it."

"She's doing well, under the circumstances. How about you?"

"I'm fine . . . under the circumstances." The lie vibrated in her ears.

"You don't sound fine."

She disliked the personal note in his voice. He had proved it was full of nothing. "How are you?"

"Nothing's changed."

The wrong answer. "Thanks for calling, but I've got to go to work now," she said.

"Toni . . ."

"Yes, Michael."

"If there's anything I can do . . . "

"There's nothing." She hung up. As soon as she did, she cried. She had to stop, or she would be weeping for the rest of her life. Drying her face on a kitchen towel, Toni put away the groceries.

At the other end of the dead line, Michael sat for a long time in the study. He took out a bottle of whiskey and a glass but didn't pour a drink.

Eavesdropping in the hall, Jenny had heard most of the conversation, but she didn't confront him about the call. It wouldn't do any good.

48

FROM THE WINDOW in her father's hospital room on the fourth floor, Toni had an excellent view of the mill, which was the last place she wanted to see. The smoke from the stacks huffed into the cold air as the mill churned night and day with the efforts of workers. She wanted to blow up the place. By blowing it up, she could save all those other men destined to die from the tiny metal razors in the air.

While she tried not to think of Michael, he came to her like a lost truth. She was grateful when Francisco groaned. "Hello, *hija*." He sat up in bed.

"I'm glad you slept. How are you?"

"Not bad. A bunch of guys from work came earlier today." The oxygen mask he wore at night and increasingly during the day made his voice as rough as a smoker's.

"Really. Who?"

"Samuel Ruiz, Primo Ortiz, Chico Alonzo and some others. They brought me a bottle of beer as a joke, but the nurse took it away."

"They miss you."

He smiled faintly. "They wanted to know when I was coming back to work."

Toni fixed the blankets around him and closed the window blinds. "Not yet, but soon."

"Don't lie to me, Toni."

She took a seat near his bed. "You have to concentrate on getting better so you can come home. Carmen is tired of my cooking."

"You're sad, and it's not all because I'm in here. Me and you are a pair of good ones. You sad and me sick."

"I'm sorry for everything."

"*¿Por qué?*"

"You know for what, you must have heard."

"I didn't hear anything."

"Now you're the one not telling the truth." She wiped the perspiration off his forehead with a tissue.

"Then you better go to confession. That's all I can say." His voice held concern, not condemnation, and Toni was thankful. She wanted no more lies between them.

"Did he hurt you, *hija?*"

"Yes and no. I never told you, but when I lived in Phoenix, I was very lonely. I missed you and Carmen a lot."

"We were lonely for you, too."

"I made friends there. But when you walk into a room of people and you're the only one who's different, you can see it in their eyes. When I came home, I ran into another kind of loneliness. Maybe Jesús was right. Maybe I did change, but I thought it was for the better."

"You stepped out of your life here to see the bigger world. Home is never the same afterward. That's what I found after I left the farm fields." Francisco coughed a little.

Toni rushed to him with water, which he sipped. "God. I don't know what's wrong with me. You're not feeling well, and I'm running on like Mrs. Hernández with diarrhea."

The water helped. "No, I want you to tell me everything," he said.

Nodding, she sat down on the edge of the bed. "I've never been ashamed of who I am, Pops. But I also wondered where I truly belonged. But this man, this man made me feel like I finally knew the answer."

"Did you ever tell him that, Antonia?"

She shook her head.

"You should have. Maybe he needed to hear it." Francisco clasped her hand.

"You probably expected better of me."

"No, Antonia. You're what's best about us. But don't forget to go to confession." He wiped at her tears.

"You don't go to confession."

"That doesn't mean you shouldn't."

49

JUDGE ANDREW PARSONS read from the paper without any emotion. "The jury finds for the plaintiff and awards her thirty thousand dollars."

Michael's client, Mrs. Woodruff Keefer, beamed as if she had married the king of England. Her wide shoulders shivered with greed at the judgment against the real estate agent who had failed to properly manage her rattrap apartment buildings on the north side of town, including one on Jackson Street, a few blocks from Toni's house.

"Mr. Shaw, I'm quite overwhelmed." Mrs. Keefer's voice rose as high as a dog whistle.

"My dear Mrs. Keefer, you'll get over it when you get my bill."

She shook off his comment, gathered her purse and left thirty thousand dollars richer, for now.

The bald head of the defense attorney, Jonathan Cole, burned red. He took out a handkerchief and swept it over his forehead. The real estate agent, a peppery-faced man, sat still at the table, absorbing the news of his loss.

Michael would have had the case won without thumping Cole, but he intentionally tortured the other attorney by crushing him in front of the jury, judge and anyone else who happened to be in the courtroom. He made shredded wheat of the defendant's witnesses with harsh questioning. All the while, he kept throwing up his hands and giving the jury one of those "I apologize this lawyer is so bad" expressions. The other attorney, meanwhile, perspired through the armpits of his suit and continually wiped his hands on a damp handkerchief. If the law had included the equivalent of a thrown towel, the other side would have tossed it in right after the opening remarks. With no towel, Michael kept throwing legal punches, because now he only existed in front of a jury of strangers.

Jonathan Cole extended his hand.

"Better luck next time." Michael took his hand, which felt like cold liver.

The real estate agent stomped out.

Martin Shaw stood at the back of the courtroom, his arms folded. "Poor Jonathan certainly offered no match. He really should have urged his client to settle."

"It might have saved us a lot of trouble if he had," Michael said.

"You were pretty vicious to ole Jonathan."

"How proud you must be."

"I'm heading to lunch . . . Like to come?"

"I have to finish up the paperwork on this case."

"Don't forget the party."

"Oh yes, the party."

Michael messed with papers until his father left and then walked out of the courtroom. Increasingly, he couldn't stand being near his father. He cut short business meetings with him and made excuses to avoid dinner at his house. Within any proximity of his father, Michael felt his essence being sucked away, and he wanted to keep what little he had.

Martin walked ahead of him, shaking hands with the judges and lawyers who walked by in the courthouse, wishing all a Merry Christmas and a Happy New Year.

Michael's pricey shoes squealed to a stop.

One of the people shaking his father's hand was Deputy Herb Bell, now Bailiff Herb Bell, with a promotion and a new uniform. Michael stepped into a doorway, close enough to hear them but not be seen. His father fidgeted at the meeting, while Bell kept up his fawning.

"Mr. Shaw." Bell took the older man's hand in both of his. "I hope all is well with you and your lovely family."

"Thank you, ah . . . "

"Herb Bell."

"Yes."

"Thanks again for your help. You, sir, know how to return a favor."

Martin stepped back and pulled his hand away, annoyed. "I have to run."

"If there's anything else I can do for you . . . "

Martin hurried out the doors of the courthouse. Bell smiled as if watching his best friend. The smile narrowed with revenge when he saw Michael.

"Hiya, Mr. Shaw. Me and your dad were shooting the breeze. We've become buddies."

"You thanked him for returning a favor. What kind of favor?"

"Whatever he needs doing. Whatever he needs to know," Bell said.

"Son of a bitch." Michael threw down his briefcase and grabbed Bell's shirt collar. "You did it."

"What?" Bell's tiny eyes watered. "I don't know what you're talking about."

Spotting the men's bathroom, Michael dragged Bell through the door. Bell could do nothing but kick his legs. Once inside, Michael slammed him against the tiled wall. "It's too bad I don't have a brick so I could ram it down your fucking throat."

"We did it for your own good, Mr. Shaw. You had no business with that woman." He was shocked at his bravery and realized he'd soon regret it.

Michael's fist crashed into Bell's face, and then he punished him with his other fist, which sent Bell skidding five feet. Bell collapsed on the floor. His nose spouted blood.

"You're goddamn nuts!"

Michael picked him up, and his fist met Bell's gut. Bell folded like an envelope and fell to his knees, gasping for breath. Michael again hauled the man to his feet. "You also like terrorizing women, don't you? Try a man on for size, you fucking piece of shit."

"Your father asked me to warn her off. I didn't mean her no harm," Bell squeaked, hoping the elder Shaw might show up to rescue him.

"No harm, you malignant asshole? Let's see how you like it."

Michael held up Bell, who took a swing and missed. Michael pounded his kidney. Bell flayed like a suffocating fish and dropped to the floor, blood dripping from his nose and mouth onto his new bailiff's uniform.

"You know, Herb, for the benefit of all humanity, I'm going to pound you into the wall. People will think you're a shit stain, and they'll be right."

Michael took a step forward but felt the vise arms of Sheriff Bobby Maxwell grab him from behind.

"Michael, what the hell are you doing?" The sheriff's placid voice was at ear level.

"Let me go." Michael resisted, but the sheriff's grip proved unbreakable.

Another deputy helped Bell to his feet.

"Settle down, Mike, or I'll hold you as tight as my old man holds onto his money."

Michael calmed his muscles but continued to stare murder at Herb.

When two men entered the bathroom, the sheriff yelled at them to get out. He ordered a deputy to stand outside the door and let no one pass.

Bell looked in the mirror at his pulpy face. "Jesus!" He spit out a front tooth.

"What the Sam Hill is going on here?" The sheriff released Michael and stepped in between him and Herb Bell.

Bell wheezed. He guessed he had a broken rib. "Sheriff, we had a misunderstanding is all. Right, Mr. Shaw?"

"Fuck you." Michael spit.

"Let's go into my office and straighten this out without any legal entanglements," Sheriff Maxwell said. "Or do you want to bring charges, Herb?" The sheriff's expression warned him against it.

"No." Bell wiped at his bleeding nose.

"See, we can be civilized men. Michael, you stay away from Herb for a while. I don't know what he did, and you probably had reason for beating him silly, but he's a peace officer, and you're an officer of the goddamn court."

"He's a goddamn piece of shit," Michael said.

"You're both sworn to uphold the law. Now, let's get outta here before somebody pees his pants waiting outside."

Michael rushed out, pushing through a crowd gathered outside the bathroom.

Sheriff Maxwell put his hand to his gun as if steadied by its force. "What happened, Herb? You bust him for drunk driving or something?"

"It's a private matter, Sheriff."

"I'll hand it to you, son. You managed to piss off one of the most powerful lawyers in town."

Concern charged through Bell, yet only momentarily. "But his daddy is a personal friend of mine."

"You better hope so. Now, get the fuck back to work."

≈ ≈ ≈

Michael's cuffs were spotted with Herb Bell's blood, as was the front of his shirt. Banging his fist on the dashboard of his car, he cursed at a slow-moving truck, swerved around it and stomped the gas pedal. As he raced to his father's house, he didn't know what he'd say or do when he got there. He only saw Toni's beaten face.

Michael's sports car threw gravel in the air as he stopped in the driveway.

Shoving open the double doors, Michael stood in the foyer. "Father, goddammit, where are you? Come out here!" His yells reverberated through the house.

From the kitchen, Josita heard the shouting and followed it to Michael. His face was slick from sweat, and his chest looked ready to explode. His hands were in fists.

"Mr. Michael, can I do anything for you?"

"Where's that old bastard? He wasn't at his office. He must be here."

The way Michael acted made Josita fear for him more than his father. "He met Miss Melody at the airport, and they flew to Palm Springs. They'll be back a couple of days before the New Year's party."

Michael staggered into the living room and fell back on a chair. Josita followed instinctively, as if he were still the child she had helped raise. She had cleaned his cuts when he crashed his bike and scrubbed him after he played in the mud at the ranch. She enjoyed his ability to accept a dare thrown at him by her sons and his attempts to speak Spanish. Even as a kid, Michael had asked lots of questions, many of which she couldn't answer.

On the day Michael learned his mother had died, he ran to Josita in the kitchen and hugged her hard. She picked him up, sat down and rocked him. He buried his wet face against her chest.

"Don't cry, my little one," she had whispered and wiped the tears with the edge of her apron. "Your mama's with the angels, and she's the prettiest one in heaven."

"I don't want her with the angels. I want her with me," he had wept. "You'll never leave me, will you, Josita?"

"Never."

Then his father had entered into the kitchen. "Michael."

The boy clung more tightly to her.

"Let him go, Josita."

She didn't want to, but she did. Michael ran to his father and grabbed his leg, but his father only pushed him away and said, "Quit sobbing like a little girl and go to your room."

Before the young Michael left, he had turned back to look at her. His small face was wet with tears. Now, the older Michael's face was also wet from crying. Not wanting to embarrass him, Josita stood at the threshold of the room where he sat.

Here again was the little boy she had rocked in the kitchen.

50

DRESSED IN A DINNER JACKET, Michael stood in the backyard of what he called the pink flamingo house. A glass in his hand, he looked down into the black square hole the previous owner had dug out for a fallout shelter. Michael sipped at the whiskey and thought about the day he had discovered what his father and Herb Bell had done to Toni. Not finding his father home, he'd driven back to Borden and contemplated wrapping his British sports car around the most convenient tree. He'd follow his mother and her easy way of wrenched metal and smashed windshield. The chicken shit route. Instead, he returned to face the severest of punishments.

By the time his father and stepmother returned from Palm Springs, Michael was ill. So much so, he couldn't get out of bed for two weeks. He slept through Christmas and sweated into his pillow. He vomited bile and culpability. If he hadn't given up Toni in the first place, she wouldn't have been hurt by them.

Actus reus. The guilty act he had committed.

Under the full moon, his shadow was long and solitary in the backyard. Inside the pink flamingo house, Jenny prepped to go to his father's annual New Year's party. He was going to attend, if only to join the rest of the guilty.

≋ ≋ ≋

Tightening a sweater about her shoulders, Josita enjoyed a short break outside the kitchen. Soon the guests would arrive. Her corns already announced them. Yet dressed up with pretty bows, candles and evergreens, the house was ready. Yet despite all the trimmings, Josita couldn't help but click her tongue in disappointment.

Each year, she hoped the Shaws would buy a nativity scene to display at the holiday. It would remind them what this holy season was all about. *Jesucristo.* Proud of the ten-piece ceramic set her sister had sent her from Jalisco, Josita delicately unwrapped each piece from tissue paper to set on a doily in her living room. Even though the set was seven years old, she admired the detail, like the gold earring the wise man Balthazar wore. He reminded her of Jim, the cook. With care, she arranged each figure, except for the baby Jesus, who would be placed on the manger after midnight Mass.

To the Shaw family, Christmas meant champagne, party dresses and the stuff on crackers resembling cat food.

Josita clicked her tongue again at what was to come. How the guests would leave small plates and glasses all over the house, even in the bathrooms. She especially hated how they would shove cigarette butts into the half-eaten food or let them float in drinks. She longed to be home with her grandchildren, who'd rub her feet and pour her a big cup of coffee with extra sugar and cream. By the time she got home from cleaning up after the party, they would all be in bed. She would have to kiss their heads to welcome the new year. She couldn't even have a drink with her husband, Diego, and older son, who parked the cars. But she grinned. No use crying over spilled champagne she'd have to clean up, anyway.

After closing the kitchen door, Josita replaced the sweater on the wooden hook. She ran a hand over her black crepe uniform with the white collar Miss Melody had bought her to wear for the party.

"I see you're wearing your slave outfit, Josita," Jim hooted.

"This is a nice dress."

"Honey, don't wear it too long, or you'll go dark as me. You Mexicans got it better than us because you're halfway to white."

The cook slapped his knee in laughter.

"I never thought of that, Jim. Well, time for business."

Josita commanded the extra help, which amounted to six young Mexican kids who tugged at ties and aprons. "Enough fooling around. Get the food out there," she ordered in Spanish.

To each young man, Josita assigned a tray to carry into the large dining room. After hauling in a tray of shrimp cocktails, she made sure the napkins were in place and the tablecloth straight. More workers prepared to check in the mink coats from the women and mohair coats from the men.

Josita walked around for a last-minute check. She did admire the fifteen-foot-tall Christmas with its luminous bulbs tree in the foyer. The beauty and size of it amazed her.

Michael stood behind her. "¿Bonito, verdad?"

She smiled. "Sí, Mr. Michael. The tree is very pretty."

Her heart tightened. She had not seen him since the day he'd busted into the house yelling for his father. His eyes now looked as empty as one of the glass ornaments on the tree. Misery lived in him like a possessing spirit. "Pardon me, sir, I must get ready. Have a nice time."

As if on cue, a small combo began playing. Martin came down the stairs with Melody on his arm. Her face was starry with the prospect of entertaining, and her silk dress clung to her curves.

"Join us, Michael." Martin touched the end of his bow tie and pointed to a spot near the door.

Michael took his place beside Melody in their traditional greeting line. His stomach churned with acid.

"Where's Jenny?" Melody asked.

"Don't know. Hold on for a second." Michael put two fingers in his mouth and let out a long and loud whistle. Then he yelled, "Jenny, front and center."

"For God's sake, Michael, you act like you're two years old." His father frowned. The old troublemaking Michael was staging a comeback that night.

Soon the tap-tap of high heels followed. Jenny rushed in pulling up black gloves. "Apologies. I was doing some touch-ups."

Melody didn't even glance at Jenny, instead keeping her eye on the front door. "You're lovely."

The door opened, and in came the first knot of guests, who chatted like careless birds. The reception line extended hands and holiday greetings. Michael soon tired of the annual shaking of many clammy palms.

≈   ≈   ≈

The silver-haired woman fanned herself with a napkin. "In a couple of hours, it'll be 1960. Another year gone."

"Don't remind me, Betheen." The woman held her hand up like a traffic cop to halt Josita, who held a tray of champagne-filled glasses. She picked one off. "The fifties were so, so . . . " her eyes flickered, searching for the word, "comfortable."

"The sixties sound like the space age." Her friend played with her pearls. "All rockets and bombs. Don't you think, Michael?"

"Huh?" After mingling with the guests, he desperately wanted to get smashed, but was sticking with club soda through the night, given his queasy stomach.

The women exchanged knowing looks.

"Michael, I asked what you think about the sixties?" one of the women repeated.

"I think they come right before the seventies." He headed off.

The other woman shook her head after Michael was out of earshot. "Drunk again."

"I guess the Mexican woman didn't change him that much."

The women twittered.

Later in the party, Michael lounged on the steps of the staircase and half-watched guests form a conga line of jiggling hips and bosoms. He was a ghost among these ghosts. Earlier in the evening, he had given in and danced with Jenny after she had pestered him. She'd kissed his neck almost as a reward and told him he was the most handsome man at the party. The compliment only made him feel more of a phantom, a missing person in a nice tux.

Michael sat down on the bottom step of the staircase, away from most of the party.

"Mike boy, how the hell are you?"

Norman Reynolds tilted so far, Michael was tempted to reach out and push the tax attorney upright. "Not bad, Norm. You certainly are celebrating."

"I'm drunk."

"Not you." Michael shook his head sarcastically.

Norman slapped Michael's back. "That's what I like about you. You're such a goddamn smart-mouth."

"And I like you because you don't bullshit like the rest of them."

"Everyone is afraid of me because I hold the fate of their taxes in my hand." Norman giggled. Red veins plumped up by gin etched his nose and cheeks. He flopped down beside Michael on a step. "Nice party. Lots of free booze. I wouldn't be surprised if your father'll try to claim the alcohol as a tax deduction. Speaking of which, I haven't seen Martin much this evening."

Michael shrugged. "He's around."

Sitting next to Michael, Norman pointed his finger to the top of the staircase. "There he is."

With both hands on the railing, Martin inspected the party like a conqueror.

"He cuts quite the figure, doesn't he?" Norman said.

"I suppose so."

Norman stared at Michael, squinted his eyes at Martin and back again to Michael. "I swear to God, Mike, you're getting to be the spitting image of your old man."

"What?"

"Pretty soon, you'll be standing at the top of those steps. The master of all you survey. Michael Shaw." Using Michael's shoulder as a crutch to help him stand, Norman left in search of another drink.

Michael rose and gazed at himself in a round ornate mirror near the stairs. "Fuck me." He ran up the stairs.

"Having a good time?" Martin said.

"We need to talk." Michael's tone was urgent and tilting toward dangerous.

"I have guests." Martin took a step down.

Michael stepped in front of him. "Screw the guests."

His father coughed in vexation. "In my study." He headed upstairs, with Michael following.

After lighting his cigar, Martin leaned against his large desk. The party noise of talk and music became a rush of air beneath their feet. "What could be so important?"

Michael, who stood by the door, walked with deliberation toward his father. "I wanted to tell you I'm quitting the firm." His voice quivered.

"What are you talking about?" Martin's face was that of a man who had heard a joke but didn't know if it was funny.

Michael straightened up. The quiver left his voice. "I said I'm leaving."

"You're drunk." He crushed the cigar out in an ashtray and stood.

Michael's hands were in tight balls. "I'm not drunk, but I am the A-number-one sap of all time."

"I have a party to host. I'm not wasting my time with this."

The son shoved his father into an overstuffed chair.

"You must be losing your mind," Martin said. His cheeks heated red.

Michael placed his hands on the chair arms and leaned in so close, he smelled his father's cigar breath. "If I killed you right now, I could claim it was self-defense. Who'd blame me? I'd wager nobody who's ever met you. A jury might even give me a fucking medal."

"Oh, my God."

Michael took a chair across from his father. "Of course, that argument of self-defense didn't work for María Curry, who really and truly deserved it. Who knows? Maybe I might get away with it, especially after what you and that asshole Herb Bell did to Toni."

The color in Martin's cheeks weakened. His chest rose and fell rapidly. For a moment, Michael feared he might cause a repeat of his father's heart problems. The fear dissipated as

Martin clutched the arms of the chair and stared straight ahead in fury.

"No one can talk to me like that. Who do you think you are?"

"Your son. The funny thing is, you probably would like Toni. She made something out of nothing, while I had everything and did shit."

"That's not true. You lead a full and rich life."

"Your definition of 'rich' and mine are on opposite sides of the universe."

"Go to her, and you'll have no job, no friends and no future. You'll be an outsider."

Michael got to his feet. Grabbing his father's jacket, he yanked him up from the chair. They were face to face. "An outsider, eh? That's no big deal, Father. I've been one all my stinking life."

"She can't give you anything."

"You're so fucking wrong." Michael pulled down on his father's jacket and brushed off his lapels.

Martin appeared confused.

"Now go back to your party and get the hell out of my sight," Michael said.

With a minor touch of sluggishness to his usual stride, Martin headed to the door. When he closed it behind him, Michael took off his tie. His body had substance again, and he wavered from the heft of it. He dried his forehead with the arm of his tux. Someone hummed behind him.

Jenny stood in the doorway between the study and a small library. "I couldn't find you."

"How long were you there?"

"Long enough." She sounded tranquil. She walked up to Michael and slapped him. Then she slapped him again. Her hand stung, and she began to feel silly.

Michael didn't try to stop her. He deserved everything.

"I guess I should scream or throw things. Isn't that what I should do, like in the movies? I'll bet Lana Turner or Joan Crawford would throw things."

"I'm a no-good husband."

"You really are."

He took her hands. "I'm sorry, if that means anything."

"Wedding ring or not, you never really belonged to me, but I kept it hidden in the back of my heart. I hoped you'd change your mind and fall madly in love with me. I was too dumb to see anything."

"You're not dumb."

Jenny took off her high heel and rubbed her arch. "I finally got my dream house, and everything goes to hell."

He grinned. "I've never heard you say 'hell' before."

"It's a good word."

"The best."

"What do we do now, Michael?"

"Find our way. You'll have to find yours, Jenny. Not to please me or your mother. But for you."

"How do we do that?"

He laughed. "Fuck if I know."

"He's going to cut you off from everything. Are you scared?"

"So much I can hardly budge."

"You're going to her, aren't you?" she asked shyly.

"If she'll have me. She may not."

"Well, I don't have a college degree and all that education, but I'm not stupid enough to hold onto you against your will."

"Thank you, Jenny girl. I'll be generous with you, that's if I have anything left. I quit my old life a few minutes ago."

She smiled a bit and put on her shoes. "My mother will beg me to take you to the cleaners in divorce court. I don't think

I will. No, sir." She smiled a bit more. Outside the door, people cheered, and the band played "Auld Lang Syne."

"It's midnight," he said. He had forgotten about the guests. "This is going to be one party nobody will forget. Least of all, me and your dad," she said. "Michael, can you do me one favor?"

"What is it?"

"Can we leave together?"

He nodded. "I'm not a complete asshole."

"Not completely."

"Jenny, you're going to do all right."

Taking her hand, Michael opened the door of the study. The music and noise from the party almost knocked them back. Michael told Jenny he had one thing to do before they left and asked her to wait near the front door.

Ducking and moving like a football player among the guests, Michael made his way to the kitchen. He found Josita vigorously wiping the counter with one hand and directing the workers with the other. She grinned when she saw him. "Mr. Michael, you need something?"

"I wanted to tell you *adiós*. I don't know if I'll see you again for a long time."

She stopped wiping. "You going somewhere, Mr. Michael?"

"You might say that. I wanted to say thank you for taking care of me all those years, above and beyond your pay." Michael hugged her. "I'm going to miss you."

"I will miss you."

He kissed her cheek and walked out the door.

51

TONI WOKE UP WITH COLD FEET and a headache, not so much from the feel of the day, but from her dream. In the dream, she wore a pretty summer dress and sat in a meadow surrounded by desert. On a green hill rising out of the meadow, she saw her father. Waving her arms frantically, she called his name, although no sound came from her throat. He took no notice of her. As the sky became orange with sunset, he finally saw her, smiled and walked down the other side of the hill. No matter how fast she ran, she could not catch up to him.

When she awoke, Toni tried to rub away the blunt ache at the back of her neck. She smelled the scent of coffee rising from the kitchen. Downstairs, Carmen sat at the table.

Toni yawned. "Morning."

"Hi." Carmen's voice was rough as coffee grounds.

"I have to work this morning, but I'll come to the hospital about three."

"That's good. I'll stay until you get there, then I'll come home and cook dinner. After that, we can both go back and tell Pops good night."

"Deal."

The hollows under her sister's eyes became darker, just like hers. "How about corn flakes, Carmen?"

"I'm not hungry."

"Then feed your baby."

"Okay, pour me a bowl of corn flakes."

≈ ≈ ≈

Colorful cardboard cutouts of Santa and his reindeer, cheery snowmen and fat snowflakes decorated the hallways and the nursing station. Whenever she walked past them, Toni wanted to rip down the decorations. No one should be happy when her father was so sick.

Carmen sat beside their father's bed reading *Life* magazine. His eyes were closed, and the plastic oxygen mask covered his nose and mouth. Carmen put her finger up to her lips when she saw Toni.

Removing her coat, Toni whispered, "How is he?"

Carmen tipped her hand back and forth. Toni sat down on the other side and opened a book about Emiliano Zapata she had picked up from the library to read to her father. Carmen stood up and stretched, her belly round and full.

Francisco's eyes fluttered. He muttered something in Spanish. His daughters drew near to listen. In the past few days his mind had landed on places and times outside the hospital room.

His eyes opened. "My girls."

They leaned in and kissed his cheek.

"I feel so sweaty." He pulled down the oxygen mask.

Carmen touched his head, which felt cool and moist. "We'll help you, Pops."

Toni filled a small pan with warm water. They both wiped his face and arms with a cloth and dried him with a towel, all with movements slow as a ritual.

"Thank you." Francisco again closed his eyes. He reached out his hand, as if to lead them somewhere. "I feel so much better." His voice was low. In a few minutes, he was asleep.

At six in the evening, Víctor didn't see Francisco's truck or Toni's car. Usually, Carmen managed to come home and fix him dinner. The one time she hadn't was a few days ago, when Francisco had choked until his lips went blue. A priest had been called for the Last Rites. But the old man recovered, although he was weaker than ever. Víctor washed quickly and changed his clothes to go to the hospital. On the way, he ate a ham sandwich he had made. His nails were still greasy from the garage where he worked.

At the hospital, Víctor sprinted up the steps to the third floor and then slowed. Carmen was crying in the hall. He enfolded her in his arms.

In the hospital room, Francisco lay in the bed, his hands folded. To one side, Toni sat in a chair, holding a book, her voice steady as she read to him.

52

VOICES ON THE OTHER SIDE of the closed door were hushed and respectful. Still, Toni dug into the covers on her father's bed. Since he'd died she couldn't get warm. No matter how much she blew on fingertips, wore socks or drank hot coffee.

"Toni's resting," someone said outside the door.

She watched the lights in the votive candles on her father's dresser. The wavering illumination made Jesus' blessed heart seem to radiate about the room. Toni wiggled her toes to warm them, making Oscar stir.

Her father's rosary was an hour away.

Weeks before, Francisco had informed her and Carmen they wouldn't have to pay for his funeral. After their mother had passed, he'd had to borrow money for burial costs. He wanted to spare his daughters, so he had started paying the Valdez Funeral Home twenty dollars a month for a casket of dark wood that would be placed in the same plot as their mother's, as well as all the fixins, as he called them.

Toni snuggled in the blanket, which still smelled of her father—a combination of Old Spice and a little sweat. The voices outside the door grew louder as more relatives and friends arrived with food and condolences. Toni put her arms around herself.

Verdict in the Desert 337

The morning of his last day, Francisco had smiled at Toni and Carmen and begun talking. Toni lifted away the oxygen mask.

"Can we do anything for you, Pops?" Carmen said.

"I'm not afraid."

"I know, Pops. You're the bravest man I know," Toni said.

"I've been worried my mamá and Maricela won't recognize me when I pass on. They'll be younger, and I'm an old man."

"They'll know you," Toni said. "I promise they will, especially mom."

"That's good." He closed his eyes. They never opened again.

Aunt Lucille peeked inside the bedroom. "Antonia. You better get ready. The rosary starts in a half an hour."

"Thank you, Auntie."

At church, the priest led the mourners through the decades of the rosary, saying Hail Marys and Our Fathers on the evening before the burial. He started the prayer: "*Bendita tú eres entre todas las mujeres, y bendito es el fruto de tu vientre, Jesús.*"

"*Santa María, Madre de Dios, ruega por nosotros pecadores, ahora y en la hora de nuestra muerte.*" The mourners finally ended their prayers.

Concentrating on the glass beads in her hands and on saying the prayers, Toni did not want to see the open casket, although Mr. Valdez was a talented undertaker. Their father could have been taking a nap. The kind of nap from which he would never awake. He wore the suit he had bought for Carmen's wedding. Sitting beside her, Carmen couldn't even pray. Her mouth was open, her lips dry.

Later at their house, relatives, compadres and friends gathered, eating and talking, some even a little drunk. Toni watched from the backyard.

So familiar a scene.

She smoked her cigarette, while Oscar put his small head on one of her shoes.

After everyone had left, Víctor went to bed, leaving Carmen and Toni sitting at the kitchen table. Toni leaned in to to touch Carmen's hand. "You tired?"

"A little. You?"

"A little."

Carmen rubbed one side of her belly. "I pray my baby won't come out sad."

"You don't have to worry. That baby will never be sad. Not with a mommy like you."

"And an aunt like you."

Carmen stood up. "I'm going to bed. It's going to be a long day tomorrow."

Toni lit another cigarette and paced the room. With Oscar at her heels, she walked to the little house. She hadn't spent much time there in the last weeks, instead sleeping in her dad's bed while he was at the hospital. Switching on the light, she smelled the dust. She smelled Michael, too. Oscar went to the pillow in the corner. As he was about to lie down, she whistled to him and flicked off the light.

The following morning, Toni and Carmen stood by the casket, which had been placed near the door of the church. Each person who entered touched Francisco's hand or made the sign of the cross over his body. Toni peeked inside the church; it was almost full. Her father would have been happy at the attendance.

After looking at his pocket watch, mortician Bob Valdez told the sisters it was time to start. That meant one last look at their father's remains, because the coffin would be closed during the Mass.

"Oh, Pops. Don't leave us." Carmen sobbed and threw her arms on his chest. Her grief caused a rush of more tears from the packed church. Víctor and Toni pulled her away.

Toni kissed her father's lips, which were solid as the steel he made. She swallowed air and stroked his hair. "I'll never say good-bye."

Aunt Lucille took her arm and led her to the front of the church.

In a dark cowboy shirt and pants, Sammy Flores sang of loss and prayer as the Mass began. Throughout, Toni shivered, although she wore her heavy wool suit. She wet her lips with her tongue, which felt so sticky. Carmen's eyes were wide and fixed. Occasionally, Toni took her sister's hand to convince herself Carmen hadn't slipped away, too. The incense and flowers turned the air sweet and dense.

During the Mass, Toni followed along and prayed at the right time. She gave the right responses and kneeled with everybody else. But her motions were disconnected from her heart. Inside, she was as dead as her father.

At the cemetery on the north side of Borden, Sammy Flores was joined by friends and relatives with guitars as they followed the dark wooden casket to the open grave.

"*Buenos días, paloma blanca,*" they sang. Good morning, white dove.

The full moon was a pale blue shadow above the cemetery as the priest said his last prayers. The group of mourners circled around the grave and huddled in their coats in the chilly morning brought on by a cold front. When the service ended, they walked back to their cars. A few briefly wondered about the stranger standing alone off to the side.

Francisco's daughters each kissed his coffin. Víctor put his arm around his wife and led her back to the car. Aunt Lucille and Juanita each took one of Toni's arms.

"Time to go," Aunt Lucille said.

"Please, a little longer," Toni replied in Spanish.

Aunt Lucille touched Juanita's back. They stepped away.

Listening to the car doors slam behind her, Toni knew she had to leave soon but didn't know where she was going.

"Toni."

She turned. Michael held out his hand. Without hesitation or even surprise at seeing him there, she reached out her own hand. He took her into his arms. At last, she found the warmth that had eluded her for so many days.

≈ ≈ ≈

Dishes of chicken enchiladas, chili, tortillas and sliced lunch meats and cheeses covered the kitchen table and every bit of counter space. Additional food filled the refrigerator in the kitchen, the one on the back porch and the one in Toni's little house. Several people remarked how Francisco García would have loved such a get-together, which spilled out into the front and back yards. When Toni came in the door with Michael, the men shook hands with him. The women nodded as she introduced him.

"Carmen, Víctor, this is Michael." Toni realized they never had met. She bit her lip, apprehensive at how her sister would react, after all that had happened.

Also unsure, Michael held out his hand, but Carmen threw her arms around him and cried. He hugged her, grateful and feeling welcome. "I'm so sorry, Carmen. I wished I had known him. It was my loss," Michael said.

Throughout the day, as friends and relatives talked with Toni, Michael sat nearby her on the couch. He made up a plate of food for her, which she barely touched, and brought her coffee and later a glass of water. He caught a few people throwing suspicion his way, as if he had wandered into the house for an evil purpose. Toni noticed and scooted closer to him on the couch.

For the past few days, he had cleared his possessions out of his office in the bank and the pink flamingo house and moved them into a motel room on Bradley Street. He was amused at how little he took away—clothes, law books, photos of his mother. Most of the items fit into his sports car. He wasn't bothered he had no job or a place to live. He only had one goal.

No one answered the door when he had gone to Toni's house. He didn't want to leave a note, fearing she would throw it away. Then he had called the hospital and learned her father had died.

For a moment at the cemetery, he'd sweated with worry that Toni would walk past and away from him. When she took his hand and let him hold her, his legs weakened with gratitude.

By ten at night, people began to leave the García house. Women started cleaning the kitchen and putting away the leftover food. They didn't allow Toni and Carmen to help. Michael offered to dump trash in the can out back. There, a group of men drank beer by the back door. .He again felt watched.

"Hey Mike, want a beer?" Víctor said at last.

"Sure." Michael smiled.

"So you're a lawyer?" a man asked.

"Yes, but don't hold that against me."

"You a good lawyer?" another man asked.

"I don't know yet. I think I can be."

"What ya charge?" another said.

"How much you got?"

The men laughed. After that, they talked about football and westerns on TV. He asked where they worked and how they were related to Toni and Carmen. They told him lots of stories about Francisco, about his cooking and his music. How everybody who entered his house was treated like family.

Michael indeed felt a loss at not having met him. He held up his beer. "To Francisco."

"*Salud*," the men answered.

"*Salud*," Michael repeated.

By midnight, the house had cleared. Carmen insisted Michael stay in the little house instead of wasting money on a motel. Carmen hugged Michael again, and Víctor shook his hand. They went upstairs. The house was still as Michael and Toni sat on the couch, his arm around her. He told her how he had left Jenny and his job and, mostly, his father.

"We're both orphans now," she said.

He kissed her lightly. They sat without speaking for a long time before Toni went to bed.

Carrying a small case with clothes and toiletries he retrieved from his car, Michael walked to the little house out back. Toni was right. He was an orphan. We're all orphans after we're born. We tumble about, lost and loose in the world, ready to float away at any moment into darkness and quandary. That is, unless we are lucky to catch something so fine it provides us a foothold.

Toni's hand had felt so sure in his at the cemetery. He prayed for strength enough to hold on. In the cold night air, he saw his breath and knew he was alive.